hunter by night

ELISABETH STAAB

sourcebooks
casablanca

Published by Sourcebooks Casablanca, an imprint of Sourcebooks, Inc.
P.O. Box 4410, Naperville, Illinois 60567-4410
(630) 961-3900
Fax: (630) 961-2168
www.sourcebooks.com

Printed and bound in Canada.
WC 10 9 8 7 6 5 4 3 2 1

To Tom, Mary, and Damon. Lee was such a big hero that it took a village.

Chapter 1

TO BE FILED UNDER THE CATEGORY OF "SHIT JUST GOT Crazy": Alexia Blackburn bled from a gash in her knee, and she was sneaking *into* a mansion full of vampires.

Her pulse pounded like a kettledrum between her ears as she made her way down the hall of the king's mansion on tiptoe. In the early Sunday morning quiet, she willed her steps, her breath, and the clang of her heart to slow the hell down and shut the hell up.

Like a champ, she managed to find every creak in every floorboard down *every* square inch of the long passage to the gilded cage she called her bedroom. The sun had risen well into the sky by now. She could only hope all the bloodsuckers were nestled snug in their beds for the day.

An ominous click when the central air kicked into action made Alexia's ticker go staccato. She paused, hearing nothing but the rush of white noise as prickly agitation and a layer of goose bumps covered her bare arms. Her tank top and cargo shorts had been just fine outside in the sticky August air. Inside the royal vampire estate where they kept the lights down and the temperature meat-locker fabulous? Not so much.

A glance up and down the hall revealed an all clear, so she eased on. She had bandages in her bedroom, all shapes and sizes. When one lived with vampires, one learned not to walk around bleeding. These guys might prefer the blood of their own, but not tempting fate was safest. Okay, so not living with vampires was probably safest. A situation she'd been thinking she should change.

Her face burned. Dammit, she'd sworn she'd never let anybody trap her again. How was she even in this mess?

Something squicky and damp worked its way between her toes. "Ew." The blood had run down her leg and into her sock. A shiver hit Alexia full force, making her pick up speed. She had to get to her room.

Another floorboard groaned. She stopped, hating the way her adrenaline spiked. Twenty-five years old, and still sneaking in and out of the house like a teenager. Worse, she lived daily with the acute awareness that no place was safe. Not even home. Even where she lived, she couldn't follow her own rules. On the upside, lately hardly anyone even noticed her. Made the occasional field trip that much easier.

From behind Alexia came a creak that her amateur ninja skills had not caused. *Fuck*. A low, deep growl froze her lungs. "Alexia."

Okay, so maybe someone noticed. After all, there was Lee. That vampire had eyes in the back of his everything.

She shifted her backpack from left shoulder to right. Carefully, she turned to face her pseudo-jailer. Lee Goram, the king's asshole in command, glared from the dark shadows.

His otherworldly blue-green eyes shone brightly in the dim hall. His tall body stood large and imposing, even from a few feet away. The prominent features of his face, his strong cheekbones and full lips, appeared unusually sharp this morning. His anger at having found her sneaking in practically punched her in the stomach.

"Hey… you." She tried for casual cheerful, but it came out sounding wobbly. There was no way to pretend that she hadn't been caught. "You're up…" Late? Early? Morning would be late for a vampire. "How come you're not in bed?"

"Because you're not in bed." He pressed close then, moving swiftly with that crazy-fast supernatural vampire speed. In a second, her back met with cool plaster and her front met… him. His square chin, thick neck… wide, solid chest. "You're bleeding," he said. Listening to Lee talk was like getting buffed all over by a loofah in a hot shower. Abrasive and raw, but at the same time decadent and delicious.

Lee had a good foot or so of height on Alexia's five feet and two inches. She couldn't ever see his face dead-on. It wasn't until he stooped to inspect her knee that she realized exactly why his face looked so weird.

Fangs. Big, fricking long-ass daggers aiming at her from his gums.

Oh, sure, she'd seen them before. But usually those babies stayed safely inside his mouth, looking longer and sharper than the average canine but more or less innocent enough. And okay, God help her, sexy as sin. She'd never seen them so large and in charge on him before.

A tremor of unease tickled the base of her spine. "Uh…" She didn't know how to answer him in a way that wouldn't draw his wrath or make him tattletale to King Thad, so she did what she always did to ease nerves in lieu of alcohol. She cracked a joke. "You know, I thought my knee felt funny."

Lee's upper lip lifted into a wicked sneer, giving her a good, gleaming eyeful of one razor-sharp tooth. "Stop fucking around, Lexi."

Her stomach tightened, and another shiver shimmied from the crown of her head to the tips of her toes. "I..." *Oh my gawd, Lexi, get it together!* She kept swearing to herself that she was over this dumb crush.

She exhaled slowly, her gaze bouncing from those hypnotic eyes that reminded her so much of tropical water on a sunny day to the furious set of his jaw, his severe buzz cut, and the tense bulk of his arms and chest. How could someone so menacing have such warm, inviting eyes?

Lee's body invaded her space, one searing hand on each of her shoulders. "You disappeared without a word. You stayed out all night. Now you come back injured and bleeding." Deep inhale. "You smell of alcohol." He took her chin in the crook of his thumb and forefinger. "This is unacceptable behavior."

Unacceptable behavior? She may have been here for her safety, but the badass mofo vampire routine was sooo last decade. She deserved to be treated as an equal in this place. "I'm not a child. I shouldn't need to ask permission to go where I want." She lifted her chin out of his grasp and crossed her arms over her chest. A little defensive? Fine. She'd challenge any gal staring up at two-hundred-plus pounds of pissed-off vampire muscle not to get defensive. Or... weak in the knees.

"You're under the king's protection. We can't protect you if we don't know where you are," he said as he pulled out his phone. He knelt before her and prodded at the cut with calloused fingers. "Sorry to wake you,

Doctor." He spoke into the phone now. Great, now she was waking the proverbial neighborhood. Frickin' fabulous. "I've got Alexia here; she's in need of stitches. I'll meet you at her room."

Lee tugged her down the hall and Alexia raced to keep pace with the long strides of his powerful legs, even though each step made knifelike pain stab into her leg. "Look, I fell. It's fine. I'm fine."

"You're not fine. You need stitches." Medical wisdom from Lee Goram.

They arrived at her door. Alexia stood tall, meeting his stare even though the intensity of his disapproval hit her full force. She lowered her voice to a whisper, mindful of all the residents who slept at this hour. "Look, I hit an after-hours rave, okay? I just wanted to go dancing. Sometimes I need to be around other humans." She'd landed here, after all, because her BFF had turned out to be the vampire queen. But being buddies with a vampire out in the human world had turned out to be a different proposition from being a solitary human living in the vampire world.

Isolating.

No response from Lee. He knelt again, fingers sliding gently over her thigh as he studied her cut. Those insane fangs of his… A quiet rumble in his throat, and her cotton thong nearly burst into flames. "What did you fall on, a knife?"

She almost smiled, but anger still simmered in his aqua-colored eyes. "Jagged rock." She reached into her pocket for the black cord that had caught her foot. "I tripped on this thing. Out by the back gate."

Raised eyebrows. "Where did you find this?" His

face darkened as he reached for the sueded string, covered with knots.

"Tied between the gateposts. The dirt from the road covered it up. You shoulda been there, I did a really epic face-plant." Still no laugh from Lee, so Alexia shrugged. "Stupid prank, I guess. Stoner teenagers." Kids around Ash Falls, Virginia, suffered from rich-with-too-much-liquor-and-free-time-itis.

Lee stopped with one hand still on her leg. "Did you mess with the string in any way?"

"Nuh-uh. No messing, swear." *Really. Please.* In a sudden moment of overwhelm, Alexia slapped at Lee's hand, backing against the door. God, if he kept running his fingers all over her, she'd lose her mind. When his body pressed close enough to share the heat from his skin and he touched her the way he was touching her now? Hard to remember Lee hated humans, and he only took care of her out of loyalty to the king and queen.

Distance was good. Distance was *very* good.

Hurried footsteps pattered up the diamond-patterned runner in the hallway. The doctor, coming to stitch Alexia's knee.

Lee glanced in Dr. Brayden's direction before licking his lips slowly and easing to his full, immense height. "Threats exist"—he raised his chin as he paused for breath—"that you can't begin to imagine. I need you to stay inside. Especially if you can't take an escort. Please." Then he departed, leaving Alexia alone with the doctor and his bag of tricks.

She searched for her voice in the wake of Lee's retreat, but found herself following the roll of his shoulders and the flex of his legs under his fatigues. *Threats exist. That you can't begin to imagine.* What the good hell did that mean? She'd seen the vampires' enemies, but she'd also learned they didn't usually go after a lone human unprovoked. And since when did Lee say "please" to anyone?

Alexia sighed. She'd been thinking for a while now that maybe it was time to leave the estate. Leave the vampire community here in Ash Falls for good. She didn't fit, and the proverbial walls were closing in.

Yes. She should go. Then she wouldn't be Lee's problem—or any vampire's—anymore.

—⁂—

"I told you to *fight*." Lee Goram threw two sweaty, young vampires to the dirt.

Next to the pit of grappling bodies, he glared down at the two recruits who had been circling carefully around each other, conserving their strength when they were supposed to be battling aggressively. Nearby, mud flew. The red clay pelted them all with stinging chunks. In the large clearing at the back of the king's estate, what would hopefully be their newest batch of fighters worked over and over to take each other to the ground.

These guys were all sturdy. Powerful. Determined. Brimming to the tops of their chunky skulls with potential. Yet in the sticky August evening, a chill of unease slithered through Lee's body.

In his pocket, the presence of the knotted black leather that had tripped Alexia weighed heavily.

No clue. She had no fucking clue what she'd stumbled upon. For the remainder of that previous day and night Lee had only avoided wringing the pretty little human's neck due to the number of other priorities on his plate. Priorities like kicking off their new round of training.

Even now, Lee's hands burned with the urge to grab hold of her and shake. Fuck priorities.

Alexia had carelessly ignored his requests that she stay indoors, convinced the daylight held no risk of evil. Now they all faced a severe threat. The knot work on that cord held meaning she couldn't know. A very old, very simple pagan magic turned wicked by its user.

Upon inspection, he'd found traces of blood on the cord. Old and dried, but familiar to Lee's sense memory nonetheless: belonging to a man Lee had believed he'd killed centuries ago.

An ancient evil had somehow been resurrected.

Lee growled down at one of the two males he'd pulled aside, the one who gasped for air as a cut leaked into his eye. "Are you too hurt to continue?"

"No. Sir."

"Then what are you doing? Get up, and fight. Until you can't, or until you're told to stop." As the young vampire struggled, Lee turned to the guy's opponent. "And you. Beyond this training ring, beyond the protection of the king's estate, do you think an opponent will back off and wait for you to recover if you get tired?"

The young male, marked with a number "four" on his shirt, stammered and went pale. Numbers were easier than names when you dealt with guys who might not last long enough to be worth the bother of getting to know them better. Things weren't looking too good for number four. Or his opponent. Given what Lee suspected, they had days at most to whip the guys into shape, and from there on out, the "training" would be trial by fire. The ones who raised doubts would go home.

To take on what lay ahead, they needed to beef up their ranks. More foot soldiers, more elite fighters. Lee couldn't be sure how many guardian helpers his old enemy Haig had brought along or when he might strike, but they needed to be prepared for any possibility. Fuck knew the humans wouldn't be ready for the plague Haig had the power to rain upon them, wandering around out there like clueless bovine with their fragile immune systems.

In the midst of the chaos, Lee's mind went to Alexia. He pictured her wide, brown eyes and her blonde hair with hints of caramel the way he'd seen it dusting her bare shoulders the previous morning. That smooth, glowing olive skin of hers. He tried not to imagine her already diminutive body affected by the rapid onset of disease, but the visions came fast and unrelenting. His gut soured.

"Forgot what a dickhead you could be during training." King Thad spoke up from where he stood behind Lee, observing the trainees.

On the far side of the pit, trainee number twelve fired sparks from his hands. The instructions had been to fight without mercy, and there were no rules against using powers. An attack could happen that way in the field. But Twelve's opponent had slow reflexes.

Lee rose onto the balls of his feet, nodding. "Have to be. Most of them figure out how to deal with it eventually." Or they didn't, and those were the ones who didn't make the cut.

"Hell, if my whiny, entitled ass made it through, anyone could, right?"

Lee swallowed the shards of emotion in his throat. Thad had nearly been a brother to Lee before taking the throne. The closest thing he had to family. He was immensely proud of the changes he'd seen in the young leader in such a short time. "You were always going to succeed."

For a second they both turned. Lee caught the shrewdness of his king's stare. "I'm glad one of us had faith."

The burn in Lee's chest intensified. "I don't have faith in anything. Some things you just know." He pointed through the mess of bodies. "Like Twelve's partner over there is about to get his ass handed to him."

The two males in question wrestled on the ground. Twelve's knee dug into his partner's chest, his hands grabbed his opponent's throat. A crackle and pop fired from Twelve's hands, and then blood flew. Screams.

"There it is," Thad said quietly.

"Yep." Lee's gums throbbed as he pushed through the group. Happened at least once a session. Good teachable-moment shit. He handed a knife to Twelve. "Give him your blood."

Twelve went pale. "What?" The young vampire took a step back from his bleeding partner, pointing to the nearby training building. "There's a doctor and a whore from Blood Service who can provide for him right over there." In fact, the doctor and an unmated female from Blood Service approached quickly.

"Now. Or you are done. And speak with respect."

Twelve's jaw hardened.

"Do you refuse?"

When the kid took one uncertain step back, Lee drew the knife blade across his own wrist and held it above Twenty-Three's open gash, drizzling blood directly into the wound. Truthfully, Lee despised giving his blood to anyone. But this was an injured trainee and they *all* had to learn.

"First of all…" He boomed loud enough that his voice echoed in the clearing, but kept his stare fixed on Twelve, broadcasting his disapproval. "Those of us who are unmated rely on help from our friends in Blood Service to stay strong. Every one of their providers is someone's mother or daughter, brother or sister, father or son. Show fucking decency."

When the doctor signaled Lee had given enough, he licked closed the cut on his wrist and gave the doctor space. The injured kid might have to go with the female from Blood Service to get a full feeding, but they had her present for such a purpose.

"Second," Lee said, "there's always the chance you get stuck. With a severe injury, even a few miles back to home can be life or death. Your patrol partner is your lifeline.

"What I just did there was not a blood exchange as it would be between mates. That's like comparing CPR to kissing. Know the difference." He motioned to Twelve. "Turn in your gear. Thanks for playing."

The young vampire schooled his wide eyes and slack mouth. He spun away, muttering about unfairness through clenched teeth.

"I'm surprised he didn't argue more," Thad said. "I thought for certain he'd give you trouble."

"He still might." Lee checked his watch, then glanced up at the sky. Heavy clouds rolled across the half moon. He nodded across the way to his other lieutenants, signaling them to finish. "You and I should head to the mansion," he said to Thad. "Check on Isabel. Review strategy." The tension of the first royal birth in a century needled everyone's nerves these days, and now of all times.

Thad nodded. "You're certain about this threat?" He shook his head. "I just can't imagine so many deaths being caused by one asshole."

"That cord came peppered with Haig's blood. I'm certain." Centuries later, Lee still remembered the smell of the blood that had originated one of their planet's greatest plagues. After all, he'd had the vile stuff slicked all over his skin. Splattered in his nostrils. "I'm surprised your father never told you about him."

Thad tightened his jaw and said nothing. The late king had tried to leave many secrets buried in the past. The past did not like to stay buried.

How had Haig survived? Lee had cut the righteous piece of shit open and set him on fire, for Christ's sake. Had seen the motherfucker burn alive with his own preternaturally enhanced eyes. He'd spent the past twenty-four hours asking himself whether or not he could have been mistaken, but in his gut he knew the answer. This meant a fight the likes of which their kind had forgotten to fear could come at any time. The likes of which humankind would never expect.

Jesus… Alexia. She could easily wind up one of the casualties if Lee didn't stop Haig in his tracks. If he didn't keep her sheltered and inside the fucking estate. Lee insisted to himself that this only mattered because she was Queen Isabel's best friend. He pushed away the dread that tried to settle in his gut.

His chest and arms ached. As he and Thad traversed

the estate grounds in the direction of the mansion, he flexed his fingers and rubbed the back of his neck, putting on a show as if the tension of training caused him discomfort. Thad walked a few steps ahead and seemed not to notice. Good.

The heartburn-like soreness had been a dull constant for many months. Lee hadn't bothered with seeing a doctor. No point. His last mission... He'd made it out alive, but nobody knew how close he'd come to death. How much his body had resisted. A vampire his age should have centuries remaining on earth, but in his core he knew what lay ahead. His body no longer functioned as it should.

Lee would fix this once and for all. Find Haig, kill him, and tear that sanctimonious monk into fucking confetti. Make sure the slaughterer stayed dead this time. See Thad and Isabel's heir into the world safely. With hope, the stupid human cattle would never be the wiser.

Then, he could die in peace.

Chapter 2

IT HAD BEEN A WEEK SINCE HER HEAD-SPINNING RUN-IN with Lee. Alexia crept through one of the estate's barn-style garages, hauling her ever-present anxiety along with her duffel bag, while the sun rose outside. The lecture she hadn't gotten from the king, the shoe that hadn't dropped yet, she expected it around every corner.

The peacefully quiet morning announced nothing out of the ordinary. Chirping birds. Squirrels or something scampered over the roof of the garage. A woodpecker did its thing out on the siding, not realizing that it wasted its effort on vinyl that only masqueraded as wood grain.

She opened the door of one of the fleet's black Land Rovers and slid behind the wheel, letting out a loud breath. She shoved her duffel into the backseat and pulled down the visor so she could slide on some lip goo and finger-comb her hair.

The passenger door opened without warning, and a shot of alarm made her go cold all over. "Fuck me."

Lee slid inside, his body overwhelming the passenger side of the car. "I wonder," he said slowly, "if you're going deaf from all that techno music you love to use to shake your brain." He scratched the side of his neck. The sweat-dampened skin over his biceps and forearms bunched as his muscles contracted. "We just had a talk a few days ago about how you were going to stay inside during the day from now on."

"You talked."

His eyes scanned her with a maddening lack of urgency. Up. Down. Up. "Willfully stubborn death wish, then. I stand corrected." Really? What the fuck? "So." He clicked his seat belt. "Where are we headed?"

What a crazy-assed dickhead. She jacked up her eyebrows. "*We* aren't headed anywhere." He accused her of having a death wish when he was the one who wanted to take a morning drive? "The sun's already started to come up. Anyway, I'm just moving the car. I left it here last time I borrowed it, and it belongs at the back of the lot."

Alexia believed in planning ahead. If she set everything up by packing what she needed and moving the vehicle to the back entrance now, she'd be all good to make her great escape after the baby came. She could leave while Isabel recovered, in the midst of all the fawning and bowing hoopla, and nobody would notice.

She took in all the grit and grime on his body, the way his clothes clung to him. "Why are you all gross and sweaty, anyway?"

"Training new fighters." He studied her. "Anyway, where do you think you're sneaking off to this time?"

Alexia's gripped the steering wheel. "Are you going to tell?" She hadn't heard word one about Lee catching her in the hall the week before, and waiting to get nailed by royal retribution had been eating her alive.

He yawned wide, turning to stare into the dark of the garage through the front windshield.

"This has nothing to do with getting a slap on the wrist for breaking the rules." She turned in her seat, eyes traveling along the hard lines of his jaw. "I just want to lead something resembling a normal life. I'm always careful. And besides, your wizard enemies mostly keep the same hours as you guys."

Lee folded his arms over his chest, still staring somewhere into the dark garage beyond the car window. "Wizards aren't our only issue." Lips pressed together, he took a deep breath and let it out slowly, like maybe he was trying to gather the patience to deal with her. He faced her again, eyes darkened. Storm clouds rolling in over the tropical water.

Alexia swallowed. Danger lurked in the obscure depths of his cloudy expression.

He leaned across the console, enveloping her with his smells. Night air, damp earth, and sweat. "I don't need to remind you that your mere association with us makes our enemies yours. A centuries-old war couldn't give half a tired fuck about one tiny human casualty, Lexi."

Alexia closed her eyes. She knew. His enemies had attacked her before. Which was why it was best for her to get the hell out of Ash Falls. Away from all the vampires, especially this one. "I haven't forgotten," she said. She opened her eyes to find him staring even more intently, nose barely an inch from hers. "But I can't hide indoors forever. It's making me all kinds of cray-cray, you know?" Heat rushed to her face and she smooshed her cheeks with her hands, as if doing so would help. "I am *not* a nocturnal bloodsucker."

The thing she couldn't say to Lee, that she couldn't say to anybody, ran so much deeper. Putting her protection in someone else's hands these past months had been an intense and fear-inducing exercise in giving up control. That thing the other day, falling down and not being able to even get her own damn knee patched on her own terms? Fuck no. She deserved control over her own body, and she'd been rendered helpless. *Helpless* was something she could not afford.

Large fingers brushed the hand she still pressed to her cheek. "I think I understand."

Her brows drew downward. "You do?" Really, she'd expected more argument.

"You're the only human living in a world of vampires. I may not like or trust your kind, but I can grasp that being told when to come and go feels stifling." His hand tightened around her wrist. "But." His face hardened. "I was dead fucking serious when I said there are threats you don't understand. What's brewing now has the potential to bring more destruction than any wizard. I need you to take this seriously."

"How—" Her mouth didn't work. "That doesn't make sense."

"A religious head case named Haig left his calling card by the back gate last week. That cord you tripped over."

What? "Religious how? Like those guys who jump around with microphones on television?"

He shook his head, appearing lost somewhere in his memory. "I killed this fucker, Lexi. Six hundred and fifty years ago. Ran a sword through his mouth. Set him on fire. Watched him burn. Somehow, he's back."

Alexia didn't say so, but she wondered if maybe this didn't actually drive home the reasons for her to go. If some major revenge blowup was about to go down, shouldn't she steer clear of the cross fire?

Lee's thumb tapped her forehead. "I see your wheels

turning. You're safer here than out in the human world right now. You have to trust me."

Alexia made every effort to match the intensity of Lee's stare. Maybe for now it would be best to agree. "You know what? You're right." She smiled. "Why don't you just let me move this car to make room in the garage?"

His eyes narrowed.

"Swear ta God." She gave him her best smile. "I'm only gonna move the car. I'll be back in five. Three." *For now.*

Slowly, he pulled away and stepped out of the SUV. A ripple in the shadows and a soft click of a door told her that he'd gone back inside the main house. Wow. She couldn't believe he'd listened. He'd believed her. She resolved to return lickety-split so as not to lose the inch of trust she'd just gained from Lee.

She put the car in gear and pulled out of the garage, down the winding drive that led to the estate's rear entrance. She was adjusting her mirrors against the sun's morning glare when movement in the rearview caught her attention.

No.

Alexia pulled onto the grass, racing out the door on shaky legs. "Oh my God." A dog on a leash yipped from the yard under a large shady tree. Isabel's dog. The leash was wrapped around Isabel's wrist. Isabel, pregnant, pink all over where her skin showed, lay motionless on the ground.

The blood rushed between Alexia's ears, and she let out a panicked scream as she dropped to the dewy grass. "Isabel!"

No response.

—◆◆—

Lee had just met the king at the end of the hall when they heard Alexia's scream.

"Thad! Lee!"

Pounding thundered on the door that led to the garage. They both tore down the hall. Alexia and a barely conscious Queen Isabel spilled through the door.

Lee had his phone in hand before Thad finished pulling Isabel through the entryway to a more comfortable position. "Brayden. Emergency with the queen. Looks like sunstroke. West hall."

Thad had bitten into his wrist before his knees hit the carpet. Isabel wore only a tank top and monkey-themed pajama pants, but every visible inch of the queen's once peachy skin glowed a glaring bright pink.

"Holy shit she's heavy," Alexia panted, sliding against the wall and down to the floor.

Lee couldn't believe that Alexia, at hardly over five feet, had managed to move the barely conscious queen at all. The petite human packed an impressive amount of might.

Lee and Thad had been getting ready to have a late meeting with Anton, mate to Thad's sister. Said former wizard who'd left the dark side for love chose that moment to mosey down the hallway. The startled male made a quick retreat back the way he came, muttering something about getting the queen some ice.

Yeah, wizard boy, ice will fix this problem.

"What the hell was she doing outside?" Lee stuffed his phone back in his pocket. Rage and frustration nailed him right between the eyes. "Where did you find her?"

Alexia pried her half-closed eyes open, chest heaving from the force of her ragged breath. "Under that crab-apple tree not too far from the garage. I guess she must have been walking the dog too close to dawn." Her eyes went wide, and she gulped audibly. "I don't know where he went. I had to let him run off. I could hardly hold up Isabel."

Lee wanted to tell Alexia, "Fuck the dog," but clearly this was a concern. Of course. Isabel loved that animal. This would matter. Lee couldn't claim to understand, but he knew it to be true.

"Fuck! She's not swallowing." Thad's words, like his face, betrayed his fear and pain.

Lee was moving closer to see if there was any way he could assist when Anton came back with a plastic bag full of ice. The wizard dropped on the other side of Thad. "Here." He reached out tentatively. "Permission to try to help her, Thad?"

Thad nodded with a thick swallow. "Go ahead."

Alexia stood and moved across the hall to give them room. Her hand rested on Lee's arm for support. Her body vibrated with tension.

Lee's stiffened, each muscle cranking tighter by the second. He kept his hands curled and ready. Heaven forbid Anton do anything to harm the queen.

Alexia tapped Lee's forearm. "He's a good guy. He's not going to hurt her."

Lee looked down at her wide, dark eyes. "Brayden is on the way over. She should be seen by a *doctor*."

Anton might be on the side of the vampires now, but the hard truth was every time Anton healed—every time he used any of his powers—they all remembered he'd stolen that ability by killing a vampire and eating its heart. Trust would not come easily for the wizard, even though he'd pledged his loyalty to the vampires. Even if he did love the king's sister.

Alexia squeezed Lee's arm. "Anton's intentions are good."

Lee kept his focus on the action at his feet. Trying not to feel the heat of her smooth fingers on his skin.

"He's been here for months. He's done a lot of good. At some point, you have to let go and trust."

Well. The human was entitled to her opinion.

With a deep inhale, Lee stepped sideways and circled the threesome on the floor, moving to stand opposite Alexia. Having her so close made his head cloudy. Made him want to take her in his arms to kiss her as much as to strangle her. Fuck, he despised how weak wanting her made him. Right now he needed his focus.

Across from him she twitched, pacing the small area with a funny jumpiness. Finally she grabbed the discarded bag of ice from Anton and dropped to the floor, resting it gently on Isabel's forehead. Lee should have thought to do that himself, dammit. Isabel shifted and moaned, rolling onto her side.

The sluggish thing in Lee's chest jumped, and Thad exhaled a heavy, relieved breath, trying again to get Isabel to take his blood.

"Oh, thankyouthankyou." Alexia's head went back as if she whispered her gratitude straight up to the heavens.

Lee kept still even though the thing inside his chest nearly burst. The queen lived. Thank fucking God.

"Thad." Dr. Brayden raced toward them from down the hall. He, too, had his hands full this week, helping

Lee with the injuries incurred during training. "I'm sorry. I came from the barracks as soon as you called."

A great deal of muttering and shuffling followed. Isabel moved and groaned again, and Lee's head got light. He sent up his own silent prayer of thanks that the queen still fought for life. This all hit far too close to home.

"I want to get her to St. Anne's," Brayden said. The doctor checked around on her stomach with a stethoscope. "I *think* I've got a fetal heartbeat…"

"Oh, thank fucking God…" Thad rocked back on his heels, slamming his hand hard enough to leave a print against the white painted wall.

"…but she should be hydrated and examined properly. She's close to her due date…"

Only a couple of weeks away. Thad had mentioned the due date many times.

Lee spotted a knotted cord around Isabel's wrist, similar to the one Alexia had tripped over the week before. He bent swiftly to cut it from her arm. This could not be good.

The doctor swiped at a sheen of droplets on the queen's arm. "This moisture was on her skin when you found her?"

Alexia nodded. "It was kind of a layer of frost at first. Like the outside of ice cream when you leave it on the counter."

Lee pressed his lips together. Leave it to Alexia to use ice cream as an analogy under pressure.

Brayden only nodded as if this made perfect sense. "She must have used her power to produce ice to cool herself down."

"Interesting," Lee said. He always figured Isabel's magic ability didn't hold much use for a sitting queen who spent her days meeting subjects and settling land disputes. Now, Lee gave thanks for that fucking power.

Lee crossed his arms and shifted against the wall, wanting to jump out of his skin. Nothing for him to do right now but watch. The sheer impotence was maddening.

Brayden nodded. "Probably saved her life." He looked at his watch. "We've got a lot of hours until dusk."

"I can drive," Anton said. "I'll pull the van around into the garage." He took off down the hall.

Lee nodded, already following the wizard as Thad lifted Isabel. "All right, let's go." Having the wizard on premises also meant one more body who could withstand the sun's rays to drive in times of emergency. Lee conceded right now that it was a tough benefit to argue.

"Wait." Alexia ran up the hall behind them. Lee turned. The rest continued down toward the exit she and Isabel had come from.

"I need to grab a change of clothes for Isabel, and I'm coming with you. I'm her birth assistant. If anything happens with the baby, I have to be there. I promised."

Fuck. The panic on Alexia's face filled Lee's gut with dread. "Fact is, given the circumstances, there's not a damn thing any of us can do for her right now. I'm sorry." He let the *least of all you* stay silent. He might be an asshole, but he had some respect. "Now we have one windowless van with a driver and it's leaving. I have to go, Lexi."

He turned but she grabbed his wrist. His pulse jumped. "I'm going with you."

They couldn't waste the time to argue. "Fine. To hell with the clothes. We'll find out what she needs when they've assessed her properly. Keep up and stay out of the way." He shook off her touch and turned to jog down the hall.

Behind him, Alexia ran.

Chapter 3

LEE'S RELUCTANT HEART BEAT STEADY AND FAST, echoing his frustration. Bad enough the king and queen had to be rushed to the hospital, that they were outside the estate where they were safest. Worse yet that a meeting of the Elders' Council had been scheduled for that very evening—not enough time to cancel after the queen's brush with sunstroke. And fuck Lee's fucking life...

"Is it just me or do these Council elders all sound like chattering monkeys?" Siddoh, his next in command, had been selected to join him. The vampire voted most likely to make Lee stab something with a salad fork.

Lee's fingers pressed into the podium. "Is it possible for you to stand still and shut the fuck up?"

Siddoh's shoulders managed a casual shrug. "I suppose anything is possible."

The muscles in Lee's neck wrung tight. He tapped a finger patiently and waited for the din to quiet. He'd seen the old bats and bat-esses chill out much faster for Thad. Maybe they still waited with hopes that the king might show. Whatever. He wouldn't give these ancient assholes the satisfaction of begging. He wasn't as far beneath them as they liked to pretend.

"You know," Siddoh whispered next to him. "In my nearly four hundred years on the planet, I have held certain truths to be universal. Females were always right, if you valued your eardrums and your testicles. Vampires were always good. Wizards were always unredeemable assholes. Cheesecake was always delicious. And if you convinced the world at large you were enough of a devil-may-care dickwad, nobody rammed the tippy-top of the chain-of-command totem pole up your ass." Siddoh took a deep breath. "Lately all my universal truths have been shot to shit."

Lee turned his head slowly and pegged Siddoh with a glare. Dammit, he didn't have a salad fork, but he *did* have a Taser. "Siddoh…"

Siddoh leaned his hand on the podium, too close to Lee's. "Except the thing about cheesecake. That shit's delicious. God help any man or beast that dares defile my love of creamy goodness with graham cracker crust."

Lee's hand curled into a fist. "We are here to make an announcement, and then I am needed at the hospital with the king and queen. You are needed to help guard the estate. If you can focus on priorities for one goddamned minute, we can do this thing and then leave."

For one maddening second it looked as if Siddoh might speak again, but just to the side, an aging male in a long coat stood to fire a shrill whistle. Immediately the cacophony faded.

"Excuse me, everyone, but I believe the speaker is waiting for our attention so that he may open the meeting."

Siddoh clapped Lee on the shoulder. "You see? Problem solved." For Siddoh, everything was always fine. Fucker made "laid-back" look like an escaped serial killer on amphetamine.

The elder, Siddoh's uncle, sat and gave Siddoh and Lee a conspiratorial wink.

"Thank you, everyone," Lee said to the room when they had all settled into their seats. He nodded politely to Siddoh's uncle.

The elders all narrowed their eyes suspiciously. Disquiet buzzed through the room. Someone in the back coughed.

"Okay," Lee said, when finally the shuffles and murmurs had ceased. "Under other circumstances we'd have canceled this meeting entirely, but there wasn't enough notice."

Hundreds of pairs of eyes widened with curiosity, and Lee's jaw clamped down. Not knowing why Thad wasn't here probably gave the elders a rash, and Lee would sooner walk naked into the sunny downtown streets looking to tango with Haig himself than tell these assholes what had just happened to their queen. Couldn't trust a single damn one of them.

"The king has been detained." He held out both palms. "Before you ask any questions, I know nothing further." Thad suspected disloyalty among some on the Council. They had hoped the actions were limited to one elder who was now under house arrest, but one couldn't be too careful.

Siddoh drummed his fingers on the podium. Lee resisted the urge to slam his fist on the guy's hand. Or bring out the Taser.

Someone popped up to the far right. A female Lee didn't recognize. She must have ascended only recently. "What of Elder Grayson? Why have we been unable to visit him to see about his well-being or to have our private Council meetings?"

Because he's a scummy piece of shit who tried to kill

a member of the royal family. That would be, as Alexia would say, "a big freaking duh."

"What the fuck is wrong with these assholes?" Lee muttered beneath his breath.

Siddoh cleared his throat. "You want me to give you the list alphabetically, or by age?"

Lee cut his gaze to Siddoh but didn't respond. "Elder Grayson is under house arrest for the assault and attempted murder of the king's half sister," he said with his voice raised again.

The din of voices swelled around them again. Siddoh leaned over. "I suggest now would be a good time to blow this lemonade stand." For once, something on which they agreed.

Lee bowed quickly to Siddoh's uncle and stalked out of the room. It was the best he could do without making his neck and back ache more from tension. If the elders thought hard, they could make the leap: the queen had been pregnant eight months. Vampire pregnancies lasted for eight and a half. The king suddenly wasn't available, and not everybody in the room was stupid enough not to do the math, even though they acted dumb as cattle.

For fuck's sake, Isabel and that baby had better survive.

He and Siddoh eyeballed each other when they reached the parking garage. "I need to get back to the hospital," Lee said. "You know what this means."

"Yep." Siddoh jammed his hands into his pockets. "Tippy-top of the totem pole." His fingers combed through his too-long hair. "Take care of them, yeah? And hurry the hell back so I don't have to be Dad anymore."

Lee nodded. "Bet your ass. Keep an eye on the human news for signs of Haig and his dirty work. I can only assume the fact that he hasn't attacked after leaving that message means he's trying to make us squirm."

"Or he's cooking something really fucked up."

Lee had no doubt.

St. Anne's Hospital made Lee's eyes burn. The bright lights, the smells, the sanitizers. Seriously, the lights. He'd held a spotlight in a wizard's eyes during interrogation that had lower candle power than the shit blazing in these hallways. Wasn't this the place where vampires came to get *well*? No way a little pale-green paint on the walls and a few pictures of flowers were going to help perk up the infirm with all that fucking glare.

As he headed up to guard Queen Isabel's room, someone walked past with objectionable-smelling greasy food and stale coffee. Burning acid shot into his throat. Again.

With a nod he took the post over from the soldier stationed at the door. Down the hall, Lexi and Anton sat close in a set of wood and vinyl chairs, talking with their heads together. The deserter wizard had his hand on the small human's leg.

You do not deserve to touch her.

Alexia acted as if the hand on her leg meant nothing, but Lee remembered. Accident or no, she'd passed out once when Anton had dared to touch her and use his healing powers. Clearly the wizard had gained better control over his ability, but it had taken weeks—months—for Lexi to return to her usual self after that night. Whatever Anton had done to her, how could she allow herself to get close again?

It defied logic.

The air beside Lee stirred. An arm brushed his. In his next sideways glance, the king's sister stood by his side. She must have just teleported in. "You still don't trust him," Tyra said.

Lee faced forward again. "If I truly distrusted him, you'd both have been out on your asses by now. Or he'd be dead."

She crossed her arms over her chest. "I love you, too, Lee."

"I do love you, Ty." Down the hall Anton brushed a tear from Lexi's face. What happened? What made her cry? The doctors had said Isabel was cooling down and the baby had a strong heartbeat. What had that bastard said to Alexia? *Why was he touching her?*

His chest thumped painfully. Lee slowed his breath. "Nevertheless, greater good is greater good. As it is, you're lucky there were no further attacks on the two of you from inside our community after he arrived."

"Yeah," she said quietly. "You'd think… He killed his own father to protect me. To protect all of them. What is there not to trust?"

Down the hall in the chairs, the defected wizard curled his fingers around Alexia's. Her free hand pushed a stray swath of mussed hair out of her face, and she smiled gratefully at him. At Anton.

Lee's own fingers clenched. "Wizards are soulless and vile," he growled. "This is knowledge burned into the hearts and minds of every vampire from childhood. One of the keys to our survival. That there is an exception to such a rule after so many centuries will be hard for some to grasp. Besides, he could have killed his father for personal gain. Revenge. Look at his brother, Petros, who used their father's death to take over as the new wizard leader."

"Hmm." Deep breath from her. "You know, I think he feels protective of her," Tyra murmured. "Because they're both outsiders. Anyway, he thinks she's got some sort of childhood trauma."

"What?" Now Lee's head ached.

She gestured slightly. "Anton. Lexi. He says he thinks she's got some sort of childhood issue. Something he gleaned from his healing touch, I guess."

An orderly pushed in front of them with an empty cart, blocking Lee's view. Shit.

He glanced at Tyra, whose brown eyes were staring at him with far too much curiosity. "Honest to God, Ty, sometimes you bust out with the weirdest shit."

"So do you." She rolled her eyes. "You keep wondering if there's something going on between them. Which is just ridiculous."

Was he being so obvious?

"I can tell. I know you. And lest we forget, I remember all those months ago when she first came to the estate. Even then, I could sense your desire for her. Anyway, I thought you'd want to know your territory is well marked."

Another of Tyra's abilities was reading emotion through touch. Damned annoying. "I've asked you not to read me. She is not my territory. I haven't marked a damn thing." Yet without intention, an image of his bite on Alexia's pale throat appeared in his mind. Jesus, imagining such a thing spun desire through his stomach.

"Well, I try not to pry. It was just so obvious then, and now…" She turned again, inclining her chin toward the two other individuals talking down the hall. "I don't have to. I can see the little muscle twitching in your jaw and the way your hands are poised like you want to grab a weapon. For the record, you should hear the way he talks about her. Like she's a kid."

Lee swept his gaze up and down Alexia's body. Tonight she wore tan cargo pants and a long-sleeved shirt. Simple, but the thin, nylon pants rode low on her hips. As she sat in the chair, they dipped to expose her lower back and a piece of one of her tribal tattoos. The shirt hugged her waist and glittered with rhinestones across the chest. Impossible not to notice the feminine lift and swell of her breasts. Her curvaceous hips. Alexia was no child.

Tyra nudged his arm. "We're in a secured vampire hospital, and you said yourself if you thought Anton was truly a danger to our race, you'd have kicked him and me both out of the estate by now. So why the need to watch her so closely?" She took a breath and lowered her voice. "Moreover, I know sometimes you check on her. I've come through the house on my way back from the shelter in the morning and caught you listening at her door."

Lee went still. He wasn't aware anybody knew he listened in on Alexia. He'd learned quickly that she didn't function well with silence. Lexi always had something playing in her room, usually music. He could tell her mood in an instant by what came out of her speakers.

"So, I think what bothers you is that you don't know what's wrong with her. Or that Anton is the one giving her comfort. Or—"

Something in the back of Lee's skull snapped. "Stop. Please. There's nothing going on with Lexi, and I wish you'd mind your own business."

The bustle of the hospital filled in their tense, contemplative silence.

"Don't you think it's been long enough since you and Agnessa—?"

"No." His teeth snapped together.

"Jeez. Sorry I said anything."

Lee's chest tightened. "Look. I don't deny that I care for Alexia. That doesn't mean anything. I care for you, too."

She rolled her eyes at him. "You know damn well it isn't the same."

No, it wasn't at all the same. It had never been the same. Against Lee's very will, he'd wanted Alexia from the darkest depths of his being since the moment he'd spotted her.

"Tyra, it's a bad fit. I can't be with a human. To be honest, I'm not sure I can be with anybody. It's not simply what Agnessa did. It's me. I like the freedom of being on my own."

"To do what? Go bowling with your bros? You have the absolute opposite of a social life."

Lee withheld a snarl at Tyra's attempt to raise his ire. "The greatest enemy our kind or humankind has ever known may be alive and well and lurking in Ash Falls. For fuck's sake, Ty, he started the plagues.

"We—I—will have our hands full if he manages to

resurrect that magic once again. I'm trying to reorganize our forces so that our fighting power is stronger. Now is not the time for relationships." *And the thing is, I'm pretty certain I'm dying. Death and relationships do not mix.*

"Yet somehow I've managed." She gestured down the hall to Anton.

He scoffed. "It took you more than a century to settle down. With someone who is helping us to fight the war. We don't have many female fighters, and I don't sleep with subordinates. Or humans."

"You're second to the king. If no humans and no subordinates are your rules, you'll never get laid. What's wrong with humans?"

"Untrustworthy. Biologically inferior."

Tyra sniffed. "Until recently, we all thought my mother was human. You never thought I was inferior."

Oh, fucking hell. All at once, Lee's skin itched everywhere. "Half human or half wizard, you always had your vampire side. Are we done with this insanity? What the fuck are you even doing here?" he whispered low and harsh.

She chuckled. "Thad wants you to take Lexi back to the estate so she can pick up Isabel's things, and he wants you to make sure things are secure there. Also, Xander and Flay have run across some suspicious goings-on out in Humanlandia. They're coming over soon to give a full report, if you want to be back for the powwow."

Lee nodded, staring down the hall while Anton handed Lexi a cup of coffee. The girl nodded at something he said, while he placed a hand on her shoulder. Lee took another slow, deep breath.

Tyra held up a slip of paper. "I have a list."

He snatched the paper from Tyra's fingers. "Great." With Tyra to guard the door, Lee shoved forward, his eyes rooted on Alexia. He tried not to take in the fullness of her lips or the tick of her pulse and the flush of her cheeks when she noticed his approach.

He failed.

Chapter 4

THERESA PACED THE WAITING AREA OUTSIDE OF PHLE-botomy at St. Anne's vampire hospital. Eamon Junior, her six-month-old, slept against her chest. Overhead, some speaker she couldn't see announced something, called a name she couldn't quite understand. Every time the address system roared to life, her nerves jangled. She was afraid this would be the time they'd announce it was his turn to get his blood drawn and she'd miss the call. A vampire covered in burns was wheeled past in the hall, surrounded by a gaggle of staff in white coats and colored scrubs. Probably attacked by wizards, probably urgent.

Her eyes burned but she held back the tears. Yes, others had urgent needs, but she was here with a starving infant who needed his blood drawn. If she and Eamon hadn't already been forced to wait through the entire day after the baby's checkup, she'd simply go home to the royal estate and tell her son's pediatrician that the old windbag could put his growth charts in his pipe and smoke them. She didn't want to have to bring her child back to go through this torture all over again.

She glanced at the clock, large and luminous against a green-and-white wall. Eight in the evening. How was it possible that they had here for more than fifteen hours? The balls of her feet begged for mercy, but she didn't dare sit. Movement kept the baby calm and asleep, and she'd been told strictly not to feed him until they could draw his blood. *Not feed a six-month-old baby.* Didn't these monsters know what they were asking?

What a nightmare.

"Theresa?" A large hand gripped her elbow.

At her startled jerk the baby jolted awake, arms flung out wide in a T. He wailed in her arms with his mouth open wide. His budding fangs peeked through inflamed gums.

"Damn." Theresa bounced and patted, uttering shushing noises into her son's ear. God bless the mother who'd given her that *Happiest Baby on the Block* DVD.

Little Eamon, poor thing, shoved a balled-up hand into his mouth. Fat tears rolled down his face. At least he wasn't screaming.

"I'm sorry. I didn't mean to wake him." The kind, green eyes of Xander, one of the king's fighters, smiled down at her. He'd watched over her and the baby for a time, after her mate had been killed in a wizard attack.

Theresa shook off her surprise and bounced with baby Eamon, humming to him once more. She'd been using her power to induce sleep when needed. After using it all day, though, she struggled to stay upright. The baby snuggled against her again, awake and hiccupping, but quiet. He stared at Xander with his wide, wet, black eyes.

"Wow, he's gotten so big. May I?" Xander reached out before Theresa could think much about it and calculate the probability that Eamon would cry again at being handed to a stranger. But he didn't cry. He stayed wide-eyed and staring as the large vampire held him up and then pulled him to his dark T-shirt-clad chest.

"That's amazing," she said. "He's been crying practically all day. I wouldn't expect him to take to a stranger so easily."

"But I'm not a stranger," Xander murmured as he touched his finger to Eamon's nose. His eyes crinkled at the corners, and his cheeks dimpled when he smiled. "I don't suppose you remember me, little guy. I held you a few times when you were just born. You were so small and fragile, I was practically afraid to pick you up." He lifted Eamon and gave him a light pretend toss, eliciting a giggle from the baby. "You've gotten heavier now, huh?"

Oh, God. Inside, it was all Theresa could do not to burst into tears. After the night and day she and Eamon had gone through, pacing the brightly lit halls with her hungry child that she'd been told not to feed, feeling so alone and helpless… She fought to keep herself together in front of him.

Xander stopped jiggling the baby and turned to her. "What's wrong, Theresa?" Who would have thought such a powerful vampire, with his rough hands and tattoos and six feet of muscle, could speak in such a gentle whisper?

She shook her head. "We're fine. I've been waiting for him to have some blood drawn." She glanced at the clock. Eight-thirty. Back over to the lab door. The tech had been gone forever. She didn't even know whom to ask at this point… "They said they needed to find someone who has experience with small babies."

"No." He gripped her arm, gentle but insistent. "I know it's been awhile since we've talked, and I don't want to pry where it's not my business, but…" He leaned close to her ear. "I can feel something bad. I've never been that good with female emotions, I have to be honest with you, but I can sense in my blood you're upset. We're still friends, right? What's wrong?"

Theresa shivered. She had given him blood as a favor when he'd looked after her and Eamon, and that hadn't been for several months. "You can still feel—"

"We're on you right now. And Eamon." He smiled quickly down at the baby and cuddled him. God, he was good with babies. "What's wrong with him?"

Her knees just didn't want to hold anymore, and finally she could sit, so she did. "I don't know. I'm still hoping for nothing. He's not gaining weight to the doctor's satisfaction. His baby fangs came in early so I started transitioning him to blood but he's not growing well. They think maybe he might have globusemia."

Xander's green eyes got wide. "Blood allergy?"

"I know," she said. She'd sobbed for so long alone in her home after getting the call about the diagnosis. Saying the word again now brought fresh tears and a lump to her throat. "It's so rare. I'm praying they're wrong."

Usually a young vampire started out getting blood from a guardian until they reached the age of consent and were allowed to feed from another of their own kind. Occasionally, a parent's own blood could be incompatible. The doctors had told her a true inability to digest all blood was rare, but vampire babies with an allergy to the one thing they needed to survive died quickly. The not knowing these past weeks had left Theresa raw and wrung out. "They want to double-check."

"Okay." Xander nodded, sitting with Eamon on the seat beside Theresa. "So this may all be fine."

She nodded. "I'm trying not to worry, but there's been little else to do all day." She gestured to a corner table scattered with magazines. "I even read *Field and Stream*." She tried to laugh at her poor joke but choked on the words.

Eamon cried out and chewed his tiny fist again. She tugged his arm, afraid he'd bite himself with his new fangs, but the gnawing seemed to calm him, so when he insisted, she let him continue.

Xander frowned. "He seems hungry."

Her chest tightened. "They won't let me feed him. The test has to be done while fasting for the results to be accurate. We've waited so long that he's starving. Usually he eats every four hours. I'm about to give up and take him home."

"No." He hooked an arm around her shoulder, bringing them both to standing. "No, you need answers. And this is ridiculous. He's only a baby. They can't leave a widow of the king's military just waiting around. Did you tell them you're a fighter's widow?"

Horrifying. "What? No. I would never use Eamon's death as some sort of bargaining chip." She hadn't even thought to. That just seemed wrong.

"Fine. I will."

"Xander—"

"Theresa, this is to help your son." He strode across the room to a blond vampire at a coffee machine. "Flay. Can you handle meeting with Thad and Lee?"

Oh God, they were going to see the king? "Xander, I'm so sorry. You've got more important things to take care of. We'll be fine."

"They've kept a hungry child waiting. It's not fine." His arm was heavy and warm around her shoulders.

"Flay, this is Eamon's widow, Theresa. They've left her waiting to get her son's blood tested all day, and the kid's starving because he can't eat before the test. I'm going to see if I can't help get this handled."

Lord. Her throat clogged with gratitude. She didn't like to think herself helpless, but Xander was large and loud and unfettered by a squalling baby. Maybe there was something more he could accomplish.

Flay bowed slightly. "Of course. I'm so sorry for your loss, ma'am."

More tears pressed behind her eyes unexpectedly. "Thank you." It was so hard to respond when people said they were sorry. What was she to say? *Thanks? It's okay? No biggie?* No answer was right. But she didn't want to be ungrateful.

Flay nodded to Xander. "We're early anyway. If you're not back in time, I'll let the king and Commander Goram know why you've been detained."

Xander pulled her away, heading down the hall past the lab door. "Come on. Not sure why, but nobody's in the lab. We'll check the information desk, and if we have to, we can go to the emergency department. Any doctor in the ER can draw blood."

She hadn't even thought of trying the emergency department. Did she have the worst problem-solving skills, or what? *I'm sorry, Eamon. Your mother is stupid.*

Xander shook his head, as if in response to her thoughts. "When you fight, you get injured frequently and eventually learn to ask the right questions."

"I kept worrying if we went somewhere, or if I gave in and fed him, that would be when they called us for the test finally, and I'd miss the window."

He squeezed her hand. "Well, now I'm here to help."

"Xander? You still have my blood in you?"

He smiled slightly. "Your blood is powerful. I've been very lucky. Now. Down here…"

"You don't need to do this, Xander. I heard you. You're supposed to be going to meet with the king and Commander Goram."

The look on his face just then melted Theresa's heart. He placed a gentle hand on hers, the other hand resting on Eamon Junior's fuzzy head. "*This* is important."

The drive back to the estate from the hospital to get Isabel's necessities had made for all sorts of fun and games. On a good day, Lee and Alexia managed to push each other's "don't make me cut you" buttons in ascending order. This time he had taken the opportunity to insult everything from her skills helping Anton navigate on the way *to* the hospital, to her desire to hit the Starbucks drive-through on the ride home… erm, *back to the estate*. In return she'd insulted his hair, his wardrobe, and his need to wear SPF-one billion.

Poor Dr. Brayden had been forced to ride bitch in the backseat so he could return to check on the guys who'd been injured recently in training. The buttoned-up physician had been scarlet-cheeked and silent for the entire duration. Lexi couldn't say she blamed him for his cheetah-out-of-hell escape when they finally returned.

At first, seeing Lee stalk stiffly down the hall to head to the estate's training quadrant had left Alexia jiggly with relief. Now though, hours had passed. She'd packed up a few belongings for Isabel and herself, and she was alone with her dangerous thoughts in her disaster of a bedroom. So now what?

She had already showered and changed, paced the fluffy beige carpet, and actually finally wondered when Lee might return. Weren't they supposed to get back to Isabel?

She kicked at the piles on the floor, pulled at the mangled sheets, and threw the fleece blankets on the queen bed into something resembling "made." The piles of clothes got tossed into a large hamper by the dresser. If she didn't straighten once in awhile, cleaning staff would creep in while she wasn't around. Then there would be guilt. Alexia had sort of resigned herself to being messy. It just didn't pay to organize and put things away when you might leave again with no notice. But she hated when others felt compelled to clean up her detritus.

She dropped the pile of clothes in her arms when a bizarre ripple swept through her, strong enough to make her body lurch. "What the…" If she believed in ghosts, she would have thought one passed through her middle and tugged at her insides on the way through. Since she lived with vampires, it wasn't such a far stretch to wonder about ghosts. Still, she was pretty sure they didn't really exist.

Okay, now she wanted Lee to come back. If nothing else, to explain what in the hell had just happened. It gave her a vague, uncomfortable impression of the "disturbance in the force" variety. Only she wasn't cool enough, or nerdy enough, or whatever enough, to be jacked into any kind of collective consciousness.

Here, she would always be an outsider.

A gentle knock sounded. "Alexia?"

A pale, fanged female with ruby eyes and platinum hair frowned at Alexia from the other side of the door. In truth, Nessa's crazy eyes had creeped Alexia out at first, but Lee's ex wasn't actually so bad once you got to know her. She was intelligent and funny. Sure, a little weird. But cool-weird, come to find out.

Alexia hated that Nessa was Lee's ex, but they simply didn't talk about the fact that Nessa had once screwed—and screwed over—the vampire that Lexi didn't quite want to acknowledge she still crushed on. Alexia didn't have a lot of friends on the estate. She'd gotten the impression Nessa didn't, either.

She might have worried it would cause other vampires on the estate to give her a wide berth on account of Nessa's bad succubus reputation, but many vampires already avoided Alexia. It was like she had a big, old "Don't touch the human" sign around her neck. Especially since that embarrassing thing with Anton. One tiny touch and Lexi had wound up sprawled out on the rug like a drunk. God. *Don't feed the bears. Don't touch the human.*

Alexia peered at the pale-skinned half succubus, nausea settling in her own gut. Nessa hardly ever looked worried, but she did now. "Is everything okay?"

"I was going to ask you the same," Agnessa said. "I felt that shift. I came to check on you."

"Shift." Alexia rubbed the goose-pimpled flesh on her arms. "Yeah, what was that weirdness? Did you get a vision or anything?"

Agnessa served as Thad's spiritual adviser. As Alexia understood things, Nessa was one of the last remaining Oracles known to vampire kind. For that reason alone, folks put up with her succubus half and her über creepiness. And Alexia liked Nessa, but she could see how it was a little creepy. Half the time she was pretty sure the scarlet-eyed lady could literally read minds. She'd come to accept that there were wacky vampire powers and whatnot that she didn't understand, but being around Nessa occasionally gave Alexia the urge to fashion herself a really kick-ass tinfoil helmet.

Nessa, dressed more conservatively than usual in designer flats and pants, turned in the hall. "I can't always command my visions. What I experienced was a powerful magical explosion. I know that much." Without warning, Nessa gripped Alexia's hands. Pulsing energy passed between them, wrapping around Alexia's arms and growing into a tangible *thing* like she held a large ball of static in her arms. "Here, you will need this," Nessa whispered.

This was not the first time Nessa had done the weird energy whatsit thing to Alexia, and once the shock had passed, it didn't seem to hurt anything. So Alexia let it slide. Times like now, the strange energy helped to calm the pterodactyls flapping around inside Lexi's body. Hopefully it wasn't a weird vampire spell, and while Alexia was off in a trance, Nessa was leaving her a quart low.

As fast as she'd gripped Alexia's hands, Nessa stepped away. "We should find Lee."

What fun. It was practically putting matter with antimatter when those two were in the same room. Alexia couldn't even picture the two of them together *that way*. Not that she'd tried. Gross. "I've been waiting for him to come back. We're supposed to take some of Isabel's things over to the hospital, but he's been gone awhile now."

"Here I am." Lee rounded the corner. He squeezed past Nessa and pushed into Alexia's small room, magically contorting himself so he didn't brush against Nessa even one iota. Right, because matter and antimatter. If they touched, there might be an explosion. An implosion. Nuclear disaster. World war. Baby hedgehogs bursting out of all the air vents.

Lee filled Alexia's untidy bedroom with his bulk. He'd changed clothes into camo pants and a dark shirt. His body dripped with weapons, guns under his arms and strapped to his thigh. Knives clipped to his pants. God knew what he had in those pockets or other places she couldn't see. His expression, dark and serious, did funny things to the place where her legs met her body.

He's a killer. That shouldn't be hot. Really shouldn't.

Siddoh followed closely behind. He, too, appeared far more subdued than usual. Siddoh was one of the few vampires Alexia had fun hanging out with, but right now he looked like he was on his way to a funeral and having trouble figuring out how to fill out the card on the flower arrangement.

Lee's look held a larger dose of grim than usual, and that was saying something. "Sorry for the wait. In case we have to be away for awhile, I wanted to be sure all the bases were covered."

Bases. "What's wrong?" Alexia and Nessa asked at once, and Lee appeared to get nauseous.

He focused on Agnessa. "Nessa, do me a favor and go with Siddoh. I want to make sure everyone is in a secure location."

Agnessa's eyes widened. She frowned and opened her mouth like she might disagree.

Siddoh took her by the arm. "I wouldn't argue, Agnessa. This isn't the time."

Lee stood stiffly with his arms at his side. He waited until the other two were down the hall and around the corner, before turning back to Alexia. "That disturbance you felt was the security system losing power."

"Whuuut?" Alexia's brows pulled together.

"The magical security system."

"Oh." She wasn't sure what else to say. It sounded bad.

"It's what helps to keep us hidden from outsiders, as well as prevent our enemies from crossing the threshold onto our land."

"Oh." Very bad. The estate covered two hundred acres and held hundreds of homes, cars, and other buildings. They were set back from a rural access road and surrounded by forest and farmland, but it would still look suspicious if one examined closely. And it would be dangerous for a lot of vampires if the property could be breached by an enemy.

"I suspect someone caught wind of Thad and Isabel leaving the estate, and may have something planned while we're vulnerable." The muscles tensed and flexed in his forearm as his hand clenched and released, lifting to rake over the back of his neck. His frustration vibrated in the air of Alexia's bedroom.

"You think this has something to do with that threat you mentioned? That guy?"

"Exactly. Which is why I've put the rest of the estate on lockdown. Thing is, taking down our magic security is beyond him, as far as I know. Then again, I also thought he died six hundred years ago."

Jeez. "Yeah, on a scale from one to ten, I'd say that's pretty spectacularly fucked-up."

Lee closed the gap between them. An awareness of warmth and clean sweat cut through the anxious confusion his last statement had injected into her stomach. "Frankly, it's safer here," he said. "I'd leave you if I could. However, I've received word Isabel is having contractions and insists on having her birth coach." The wave of his hand conveyed his apparent belief that such an idea was preposterous.

Alexia stepped close, craning her neck to meet his arrogant stare. "What, you think the queen's birth coach isn't a priority?"

Lee's large hand rubbed his forehead like it ached. "In my youth, females gave birth. No birthing tub, no special class, no self-hypnosis CDs, no coach."

What. A phenomenal dick. "Excuse me." She poked a finger that was supposed to jab into his chest, but anger and her refusal to break eye contact effed up her aim. She ended up poking at the firm, fine muscles of his belly. Pride kept the finger in place as if the landing had been intentional. "First of all, no uterus, no opinion. Second, Isabel got completely fried this morning, so it's kind of a special circumstance. Third, quit being an asshole. Fourth? Quit being an asshole."

It bore repeating.

"Fifth, Isabel's the queen. She can request whatever the hell she wants."

Lee dipped his chin. "Yes." His fingers closed around the one still sunk into his abs and pulled it aside. "She can. So. In spite of the fact that we may have an insane plague-spreading nutcase bearing down on us at any given moment, it's royal baby time. Let's move."

Again… What the fuck?

She opened her mouth but Lee pulled her forward before she could speak. Alexia ignored the tremor that traveled from the place where their hands touched, along her arm and down her body, landing a quiver of want deep in her core. Any time now, it would be fan-fricking-tastic if her body could stop reacting to him like he'd been double-dipped in her favorite brand of pheromones.

She reached for her blue JanSport backpack, just next to the bedroom door. He made no move to let go or get out of her way, and she was forced to squeeze past his tree-trunk thigh in the process. She failed horribly at ignoring how frigging huge those legs of his were. How the vee of her thighs brushed his leg when she passed, and how her body temperature climbed. *Stop staring at his ass*. "Right. Got everything ready to go, right here." She cleared her throat.

"Great. I'll drive," he grumbled.

Did he realize, as he tugged her down the hall, that his fingers were still wrapped around her hand?

Chapter 5

LEE'S NOSE PICKED UP THE ELECTRIC TANG OF A STORM brewing in the air. The static prickled his skin. Without hesitation, he clasped Alexia's shoulder and drew her against his side as they exited the mansion's side door at the end of the east hall.

She scowled up at him with a mix of irritation and confusion. Far from the first time. They certainly had a way of tripping each other's wires. They could pretend otherwise all they wanted—Lee would fucking love to pretend—but from the moment Alexia had followed Isabel to the estate, she'd seemed hell-bent on raising his ire. Centuries of building a carefully controlled facade, and he couldn't keep his grip around one tiny human.

He adjusted his hold. "I told you. The security system is down. I want you close." He pointed toward one of the open parking areas. "I'm getting one of the smaller cars."

They trekked in silence down a long gravel path that led to a parking area where most of the vehicles were located. At the front of the property stood a large barn and a cover of trees, to help the illusion that the property was nothing more than a very nicely kept farm. Everything was masked further by vampire illusion. Alexia's body stiffened, and when he had the sense she might tug away, he slid his hand to her waist. The shift secured his hold but made it less awkward, more gentle. She didn't quite relax, but she stopped fighting.

Her frame was small even by human standards—just above five feet in height. With his rangy six feet and four inches, he hadn't really expected she'd fit against him so nicely. Yet his hand spanned the curve of her waist. Her head, if she moved just so, would go right in the crook of his arm.

Her human teeth sank into her pouty bottom lip. "So what's the deal with this Haig guy? How can you be sure this dude is back from the dead after six hundred and whatever years?"

Lee spread his fingers against the hourglass of Alexia's waist. How could the curves of one human be so perfect? And why were males wired to think of sex at all moments of the day, even when things such as war and illness held the greater priority? "You've heard that old saying about keeping friends close and enemies closer?"

"Oh. Damn skippy." She shrugged against him. "In seventh grade, my 'friend'"—she made air quotes— "Alethea Darrington thought she was badass because she developed early. She not only stole my boyfriend but also started a rumor that I stuffed my bra and had gone 'all the way' with her brother in the back of his 'hot rod.'" More air quotes. Her head swiveled around.

"The only place I went with him was to the library to study for algebra, and his so-called hot rod was a Honda Civic with a rusted grapefruit launcher where his muffler should have been. She said I spread crabs to his entire track team, so I said, 'Let's bury the hatchet,' and invited her over for a slumber party so I could do that warm-water trick to make her pee in the bed."

Lee shook his head, half surprised she'd never attempted such a stunt with him. "All right. So I suppose you understand. I once knew Haig better than anyone."

"Okay, but I wouldn't know Alethea now if she passed mc on the street."

"You might surprise yourself. Anyway, let's say your enemy Alethea had not only wronged you personally. Let's say she killed millions of people."

Alexia sucked in a breath.

"Trust me. I once knew this bastard as well as I knew myself."

"But… the fence." She looked around. "I thought we had double security. There's a human-installed system, too, right? The fence has motion sensors and video monitors and all that jazz, and then there's the magical protection. So without one, you've still got the other, and the estate should still be relatively safe." As she chattered, her warmth pressed closer to his.

Sure, when she was this nervous, she didn't think he was such a motherfucker.

Lee's jaw muscle twitched. "I don't like 'relative.' I don't believe in coincidences. That this happened on a rare occasion when the king and queen are away from the estate for an extended time says nothing good." Lightning flashed a bright spiderweb across the sky. "And I don't like the fucking weather." The fact that this risk of plague would be of far greater harm to her than to him died on Lee's tongue.

Alexia stopped. He pressed his fingertips into her waist to make her continue. "You can't control the weather, Lee."

That was why he hated the weather.

Thunder rolled overhead, too fast after the lightning. They needed to haul ass. "Sky's going to open up soon. Let's move." Nothing frightened him anymore. He'd grown too old for life to throw him true surprises. Still, bad weather added an extra layer of complication. He experienced a healthy sense of urgency in light of the coming rain.

They made their way to his favorite car, a black Honda Accord sedan. Screw the big SUVs that screamed, "Sorry about my small penis." This thing had a V-6 and handled like a dream. He opened the door for Alexia and ignored her angry glare when he all but shoved her inside, scanning the surrounding area for activity. *Sorry, Lexi. Priorities.*

He'd given the order for all residents to remain inside. An eerie quiet hung over the estate as far as the eye could see. B Team patrolled the primary vampire-housing areas in Ash Falls. C Team was staying close to the estate tonight. Siddoh had been given the task of wrangling the elders into putting the mojo back in place for the perimeter. Dammit, they needed a better plan for the estate security. They couldn't count on a bunch of aging assholes who were all against the king as their primary line of defense. Lee pushed Alexia's door closed, went around to the driver's seat, and took off.

They'd made it less than a quarter mile down the road when the sight of a person stumbling into the road from just off the woods made Lee hit the brakes. "Shit."

"Oh God. What happened?"

"Hard to say."

He had a suspicion. The car hadn't hit the man, Lee was certain. Yet the human who'd stumbled into the road had fallen. With his superior vision, Lee had spotted lesions on the guy's face. The Big Bad that Lee had been expecting might well have begun. He could only hope that Haig and his crew were nearby so he could kick their asses.

He pushed open the door. "Stay here, Lexi. I don't like leaving you by yourself, but I have to see what's going on out there. Lock the doors and call Tyra immediately. She can come and give you an airlift." Times like these, Tyra's ability to teleport proved useful.

Alexia bit her lip again. Scared. Angry, maybe. He couldn't make this better for her. And as much of a bastard as he could be, he would smooth her fears over if he could. They had no time for arguments. "There are nearby patrols. Soon as I see anything strange, I'm calling for backup. I'll be fine, okay?"

She nodded but said nothing.

He took that as his cue to leave.

—ᴗᴗᴗ—

Alexia's call to Tyra did not go through. Neither did the next three rapid redials. She lasted maybe a minute, two tops, before she developed an extreme case of the panicked squirmies. Sure, easy for Lee to tell her everything would be fine. He was the one running off through the woods with guns and knives strapped to his brawny vampire bod.

Why was he running off through the woods, anyway? What about that kid who had taken a nosedive right in front of the car?

Blackness surrounded her, save for the eerie glow of the moon blocked by trees and clouds. Lee had pulled off the main road onto a tree-lined shoulder, so she couldn't see much beyond the cockpit of the Honda Accord and the surrounding forest. Unnatural thumps through the woods in the near distance did nothing to help her level of discomfort.

Her wild imagination conjured up all sorts of scenarios, most of them involving Lee being beaten to a bloody pulp, even though she knew damn well he could take care of himself. It didn't escape her that this was probably somewhere in the vicinity of what he imagined when she went outside alone during the day. She could see now that she'd been a bit one-sided in her thinking.

A flash of lightning and a sonic boom made her jump. "Fuck." She clutched her shirt in the center of her chest, grateful for a lack of witnesses. Where the hell did Lee go? Hopefully, he'd met up with the other patrol guys, and they were all kicking names and taking ass. Maybe Lee was even kicking ass all on his own.

She pulled her phone out again and thought of calling someone else, but all the someones she could think to call would either be guarding the estate—very important—or guarding the king and queen—ridiculously important. She couldn't ask someone to drop everything just to come and get her.

Morbid curiosity made Alexia wonder about the guy on the ground in front of the car, and she wanted to know if she could hear the sound of Lee's voice anywhere. Slowly, she pushed her way out of the car. Sticky August air permeated her clothes the second she got out.

The night sky lit up daytime-bright with another flash of lightning, giving her a clear view of the dude on the ground. "Oh. Fuckballs. This guy's totally messed up." She barely whispered the declaration, wishing Lee hadn't disappeared into the woods.

In terms of options, sticking by the side of a vampire who made her want to break out the bitch-slap hand stood head and shoulders above hanging out with a dead guy. Well… now she had set her bar.

Alexia stooped down. She didn't want to touch the body, but damn, she'd seen shit like this in old science-class textbooks. Waaay back, like in middle school. The ugly patches of skin, the blackened fingers. The Black Plague. This was what Lee had talked about. It must have been what spurred him to head for the trees. Clearly, whatever caused this guy's lesions had caused his death. Far grosser in person, this plague thing.

"Oh hell," she murmured. "That can't be right. Didn't they eradicate the plague? Is this some kind of zombie apocalypse?"

When Lee had said something far more dangerous was on the horizon, she'd thought he was being ominous and threatening to keep her in line. Looking at the disease-riddled corpse at her feet, she rethought her position. God, he'd said something about millions dying. She tried hard to remember those plague symptoms, but all she could remember about eighth-grade science was trying to get Eric Garmeneski to bump elbows with her during lectures.

She'd still been innocent then.

Crackles came through the trees like fireworks. She had to find Lee. She couldn't stay here with the car and the dead guy. But running into the dark woods…

The sky lit up daytime-bright with lightning. Movement through the trees caught her attention. She strained to see. She recognized a few vampires from around the estate, but she didn't see Lee. The guys they were fighting… "What the—"

They wore robes. Nothing she'd seen before; these reminded her of something old and clerical. Something a monk or a priest might parade around in, only Alexia didn't attend church enough to know for sure.

And their hands glowed. As in seriously, if she didn't know better, she'd think they were all walking around out there with *E.T. phone home* going on in their palms. Had these guys just shown up, or she been too distracted looking at the dead dude to notice?

The really freaky-deaky part, though, was the low, melodic chanting that echoed through the trees. About a half dozen of them fought as they murmured their creepy incantations, but nearest to where she crouched, a young vampire had been separated from the group by one of the monkish-looking freaks. Somehow the spell or whatever held the young vampire ensnared and un-able to move. One of the robed weirdos held up a huge fucking knife, and the vampire just stood there. Like he was waiting to get sliced apart.

Alexia couldn't just stand there and watch him get killed. She grabbed a big-ass tree branch from the ground and ran as fast as she could. She managed to swing and connect squarely with the back of the big asshole's head. The man in robes turned on her, still holding the psycho-killer knife. The vampire crumpled to the ground.

She blocked the knife with the branch, but the robed dude got her good in the face with his fist, bringing blood and tears with the stunning wallop. He drew up high, and through her watery vision, the dagger gave a threatening gleam in the moonlight.

She stepped back, landing a kick right to his jewels with her Doc Martens. The knife disappeared onto the ground, and Alexia kicked again. The guy went down, but she kept whaling away with the tree branch, even though her arms shook and burned from adrenaline and effort. She didn't know who or what this guy was. She only knew she needed him to stay down.

Something exploded in the direction of the car, and voices came closer. She ought to go check on that vampire. The asshole on the ground had stopped moving. She crouched to check him out, and pain bit her in the knee as her stitches popped open.

"Lexi." Someone grabbed her from behind. "Stop."

Lee stepped up beside her with his arm raised. A couple of shots, and the creep was done. Definitely dead.

He sliced the dead guy at the wrists and throat to make the body bleed out, and Alexia watched in fascination while the body turned to ash as it drained right before their eyes.

Wait. What?

A large hand grabbed her chin and brought her face around. Right. Lee. "Jesus, are you okay? You're bleeding everywhere. What the hell happened? Why would you try to beat an unknown enemy with a fucking stick?"

A big branch, not a stick. A stick would have been stupid. She almost laughed.

She shook her head but that made her dizzy. Everything shook. Good God, she'd just beaten the shit out of some guy. Months ago, she'd hit an enemy wizard with a car. She wasn't sure she'd killed that one. It had been self-defense then, but still… What was she turning into? She dropped the tree branch.

Lee grabbed her hand. "Lexi, I need an answer. Are you okay? Can you move on your own?"

"Yeah." She nodded. Her voice came out scratchy. "I can." She hoped. Her legs shook like a mofo.

"Good." He glanced around and grabbed her arm, heading deeper into the woods. "Then I'm sorry, but we need to run."

Chapter 6

LEE GRIPPED ALEXIA BY THE FOREARM. BEHIND HIM, her footsteps tripped and tumbled. For once, remorse burned in his belly when he yanked her forward so they could tromp deeper into the woods.

"Lee, I can't keep up."

"You have to." The sticky, humid night air clogged his nostrils. Giant mosquitoes buzzed around his face, flying into his eyes and ears. Fucking nature. "You're injured. Going back to the estate is not an option. You may not have noticed, but the car got blown up back there while you were busy playing pint-sized vigilante. We need cover so I can get you healed."

More hustled footsteps. She actually kept up fairly well for an injured human. He'd noticed her legs were rather long for her height. Just not long enough.

"Who the hell were those guys?"

"Magic wielders from an ancient religious order. Guardians."

"What?" She huffed and ran behind him again. Coughing and sputtering ensued. Probably blood from her nose getting into her mouth. It sucked when that happened. "Where the hell are we going, anyway?"

He shook his head. "I don't know their plan. They never before strayed so far from their leader's tomb. Come on. This isn't the place to chitchat." He pointed up ahead, slowing slightly so he could fall in beside her.

"Through these woods is a farm for sale. I'm hoping the property is still empty. I want to get you healed. I'm concerned about the amount of blood you've lost."

"Yeah, right." She all but snorted the words, as if the idea of his concern was preposterous.

Lee turned to look at her. The sight of all that blood jarred his brain. He couldn't believe she'd tried to fight a guardian with nothing more than a tree branch. "What does that mean?"

"Like you're actually worried about my health and well-being."

He growled his annoyance. "It behooves me to get you back in one piece and not looking like you got the hell beaten out of you. I also think you're not nearly as excited to be captured and killed as you'd have your sass and defiance make me believe."

She threw her hands in the air. "Give the vampire a gold fucking star."

God save me, I am trying to be patient with her. The word here is "trying." He rubbed his tender jaw. "Then let me carry you. I know I've been an asshole about things in the past. Let's both forget about pride for a minute. If I'd been doing the walking for both of us, we'd be to cover by now. Every minute we spend in these woods, we risk our lives, especially with you injured."

She stopped, bit her lip, and mumbled a quiet "fine." Dammit, she looked terribly vulnerable covered in all that blood. Vulnerable and appetizing.

Lee scooped her up, cradling her in his arms rather than over the shoulder. He knew from experience that she wouldn't stand for being treated like a sack of flour.

The sky opened.

"Dammit." After that, Alexia didn't argue about Lee carrying her.

His boots sped over the damp earth. Moments later, they arrived at one of the local properties where show horses had once been trained. The economy was tough these days, especially for humans. Dilapidated fences ringed the perimeter, and downed dressage posts lay on the ground in a dirt ring in front of the house. The humans had clearly loved their horses. The nicest kept building on the property was the barn. It stood close to the house. Closer than some people kept them.

He went there instead of the main house. The building appeared sturdy, and it would be a less obvious place to hide. Upon inspection, Lee found that some straw remained in the upper loft area.

He sat her against a bale of hay. Her clothes, soaked with blood and rain and spattered with dirt and tree sap, had seen better days. Still, after everything she'd just gone through, her dark eyes challenged him.

"Are you okay?" She nodded and brought her hand to her face, but he grabbed it preemptively. "Don't touch. Do me a favor and look to the left."

She complied. A deep cut across her cheek oozed steadily. Unexpectedly dark and lovely... for human blood.

Lee's fangs thrust into his mouth. He ignored the pulsing ache in his cheeks and gums. All that life-giving fluid of hers. All... over... her. "I'm going to stop the bleeding."

A blink and slight nod was all he got in the way of approval. She sat still, even though she probably didn't know what he was about to do. And he didn't explain, because around Alexia, he barely kept his will on a leash. Darkness pressed in around them, but she didn't complain and didn't act nervous as he pushed against her. His cheek brushed against hers as he swept his tongue over her cut. The smooth, delicious warmth of her human blood slid down his throat and deep into his gut. A throbbing need took root. *Merciful heaven.*

He'd dealt with his share of human fluid over the centuries. In battles, prisons… The odor pungent and reminiscent of dirty pennies. Alexia might have soft, olive skin and doe-like eyes, but he'd expected nothing more of her blood than the same astringent copper.

He sucked a deep breath and took another swallow, trailing his tongue again gently over warm, wet skin. Alexia's blood tasted pure. Clean, with hints of all that tea and raw honey she loved to consume. Lee had never perceived anything so refreshing.

"Lexi…" Unable to say anything else, he licked from collarbone to chin, cleaning the blood from her skin. Across her jaw. *More.* Dear fucking God… like breathing, he wanted more.

—⁓—

Alexia held herself perfectly rigid. Her fingers dug into the straw beneath her as the near-dark and the quiet hum of the night air wrapped around them. Rain drummed steadily on the barn roof, a soothing white noise. Lee's tongue slid soft and warm along her cheek.

Gentle.

She hadn't been prepared for gentle. The surprise of his careful touch tripped her heartbeat, making it stutter and stumble. Lee stood tall and broad, like a Sherman tank with arms and legs and deceptively tranquil eyes.

He projected "fuck off" to anyone who dared look at him askance. He killed bad guys for fun and games. He did *not* clean blood off silly humans the way a mama cat would bathe her kittens.

Oh, but... His tongue traced along her jaw, and a breeze in its wake made her shiver.

"Cold?"

She squeezed her eyes shut. "No." She shook her head. Another breeze, another shiver gave her away. The rain had caught them outside, and her clothes were soaked. "Okay, a little. I get cold easily, and my clothes are wet." *Also, your tongue is on my neck.*

"Here." He pulled off his jacket and slid it around her shoulders, tugging the lapels together. The jacket, with its fleece lining and its warm, dry interior, swallowed her whole.

"It's okay. I'll be fine. You don't need to give me your coat." She shrugged it off again.

Strong hands returned the jacket to her shoulders. "I know you take great pride in making up for your size by being unbearably stubborn, but wear the damn thing. Please. This isn't fucking chivalry. This is about keeping you from getting sick and getting you to the queen intact. Now." He grasped her chin gently in the crook of his thumb and forefinger. "Hold still. I need to finish cleaning your face. Make sure your nose is set. I'm going to give you some blood to make sure the break heals quickly. Okay?"

His blood. Hooooboy. She swallowed. "Okay."

Alexia tried to stay nice and calm on the outside. Inside, her body heated at the suggestion. To her own personal embarrassment, she even got a pleasant, tingly little throb going between her legs. She'd drunk Lee's blood once before, after being attacked by a wizard. The experience of putting her lips on his skin and sucking his blood had been startlingly erotic.

She wasn't sure if it was the blood itself, or the two hundred and fifty pounds of alpha male that she'd been sucking the stuff from, but day-um. Doing that again? Not a good idea, not in the slightest. Not if she wanted to keep her dignity. She'd decided unequivocally since then that staying far away from the emotionally un-available, bad-guy-slaying vampire was the best idea ever. Especially since he clearly viewed humans as a subpar species.

But Lord, that vampire had been tasty…

"The best thing," he said, "would be to have you re-move your wet clothes. But we need to be ready to move again soon, and it seems your pack was left at the car."

Killing her. Absolutely killing her. Her fingers dug deeper into the dry, prickly straw. She shivered again, this time not so much from the cold. "Sorry."

"It's okay. Let me finish." He touched gently around her nose, then swept his tongue over her jaw, her chin, and her neck. He lingered there, and she couldn't be cer-tain, but gentle huffs gave the impression that he was… sniffing. She indulged for a moment in a fantasy of him biting her, drinking from her. Pulling her body against his while he—*No*. She swallowed.

Why would he even want her? He'd made it clear: humans weren't good enough for a fighter like him. He needed someone with stronger blood. *Why do you want to be with someone who doesn't like you as a person, anyway? Get over him, Lexi.*

Except right then, it was so easy to get lost in the considerate way he held her. In the near eroticism of… Oh. Heaven. His tongue brushed the corner of her mouth. It wasn't a kiss. Not a kiss. *He's cleaning off the blood.* But so nearly something, almost, if she closed her eyes and pretended.

"Ow." Her arousal cooled when the solid grip of his hands left her arms and went to work prodding at her nose. "*Owww.*"

"That hurts?"

Were all vampire guys so dense? "Holy fuckingheimer, are you kidding? Yes, it freaking hurts."

"I'm trying to help," he said. "And your bastardization of the word 'fuck' would make some of my soldiers blush."

A gust of wind brought a fresh round of teeth-punishing shivers. "I totally feel that fact, and thank you. But you know, I fought some freak back there in the woods. I'm pretty sure my nose is broken, and I'm soggy and cold. My apologies for being cranky."

He huffed a breath, and in the dark of the loft all she could see was the shadowy outline of his body. Tough to tell if he was happy or pissed or somewhere in between.

It was also tough to stay mad with his body pressed so close.

"Here," he said. "Drink."

Something warm and wet pressed to her lips. The familiar tang of his blood, salty with hints of anise, slid over her tongue. She wrapped her lips around his wrist, sucking tentatively at first, then harder. His blood was thicker than human blood; it reminded her of drinking warm bisque. She had forgotten how much she enjoyed the taste. Maybe she'd blocked it out for the good of her sanity.

The last time she'd drunk from him, she'd hardly sipped much before he put on the brakes. So she pulled away after a few moments, surprised and secretly thrilled when his hand pressed into her hair. "Take more." When she hesitated, he said, "You've got a broken nose. Go ahead."

More warmth flowed into her mouth, leaving her little choice but to gulp and swallow. Alexia's blood hummed, and desire spiraled through her insides. Forgetting all restraint, she dug her fingers into his arm and sucked harder, eliciting a murmur from Lee and a tightening of the hand in her hair. In the quiet dark of the barn, his warm body pressed against hers. His breath puffed against her ear.

Alexia's blood flew through her veins. Her body pulsed head to toe, from a pleasant tingle in the tips of her fingers to the intense swell of pleasure that centered in her core. God, the way his thigh was wedged between hers, if she just squeezed only... a little... *Gah! Don't embarrass yourself.*

She had to remember this couldn't be real. This was the two of them in the isolation of a hayloft after a high-stress moment. This was him healing her because it was his job. As Thad's numero uno, taking care of Thad meant taking care of Isabel, and Alexia couldn't walk into the hospital and scare the queen while she was in labor by looking all battered and bloody.

But for that one moment, the power of his blood, of knowing that for just a little while he wanted her the way she wanted him? She reveled in that delicious power. Rarely in her life had she held something so precious.

Chapter 7

SIDDOH IGNORED THE RAIN THAT SOAKED HIS CLOTH-ing. He marched the path toward the perimeter fence gate ahead of his uncle, flanked by the doctor and another soldier. "You're sure you can do this, Uncle?"

"I'm not convinced it's necessary, but I can."

Siddoh's eyeball throbbed. So many of the elder vampires had issues with humans, particularly those in his godforsaken bloodline. "Commander Goram sent word of threats in the surrounding area. I've sent backup but the security system must be fortified."

"The quarantine—"

"Cannot be kept in place indefinitely." Siddoh cracked his knuckles, hating his current position. Being the drunk fuckup held far more comfort than the guy in charge of making sure the estate didn't get flattened.

"It can be kept in place until the human plague has run its course."

Siddoh stopped. He turned slowly, stabbing a finger at his uncle, who hid under the cover of a large umbrella. "The king and queen are not at the estate. St. Anne's Hospital has not been sealed, and the handful of vampires in our community with human blood in their veins may not be immune." He drew close to the elder, injecting a threat into his growl. "We will not have this conversation."

They had reached the edge of the estate. Siddoh's

uncle drew up straight, nostrils flaring in the soggy, stormy night. Lightning flashed overhead and showed everybody's grim faces. "You're right. Of course," said Elder Esmerian. He drew a deep breath but still hesitated, staring off into the night.

Siddoh strode forward. "Are you too ill for this, Uncle? Is that the trouble? Perhaps I need to find someone else." Uncle Sion was no fucking unicorn. His power, while rare, could be found elsewhere in their community. "You haven't taken blood since Aunt—"

"I have the ability," Elder Esmerian snapped. "I helped to erect that fence when this estate first broke ground, and I can damn well restore it to power."

All righty, then. Siddoh nodded. "Very well."

The different possibilities beat their bloody knuckles against each other in Siddoh's churning gut: his uncle lying to him versus his uncle sapping what power remained in his body after the death of his mate and subsequent refusal to feed. The royal estate spanned a good couple hundred acres. This would not be easy.

Elder Esmerian had dropped his umbrella to the ground and returned to staring into the dark night. Counting raindrops for all Siddoh bloody knew.

"Uncle Sion. I need to remind you that we have literally hundreds living on this piece of property. We've got a gaggle of Haig's guardians spotted less than a mile from the estate."

Sion closed his eyes. "Step back," he commanded.

Everybody complied except Siddoh. He nodded to the doctor. "Stand by, just in case."

The elder's hands went to the sky, and lightning flashed. Again. And again. And again.

He's drawing the lightning.

Channeling it was more accurate. Like yarn on a spindle, the bright strands of electricity coiled and bounced along the fence, like a concertina of razor wire. The image glowed and stretched as far as the eye could see. Siddoh kept watch on the elder's hands while the coil of light grew longer and longer. The older male's arms shook, his face red and rain-slicked. Two hundred acres was a shit-ton of ground to cover.

Thunder rolled overhead.

The elder male channeled more lightning, and more again, until at last the ends met. They fused together with a sizzling firework of spark and sound. Then the entire thing disappeared.

For a moment nobody spoke. Uncle Sion's hands dropped to his side, his breathing deep. "That… that should do it. No evil will get inside these bounds. I swear."

Siddoh approached slowly and put a hand on his shoulder. "You gonna make it, Uncle?"

"I think I will, yes."

"Need help getting back?"

"No, I…" The old male took a step but before he could continue, he crumpled to the ground.

Siddoh took a knee in the muddy grass and hoped to hell the only family member who still spoke to him wasn't dead.

A boom of thunder overhead drew Lee's attention. The heavy bang, reminiscent of cannon fire, also startled Alexia enough to unlatch from his arm. Which was for the best. The only excuse he had for his appalling distraction and letting her feed so long was that the pounding in his pants had managed to relieve the ache in his chest.

Lee needed to find his discipline. He'd tasted her blood, and she'd consumed his. Now her hands on his body, her lips and tongue on his skin brought him alive with need like he couldn't remember. Ever. For the first time in months, the steadily growing certainty that Lee would soon be fodder for the sun gods faded into the surrounding blackness.

It was good to forget. Amazingly easy, until that boom of thunder had yanked him back to the present. For a moment he'd been taken back to the battles of his youth. The plagues, the human land disputes, the greed, and all the trouble that came after. He closed his eyes and shook his head.

He'd lost his mother and sister, thanks to all of that bullshit—thanks to Haig and greedy humans mistreating each other, and his mother getting in the middle. No good came from revisiting those memories. From getting too close to humans. Now, it could all happen again.

Lee licked closed the punctures on his wrist. Alexia's throat made hard, wet swallowing sounds, and her hot breath ghosted over his jaw. *Hell.* "What should we do now?"

He put his hand to the side of her face. God willing, his blood still held the strength necessary for her to heal quickly. Sure enough, as they sat quietly in the dark, the bruises slowly faded and the swelling on that tiny nose receded. The bump on the bridge straightened. Good. Excellent.

"We just need to get you healed and make sure the

coast is clear, and then you can head to the hospital."
He pulled out his phone. "I'm going to call and see if I
can get Tyra over here to teleport you back." Lee could
manage fine on his own. Getting Lexi to safety was
paramount. What he really needed was to follow up with
those guardians they'd found in the woods. Make sure
they had truly met their end.

"Good luck. I tried earlier and it went straight to
voice mail." She wriggled and shifted, pressing closer
between his thighs as he crouched there on the loft floor.
"Jeez, this hay is scratchy."

Scratchy hay fell dead last on their list of problems.
He could have, should have moved away. He didn't.
If he insisted on torturing himself, he may as well
go balls out. He'd already admitted that he wanted
Alexia. He saw nothing to be gained in lying to himself about his desire. He wanted her physically, and
he could even acknowledge that he cared for her, after
spending time in her presence these long months. Of
course he did. It just didn't change anything. Their
situations were immutable.

Human. Vampire. Biology could not be altered.

Nor could deeply held mistrust. Were it not for humans, his family might still be alive.

"I need to get you to the hospital." Lee's phone
blasted light into the dark, nearly blinding his sensitive
eyes. Fuck, no phone existed with a screen he could
make dim enough at times like these. He eased against
the wall of the loft, suddenly light-headed from the shot
of brightness.

"Lee, are you okay?"

How does she know? He pushed down a burst of rage.

His blood. This was one of the reasons he never shared. Privacy. Even if she wasn't aware of what she was feeling, she sensed his weakness in her veins. Without cause, he hated them both for his vulnerability. "I'm fine," he said quietly.

Her doubt lingered in the air, crackling like the electricity from the storm, but they both remained silent.

Sure enough, Tyra's phone went to voice mail. As did everyone else he tried. Finally, he called Thad, who answered on the third ring.

"Lee, I was beginning to worry, man. I tried calling but I couldn't get through."

"I've tried calling as well," Lee said. "Nobody's answering."

"Reception might be spotty due to the storm. Also, Saint Anne's doesn't allow phones to be on in the maternity ward. They'll make an exception for the king, but I'm still getting nasty glares. What's your status?"

Across the way, Alexia had given up and leaned her arm back down on one of the blocks of hay. She appeared smaller than usual, still dwarfed in Lee's jacket. Her eyes drifted closed. No doubt, the feeding and the night's earlier effort had worn her out. Now cleaned of blood, her face looked pale and etched with exhaustion.

But… beautiful.

"Siddoh's trying to work with his uncle on the fence. Lexi and I were forced to take a detour." He dropped his voice and cupped his hand over the phone. "She nearly killed a guardian, Thad. I secured her out of harm's way, but she saw Parinon being attacked while everyone else was occupied. She beat the asshole with a damn tree branch."

On the other end of the line, Thad sucked in a breath. "That's twice now, including the wizard she ran over last winter."

"I know," Lee murmured.

"I hope she can handle this," Thad said. "Unfortunately, I've got bigger issues. They're saying the baby is in distress and Isabel's not ready to give birth. I may be unavailable if they take her down to surgery. The storm must be getting bad because the lights have gone dim here twice already."

Lee bit back a curse. "Understood. Can you send Tyra for pickup? I need to make sure the coast is clear, but if she can get Lexi over to Isabel—"

A flash-bang of lightning and thunder came through the slats in the barn, followed by an obnoxious beep from Lee's phone. He tried to redial, but there was no service. "Fuck."

Alexia raised her head, looking heavy-lidded and drunk. From his blood. "What's wrong?"

A stiff wind blew. "The storm must have knocked out cell service. I have no way to tell Thad where we are so Tyra can pick you up."

She sat straighter. "So what now?"

"We get you to the hospital some other way. Hopefully we can make it before Isabel has the baby." Lee kept the surgery thing to himself. He kept a lot to himself. Alexia needed to keep her head together, not worry about Isabel. Not now.

"How do you feel?" He looked her up and down. Already her skin glowed with renewed health and her wounds had faded. The inflammation had gone down in her nose.

Lee's chest swelled. He'd healed her. His blood. His body. *Him*. Something so simple, but it fluffed his feathers nonetheless.

"Good." Her smile lit the darkened barn. "Stronger."

Good. "Ready to move?"

She drew a deep breath and pulled her shoulders back. "Yeah."

"Okay. Let me help you climb down. I don't want you to burn up all your brand-new energy."

He reached for her arm and pulled her close. Instantly he returned to where he'd been only a few minutes before when he'd lapped that blood from her face, when he'd swept his tongue over her lips. When he'd nearly given in to the urge for more.

All over again, he wanted. Craved.

They'd nearly finished descending the ladder when the short hairs of his buzz cut tingled. His sensitive ears picked up subtle scrapes of movement at the back of the house. The quiet warning of an arrow hitting wood. Only a guardian would use such a weapon.

Lee's fingers tightened around the lean arm in his grasp. For the first time in centuries, something acrid burned his nostrils that smelled very much like his own fear. He had to get Alexia out of these woods. "Lexi, we have company."

Chapter 8

THERESA PERCHED ON A BENCH NEAR THE FRONT DOOR of the vampire hospital and peered into the dark, ceaseless downpour. Eamon Junior nuzzled against her collarbone, finally asleep, bundled in a fuzzy knitted blanket from one of the soldiers' mates. Her son had been conceived on a night like this: full moon, pouring rain, a rare night when her mate wasn't on patrol and the power had gone out. Nothing to do to pass the time but make love. That night may as well have been a century ago.

The lab had finished with Eamon's tests, thanks to whatever strings Xander had pulled. Thank God. Little Eamon was finally fed, finally content.

Her, on the other hand? Her body trembled and her ears rang, a sign that she'd overused her powers. She needed to get herself and her baby home. She needed sleep.

The torrent poured relentlessly, though, and Eamon had been through an awful ordeal. She hated to take him out in the cold and wet that would surely wake him, into the parking lot that from her current vantage point appeared to stretch the distance of a football field. She'd parked all the way at the far end. Why hadn't she thought to bring an umbrella? Perhaps she and Eamon could just rest here for a little while.

"Theresa." Xander's voice silenced the echoes between her ears.

She glanced up. Xander stood above them in the

alcove's purplish lighting, wet from the rain. Cast in shadow with his short, dark hair plastered to his forehead, he showed a fierceness that Theresa hadn't seen before.

"The woman at the checkout desk said you'd just left, but I couldn't find you in the parking lot." He let out a breath and sat down next to her. "I was worried."

She frowned. "Is something wrong?"

"I just met with the king. They've called a bunker at the estate. Nobody's to go in or out." He shook his head. "You've been busy with Eamon so you wouldn't have heard. The magical security around the perimeter went down."

"Oh, no." Her head shot up. Her eyes met his. "Aren't they going to evacuate? What about everyone else?"

He shook his head. "It could be just as dangerous, trying to move so many residents. We've got the ability to close off the inside tunnels, so that's what we're doing for now. Nobody is allowed outdoors on the grounds without authorization. Which means I can't let you go back. It isn't safe. Don't leave, okay?"

Her heart flopped desperately. She was so tired. "But what about Eamon? I have enough clothes and supplies for him to last the night, at best. We've already been here throughout the last day. I haven't slept, Xander." How had she never noticed the vividness of his eyes before? So deep and green, like emeralds. Goodness, her muscles ached.

His fingers wrapped around hers. They had both been widowed, had become unlikely friends of sorts, but in the months since, they'd hardly spoken. Theresa had been consumed by motherhood. Xander had rejoined the fight to keep their vampire kind protected from wizards. Now, with his hand on hers, it was like coming home. The familiarity in his touch nearly melted her, and she hardly thought before she leaned toward him, cradling Eamon's fuzzy head with her other arm. "What are we supposed to do?"

Xander leaned close to her ear. "I'm going to take you out of here, okay? You and Eamon," he whispered. "I've got Flay paired with Anton for the remainder of the night while Tyra guards the king and queen," he continued quietly. "Right now my job is to take care of you and Eamon. Everything will be fine."

She nodded. Damp clothes and wetter hair clung to her cold skin. At that moment she nearly would have paid someone to let her sleep there on the stone bench that had turned her right hip numb. She couldn't bring herself to argue.

"Okay," he said. "Let's find your car, find a place to get you some clothes, and go get some rest. I'm going to take you into DC, find a place with electricity, and keep an eye out while you and Eamon recharge. Word has it that something big is going down, and I want you guys far away."

She had been so proud of not needing any help since Eamon Senior had been killed. When Xander had said he needed to leave guarding her and the baby to return to fighting, she had let him go and tried not to miss him much. Had insisted to herself that it was only the hole in her heart left by her mate's passing that had made her want him to stay.

Now... having him go out of his way to help her like this made her so warm inside. But was he doing it out of duty, or because he wanted to? Was it awful that she cared?

Best to stick with duty. The king and queen had both been very upset about Eamon's death. That he'd fallen while rescuing the queen from being kidnapped had hit the queen especially hard. And protecting the next generation of vampires was important due to their dwindling numbers.

But when Theresa looked into Xander's intent eyes, she thought of the comfort he promised and wished just a little that he was taking her home. *Really* taking her home. That he would stay with her there, the way he had when Eamon was first born. Was that so wrong?

———

Fire burned in Alexia's lungs and her muscles screamed for mercy, but she stayed right on Lee's heels, ignoring the clumps of mud that flew from his boots to hit her favorite Kikgirl pants. She felt like she was on one of those Warrior Runs—only amped up to the max because they were running from actual bad guys—and God only knew how much adrenaline and vampire blood charged through her body.

"Holy shit, Lee." He glanced back and tightened his hold on her wrist but didn't respond. "Lee," she hissed.

"Shh."

They zigzagged around trees and jumped over mossy logs. She wanted to ask what the hell they were running from, because she couldn't see or hear anything. But holy cow, did she have a whole lotta rocket fuel in her zoom all of a sudden, and keeping up with Lee was super easy.

"Are we going to run all the way to the hospital?"

"Until I feel like we're clear of the threat, we need to keep moving. Hopefully I'll find a vehicle I can borrow."

A spiderweb clung to Alexia's face. *Ew. Gah.* She brushed at the cloying strands and pushed forward even as surprise plucked at her eyebrows. "You're going to steal a car."

"Borrow."

"Hmm."

Alexia bit her lip. Ish, did she get the entire spiderweb off her face? She rubbed her mouth again. From getting licked by Lee to attacked by a spiderweb all in one night. Talk about your sexy times.

"Somehow I find it surprising that my taking a vehicle to get us to safety would bother you, Lexi." He slowed slightly, allowing her to catch up.

"I find it surprising that *you* would steal. You're so by the book."

He halted, pulling her to his side. "Yes, well I'm also so very fond of not dying in the woods." He raised a gun she hadn't noticed in his other hand before and fired, backing to a large rock face as he did. "You telling me you'd rather I uphold some human law even though we've got guys shooting at us?"

"That's not what I said."

"Uh-huh."

Coulda been wrong, but it sounded a lot like he chuckled. Lee. A chuckle.

"Whatever you do, Lexi, keep touching me, understand? I've got my shields up. Not much they can throw at us that will hurt you, so long as we stay in contact."

Alexia thought of Lee's power as some sort of force field. Very sci-fi. She suspected that was the source of the electric prickles and shivers that danced along her skin where he touched her. She'd *hoped* it was lingering sexual chemistry, not that she should.

She glanced down at his gun. "Do you have another one of those?"

"Seriously?" He exhaled and squeezed the trigger smoothly once, twice, without any change in his expression.

She huffed in frustration. She'd dated guys with gun collections and even taken the odd firearm refresher. "I know how to use a gun."

Lee raised a hand, which she took as a sign for her to shut the hell up, and that only pissed her off more. Still, she shut up anyway because she was definitely down with that whole not dying plan.

A soft click caught her attention in the dark over her left shoulder, and another over her right. Holy crap. In all, she made out roughly five of them. Lee had skills, but they had to be outnumbered here. "Lee, they're all around us." And why hadn't they attacked? Lee had already shot two others. They were lying in wait for something. She shivered.

"I know," he whispered. "I'm going to count to three and step forward. I want you to glue yourself to my back. Do you understand? Do *not* let go."

She nodded. "Okay."

"No matter what. Don't you dare let go."

"I'm cool," she whispered. Only she wasn't. Not really. Honestly, she'd kept it together. She'd followed his lead, and she'd been pretty damn proud of herself for handling what was unarguably an extremely stressful situation without flipping her wig. But all at once, Alexia fought the urge to flee and the inability to draw the stifling night air into her lungs. Hot, fat raindrops pounded incessantly down the back of her neck. Her hands went to his sides and dug into the lean flesh for dear life.

There were a lot of guys in those trees. As badass as Lee was, Alexia didn't see a way out.

He put his hand over hers. "Stay with me. We can do this."

She pulled in a shallow breath. "Okay." She had to trust. She was a goner if she ran. That much she knew.

"They haven't attacked yet because they think they have us outnumbered. They probably don't yet realize you're human. They're trying to get us in one piece and keep our hearts intact to steal our powers," he whispered.

Acid rose in Lexi's throat. So these were wizards then, not the guardian whatchamahoozits they'd run into earlier. She knew wizards—the vampires had been fighting against them for years.

For only a second his hand tapped hers. "Not happening, okay? Here we go. On three. One… two… three."

She stepped in time with Lee away from the rock face, her muddy, red Doc Martens following behind his black military boots. The charge of his shield got stronger. She sensed so in the hum of her blood and the electric buzz over her skin.

Lee rotated them both clockwise, firing on the nearest wizard. He narrowly missed clipping the guy's shoulder. It angered the wizard into advancing on them, and the others followed suit. Not for the first time, Alexia thanked her lucky stars for good bladder control. The icky, nauseating nastiness of five wizards surrounding them made her gag. Her fingers dug harder into Lee's sides.

"Hang tight, Lexi."

Oh, she was hanging, all right. Her hands gripped Lee's sides. The rest of her trembled. She couldn't stop, no matter what assurances she gave herself.

Lee stood completely still. He was so calm that she might have wondered whether or not his heart was still beating, but her ear pressed against his back. The steady *glub, glub* offered limited reassurance. Was he confident enough to be so calm, or just insane?

All at once Lee turned them both toward a wizard who threw out what looked like a long, white rope of electricity. Not unlike a sizzling bolt of lightning, only way hella scarier up close and personal.

The shaft of light flew right at them. Alexia's heart stopped. They were toast. They were so fucking going dow—

Only Lee grabbed the beam of light. *Actually* managed to grip hold of the end like it was a handle or a rope or something.

And then… Oh, holy shit.

Pain screamed through Alexia's body. One look up at the intense concentration on Lee's face, the strain of his muscles against her hands, and she had the source. What she didn't know was why. What in God's name was he doing?

Come on, Lee. Let go.

But he held on to the beam of light, his arm straining with the effort. The others around the perimeter shot projectiles, but they couldn't get through whatever bubble Lee had built around them. Without warning, there was a rumble and a boom. If Alexia hadn't been standing in the center of it, she'd have thought it was more thunder overhead. It came from Lee.

With a blinding flash, the rope of energy scattered outward in a burst of white flame.

In a knee-jerk response, Alexia wrapped her arms tight around Lee's waist and buried her face in his back.

She stayed that way even for a moment after he slumped and put his hands on his knees. "Is everything okay?" His body expanded and contracted against hers, but no answer came. "Lee?"

She looked up. Oh, cheesus. The wizards lay dead on the ground. The whole evil-assed lot of them. Burned. Ashes. So were some of the trees that had been unfortunate enough to bear witness to Lee's display.

Her ear at his back told her that his heart maintained that reassuring *glub, glub*, albeit at a faster gallop. Still, the reassurance was there. Minimal, but there.

He gripped her hand. "We need to g—"

A large, dark oval appeared across from them in the woods. "Uh, Lee?"

A man stepped out. He bore a striking resemblance to Tyra's mate, Anton. Only his eyes conveyed such evil intent that she could practically feel the knife sliding between her ribs.

Lee's hand tightened around hers. His back expanded against her front with the force of his inhale. "Petros." That name. Anton's brother.

The wizard leader.

Before she could blink, Lee took aim with his gun.

"Oh, come on, Commander." The wizard grinned and held his arms wide. "I'm here to make a deal."

That tidbit shocked Alexia enough to make her stick her head farther around the side of Lee's body, but Lee brought his arm down and pushed her head back again.

No way in hell would Lee deal with an enemy. That would be like making a deal with the devil's fucked-up cousin. The ugly one with the meth addiction and a penchant for stealing candy from old ladies. No, Lee would sooner drown a box full of puppies and babies. He'd rather kill—

"I'm listening."

What. Thah. Crap? Alexia's fingers clenched.

Across the way, Petros stepped into a patch of watery moonlight. He gazed up to the sky, head tipped back, unconcerned about the rain or what Lee might do while he wasn't looking. If the creep had henchmen lurking off to the side, Alexia couldn't see them. Finally, Dr. Weirdo took a deep breath and stepped forward. "I thought you would. The enemy of my enemy is my friend, after all."

What in the goofy hell was that about?

Against her, Lee turned into granite. "I suppose. Your father did help to kill Haig once."

It kinda seemed like Lee was trying to ruffle the big wizard's feathers, but Petros only smiled. "I am not my father. Or my siblings. What I am is practical. Haig's magic long predates ours, and if the plague takes root, it will kill our kind faster than yours. So." He clasped his hands behind his back. "I propose a truce. Until Haig is no more. Does this squeak your rubber ducky, Commander?"

A snarl rumbled in Lee's throat. Alexia didn't figure this angry vampire's ducky would be squeaking any time soon. "Petros. He's mine," Lee said.

"Of course." Petros stepped backward into the shadowy dark portal from which he'd arrived. "Unless I kill him first." Then he was gone.

"What a weird asshole." Dull pain smacked Alexia all at once, as if she'd been walloped by a brick barricade.

"Fuck!" Lee went down on one knee.

"Lee, what's wrong?"

He gripped her arm. "Don't tell anybody."

Chapter 9

Lee could hardly understand Alexia as they trudged to the cave opening she'd located nearby. Had she been gargling marbles?

"You know, I'm all for equality but you've got like two hundred pounds on me. This is worse than trying to hoist a half-conscious and pregnant queen."

"Sorry." He allowed himself to ease onto the stone floor of the cave once they got inside. "Jesus, Lexi." The opening was deeper than expected, but he did not like tight spaces.

"What's wrong?"

Hell, now her hands were all over him. Sliding over his jaw. His neck. A frisson of heady arousal bolted through him when her fingers dusted over one nipple on their way to check a scrape by his collar. He should have kept his mouth closed.

"Are you okay?"

He groaned quietly. "Blew my powers. Couldn't let it show in front of Petros."

"I suppose I can understand. What was all that shit about? What was that explosion? How'd you knock all those guys down at once? I can't believe he didn't get pissed." The questions fired in rapid succession.

"I'm sure it was intended." Slow, deep breaths. "He probably set those guys up as pawns so I'd be too weakened to attack him when he approached us with his little deal." Fuck's sake. Not for a second did he trust Petros. But this was the hand they'd been dealt, for now. "The wizard with the ability to channel lightning, I used his power against him. Instead of blocking it with my shield, I amplified the energy. Kept it building until it overloaded. Made them all eat dust."

He chuckled slightly. "Actually worked very well." Best effect he'd ever gotten. "Except for the backlash." His head spun, his chest thumping hard. "But nobody knows I can do something of that magnitude. I'd rather it stay under wraps. Please."

She stopped with her hand on his shoulder, near his neck. One thumb rubbed near his pulse point. "Not even Thad?"

"Not even Thad." It took a great deal of blood to create that kind of power boost. Lee had worked hard to rein in his bad habits. But letting anyone know this was an issue, especially the king? It would cause unnecessary worry. Jeopardize his position.

She shook her head. "You can't honestly trust the wizard leader."

He closed his eyes and the world tilted. "No, but they fear Haig. His magic predates theirs." Agony lanced through Lee's arm. He closed his eyes against the pain. "Haig was the first to divine how to create the magic that the wizards use today, by using blood. In the name of God, so he claimed, but his love of the Lord turned into something sick and twisted. He and Petros's father were friends before they turned on one another. If anybody wants him dead more than we do, it's Petros."

"The magic in their blood. That's how you can make their bodies disintegrate when they die?"

Lee nodded carefully. "Like wizards, their blood destabilizes as they age. Particularly if they have consumed vampire blood to enhance their magic."

Lee waited for more questions. Or one of Alexia's finger-wagging rants. What he got instead was her tight human body pressed against his chest like a second skin. "All right then, buddy. Let's get this over with."

He didn't have to ask what she meant. Her neck hovered by his mouth, and his fangs shot out at the mere suggestion. "Alexia, you're—"

"Okay, look." Her hands pressed against his chest. "Don't even start with that whole 'You're human, so your blood isn't good enough' business. It kept Isabel partying like a rock star for two whole years while she and I were roommates. No, she wasn't a fighter, but this is an emergency. Right now I'm the safety net you've got."

She pulled back, he supposed to give him a stern look, but her nose rubbing against his negated such an effect. "I assume the goal is to get you vertical and get out of here fast. We don't know where Petros went, and I don't see how we get anywhere unless we're going to just hang out here and wait for your energy to return."

Lee nearly bit through his own tongue. He hated that she was right.

"You're hating this, aren't you?"

He didn't answer. His blood flowed in her body now. She could sense his emotions. And he didn't have the energy to keep a lid on them in his present state.

"I'm sorry you have to trust me with your secret, and I'm sorry you have to put up with using my inferior blood, but let's both be adults."

He nodded. She had no idea. No idea at all what trusting his life to a human cost him. What humans had once cost everyone he loved. He'd made it seven centuries without consuming one drop of human blood.

That's only true if I discount the blood I cleaned from her wounds back in that barn. I cannot ignore the fact that it tasted better than anything I can remember in my life.

He could not justify sitting on his hands in a cave waiting to heal when Alexia's blood could help him regain his strength. It might not be as potent as blood from one of his own kind, but right now blood was blood. Hers would get him back on his feet long enough to deliver her to the queen. They could not afford his pride.

Admittedly, her blood had been so sweet.

He lifted a hand and swept her wet hair from her face, rubbing a thumb over one dark eyebrow. Such a stark contrast to her honey and almond hair. "Why don't you let your hair go back to its natural color? I imagine this ebony of your eyebrows would look lovely with your olive skin."

Her lips curved slightly. "Make it through feeding from me without tossing your cookies, and maybe I'll tell you."

She did have quite a way with words.

Her hair slipped silky and damp through his fingers. Her chin tipped. He hardly knew he'd struck until her skin touched his lips. The familiar scent of her filled his nostrils even though the cave was musty. Her blood was thinner and warmer, and the flavor of honey and tea burst on his tongue. So delicious.

These days he fed from whatever unmated vampire

came courtesy of Blood Service. Feedings could get intimate and sometimes arousing, but he never crossed lines. Never took more than the necessary life-giving fluid. Out in the field was different. Emergency care.

This… this was Alexia.

His pulse rushed, and the horrible tightness around his chest released as her blood flowed into his body. More. Yes. *More…*

He hardly noticed the moment when he pulled her into his lap. Her skin burned so hot. She provided warmth and comfort, and he was too tired to fight.

She squirmed against him. The peaks of her breasts brushed gently through wet layers of clothes. His nerves and veins roared to life with surprising power as he drank. The tangy, coppery elixir with hints of honey slid down his throat so easily that he completely forgot himself. Lee burned with the urge to lay her out on the stone floor and taste her from head to toe. Any amount of money, guaranteed, she tasted this delicious everywhere.

He needed to stop. This had already gone too far. *Where's your control, Lee?* He'd left it out in the woods with all their dead fucking enemies.

For weeks, months, he'd ignored this craving for Alexia. And God, this blood. Her blood.

Lee's growls and snarls filled the cave. Feral noises that reminded him of who he was deep inside. Inhuman. Animal. *Stop*.

Alexia whimpered, high-pitched and needy. Her thighs clasped firmly around him. Fingers splayed across his chest. Her thumbs stroked his nipples through the soaked fabric of his shirt.

A strange sensation came from Alexia's hands, a gentle throb against his chest. He pulled back, licking closed the punctures on her throat. "What are you doing?"

Her breath shuddered, deep and heavy. "What do you mean?"

"Your hands. That... pulse. What are you doing?"

"Oh." She wiggled her fingers. "I'm not sure, to be honest. Agnessa did this weird thing a couple of times, some sort of energy transfer I think, and ever since then—"

Nessa. She'd gotten her hooks into Alexia somehow? Lee should have known. For God's sake, nothing in Lee's life was sacred to his scheming, conniving ex. "What sort of energy? What did she do to you?"

Alexia shook her head, suddenly eyes wide and body frozen in Lee's lap. "I—I don't know. It seems to relax me. I could tell you were in pain, so I thought maybe it could... I don't know, help I guess."

Shit. Lee's head clunked the rock behind him. Whatever it was, anything to do with that bitch was tainted. Lord knew Lee himself was fucked in the head, thanks to his ex.

Thinking of Nessa dumped a bucket of cold water on Lee's head. A reminder of what happened the last time he'd allowed himself to get involved with someone not of his own species. He put his hands on Alexia's shoulders, nudging her off him. "Come on," he said. "We need to get going."

—◆◆◆—

Siddoh carried Elder Esmerian's lifeless body to the king's mansion. The old male's home sat a ridiculous trek across the estate. He'd gathered his uncle, surprisingly hefty as a heap of unconscious vampire, and shouted for everyone to follow. "The guest room next to Alexia's room is free. I'll put him in there."

The doctor ran ahead of them into the front hall. "Good. We can move him once he's stable." He motioned toward the rest of the group. "I need one of you. Everybody else, give me space."

Ivy, Thad's property manager, rushed up the hall as Siddoh backed out of the room. "Is everything okay?"

Siddoh caught her arm. "Lee called a quarantine. What are you doing here?"

"I was out running errands. Once I found out about the lockdown, I figured it was too late so I might as well stay and get the house in order for when the king and queen return."

Fuck. She should have been sealed in the storm cellar with the other women and children. He studied her face. Dark skin, dark hair. Very sharp fangs. He didn't know Ivy well, but it was Siddoh's understanding that she came from a traditional family. Old, pure bloodlines. "You don't have any human blood?" For those with pure vampire blood, the threat from the guardians held less concern. With the perimeter secured, Ivy probably hadn't risked as much as Alexia risked now, being out there who the fuck knew where.

Ivy rolled her eyes, which took Siddoh by surprise. She'd always struck him as... proper.

He turned and snapped at one of the other soldiers. "Go with Dr. Brayden. Also, try calling Lee so he knows the fence is back online. Text me with a status if you get through. The rest of you, pair up with the newbies and patrol the perimeter. If this new defense is doing its job, we shouldn't see any guardians. Just the same, keep your eyes peeled," he said quietly. He nodded to Brayden as the doctor slipped through the door.

After a moment of mumbling and shuffling, Siddoh and Ivy were alone in the hall. "No," she said softly. "No human in me. One hundred percent, gold star vampire." Something strange lingered in her eyes. In a case of blink-and-you'll-miss-it, she went from something that seemed like humor to shrewdly assessing him, eyes narrowed and cold.

"Excuse me?"

"Poor joke." She shrugged her shoulders. "Can I get you anything, sir? Coffee? Tea? Gauntlets of almighty power?"

What a strange young female. Alexia says strange shit on occasion, but I figure it's her humanity, right? Or all that partying she used to do. I honestly have no idea how to respond to Ivy right now, and I don't know when I was last at a loss.

It hit Siddoh then: Ivy's father had been put under house arrest for crimes against the king, and Siddoh had been instrumental in sentencing and locking up the elder male. In spite of her father's crimes, Ivy remained a trusted member of Thad's staff, but the logic certainly followed that she would have her issues with Siddoh.

Perhaps that explained the sarcasm and the strange undercurrent of hostility. The just plain strangeness.

"I'm... all stocked on gauntlets. Thanks." Strange. Unspeakably so. Siddoh turned toward the kitchen anyway, dying for a stronger drink than he'd find there. He was surprised when she followed, given her apparent aura of hostility. "Hungry?" He flipped the light on. Given the slights she perceived he'd committed against her family, the least Siddoh supposed he could do was make the young lady a meal.

"No, thank you." Her body remained stiff and stilted, her eyes narrowed as if she were picturing his head above her mantel. Sure. In a way, he was the bad guy. Made sense.

He put the kettle on for tea without asking. Not many things a hot mug of tea wouldn't fix. He'd bonded with Alexia over many a late-night cup of tea and good conversation. He stayed away from that newfangled electric kettle she used. Hell, if he could, he would do this over the fire pit in his backyard. Nothing like cooking outside. Modern kitchens were one thing Siddoh had never embraced. Or boxer shorts, for that matter. Dammit, his boys needed a snug fit.

"Have a seat." He steered her toward one of the bistro chairs on his way across the kitchen.

"I'm not sure I'm in the mood for tea."

"Well, then. If you followed me in here because you have devious plans to come after me with the cutlery, I suggest that big French chef knife. Maybe the meat cleaver." He pulled out a box of something Alexia kept in the pantry called "Calm." Highly ambitious claim for a tea to make, but what the hell. He tossed Ivy a fangy grin, the kind that often pissed folks off because it gave the impression that he wasn't taking anything seriously. "I should warn you, though. I'm fast."

This time he was rewarded with a weak smile on his return trip with his tea bags and Alexia's gallon-sized jar of raw honey.

"I suppose I could have a cup of tea," Ivy murmured. Letting her anger slip, she rested her cheek on her arm, showing her fatigue. Poor thing. Until tonight she'd always come off as so easygoing. Mellow. Was she like him? Always struggling to hide herself? Helping to run the royal estate had to be exhausting. And having her father in trouble with the king...

Siddoh shook his head. He found himself wondering inappropriately what she did for blood. Why such a beautiful female was single. She was young, but old enough to have been mated by now. Asking would be rude. Right? Right.

He threw the tea into two mugs, one with cow spots and one with a logo for some old show called *The X-Files* that Alexia loved. The mug said "I WANT TO BELIEVE." Believe *what*? Siddoh didn't have a clue. He'd seen shit in his life, with his own two headlamps, that he didn't want to fucking believe. If he could, he'd go into his brain and root that junk out with industrial bleach and a chisel. Forget about space aliens and hovercrafts.

"Here," he said, after adding the water and honey, and settling across from her at the table. He gave her the mug with the cow spots. The side said "I udderly adore you," and it always guaranteed a smile.

Bingo. He got a small smile, but still a smile. She sat up straighter, tapping the handle of her mug. "So what happened tonight? Will your uncle be okay?"

"It's a good question." In more ways than one. Siddoh's gut said this all smelled like sabotage. Someone had dicked around with the estate's magical barrier, and had done so deliberately on a night when

Thad was away from the helm. An exceptionally rare occurrence since his queen had become pregnant. So the estate was vulnerable, less on guard.

Siddoh drank his tea too soon and ignored the burn down his throat. Maybe the motive was to make Thad look like a dipstick. Maybe the motive had been far more malicious. The options were bad, very bad, and who the fuck did he have to kill?

If they hadn't gotten the perimeter reinforced fast? If it didn't hold? Maybe a few hundred dead vampires. *No biggie*. Thank God his uncle had been able to help.

Come to think of it, they'd almost fixed the fence *too easily*. Maybe it hadn't been completely drained of power. Maybe the motive *had* been to make Thad look like a moron. "I know Thad has his dissenters on the Council, but who wants to make it look like he can't keep the estate protected?" he mused aloud.

Siddoh studied Ivy in the silence of the kitchen as she blew ripples across her tea. He couldn't believe he'd slipped and said such a thing aloud in front of someone whose father had committed crimes against the royal family. Just because Thad still trusted her—

"Anyone who wants to take his place," Ivy said. "You know, I recall shortly before Thad's father died there were complaints filed about the human interaction bill. A lot of the elders on the Council had issues. Maybe it's related somehow. I don't remember who filed the grievances, but the records would be archived in my office."

Siddoh took another swig of the hot stuff that tasted something to him like dried-out dandelions. Surely Ivy had her wires crossed. "The human interaction bill didn't come up until after Thad's father died," he said.

"No." She blew on her tea again, looking thoughtful. "I mean, yes. This time. But it's come up before. At least once, a few years ago. Just like Thad, his father dismissed the proposal outright. As I recall, it sparked a lot of anger. I open the king's mail. I saw the letters. There were threats."

Cheese on rice. Siddoh jumped up from the table, hardly paying attention when he splashed scalding tea over his hand and knocked a bistro chair to the floor. "Ivy, show me what you've got. Please."

Chapter 10

ALEXIA AND LEE FOUND A BATTERED, MULTICOLORED pickup truck on the edge of Route 9 that they hoped nobody would miss much. Alexia was too soggy and bone-weary to employ any kind of brain-to-mouth filter when Lee bitched about the fact that it had manual transmission. "Seven hundred years of badassery and you don't know how to drive a stick?"

He leveled a glare at her while his hand hovered over the ignition. "Of course I know how to drive a stick. My hand got cut open by evil-powered lightning. Needs a little longer to heal over."

Oh. Well. Wasn't she an asshole? "I'll drive."

Alexia jumped on the running board and behind the wheel, sliding right alongside him. She kept her face serious but smiled inside. The power boost of Lee's blood made her fly. Hell, without it to heal her cuts and broken places, she might not have made it through those woods without collapsing. She was grateful.

And yes, so sue her, she was enjoying how uncomfortable she made Lee right then. He'd shown his hand back there in that cave. After all the time they'd danced around each other, he *did* want her. He was stuck in the same unpleasant situation she was: whether he should be or not, he was attracted. Lord knew misery demanded company.

Alexia nudged Lee's side gently when he seemed

reluctant to give up the driver's seat. "C'mon, scoot. I can tell you're still wiped out from that big magic trick you pulled back in the woods. I won't tell anybody you had to rest for five minutes, I swear." She'd meant it as a joke, but he didn't laugh. He was probably still concerned she might open her big yap.

She really wouldn't tell a soul. In her opinion, the toughest men alive were the ones who knew how to bend before they broke. It actually reassured her to see him a little vulnerable. He'd asked her to keep his confidence, and she could keep her mouth shut. Alexia could definitely do silence.

"So," she said as he grudgingly slid over. "You don't like humans, wizards, those guardian guys, or cars with manual transmission. I've also noticed you don't like alcoholic beverages or any music that came after the Romantic period." She punctuated the last part by turning the station to the local hard rock channel.

"All justified."

She bit her lips together and turned the radio back off. Now would be a good time to be silent. *Keep that big yap shut*. "Wizards and guardians I get. Humans because we're what? Stupid, weak, and inferior?"

Oops. So much for shutting the big yap.

He grunted a macho, jerk-head grunt. "For starters." Ouch. She waited. They rolled down an unusually dark Route 9 and into downtown.

Holy hurricanes, all the lights were out. Everything looked dead and deserted. Thank goodness for the full moon, and that the rain had changed from an angry pound to an irritating but light drizzle.

She glanced at Lee. "And for finishers?"

"That we manage to stay hidden in this millennium guarantees our safety. In the older ages we were not so lucky. Your kind thought we were murderous monsters and treated us accordingly. Or used and abused us for fun. Killed us and siphoned our blood for its healing properties. Think about what you've read in your folktales. Old horror movies. What do you think those myths and legends were based upon?"

Monsters. She had no flip response. Lee could scare the rainbows from a unicorn. If she didn't know him the way that she knew him, she'd wet her pants running into him in a dark alley.

"Let's not forget about how your kind treats each other, Lexi."

She'd clearly pressed a button. His words came fast and hard like a verbal battering ram.

"Terrorist attacks, murders, parents beating their own children and putting them on the street, theft, rape, abuse, kidnapping, drugs… I can't turn on the news without—"

Alexia couldn't sit still. Her heart raced, trying to escape his vocal assault, but there was nowhere to go. Her arms propelled out from her sides. "Okay, you've made your point!" She was forced to grab the wheel again in a hurry. Lee didn't need to give her the laundry list of awful things humans did. She'd been on the receiving end of enough. "Not like you vampires are all poster children for sainthood."

"We abide by a strong moral code," he said.

"Right." She slowed at a stoplight that had no power. She needed to go left, and there was mass confusion. "Except that you've got someone conveniently monkeying with the magical security system on the night Isabel goes into labor." She leaned her head in his direction, accidentally bumping his hard shoulder.

"We're not certain that was an inside job," he said.

Hellooo, denial. She didn't answer, focusing instead on getting across traffic and down Seventh Street toward Saint Anne's. She'd only been to the vampire hospital once with Isabel for an ultrasound. Most checkups had been done at the estate by a midwife, thank the great goddess. They'd been so rude to Alexia at the vampire hospital. She'd left the place very grateful *she'd* never be the one putting her feet in those stirrups. She craned her neck to see the street signs in the dark, unwilling to admit to Lee that she didn't remember exactly where to turn.

Alexia had finally spotted the right street when a horrific burn shot through her chest and arm. The pain weakened her grip on the steering wheel, and this time she couldn't get it back. The truck had shitty alignment. She was forced to pull off near their turn by a strip of historic shops.

"God, Lee, what is wrong with you?"

"Fine," he said. "Sometimes vampires are dishonorable, too. Is that what you want me to say?"

"No." She looked him over before sliding across the bench seat and straddling his lap like before in the cave. She paid no attention to his grunt of protest or the concept of personal space as she held his right arm against hers. "This arm hurts, but it's an echo or something. It's you; I can tell. And my chest burns. What's wrong? You're not having a heart attack or something, are you?"

The corner of his mouth quirked. "I don't think so."

He shoved against her shoulders. "Please get off me. The detour back in the woods distracted us both, but we're supposed to be getting you to Isabel. Remember? I need to talk with Thad and get back to the estate to make sure things are being handled. Whatever happened between you and me back there in the cave shouldn't happen again. It was the blood exchange and adrenaline, nothing more."

She gave him "the face." "Don't give me that bullshit."

He bit down so hard that his fang clipped his own lip, drawing a bead of blood. Was it weird to find that sexy? Especially when he was kind of being a dick? "Sure, Lexi. You're attractive. I care about your well-being. That does not a long-term mating make. Sure as hell not when you're a human and I'm—"

He winced, and the pain surged again in Alexia's chest. "Okay, first? If you think every woman wants a long-term commitment from one feeding and a little bump and grind, you've read too many romance novels."

He snorted.

She smiled, hoping the fact that she'd amused him had distracted him from his discomfort. "And second, you know damn well that's not what I meant. When we get to the hospital, I think you need to be the one to see a doctor."

He stared out the window, head back against the seat rest. "I'm not seeing a doctor. I'm fine."

"Are you kidding?" Her palms smacked his damp, T-shirt-clad pecs. "Why not?"

He licked his lip, giving her a serious, dead-on stare. "Because whatever this is, it's been going on a long damn time. I can't afford to dick around with getting checked into the hospital and sitting in an assless gown while someone makes me eat flavorless food. I need to get shit nailed down. Kill Haig. Train a replacement. Make sure my king and my kind are safe."

Her stomach heaved. "Get your ducks in a row."

"Yes," he said quietly. "I've never entirely understood the meaning of that statement, but yes." He exhaled long and hard, bringing a hand to her back and then dropping it. The hand, large with long, calloused fingers, came to rest in the curve of her waist.

Her heart had slowed some, but it maintained a firm, steady pound. "So, how long has this gone on?"

He hesitated. "Months. Close to a year."

Close to a year? She'd barely passed her biology classes, but if this was actually his heart… "Lee, you have to get this examined."

The moon and rain through the window of the truck made his aqua eyes glimmer so beautifully. Even when he said, "No. I don't."

She closed her eyes and pushed back an absurd press of tears. Why did this mean so damn much? It shouldn't. He pissed her off, and so what if there was some dysfunctional, awkward attraction between them?

So… so she'd miss him if he was gone. Whether she should or not.

But is this really your concern? You're the one who's been wanting to leave Ash Falls. Leave him. He's old and wise enough to handle his own affairs.

When she opened her eyes, beneath the lingering pain and fatigue of their night, a primal hunger rose in his veins. Her veins? Both, she supposed. The heat of it raced through her as the cool air from the car vent blew on the back of her neck. She couldn't help but shiver.

The dark part of his eyes widened, mesmerizing her. Pulling her closer. She licked her lips, and he responded in kind.

A loud bang and screeching brakes from across the way made them both stop. Before she could blink, Alexia had been shoved aside and dumped on her ass. "Let me drive," Lee said, starting the truck and pulling back onto the road with a gut-grabbing lurch. "Whatever that was can't have been anything good."

"Commander." Xander sped toward Lee and Alexia from across the road, hauling someone behind him by the arm. "Accidentally bounced this guy off the hood of Theresa's car. Said he had a run-in with a cluster of guardians."

Lee recognized the second male as the other two drew closer: that bratty SOB from assessment who'd refused to share blood with his training partner. Damn, the kid looked shittier than shit. Banged up, dirt caked on his face and hair. Bloody lip. Last fucking thing Lee needed.

Xander stepped forward. "Call it a really bad plan to try to get you to reconsider his training application. I already gave him a lecture and made him apologize to Theresa for bodysurfing across her hood without paying attention. He's injured, and he needs to be seen by a doctor. Then I suspect you'll need to interview him."

How would Alexia say it? *Fuckballs. Fucksicles? Fuck a fucking hand grenade.* That one sounded especially appropriate at the moment.

Lee gripped the washed-out trainee's shoulder with

one hand and yanked the truck door open with the other. "Come on," he barked inside to Lexi. "I gotta get this guy inside, and we're both already soaked. We'll just run across the parking lot."

No way in hell was he letting this idiot inside a truck cab with a wet human who could still have traces of blood on her skin.

"Sir…" the kid began.

"Save your breath," Lee growled. His chest seized. One glance down to his side at Alexia let him know she felt his pain and worried. Jesus, he was going to rue the day that he had let her drink his blood. That he had trusted her with his secrets. There was nobody to trust. He should never have forgotten. He should never have done many of the things he'd done tonight.

The surge of anger in his system brought a cloud across her features, already dark and wet. The raindrops on her parted lips made him want to wipe them clean with his tongue.

Her cheeks flushed crimson in the moonlight, even as her forehead tightened into a frown. No question, she sensed the direction of his thoughts. His desire.

"You have a terrible poker face, Lexi."

"I know." She huffed and puffed a little, but kept up respectably. "Isabel used to tell me I should never gamble."

"Just do me a favor and keep your observations quiet."

Her pink lips pursed into the beginnings of a frown but she stayed silent.

Thank fuck. He didn't need her blabbing his shit, especially not in front of this guy. "Okay, tell me what went down," he said to the kid.

"I didn't want my parents to know you'd sent me

home. I stayed a few days at my girlfriend's after I left the estate. She's over in the old Landhorn place." The kid jerked his thumb.

Ah. Not far from Thad's estate, the property had stood empty until only a year before. Lee had not seen the new owners. "Continue."

"So yeah. I took my time getting home because I knew my father would be pissed. I'm kind of a screwup. He'd been really excited for me to join the cause, you know?"

"The cause." That was what the kids were calling it lately? "We're not having a party over there, kid."

The young vampire's arms flinched under Lee's fingers as if he'd been smacked. It was a fair difference from the cocky little shit Lee had seen during evaluation. "Still, it was important for him that I get accepted. My mother and sister were killed by wizards walking home from the grocery store one night. He's got blood disease and can't serve. He was counting on me, and I fucked it up by being stupid—"

Lee didn't realize until the kid's body pulled against his hands that he'd stopped moving. He started again, swearing internally as the pressure intensified in his chest. *Fuck it all*. Hardly anything plucked at his heartstrings. Most days he didn't believe he had heartstrings.

"Okay," Lee said. "So you were coming home from your girl's place and you ran into guardians. Then what?"

"There were four of them," the guy said with excitement. "They came out of the fuckin—" The kid glanced down at Alexia, as if chagrined about his language choice. Little did the kid know. "Freaking alley, behind the 7-Eleven and the car wash and stuff."

Alexia sneezed.

The young vampire made a point of blessing her, and Lee fought back an unnecessary snarl when she smiled up at him gratefully. No, it wasn't the smile so much as the stir in Lee's blood that told him the young trainee's attention made Alexia feel pleasure. Lee loathed that he had such a base reaction. Their kind—their community—was the world in which she lived. She'd been brought to live in their territory and had been handed a stack of rules. He couldn't expect her not to even speak with other vampires.

This was no safety issue, unlike telling her to stay indoors during the daylight hours. Lee disliked that she appreciated the attention from somebody other than him. Plain and simple. He was big enough to admit he was being a dick. Gun to his head, this was jealousy. Lee wanted to be the one to please Alexia. Nobody but him.

Life is discomfort, Lee. You're on borrowed time. Suck it up and let her be happy.

Even so, when Alexia slowed down in front of him, reaching to nudge the small of her back with the flat of his hand came so automatically that Lee hardly gave it a second thought. Fuck, but his palm fit perfectly in that sexy slope above her ass. He wanted to touch her there forever. Touch her everywhere. To claim her. Possess her. Had they lived in another time and place, if they had the means to get around their biological barriers, Lee might have given thought to those luxuries.

They approached the entryway for St. Anne's, which appeared to be running on generator power. The lights still blazed inside but dimmer than before.

No, Lee could not afford any such luxury. Even if he could, it would never be fair to Alexia. He would find Thad and Isabel, deposit Alexia, and question this asshole. Find Haig and his followers and separate every last one of their heads from their shoulders.

"You used your power to take them out?"

The male nodded with apparent pride. "Sure did."

"Need to learn not to rely on power."

Alexia scowled up at Lee like he'd just kicked a puppy. Fuck that shit. Newbie wanted to fight, newbie needed to learn.

The young trainee's face fell. "I didn't have a weapon. My power was all I had."

"Yeah, well, this was your problem in assessment. Your energy flagged so you brought out the big guns. Need to work on your hand-to-hand skills. Your strength. You won't have the stamina to last out in the field if that's your go-to tactic. And when you're not in training, at minimum always carry a knife."

The male nodded, eyes unfocused. He was thinking. Good. "Roger, sir."

Alexia's eyes narrowed at Lee again. He could practically see the wheels spin in that pretty, disheveled head. No doubt she remembered the fact that Lee had hauled out the biggest gun he had when they'd been up against that circle of wizards in the woods. Those guys had been many more and stronger, and Lee was trying to teach this kid something. Which he'd never before taken the time to do with someone he'd already cut from consideration.

But the kid had trotted out a sob story that was just a little too close to Lee's. On a night when Lee was too wet, cold, tired, and in too much pain to not be touched.

"Jeez." Even dimmed, the hospital lights seared Lee's eyes as they walked through the halls and up to the maternity ward. The sooner he handed this young vampire off to Tyra, the better. He could use the break of guarding Thad and Isabel for awhile. Anything would be preferred over Alexia's curious stares.

"Lee." Tyra jogged up when they hit the floor. The door to Isabel's room stood open. "What happened to you guys? You look awful."

He only shook his head. "Where's Thad?"

She gestured to a nearby set of double doors. "They're prepping Isabel for surgery, and he's not allowed in the room. I've had one angry king on my hands."

Lee nodded. "I'll keep an eye out. Do me a favor. Take this guy to get checked out and help Alexia get cleaned up." His chest burned again. The searing pain spread through his neck and arms, making him sweat. He would stab somebody with a spoon for a moment alone.

Alexia grabbed his arm. "Are you going to be okay? Don't you want to get cleaned up, too?"

Unexpected guilt cropped up over her concern. When had he last felt guilty over anything? A night of surprises all around. He made a show of giving her a genuine smile. "No worries. I'm sturdy. I'll get cleaned up once you're done."

The night Lee had first met Alexia, first seen her face, she'd been wearing party clothes and angel wings, looking like any other of a hundred young women in a warehouse rave. But a guardedly *aware* pair of brown eyes had marched up and challenged him from underneath her glittery, gunked-up lids. He'd never have admitted so to a soul, but that challenging glare had nearly leveled him.

Nobody challenged Lee.

Alexia had challenged him repeatedly since. She did so now, the very same set to her stance telling Lee that his assurance of "I'm sturdy" had not hidden the fact that he struggled for breath like a vise was pressing his chest.

"Stop fucking around, Lee." Throwing his words back at him? Fantastic.

Lee's scalp tingled. That Alexia always had her proverbial human finger on his pulse lately struck him as strange. The blood bond typically started off weak and tenuous unless feeding remained consistent. Lee hadn't been physically bonded to anyone in decades, not since he'd parted ways with Agnessa. He hadn't fed from the same host twice since.

Still, he'd had no experience feeding from humans. Alexia's shrewd gaze showed that he kept no secrets. He may as well have stood in front of her naked. That thought flushed his body with a pleasured heat. As did the sight of the boldly beating pulse in her neck.

At the sight of that throbbing artery, his mouth watered. His fangs lengthened, poking into his tongue. The memory of that honey aftertaste in his mouth turned him on.

Moreover, his body knew a deep truth now that Lee's mind could not erase. In spite of all he knew of human blood, the one time his pain had eased had been when her blood had been sliding down his throat.

Chapter 11

SIDDOH SWIVELED IN A CHAIR IN IVY'S OFFICE, TRYING hard to show patience. What started as a promising idea had turned up jack shit. He'd passed the time while Ivy searched the records on her laptop by mussing her pristine desk, making baskets in the tiny trash can with crumpled pink sticky notes, and doodling a cartoon bunny on her clean, white desk blotter.

The amusement faded fast when he returned the pen to Ivy's desk drawer and laid eyes on something he'd bet every single pair of his boots shouldn't belong. A lighter, a rather nice one with brass and engravings, and the biggest damn sewing needle Siddoh had ever seen. Smoky darkness scorched the ends of the needle, clearly showing it had been seared by fire.

"That's so funny," Ivy murmured as she scrolled through a computer spreadsheet. "I thought for sure I had something in my files. We've kept electronic archives of all complaints and motions for the last five years. I should have some reference to it somewhere."

Siddoh shoved the drawer shut. Could Ivy be fucking with him? Paying Siddoh back for his part in her father having been put on house arrest? He'd heard the elder currently tapped at death's door.

"Well." Siddoh stood. "Maybe you misremembered." Something about that needle made him ill. He couldn't discern its purpose, but its presence in Ivy's drawer spurred him to want to leave.

"No." She pushed her chair back. "I remember it was a big deal." Her brow furrowed, the crevices lit horror-movie-style by an older-style halogen lamp. She pushed her chair out, staring into the middle distance. "Give me a second to think." Her fingers tapped maddeningly on the desk. "I just… I know there was something about humans. Specifically humans." Her voice cracked. "I know my father did very bad things, but however mis-guided, his intentions were good. He wasn't after Alexia for being human. He was after Anton because he's a wizard. Right?"

Siddoh brushed off a chill from the air vent blasting over his head. "As far as we know."

"So this other complaint I'm thinking of had to have been filed by someone else. I try to stay out of it all, you know? Politics, honestly, I wish everybody could agree to disagree. And because of my position, I'm supposed to be neutral. I file the paperwork, though. It's hard not to notice. I mean, I have to know what it says to enter it into the system. I remember thinking back then that this was going to be trouble. I was kind of surprised it died in the water so fast."

A sliver of agitation slipped through Ivy's graceful exterior. She'd long ago removed her shoes for comfort. Her bare, red-polished toes pushed slowly around on the cabbage-rose area rug until she faced a bank of large file cabinets on the rear wall of the office. The painted toenails added an unexpected touch of shine.

Ivy certainly looked pretty, no argument, but… a plain, unadorned pretty. Natural pretty. Golden skin and soft features. He'd never noticed heavy makeup or designer accessories. Her family clearly had "traditional" stamped all over it, like Siddoh's. She didn't go around trying to get noticed. More like she went around trying to blend in with the paintings and the drywall.

Her full bottom lip pulled underneath one fang and got worked over something crazy while she mulled over whatever she needed to mull. "Gah." All at once she shook her hands and smacked herself on either side of the face, leaving a rosy blush of handprints on her golden skin that made Siddoh sit up straighter. "This is going to drive me crazy. I *know* what I saw."

Siddoh had about reached his limit. He'd gone from deciding this female was maddening as hell to maybe just completely nucking futs. Maybe *this* was a clue about why she still had no mate.

"Okay, Ivy," he said slowly. "Just tell me exactly what you think you saw. Let's go from there." He needed to go see how his uncle had pulled through after fixing the perimeter security. The elder had really done them an immeasurable favor.

"I already explained." She laid the phrase down carefully, as if Siddoh couldn't follow along with his primitive mind. "The proposal to limit interaction between humans and vampires. You know, to officially ban us from bumping our pure vampire parts against their impure human parts." She flashed a mischievous smile. "It's been brought before the Council more than once."

She rose from her chair and approached one of the cabinets, bending low to dig in the back of a bottom drawer. Her jeans had that low-rise hip-hugger thing happening, and the thin Y of a skimpy thong and a tramp stamp of a coiled snake did not mesh with the good-girl image that Ivy presented to the world. Until tonight, she'd seemed like a quiet female, someone Siddoh had always assumed to be somewhat conservative. She did not possess sexy, skimpy underwear and snake tattoos.

Well? It would appear that she did.

"Of course the bill has been proposed more than once," Siddoh said. Some flashy little charm where the three strings of her underwear met caught the light from overhead when she moved. Distracted the direction of his thoughts. "Thad smacked the proposal down, and then the elders raised it again."

"No. This was before Thad's father was killed," she muttered absently. She'd practically climbed headfirst into the file cabinet at this point. Her shirt rode up. Mary and Joseph, all that toasted skin. He wasn't blind.

Not blind at all. It was then that he spotted the angry red lines on her side. Short, puffy hash marks. Fresh wounds. His mind returned to the burnt needle in the drawer. Jesus, could she be — ? No... Ivy always seemed so mellow. Cheerful.

Siddoh forced himself to focus on her words, despite his growing unease. "Okay, so there have been a lot of vampires here and there who were against the mixing of the species. It remains one of our biggest no-nos." He shifted in his chair.

"Playing devil's advocate..." He cleared his throat. "What would that have to do with trying to take Thad down or setting up the estate for an attack? It stands to reason that if you're against mixing humans and vampires, you're out to keep the species safe. Why sabotage?"

"To make a point, right?" Ivy waved a hand impatiently

at the pile of hair on her head and pulled at whatever held it up. A tumble of inky black waves spilled over her back, covering the focus of Siddoh's gaze. She worked a hand over her scalp, massaging like it was itchy or sore. "Maybe it's sabotage, or maybe someone's out to prove Thad's a shitty king. Didn't you say so yourself?"

Swearing, now? Siddoh coughed and pretended her World Wildlife Fund wall calendar was real interesting when she shot a narrowed glance shot over her shoulder. *Oh, look. It's the month of the blue-footed booby.* His previous image of Ivy disintegrated before his eyes.

"Oh my God, here." She scooted back from the open drawer with a faded stack of forms in her hand. "Dated September 2000. The issue stated has to do with human and vampire interaction and quote 'the regulation of interspecies relations on the basis of protecting and maintaining the purity and safety of the vampire population.' It cites a specific case in which a female vampire mated with a male human in secret without revealing her heritage. When the human found out, he became violent, killing her and her unborn child—along with his visiting mother-in-law—in their home before finally turning the gun on himself." Ivy looked up at Siddoh with wide, wet eyes. "Oh, that's terrible."

Fucking horrifying. Without comment, Siddoh held his hand out for the form. His blood made a full stop in his veins. The form listed a single named complainant: one Elder Sion Esmerian, Siddoh's uncle.

—⁓—

"Okay. You're coming with me." Alexia would bet her favorite collection of coffee mugs that something was big time wrong with Lee. *Big time*.

With his huge arm clasped in both of hers, Alexia hauled ass to grab the first vampire she could find wearing a stethoscope. They'd passed the check-in desk downstairs and no way in hell was this following any kind of protocol, but she wasn't convinced they had time for procedure. She marched a short distance to the station at the end of the hall, a square area with raised counters that looked like a holding pen for the nurses.

"Hi. Yeah. 'Scuse me. I need to get this guy looked at. I think he might be having a heart attack or something."

Behind her, Lee hissed. A surge of pressure in her chest told her he was riding out another wave of pain. As if the fact that he wasn't fighting her on being led down the hall like a disobedient child wasn't enough proof. "Lexi, vampires don't have heart attacks."

"Oh? Then what—"

"Oh my God." The tall, blonde vampire wearing ice cream–decorated scrubs and a severe bun in her hair, gasped and withdrew from Alexia's shoulder tap like she'd been burned. "There's a human in here?"

Alexia snapped her fingers. "For fuck's sake, lady. So not the time." She pointed to Lee. "Vampire. Chest pain. This is the king's top banana, by the way. You know the king who's up in surgery right now because your queen is having a baby?"

Oh hell, now multiple fanged staff members were staring at Lexi like she'd marched in parading the freak flag. "Uhm, hellooo? *Do something*."

With the sound of slapping cardboard, the woman

closed the manila folder she'd been making notes in and scurried away.

"Lexi," Lee said under his breath. He leaned against the information desk. "This is ridiculous."

She turned, hitting her palm on the counter with a painful but satisfying *smack*. "Yes, it is ridiculous. It's ridiculous that you have been hanging out with this condition for God knows how long, so you're going to leave us all in a lurch because you were too stupid to get help." His brow furrowed, and she wanted so, so badly to thump him right in the center of that smug-looking crevice.

Alexia never thought she'd find herself wishing so freaking badly that Lee's ex was around, but day-um. She'd give her proverbial left nut for Agnessa to show her freaky-deaky face right about now. She had to admit that part of Lee's past made Alexia uncomfortable, but Nessa could certainly spur Lee into action.

Then Nessa could help get Alexia out of Ash Falls. She'd promised.

Her nose throbbed. First time it had hurt since he'd given her his blood. Blood in lieu of having a bone set. *There* was a wacky notion she hadn't learned about in high-school health class. Not that it could even rate on her top ten list of "things I never thought I'd do" that she'd managed to check off in the months since coming to live in "Vampire Falls." Because just when she thought she'd experienced every possible level of crazy, she found out her crazy had a basement. And a subbasement. And an adjacent crawl space with some old junk from the sixties.

The throbbing pain in her nose spread to her cheek

and jaw, and she rubbed a hand over her face. She probably couldn't even ask for Tylenol in this place without getting looked at like they wanted to put her in a crate and give her a rabies vaccine. How did Lee have the nerve to call *her* stubborn?

Tonight had reminded her of all the reasons why she couldn't be a part of this life… this vampire world, no matter how much she might want otherwise. Being near humans but not with humans confused things for her and everybody else involved. For her sanity she had to *go*.

She had thought that by running away from home as a teenager she'd left behind all the isolation, the violence, the mistrust, and the fear. Somehow when Thad found Isabel, Alexia had landed back at square one. Now she lived smack in the middle of a war between two species… no, three? She still didn't entirely understand this guardian threat that Lee worried about so much. Could they honestly be so dangerous that he'd make a deal with the wizard leader?

That was like no fucking way territory.

What she *did* know for sure? On top of it all, she was worrying—not just worrying, literally physically hurting—over a guy who was intent on killing himself slowly. The whole thing would drive her to madness.

"I'm sure she'll be right back," Alexia said to Lee. She craned her neck to see down the hall in the direction the startled nurse had gone and reassured herself that soon this could all be over. Isabel had been taken to surgery. God willing, the baby and Isabel would come out of everything safe and sound. Then Alexia could leave. Then she *would* leave.

"I'm sure she will. I'm going to go." Lee's large

chest rose and fell slowly as he put his hand down on the counter to push away. "I don't know why I let you drag me down here. I will handle this when I'm ready."

Alexia paused with her hand in midair, but this time she didn't try to stop him. From here on out, Lee and his death wish needed to be his own problem. If her parents had taught her anything, it was that people intent on destroying themselves could not be saved. If you tried too hard or too long, you might just go down with the ship.

"Fuck." *Jeez*. In her next breath Alexia nearly doubled over, slammed by an invisible fist that had punched her in the throat and ripped out her lungs. Lee's fingertips pressed against the countertop, heavy and tipped with white.

No passerby would notice. He stood tall, handsome as ever, looking deadly. Nobody but Alexia knew that his firm jaw clenched tighter and the crinkly lines around his eyes carved deeper because of the pain.

She took in a slow, deep lungful of air, surprised to find that she still could. "It's getting worse." A statement, not a question. That phantom pressure in her chest, the dizziness… the intensity overwhelmed her.

"Yes." He pushed away from the counter with a breath. "Now, please. Go and find Tyra. I will not create a scene here fighting with you in this hospital. There is too much to be done for me to just stand here waiting all night. I'll survive."

Points for effort. The words rolled off his tongue so smooth and calm, but his face couldn't quite mask the undercurrent of strain. And besides, whatever tied her to his pain, he couldn't hide from her. She *knew*.

"For how much longer?" She peered through the

space between his body and his arm, willing the nurse to return with a damn doctor. She shifted restlessly, and the back of her neck prickled hot and sweaty. "This is insane. You're a walking time bomb. You can't help your kind or your cause, Mr. High and Mighty, if you land toes up on the asphalt." Alexia's body chilled, even though her heart went speeding for the door. She had no doubt that rant would hit him right in the ego. From his red-faced expression of rage, it landed.

But Lee didn't walk away. He eliminated the gap between them. One hand came to her back when he pressed close. "You know, you're right."

Her eyes popped wide. Did he really just agree with her?

"There's one thing that has eased the pain," he whispered.

Stirring arousal swept through her at the promise in his words. The gentle grind of his hip at her side. That otherworldly, husky, suggestive growl. She had a guess as to what he would say even before she asked, "And what's that one thing?"

He stared for awhile, straightening to his full height. With his shoulders back and his chest broad, he looked like the Lee she'd always known. She could almost pretend nothing was wrong. Just the two of them standing in the hospital, waiting for Thad and Isabel to have a baby. Except for that burn in her chest. Even more prominent were the butterflies in her belly and the moisture in her itsy-bitsy thong that she couldn't blame on the rain.

"I hate to ask, but do you feel you can spare more of your blood?"

She licked her lips and rocked back on her heels. Hell, she'd give it all to him if he asked.

Way to stick to your guns, Lexi. Weren't you just telling yourself you wanted to get the hell out of here because you couldn't help him? Wouldn't help him?

But that didn't mean she didn't want to help him. She'd wanted to from the second she'd laid eyes on him. That whole I-am-an-island thing had practically been like her own personal Bat-Signal.

Still, she burned from his many months of insults about her biological inferiority. Pride refused to let that shit go unanswered. She leaned close to avoid being heard by all the sensitive ears in the room. "We're out of the literal and metaphorical woods. You can get blood from anyone. I thought drinking human blood was, like, worse than licking bat guano off a wizard's shoe."

The softness of his laugh shimmied straight down her spine. *Dear merciful Lord.* "I don't claim to understand." His lips feathered against her ear. "In the cave, the pain abated when I drank from you." He pushed closer, his breath soft and hot. "Nothing has eased it in a long time. No one. Whatever this… problem… is, drinking from you eased the pain. It's the one thing I know for certain."

Oh, hell. Only her blood? Talk about making a gal melt in the weirdest way possible. She wanted to be all snarky and make him beg or apologize or something, but fuckballs, that was the most beautiful thing ever. Besides, she wanted to ease his hurt more than she wanted to get even.

Alexia glanced around and pulled him into an empty room next to the nurse's station. To be safe, she locked the door and pulled the curtain thingy. Two comfy chairs sat by the hospital bed. She tugged one close and offered her wrist. It seemed the fastest way, and this was urgent.

The strike of his fangs hardly surprised her this time. Much like a tattoo or a piercing, you got used to the pinch. Isabel had drunk from her a few times when they'd first become friends, but that had been different. That hadn't been a two-hundred-and-whatever-pound vampire male in a desperate amount of pain.

Oh, holy… Wow.

The relief was amazing. Fireworks and dynamite. The pressure flowed out of her along with the blood. What rushed in to take its place, though, was a disturbing sense of rightness. In giving herself to him in a way she had never wanted to give to anyone. Somehow her other arm wound around his neck, and either he didn't notice or he didn't actually mind. *It's just the blood, like he said before*.

But then his fingers crept into her hair. Her body slid down into the large, comfy chair. Lee pressed closer, on his knees now in front of her, her arm held aloft by his efforts as he lapped at her wrist. His tongue trailed down her arm to catch a wayward drip. On his knees with his long legs, Lee's pelvis pressed against hers through their pants, his erection hard and thick and throwing off heat.

Alexia couldn't stop herself from wrapping her legs around his waist and bringing him closer. Her hand grasped his free arm, which had moved from the chair to her leg. Their fingers laced together.

Lee's groan vibrated against her wrist.

A knock sounded at the door.

"Mr. Goram, are you in there? This is Dr. Farrington. I was told you were having pain and were in need of an evaluation."

Chapter 12

THIS DOCTOR IS A PUNK. LEE HAD LONG PASSED THE AGE where he could expect seniority from his medical professionals, but this kid was highly questionable. Was he even above the legal drinking age? He had a Mohawk, for the love of all things holy. *Aren't you late for practice with your band?* It didn't help Lee's mood that they'd put him in a pediatric exam room, brightly painted with rainbows and fluffy bunnies.

"Dude, your blood is the most fascinating thing I've seen in my career."

Lee crossed his arms and sat up straight on the exam table. Centuries of tactical expertise and he couldn't move a damn centimeter without making the paper on the fucking table crinkle under his ass. "And how long has that been exactly? Dude."

The vampire in the white coat smirked and sat himself on a rolling stool while he looked over an electronic tablet in his hand. "Tell me, Mr. Goram, when did you last consume blood?"

Never one to mince words, Lee now had reason not to answer. "This evening."

The doctor tapped his tablet with a stylus. "Vampire blood?"

"Human blood." Lee's skin crawled.

"Uh-huh. And how frequently do you consume human blood?"

"I don't."

The doctor looked up then, eyebrows raised in either interest or confusion.

"Tonight only." Paper crackled under Lee's hands as he dug his fingers into the exam table. Did he really need his shirt off for this conversation?

"All right." More tapping. "So prior to today, vampire blood?"

"Yes."

"When last?"

Lee's gaze went to the ceiling. "Last week." He'd called Blood Service after a training accident. The days between then and now seemed like ages.

"And how frequently, on average?"

Lee flicked a fang with his tongue. "Weekly, I suppose. Maybe every other week." Sometimes more, but Lee refused to say.

The doctor's head lifted. "Weekly for how long?" The doc's somber expression and his now-hard stare stated that Lee's reasons likely wouldn't be understood. They had left "dude" territory.

"Awhile."

Dr. Farrington scooted into Lee's personal-boundary zone. With his shiny, polished loafers and pressed khakis, the young doctor had probably never had a scratch more serious than a hangnail. "The average adult vampire needs blood in roughly one- to six-month intervals, barring illness, injury, or extreme stress."

"Pay attention to your own caveat, doctor. Every night I'm fighting, or I'm in hands-on training so my guys can go out there and keep our kind safe, or I'm *guarding the king*. I have everything you just listed by the truckload. My job is to stay at one hundred percent."

The doctor cocked his hooligan head to one side. "Have you ever changed the oil in a car, Mr. Goram?"

Lee glanced around the room, from the posters explaining the importance of proper fang care to a diagram showing an eyeball and a bunch of veins and nerves. Where was this shit going? "Sure." Lee's back teeth ground together. "Why don't you spare me the automotive analogy and just cut to the lecture I can see you're dying to spank me with."

The doctor leaned forward, hands planted on thighs, lips curled into an almost sneer. "For how long have you been feeding at a near-weekly frequency?"

Lee met Dr. Farrington's stare. "Years," he ground out. More than a quarter century, to be exact. Since he'd split from Agnessa. Some weeks, more than once a week. No need to clarify. He'd dug the hole plenty deep.

It had started as a quest to purge Agnessa from his system. Then a string of injuries had required more frequent feeding. Next thing Lee knew, he'd developed a habit. He found he functioned better with a topped-off tank. His power charged faster, and he accomplished more. He could not only use his power as a shield but as a reflector, turning an enemy's power back upon itself. Rebounding it, as he had earlier in the night when he and Alexia had been attacked in the woods. He hardly needed to sleep. He could damn near move mountains.

For a long while, the frequency of his feedings had worked magnificently, and Lee had been in the optimum shape of his life. Over the course of the last year or so, he had noticed diminishing returns. First, only pain once in awhile if he stayed at rest for too long. Then, pain more consistently. Like he'd told Lexi, he hadn't known exactly what was wrong. He had, however, suspected the cause. He'd known there was no going back.

He'd decided more good could be accomplished in getting his shit organized, making sure his kind was protected, and going out with a bang. Sitting here getting lectured by a doctor for something he'd already done that he couldn't fix? Pointless. Once mixed, blood couldn't be separated.

Given the life he lived, he risked his death every night anyway.

Dr. Farrington snaked his tongue thoughtfully around one fang, eyeballing Lee.

Lee avoided direct eye contact and instead stared mindlessly at a fake vampire skeleton in the corner, letting his vision blur. *This was why I didn't want to see a doctor.*

"You're about a decade overdue for an oil change, Mr. Goram. Your blood is like sludge."

Lee's heart thumped slow and hard in response. Well, that was certainly interesting. He supposed he shouldn't be surprised.

"If you were human," the doctor continued slowly, "you'd have gone fangs up by now." The wheels on the little stool squeaked as the doctor repositioned to maneuver his way into Lee's line of sight. Fucker. "Frankly, I'm surprised you're still alive anyway. I figure you're damn lucky. You're pretty strong, and ultimately, it might be the human blood that saved your ass."

The human bloo— "You're certain?" That thing he'd

said to Lexi about her blood easing his pain was heat-of-the-moment stuff. He hadn't been sure.

"Reduced the viscosity of what was already in your system. Not much, but enough to provide a Band-Aid. You've been straining that ticker of yours something awful."

"I see." Confirmation of the thing he'd suspected and feared made his vision swim. He didn't see jack shit. Still, it seemed the appropriate thing to say.

The young doctor picked up his tablet again, tapping as he spoke. "Now, what I'd like to do to get this problem under control quickly is put you on a blood thinner. Then we can—"

"No." Lee's insides froze. Absolutely unacceptable. The thought of popping pills made Lee's chest ache all over again. "I can't be on blood thinners. I go out in the field and get hit, I'm screwed."

The doctor nodded slowly. "It would mean a lifestyle change. No high-risk activity, no fighting."

Hell cocksucking no.

Not in a million years. He'd already accepted that he was probably on the verge of death. He'd rather go out fighting. No way would he take any medicine that turned him into some fragile old man. "Thanks, Doc. Honestly." He grabbed his shirt and threw it on over his head. "I'll take my chances."

Alexia scanned the hospital cafeteria where the offerings ranged from "yuck" to "oh *hell* no." Burgers. Jell-O. Fries. Coffee that, from the smell of burnt desperation, had been sitting on the burner for days.

All of it horrifyingly displayed under the glare of

unappetizing fluorescence. It was no better than anything she'd managed to find the last time she was in a
high-school cafeteria. "I'd expected better," she mumbled with a dubious-looking yogurt parfait in her hand.
How old were those strawberries? She didn't much care
for penicillin on her fruit.

She found nothing appetizing under the warming
lamps. The busy checkerboard tile on the floor didn't
make anything look tastier. Jeez. Superior species.
Wouldn't that "superior species" include better cooking
skills? Then again, maybe when you had the strength to
live for more than a thousand years, you didn't so much
give a shit about a little extra cholesterol.

A basket of fresh fruit caught her eye. She grabbed
a banana and some coffee, and decided a healthy dose
of refrigerated milk in the coffee was probably a safer
protein source than the yogurt. She longed for a massive
peanut butter and jelly sandwich, but as desperately as
she needed to get her strength up, she couldn't bring
herself to go for what they called "burgers" around here.

She usually avoided red meat and commercial dairy
products. She shook a little, though, from giving Lee her
blood and needed something to re-energize. She'd gotten spoiled lately living on land that snuggled up against
a bunch of farms and being able to sneak out early in the
morning once in awhile to get fresh eggs and raw milk
and honey.

She'd miss those little things when she left. Stuff
like knowing the milk in her morning coffee came
from a cow named Sally at the farm down the road
from the estate.

Alexia smiled to herself as she approached the

checkout. Despite her exhaustion, pride about having been able to help Lee filled her with a deep inner glow. At least, she hoped she'd helped him. Aside from the ache in her wrist, no more phantom pain had nagged at her since they'd parted ways in that room. Seemed like a good sign.

"That'll be four fift… y. Oh."

The thoughtful smile died on Alexia's face, and she could only imagine what the severe vampire female ringing her up took in right then. She'd tried to clean up in the bathroom, but her clothes were dirty from being out in the woods with Lee. Plus, *ohrightyeah*, her damn teeth. She never remembered to hide that she didn't have fangs around other vampires. On the royal estate, pretty much everyone knew, and usually if she left the estate, it was to spend time around other humans.

"Four fifty?" Alexia repeated. She reached to pull out the twenty she'd borrowed from Tyra. The look from this stuck-up bitch showed obvious disgust, and Alexia itched to salute with her middle finger right before she smacked the righteous judgment—and the hairnet—off her face.

She was tired of being treated like slime because of her species. *Born this way,* right, bitches? Well, hey, she could go out in daylight and they'd fry. She could survive without drinking blood. Then again, her life would pass in a blip of time compared to theirs.

Trade-offs.

Alexia thrust the money toward the now stiff and stern-looking female, suspecting how this was about to end. She straightened her spine, raised her chin, and pasted on her friendliest smile.

"Sorry, it looks like my register's broken."

"Uh-huh." Alexia glanced down at the blue numbers on the thing. "The numbers are still lit."

The female smiled to reveal her fangs. "I'm not a technical expert, honey. But I do give good directions. Shall I point you in the direction of the nearest human bus station?"

Oh, wow. *Wow*. Alexia worked hard to keep still. She'd had plenty of vampires treat her plenty of ways these past months. Some had been frosty and some had been a little rude, but this one was actively suggesting that she promptly leave town. How completely disrespectful.

You're planning on leaving town anyway.

But still. The nerve.

Alexia forgot her polite smile. "Listen, I've got money. If your register's broken, then I'm up for sainthood, so you can forget that crap. I am happy to get the hell out of here after you let me buy my food."

The woman didn't budge.

"No? Fine. Here." She slapped the twenty down and walked away with her food.

"Security!"

Alexia stopped, huffed a breath, and rolled her eyes. "Are you freaking kidding me? I just overpaid—"

Meaty hands gripped her shoulders and pulled her arms behind her back. Coffee splashed all over the floor. Her banana flew to who knew where. Seriously? This was honestly how humans were treated in this hospital? Totally ridiculous. And Lee would probably get pissed at her for acting stupid. She really did need to get away.

She wriggled from the guard's grip and spun around.

"I didn't steal." She aimed her finger at the cashier lady. "Don't you *dare* say I tried to steal." Tears sprung to her eyes. How did she manage to get into this shit? She'd done some things she wasn't proud of back in the day, but she would never steal. Not after what her mother—

"Alexia."

The voice calling from behind her sounded familiar.

"Alexia."

She turned. Flay, one of Thad's fighters, charged forward. She didn't know him well but they'd spoken to each other at the mansion. Oh, thank the great flying teakettle. Except... he looked angry. Why wasn't she surprised? "Look, I didn't steal anything. I swear." Her hand went into the air. God, was she twelve?

Flay ripped the guard's hands away from her shoulders and jerked his chin. "Money's on the counter. This human is under the protection of the king. Back it up before I report you." He slung an arm around her shoulder. "Come on. Anton and I ran into some trouble so we had to double back. I'm waiting for him to check in. The rain's let up, and there's a convenience store up the street. Let's go find you some food elsewhere."

Alexia stared sadly at the floor. At her squashed banana and spilled coffee. She willed her frantically flailing pulse to settle down and smiled her gratitude at Flay as she put a trembling arm around his waist for support. She wasn't hungry anymore, but she wouldn't stay another minute in this place.

Chapter 13

THERESA APPROACHED XANDER SLOWLY. HE STOOD STILL, staring out the window of the hotel suite he'd secured for them, but his body vibrated with restless energy. She remembered this sort of barely contained tension from Eamon before his passing. Something weighed on Xander's mind that he felt he couldn't share. Something about the fight beyond that window.

Her eye fell to a scrape on his arm. "You're hurt."

"I'm okay." He kept staring out the window of their hotel suite into the dark. He smelled of rain. Night air. That small scrape on his arm should have healed already. What was he doing for blood?

As she drew close, he turned toward her. "You seem restless. I thought you would want to sleep. I'll keep watch. Do you need me to call up for food?"

She stepped next to him, unwilling to admit her hunger. She suspected Xander denied his needs as well. "This place is lovely, but you didn't have to go to so much trouble." In her stress, she hadn't paid close attention to where they were, the Intercontinental something or another. What she *had* heard was the clerk telling Xander that the hotel was booked except for the horribly expensive suites. Xander had simply nodded and asked for whatever room they could provide. With three bedrooms, a living room, and a full-sized dining area, this hotel room put Theresa's tiny colonial home on the corner of the king's property to shame.

He shook his head, turning back to the window. Down on the street below, headlights plodded along. Not many out tonight, but a brave few still roamed in the wake of the worst part of the storm. "We needed to go somewhere, and this place is easy. The concierge service is top-notch. We can stay through the day without having to worry about leaving for anything we need. I've got it covered. Everything's fine."

She tapped at the wound on his arm. "Do you have this covered as well? Do you need blood, Xander?"

"I told you. I'm fine." He stepped back from the window and threw her a quick glance, appearing to keep one eye on the door. "You're exhausted. Go. Lie down with Eamon. I'll order you some food."

Xander reached for the room service menus on the coffee table and held them up just as Theresa stepped backwards into the living area sofa. She'd forgotten until tonight how being around him made her skin prickle and her steps clumsy.

"Oh." Theresa stepped toward him with her hand out. If he didn't wish to discuss anything else, she supposed food was a safe enough topic. "Thank you. I guess I can take a look at the menu."

"Let's see..." He scanned quickly. "You'd like the chicken salad. Tea. Juice. Maybe the flourless chocolate cake." They hadn't turned on any lights but a lamp next to the sofa, and in its golden glow, his green eyes and dazzling smile seemed to assure that everything truly would be fine, in spite of the storm outside. In spite of all the enemies and other threats.

She stopped short of reaching to take the menu from his hand and laughed. "You're very good."

Xander returned to his careful study of the menu. "I guarded you for weeks after Eamon Junior's birth, Theresa. I know what you like."

Her laughter stopped. So did the rest of her. She hoped the heat suffusing her body wasn't too obvious. "You know, I think I'm just going to check the thermostat…"

Damn. The little white box on the far wall read sixty-five degrees. Perfectly cool for a vampire. Should have been, anyway. Eamon slept under a pile of blankets in the next room, so she went ahead and dialed it down another couple of degrees. When she turned back toward Xander, he seemed to be studying her. So much for cooling off.

"You do know me fairly well," she said quietly. "I guess I hadn't realized. And you're right. I am exhausted. This whole thing with Eamon's blood test, and the storm… Not being able to go home is especially stressful." *But having you near again is wonderful. I'd missed you.* "Are you sure you're okay?"

Xander rose to circle the suite. He checked the bathrooms, the closets, the empty bedrooms. Everything he'd done when they first entered the room. "Well, we're as secure as possible for now. Until I get word otherwise, here is where we'll stay."

It didn't escape Theresa's notice that he hadn't answered her question, not exactly. She crossed her arms over her chest.

"Theresa. Let me be the one to worry," he said. "It's my job."

Yes, let's stress that point clearly, Theresa. He is here because of duty.

She nodded slowly, backing toward the bedroom. "All right then. Wake me when the food comes, will you? I am pretty starved."

"Of course."

She turned to go then. In spite of her exhaustion, she wasn't certain she could sleep. Nevertheless, she couldn't think of anything further to say.

—⁓—

Lee paced the hospital hallway, angry and restless like a wounded animal. Itching to smash every single cheery watercolor painting from the high-gloss wall. Oh yes, he could admit he was cranked up. Big time.

He'd conferred briefly with Thad and had finally managed a quick call back to Siddoh. Extremely quick. The phone situation remained spotty. He could only gather that tensions ran high over at the estate. Siddoh's most annoying trait was being laid back to a disturbing degree. He'd never known the male's voice to hold so much strain.

The queen and the baby had come through surgery, thank fuck. Lee was grateful they hadn't needed to put the baby in the VNICU. Such a thing would have only placed further strain on the king and queen.

Selfishly, he was equally grateful they were not yet being allowed visitors. He'd managed to stave off an important part of the birth: the Oracle ritual. As the royal seer, Agnessa would need to be brought to bless the baby. Spending time with his former mate gave Lee the urge to stab someone in the stomach. Yes, with a salad fork.

Now Alexia had disappeared from the hospital. In a

bitter stroke of luck, Isabel's need for emergency surgery had rendered the frustrating little human's position
as the birth assistant null and void. Otherwise, Lee could
have had an even bigger mess in explaining her sudden
disappearance to the queen. But hell, if Lee didn't find
that woman before Isabel was allowed to have visitors,
he'd kill her once she was located. The queen was going
to want her best friend.

And Lee wanted Alexia back.

He stopped dead in the hallway when he spotted her.
Alexia and Flay came toward him from down the hall,
holding coffee cups and with plastic bags slung over
their arms. Talking. Laughing. Not a care in the godforsaken world. Fuck the salad fork. He would strangle her.

"Lexi." He charged forward, his boots pushing across
the speckled tile floor with a squeak.

She paused and put a hand on Flay's arm, like he
might do something to defend her. *Think again, sweetheart. He works for me.*

"May I ask what the two of you were doing?"

Flay held up his cup. "Food, sir. Alexia was unable
to acquire any in the cafeteria downstairs so I escorted
her to the 7-Eleven."

Lee focused on Alexia. "What the hell's wrong with
the food downstairs?"

She wrinkled her nose at him and sipped from her
coffee. For fuck's sake, a cup of coffee in one hand and
a drink made of sugar and artificial dyes in the other?
And yet back at home—at the estate—she filled herself
with organic vegetables and raw honey. He would never
claim to understand this woman.

"Aside from the fact that it all smelled as bad as it

probably tasted, they wouldn't let me buy anything. When I tried, they accused me of stealing."

Lee looked from Alexia to Flay and back again. "I don't understand." He might not like humans, but he wouldn't be discriminatory toward one without cause.

Are you sure, Lee? The acid twist of Alexia's anger and disappointment soured in his veins, but the strength of his own fury won. "You left unannounced. I didn't have a clue where you were. There's no power out there. Enemies, both yours and mine, are *every-fucking-where*. We call that a security risk."

She took a defensive stance. Feet planted, arms crossed over her sparkly T-shirt, which seemed to have shrunk a size since drying. Even in his frustration he noticed the way it hugged the curve of her breasts, the hourglass at her waist. "Tyra knew I went to get something to eat."

"You told her the cafeteria. I got finished checking there an hour ago. How the hell long does it take to walk a couple of blocks and pick up some junk food?"

Flay stepped forward. Guarding her. Guarding Alexia from Lee. Jesus, he was no danger to Alexia. He'd just had his mouth on her skin. His hands on her—

"Sir, security manhandled and insulted her. We took a time-out to cool off and talk privately, since the rain had lifted. The power's back on down the block, and she never left my side. Perfectly safe." Flay's face was so fucking earnest. Damned kid had blond hair and freckles. Freckles. "I'd never let any harm come to her, I swear."

With his knuckles jammed into his hips, Lee stared up at the tile ceiling. Maybe Flay only intended to be helpful, but the young vampire had a legendary fascination with humans. Everybody knew. Lee wouldn't put it past him to cozy up to Alexia for less than honorable intentions.

Lee should have been the one protecting Alexia. Instead, when she had been in need of help, Lee had been getting lectured by Dr. Mohawk.

He fixed his stare on Flay. "Report to Tyra. Find out if Anton is ready to go back on patrol. You've got a couple of hours left before dawn, and you need to cover what ground you can in that time. If she's had a chance to finish questioning that washed-out recruit, do me the favor of escorting him home."

Flay nodded and made himself vanish.

Lee focused then on Alexia, who was doing her usual arms crossed, chin up, go-ahead-and-try-me stance. Her hair had dried in sexy, disheveled waves. Dammit, when she stood that way, her challenging glare got him hard instantly. She had no idea. "I need to make a trip back to the estate," he said. "I want you to come with me."

"You do." Irritated glare. "Well, gee, after your verbal assault, that sounds mighty tempting."

"If I have you by my side, I don't have to worry about you."

His heart hammered fast and hard again, tension climbing in his chest. This time the squeeze wasn't simply his medical bullshit. He couldn't pretend otherwise. He hated that Alexia had leaned on someone other than him. Again.

Anton. Siddoh. Flay. For so long, Lee had insisted he wanted her *not* to need him, but tonight had been one proverbial slap in the face after another. That protective look from Flay…

Not knowing where she'd gone just now had been the final, bone-chilling straw. If something had happened to Alexia, Lee wouldn't have been there. Not fast enough.

Alexia shifted her feet, planting them wide. Her glare of mistrust plunged a cold knife into Lee's stomach. Hot and heavy, Lee's guts spilled onto the floor.

Okay, no. *This* was the final straw.

Lee pointed to an empty room, the one they'd used before when he'd fed from her. They needed to resolve this, and he refused to use the hallway for a public showdown. "In there. Now." His fingers clenched and released, fighting the urge to grab hold of her and make her go. "We will not discuss this in full view of everyone. Please."

With an angry glare, she finally went. Once the door shut behind them, he urged her into one of the large chairs. He knelt on the floor to make eye contact. *Forced her* to make eye contact, one knuckle under her chin. "Lexi, I'm not trying to be a hard-ass. I had no idea where the fuck you'd gone. I need to keep you safe."

She squared her shoulders and leaned forward, extending the long column of her gorgeous neck. The full moon through the rain-spattered window gave a liquid glow to her deep brown eyes. "Right. Your job. Your job is about protecting Thad and protecting Isabel. In the long run, I'm incidental. You've as much as said so in the past. You only protect me because I'm important to the queen. And sooner or later I'm going to be gone anyway, because I'm a basic, boring human. So let's just stop pretending like you honestly give a shit."

God damn. The pain on her face and the venom of

her words reached into his chest like a claw and yanked his heart out clean. Better than any enemy ever could.

He'd spent so much energy on pushing her away. Because he was a dick. Because no matter what either of them might want, a human and a vampire together could not work over the long centuries that should span a vampire's lifetime. Sure as hell not if he faced death's door. But those words had been said in defense many months ago. After everything that had happened to them tonight, did she honestly still think she held no meaning for him?

Lee's fingers dug into her arms. His vision blurred. "For fuck's sake... *you matter*. If I didn't give a shit, you wouldn't drive me so fucking crazy."

Her eyes widened. "I make you crazy?"

"Completely, certifiably insane." The next thing Lee knew for sure, his lips, his body, his aching cock all slammed against her. Their chests rose and fell fast, in sync.

Had it been only a question of desire, he could have withstood desire. Maybe he could have also withstood jealousy. Piled on top of those foreign things he hadn't felt in so long, was the passion of Alexia's giving intention when she'd offered her blood. When he'd finally dropped his guard and allowed her to seek help on his behalf. And dear God, the white-hot knife that had gone through him when she resisted his protection.

Alexia's moment of mistrust toward Lee had ripped through his veins like shards of shrapnel. Her rejection should not have burned so forcefully, but it had.

He'd never known much of the vampire-human blood tie, but this avalanche of emotion, his own and the ones that swirled within him thanks to her blood, threatened to knock him down. He wanted to wrap around her, to bury himself inside her forever. To make promises he should not make.

To forget everything but only the two of them.

Alexia's hands found the back of his neck. Fingertips dug into the base of his skull. "Lee?" The quiet syllable of his name vibrated against his lips.

He didn't know how to answer her silent questions. What were they doing? Where might this go? Humans had been responsible for the death of his family. Yet Alexia had given up her existence for Isabel's safety, had attacked an enemy to help his kind. Had given her blood to him so selflessly. He had been an ass to her right and left, and her worry for him—her concern—had stirred in his veins even as he consumed her blood. He couldn't blame Alexia for another human's sins.

Her spirit humbled him. God, he'd wanted her from the night he'd set eyes on her. How many times had he managed to pull away? He was no fucking saint.

Lee's walls, his resolve, the reasons he'd held his want for her at bay, all crumbled like so much wet sand. His arms went around her waist, hands under her shirt. His coarse, overlarge fingers caressed her smooth, delicious skin. He cupped one firm, round breast in his palm. "Alexia…"

A low moan. Her fingers tightened, digging into his back. "Yes. Oh… God."

It was all he needed. Lee did something then he'd never done in centuries of living. Not for any vampire, any enemy, or any human.

Lee surrendered.

Chapter 14

SIDDOH'S KNUCKLES CONNECTED WITH THE UNDERSIDE of his uncle's jaw as soon as the door to the cozy colonial opened.

"What in hell's name—"

"Yeah, that's what I'd like to know," Siddoh said. "Glad to see you're back at home and on your feet so soon, Uncle."

Sion stumbled against the couch that sat just beyond the foyer. An ugly, dusty green monstrosity, chosen by Siddoh's aunt before her death.

"Goodness, Uncle. I'd say it's been quite an evening. With the perimeter protection going down, leaving the estate exposed. The king unavailable because the queen's in labor. Tell me, how do you feel about the new king? His laws. He vetoed the human interaction bill. You've been sort of quiet on the subject this go-round. Did you know the queen's best friend is human?"

His uncle frowned. "I think it is a universally accepted truth that the species are best kept apart," he said slowly.

"Bullshit," Siddoh barked. His palms slapped his uncle's shoulders. Yeah, he'd been taught all that respect his elders business, but tonight this one had nearly put their entire compound at risk. Siddoh would bet his right eyeball.

"One of my own fucking blood. I should have known."

He shook his head, white light swimming in front of his eyes. "Are your old hurts really worth betraying the king? Betraying all of us? How many could have been killed tonight?"

Siddoh caught a glimpse of himself in a mirror above his uncle's mantel. His face blotched red with anger and his hair stood out in all directions. He looked insane. Actually, that was pretty fucking appropriate.

He slowly paced in front of his uncle while awaiting an answer. *It's official. This place is crumbling to pieces. My entire family hates my ass. My king. My life. All in jeopardy over some archaic notion that mixing with humans will taint our blood and curse us all to hell.*

Siddoh hadn't spoken to his own parents in decades. A century?

His uncle straightened. The old male's face betrayed equal parts disgust and sadness. "You wouldn't understand. You've been blinded by serving the monarchy. By fucking a half-breed."

Siddoh stopped mid-pace with a squeak in the tiled foyer and turned abruptly. "I'd suggest," he said slowly, "that you leave the king's sister out of this. You're already in pretty damn deep, sir." He pressed forward. The crook of his hand pressed a little too firmly at his uncle's throat.

If his uncle intended to jab at a lingering hurt, he'd succeeded. Siddoh appreciated that Tyra had moved on and found love, but the fact that she'd done so right after cutting ties with him had wounded his pride. With a former enemy of their race, no less.

"Siddoh, I am your uncle. What of your loyalty to your family?" the old vampire hissed.

"Yes," Siddoh replied evenly. Deep inside where nobody could see, his stomach wrung itself tight. "And that is what makes this so shitty. I don't know how you could be so shortsighted as to put the pain of losing your child over the safety of so many of us here on the estate. Hell, in the entire community. If we lose the king's military wing, who's to keep the evils that threaten our kind from running unchecked through the civilian population? All because you'd rather not have the occasional hanky-panky between humans and vampires." He swallowed back a throat full of bile.

The old male shook. "A little hanky-panky? My daughter and her child were *slaughtered* because she loved a human. We risk destruction from them as much as from the wizards who cut us open for blood sacrifice. Our species, our blood, should not mix."

"Are you shitting me? You have no idea about the cause and effect, old man," Siddoh snarled. "Some humans are able to handle the truth better than your son-in-law clearly did. The human who killed your child could have been a nut job to start. Kind of like, I don't know, an elder who would throw the whole estate under the crazy train just to make his king look bad. Am I close, Uncle?"

"Those guardians were never going to get close enough to attack."

Oh? Oh really?

Siddoh drew up short. "All right, lay it out for me."

Sion clamped his mouth shut.

"Might as well. I'm already on the verge of walking you out the door, old man."

"Siddoh, that king will flush our society down the drain. He's too young. Too—"

"So your solution was to leave us all vulnerable to attack intentionally? Hundreds. *Hundreds* of vampires on this estate." Swear ta God, any moment now the top of his head would blow sky-high.

"I knew I had the power to put it back."

"Lucky thing." Siddoh's hoarse yell echoed in the small room. He thrust a finger into his uncle's shoulder. "And lucky for us all, the fighters you so judge and despise had their shit together, so you're right. Nobody got close. Nothing more than a few isolated human cases of Haig and his disgusting plague, according to the human news. It hasn't spread, at least not yet. Lucky nobody slipped through, and you didn't fuck up or buy the big vampire farm instead. Hell of a gamble, though. And for what? All that effort to force the king to pass the human interaction bill?"

His uncle straightened. "We want to bring the age down on the Elders' Council. Increase our numbers. Make it a governing body."

Siddoh repressed a shiver and crossed his arms over his chest. "You want to be in charge."

"We have a collective wisdom that spans millennia. This... this... child..."

"He is the king," Siddoh said tersely. "And he is a century old." Jesus, had these assholes honestly thought they could overthrow the monarchy they'd had in place since the Iron Age? "He may be younger than you and me, but he was trained for the job. His interests lie in protecting us all. *My* interest lies in protecting us all. I don't need to tell you that you've put me in one hell of a position right now."

The old vampire swallowed. "Siddoh, I'm your family."

Yes, he was. That fact had caused an unholy tangle of guilt in Siddoh's nerves. Still? Fuck this guy. Fuck him and his fucking superiority. Whatever Siddoh's uncle and the Council thought they knew, they had endangered lives tonight. *That* was the bottom line.

Siddoh had no choice but to focus on the law. The greater good. "You are a traitor." His mouth twisted at the taste of all the acid in his throat. "I can't tell you how much I hate to say this, but with the king and Commander Goram away from the estate, this is my problem to handle. And you've really given me a doozy, you selfish prick." He pressed his lips together. His eyes and throat were on fire.

The old man was crying now. "My daughter, Siddoh."

"Yeah, that must have been hell. You have no idea how sorry I am." Truly. Siddoh couldn't imagine the grief that had pushed his uncle to this place. "You should have gone through the proper channels."

"The proper channels didn't work. Repeatedly, I was dismissed."

Siddoh softened his voice. "Perhaps if you'd met privately with Thad, he could have discussed the matter further. I don't have all the answers. Trouble is, now you've left me without any other solutions. Trying to mandate who folks can mate with gets to be a slippery damn slope. What happened to your daughter was a tragic anomaly. We've carefully lived side by side with humans for centuries by teaching caution. Safety is the key."

Alexia and Lee came to mind. No question something was brewing between those two. Their relationship would be directly impacted by any sort of bill preventing "interaction" with humans. No good.

Sion sniffed. "Spoken like a true follower."

Siddoh blew out a breath. There was no arguing his uncle's statement. Youth aside, Siddoh trusted Thad. Siddoh had witnessed some real piece of shit, power-hungry leaders in his years, human and otherwise. That kid was a good vampire. Thad cared.

These were troubled times. The vampires *needed* a good leader.

Siddoh pulled out his cuffs. Damned things weighed fifty pounds right then. "Come on, Uncle. I'm sorry but I can't let what you've done go unanswered."

Once upon a time, Lee first made love to a female as a fumbling teenager in a quiet vegetable cellar. That night he'd been focused on trying desperately not to make any noise that would give away their location or orgasm before she did.

Tonight, needing Alexia so desperately that he shook, he fumbled between the thighs of this gorgeous human woman in a dark room while he tried to keep quiet and not come too fast. Nearly seven hundred years later, a teenager all over again. Even the heavy beat of Alexia's pulse sounded obscenely loud in the silence as he parted her legs wider.

She moaned into his mouth while he unsnapped her pants and peeled down the drying material. He murmured a quick thanks that it came off easily, save for the fact that he had to stop and yank off those damned boots. Chilly lips pushed against his, her aggressive human teeth nibbling and tasting. And when her tongue swept inside his mouth...

His fangs grazed her tongue.

She gasped and ground against him.

A hint of blood filled his mouth. Burst on his tongue. "Sorry." Hard to be truly sorry when she tasted so sweet.

How could he not have known her blood could bring him so close to heaven? Tasting Alexia… Jesus, he was finally truly quenching his thirst. How had he not known he'd been thirsty his whole lifetime?

"No sorries." She teased inside his mouth again, offering more.

From that alone, Lee might go up in flames. He sucked gently, tasting her. "Fucking delicious." He breathed hard, longing to kiss her deeper, but his fangs were overextended. He longed for more of her blood. The pressure had eased in his chest. His heart beat fast. Freely. He would not take from her unnecessarily.

Guilt tapped on his shoulder. If they hadn't passed the point of no return, they'd be there soon. "God damn it, Lexi. We should stop."

"Okay," she breathed. "Then you should give me back my pants."

His snarl of disappointment pried her eyes wide again, and she pulled her head back against the chair to look at him with a teasing smile. Her legs wrapped around his waist. No, she didn't want to stop and neither did he. Not now. How many times had he pulled himself back from the brink? He would if she asked, but heaven… please…

He braced his arms over her on the chair. "Lexi, I'm doing my best to be serious. You have about ten seconds before I'm too far gone and stopping is impossible." He fought to control the way his body shook. From cold…

from fear. She was so small. He had held back from this for months. He was flying high on fresh blood. He gripped her arms. "I don't want to hurt you." His lungs burned with each attempt to draw breath.

Alexia's teeth sank into her lower lip. Without a word, she reached forward and tugged at his shirt, helping him pull it over his head. "I'm stronger than you think," she whispered.

Lee growled low in his throat. He knew she was strong. He knew.

He helped her with her shirt in return. Nuzzling along her collarbone and cleavage, he bit apart the bra, one fang slicing through pink satin. He'd always hated those things.

She lay spread out and reclined in the chair, hair tousled, chest rising and falling. Nipples... dark and pink surrounded by smooth, warm flesh. For him. All for him. Heaven.

He leaned down and took one nipple in his mouth. The smooth skin wrinkled and peaked under the touch of his tongue. The jerk of her body and tightening of her grip, the catch of her breath, such small but potent responses drove him wild.

Lee growled and pressed forward. He popped the buttons on his fly, shoving his pants and boots to the floor. No patience remained for the barriers between them.

He ripped off the tiny scrap of fabric that passed for her underwear and guided his cock into her tight, wet heat. After that, he couldn't remember his own name. Alexia's muscles squeezed around his shaft, as she wrapped her arms tighter around his neck and her legs around his waist. Pulling him deeper. "Oh God. Lexi."

Need. He needed her. This intensity… How many times had he dreamed of being with Alexia this way? He'd never known this kind of connection.

He'd intended to be careful. He had. He slowly thrust once, then twice. The softness and heat, the warmth of her when he'd been cold for so long, were all-consuming. Gums throbbing, Lee reared back with a mighty snarl.

Everything went red. Lee bared his elongated fangs. All his good intentions were drowned out by the rush of blood in his head. His fingers dug into Alexia's hips as he pumped hard. Deep. Fast. Only for a moment did he wonder what he must look like to her right then. A beast? A monster?

"Lee. Yes…" Damned if she didn't dig her heels into his ass and meet him for every thrust. The curl of her hands around each arm, pinching in each shoulder, told him that she'd dug in with her nails.

Yes. God. Hurt me.

Her head thrown back exposed that gorgeous narrow column of neck. He wanted more. So much more.

Their eyes met. He leaned down to kiss her, and their tongues tangled. His fangs pricked her lip and he sucked the blood from the plump, pouty spot on her mouth while he thrust hard inside her.

Alexia moaned and stroked her hands over his arms, his back. Her nails raked his neck, his chest. Her arms slid under his and she rose up, giving attention to his nipples. Biting across his chest and shoulder. *Fuck yes*.

He shuddered and pumped faster. The biting. He loved the biting. How could he not?

"Please…" One of her hands threaded her fingers

through his and pulled until his hand landed on top of her breast.

He huffed a laugh, leaning down to kiss her again before slowing his pace so that he could hunch over and lavish affection where she asked. He was more than willing to put his hands, his mouth, on those perfect breasts. He grazed one wrinkled peak, then the other, with his fangs. Kissed along her collarbone. "Good? You like when I touch you there?" His put his hand where his mouth had been, swiping his thumb across one hardened nipple.

A soft cry escaped her throat. A nod. Her breath got shallow. Faster.

Good. *So good*. He buried his face in the crook of her neck. His fangs were still extended. He wouldn't drink from her again. He couldn't. He just wanted to be close to the tick of her pulse.

He breathed her scent, like fresh rain and sweat. Her honeyed blood.

"Lee. Oh God, Lee!" Short gasps of breath. Her legs tightened, her muscles squeezed his shaft. Her sweat-slicked body trembled and writhed, meeting him with every thrust.

He slid his hand over the softness of her stomach, tracing with his thumb through the thicket of curls between her legs. He moved in small circles over her clit, pulling a delightful symphony of whimpers and moans from her throat. "God, yes. You're so fucking gorgeous. Come for me, Lexi."

He rested his forehead on her shoulder, focused on getting her off and avoiding the temptation of sinking his fangs into her lovely body. So close. So goddamned close, and he ached all over. He needed her to be the one to come first.

"Lee… Yesss."

Her orgasmic cry brought his head up. He needed to see her face.

Eyes glazed in ecstasy, she reared up and sank her teeth into his arm. Lee cried out from the surprise, the pain, and the thrill of Alexia's human teeth sinking into his skin.

Chapter 15

ALEXIA GASPED AT THE SENSATION OF HER TEETH SINK-ing into Lee's solid muscle.

Lee roared his release, pulsing hot and hard inside of her. His skin gave way under her teeth as the aftershocks of her orgasm rocked her body.

He thrust hard one last time, creating a good ache in her belly before he stilled. All at once, Lee's massive body was remarkably tense for a guy who had just gotten his rocks off. His head turned toward the uncovered window. "Wait. There's a full moon. Are humans fertile during the full moon?"

What? "Not even. Why, what's wrong?"

No answer.

"Lee. What?"

He straightened so fast he pulled out of her, tugging his pants up in one quick jerk.

She sat up quickly in the chair. *Ow.* "What's the problem?" Even though she was vulnerable and exposed and suddenly chilly, she made a point not to curl up or cover to hide her nudity.

As buttoned up as Lee was, she should have known he'd freak. Alexia refused to apologize for what they'd done. Instead, she planted her hands on either side of the chair and stood, moving toward him slowly like he was a trapped bear. *Easy, big fella.*

He backed against a wall papered with little mauve

flowers. He finished fastening his pants and gained control of his breathing. He brought his hand to his arm, to the place she'd bitten him only a minute ago. No blood there, but she'd left a mark.

Oops. Damn. Really, what had she been thinking? She shook her head. "Yeah, sorry. I got carried away." She glanced out the window at her barely there, runny reflection. Heat rushed to her cheeks. "It seemed like you didn't mind." It hadn't seemed that way, but now, of course, he was being all Sketchy McSketcherton.

Did he just shiver? The moonlight coming in through the window caught his eyes with a dramatic twinkle. "Anyway," she said, "if you did, sorry." Looking at it sort of logically now, she'd think maybe a vampire wouldn't mind taking a tumble with a girl who liked to nibble on her lover. But logic and Lee didn't always seem to apply where she was concerned.

"It's fine." His breath slow and steady now, shoulders back against the wall like everything was normal. Were he not shirtless, ripped abs and help-me-Jesus pectorals shiny with sweat, perhaps he could have pulled off normal and fine. Not so.

She bit her lip. "Uh, stupid question. You can't… turn me or anything, right? I mean we've swapped an awful lot of fluids so I thought I'd make sure."

He chuckled low in his throat. "Of course I can't turn you. Humans are born human. Vampires are born vampire."

The corner of her mouth lifted again. "Sure. Yeah. I was kidding. Mostly." Not that she hadn't gotten aggressive in bed before. It was just that the urge to sink her teeth into him had taken hold of her and that craving had been so *very* intense. What she'd wanted was to bite his throat. She'd wanted another taste of his blood.

Frankly, that kind of urge had freaked her out.

His eyes softened. "You probably acted on my urge to bite you. The strength of our blood tie is why you were so compelled. At least, I believe so."

"Huh. Weird." She pressed her lips together. She definitely looked forward to whenever that blood-tie thing would fade. A little rough sex was one thing, but she didn't want to go around craving blood.

He nodded slowly. "This is unfamiliar. Human blood must bond differently than the way vampire blood does. Maybe the number of times we've shared tonight boosted the effect. It's obviously not something I've thought about before. Either way, this intensity seems unusual." He rubbed his forehead and dropped his head against the wall. He glanced out the window again. "Lexi, you're sure human fertility isn't affected by the phases of the moon?"

She shook her head and laughed. "Oh my God, what a revolting thought." She frowned. "That's how it works with vampires?" She put her hands on her hips, looking around for her pants. "God, I couldn't imagine every human woman on the face of the planet hitting her time of the month the same week. Think of the chocolate shortages."

He cocked his head, brows pulled tight. Confused. Of course.

She pulled on her *ohthankyoujesus* dry pants and shirt, holding her torn bra aloft. "Thanks for this, by the way. Do you *know* what Victoria's Secret charges these days?"

No answer to that joke, either. Not that she expected one.

"Lucky for you my boobs aren't that big."

An exasperated sigh.

Great. So this was gonna be weird. "I'm on the pill," she said finally. His irritation was clearly ratcheting over the fact that she hadn't answered the bizarro fertility question. Best to put him out of his misery. When his face remained blank, she added, "Birth control. Surely you've heard of it in seven hundred years."

He nodded finally.

"Or maybe you don't know as much about humans as you think you do," she said. Sure, it wasn't the most mature thing to say, but he was harshing her afterglow. And at least she didn't do the "I told ya so" dance.

Silence from Lee.

"You don't know as much about *me* as you think you do."

"I'm getting there." Was that a smile? It was tough to read his face with all these shadows, and the vibe right now was so strange.

He took a deep breath and Alexia spotted something she hadn't seen before. On his rib cage, where the shadow of his arm nearly covered the marks, two dark circles. Or were those hearts? "Wait, I didn't know you had tattoos."

She took a step forward but he moved away, restlessly grabbing for his shirt. "It's more of a mark of remembrance."

Alexia wanted to ask. She was dying to ask, but the icy tremor that shimmied through her kept her jaw clamped tight. This was something painful, and she couldn't bring herself to pry. That ghost of emotion told her it wouldn't go well. She focused instead on pulling herself together.

She was lacing up her boots when he said, "My mother and sister. They were killed by humans during the plagues."

Oh. Shit. Her heart and lungs took a pause while she absorbed that info. Hadn't she heard a rumor around the estate about his mother dying in childbirth? Whatever she'd heard, it must have been wrong.

She took a deep, steadying breath. "So this is the real reason you hate humans."

He licked his lips. "I suppose. Yes."

Alexia's gut churned. She ached for him and whatever he had gone through. For his loss. But to blame all humans for what someone else had done? Neither thing was right. She closed her eyes and nodded her head. "I understand, and I'm so sorry." She reached to touch lightly on the back of his hand, unsure now about where they stood. "It would be nice, though, if you didn't lump me in with all the rest of the people who destroyed your family."

Lee tipped his head silently in what she hoped was a sign of agreement. He made a show of looking down at his watch. "We should go," he said.

That certainly seemed the best sentiment of the night, didn't it?

—⁓—

Once they'd gotten themselves fixed up, Lee strode into the hall on Alexia's heels. Just in time to see Thad storming toward them. Fantastic.

"Good, I was hoping to catch you two before you left." He looked from Alexia to Lee and back again. "Everything all right?"

"Fine." They both said it in unison.

Alexia's face displayed a pasted-on smile, but the chill that passed through Lee's system broadcast her unease to him as clearly as if she'd painted it across her naked body. God damn, what a body.

Well done, Lee. You've exposed the darkest parts of yourself and made love to her, and now it's time to move on with business as usual. Good luck forgetting the taste of her on your tongue. How smooth her naked skin feels beneath your hands. Or that she's seen and heard things you've never shared with anyone.

Alexia gave him a curious stare.

Thad cleared his throat. He gave Alexia a visual sweep. "You sure you're okay? You look a little banged up."

She glanced away, jamming her hands into her pockets. Hiding the bite on her wrist? Fuck, she was. Probably for the best if nobody knew. They weren't... *anything*, were they?

All the same, something primal in Lee's center screamed that those marks proved his possession of Alexia. He wanted them on display for the world. Her hiding them away made him want to roar until the windows shook. "She had an unpleasant tangle with security a little while ago," Lee supplied. "On top of the run-in I already told you about in the woods. It's been a trying night." *Nice bogus story, jerkhole.*

This earned him a glare from Alexia. "I can speak for myself, but yes. I'll feel better once I'm able to get cleaned up and everything."

Thad nodded, but he nearly crossed his eyes at Lee. Something was wrong. Thad wasn't stupid. Lee wasn't thinking clearly, but something nudged at the back of his mind. What piece of the puzzle was he missing?

Thad nodded finally to Alexia. "Do me a favor and come see Isabel and the baby before Lee takes you back to the estate. She's still groggy from surgery, but she's been asking for you." He pointed. "Go on ahead. Last door on the right after you turn down that hall. Tyra's guarding outside."

Thad hung back to walk next to Lee. "You want to talk?"

Lee shook his head. "Nothing to talk about."

"Sure." Thad rounded on Lee, stopping him with an arm to the shoulder. "Then listen." His voice was a harsh whisper. "I know you like to keep things close to the vest, and I respect and trust you enough to honor your wishes. I trust you. I love you like a brother. I killed that shit with the Elders' Council trying to lower the induction age because you asked me to, and I didn't ask any questions about why."

Lee stiffened. The Council had wanted to lower the mandatory age at which upper-class and military vampires retired. Lee had all but begged Thad to have the proposal tabled because even then he'd known his health was declining. He wanted to go out fighting, not sitting on the Council like some stooge. Too late now, he realized it wouldn't matter. Who knew if he had even weeks left? Days? "I know, Thad."

"And things could have been handled better with Tyra's disappearance this past winter. I've been understanding about the friction between you and

Agnessa, which despite decades seems only to have gotten worse."

Lee wrapped his lips around his fangs and bit down. He counted to three before he said, "I already offered to resign."

Nobody needed to tell Lee he was losing his grip. He'd have canned his own ass easily for some of the shit he'd pulled these last several months. And those were the things the others knew he'd done. He hadn't mentioned his underlying health problems and his blood abuse, both of which made him a walking liability.

Thanks to Alexia's blood, at least he finally had hope he wouldn't eat it in the middle of a fight and leave everybody hanging. Not tonight, anyway. *Thanks to Alexia's blood. A human's blood. Unbelievable.*

Still, it behooved him to appoint a replacement. The sooner, the better.

Thad's blue eyes pegged Lee with a chilly, knowing stare. The grip of Thad's hand on Lee's shoulder had tugged his shirt collar to one side, and Thad's lips pursed thoughtfully even as his fingers dug into Lee's shoulder. The king was eyeballing the scratches and bites Alexia had left on Lee's skin.

Lee stilled like a stone under the king's scrutiny. Inside, his temperature rose again, remembering the ferocity of Alexia's lovemaking. So many times he'd wondered what she'd be like in bed...

With a final squeeze, Thad stepped back. "I know it's been a rough year for you, and I've been happy to let you deal. I respect that you're older and wiser. If it weren't for your position relative to mine, it wouldn't be any of my damned business." He glanced down the hall. "Isabel tells me that girl's been through some shit she won't discuss. I know you work to keep everyone at a distance. But if this becomes a problem—"

"It won't."

Thad maintained his silent glare. An orderly with a cart stopped just shy of hitting them both and awkwardly maneuvered around rather than pass in between their standoff. "Be very sure," Thad said finally.

Lee nodded. He would resolve things with Alexia. He didn't know how, but he would.

As they entered Isabel's semi-dark room, Alexia leaned over the bed, speaking softly to Isabel. She cuddled a tiny, scrunched-up ball of wrapped-up newborn in her arms. She'd laid a striped hospital blanket over her shoulder, and with her eyes closed and her face nuzzled against the pink-cap-covered newborn, it was easy to forget the way he'd seen her minutes before. Hours before. Alexia wore boots and tromped through the woods and stuck her middle finger up at the world. Now, she snuggled a tiny baby and looked incredibly right doing so.

Even at his age there was clearly a great deal Lee didn't know. Especially when it came to females. Humans. So easy to forget.

Isabel, who'd seemed on the verge of sleep, looked up at him just then. Her skin appeared pale and puffy. Lee sympathized with her exhaustion but squirmed with an uncomfortable urge to leave the room. Even after so long, he had difficulty being around pregnancy and babies. All the happiness.

"Would you like to hold her?"

"Of course." He smiled. He didn't want to at all, but

he couldn't refuse. Such an offer from the queen was an honor, and it would have been rude to say no.

With hope, nobody noticed that his arms shook. That baby was so tiny. Innocent. Fragile.

Alexia avoided eye contact as she handed the bundle over.

Whoa. Light as a feather. He hadn't done this in so long. Centuries. "She's beautiful." Unexpected warmth slid over him, settling in his chest.

"We're still working on a name," Thad murmured. "We'd been expecting a boy."

Lee refrained from asking for details. Truthfully, holding this tiny baby girl put a hard and painful squeeze on his lungs, and he wasn't sure he could even speak. Not only for the loss of his mother and sister... He realized then that he would never be a father. He never thought that mattered. Now, the knowledge came heavily infused with regret.

Alexia leaned over to kiss Isabel on the forehead. "I'm gonna get cleaned up, and since the clothes I tried to bring you got lost in the woods, I'm gonna pack up more for Lee to bring you. And some books to read. Feel better. She's perfect, sweetie."

Isabel smiled weakly. "Thanks, Lexi."

Alexia slid past Lee on the way out the door. "I'm going to grab more coffee from next to the nurse's station. I'll wait in the hall."

More coffee. Was all this unhealthy behavior a ploy to antagonize him? *If you want her to be healthier, perhaps you should try being healthier yourself.* What a novel concept. He shook his head at himself.

"Isabel, if I may ask one question. You had a knotted

bracelet on your wrist when you were found outside. Where did it come from?"

She frowned as if doing so took effort. "It arrived in an unmarked box with the mail the previous evening. I assumed it was a gift from someone in the community. Stuff like that comes in all the time."

Lee nodded and placed the baby into the crook of Isabel's arm. They'd need to watch for this sort of thing more carefully from now on. "Congratulations to both of you. I'm going to square things away with Siddoh and bring Agnessa back for the blessing." He checked his watch. "It may have to wait the day."

Thad nodded.

Lee met his stare. "I'll work it out, no worries."

Thad nodded again. "Please."

Lee turned to find Alexia. He could admit he was at a loss, but he would make things right. If it was the last thing he did. And it might well be.

Chapter 16

UPON RETURN TO THE ESTATE, LEE FOUND SIDDOH pacing a section of tunnels that led to an underground storage facility. The tunnel lights hadn't been turned back on after the power had come back. The underground walkway stretched for foot after foot of pitch dark, ending with a set of double metal doors on either end. Lee stretched his natural night vision as he entered from the hall tunnel, disturbed by the agitated prowling. This was very unlike Siddoh. Very.

Despite the all-quiet report he'd gotten from the guys he checked with on the way in, it was immediately apparent to Lee that Siddoh had a problem.

At first, a quick jerk of Siddoh's hand was the only acknowledgment Lee received. "What's going on, Lee?"

Lee pulled up short just as Siddoh's pacing was about to involve an about-face to loop around and head the other way. Lee reached out and gripped Siddoh's shoulder. "You tell me."

Siddoh stopped and shook his head hard. "Doing okay. The magical power to the fence has been reactivated. Everybody's still quarantined except for the guys patrolling the property. So far it looks like it's going to hold."

So this did not explain Siddoh's apparent discomfort. Ah, wait… No doubt Siddoh could smell Alexia on Lee. Was that the source of Siddoh's anger? Alexia and Siddoh were friends, hung out on occasion. Perhaps those feelings extended beyond friendship.

Lee's shoulders tightened. "Siddoh, do we need to talk?"

Siddoh shifted uncomfortably. He moved side to side and then in a boxlike fashion, like an animal in a cage. "I've got guys stationed along all the tunnel access points to the outside, as you instructed. The single females are in the natural disaster vault area at the center of the estate. Except Agnessa. I escorted her down there, but she insisted on leaving and things were well enough settled at that point. Anyway, her presence made the other females nervous."

Lee gave a short nod. "What else?"

"I've got patrols ready to go out at dusk. The newly hatched assessment trainees that are ready will shadow someone with experience on patrol close to the grounds. I don't think any of those guardians got close enough last night to pinpoint our exact location, but I want to keep it that way. I'll switch up the rotation short-term until we're sure the coast is clear given this latest attempt. We're gonna continue to check in with the human hospitals to make sure there haven't been any more bodies reported."

"Fine." Lee gritted his teeth. "What else?" *Come on, asshole, the thing you're cranked about that you're not saying. You're angry because I fucked Alexia. Spit it the hell out so we can kick each other's asses like we've been meaning to do and get on with our lives.*

Finally, Siddoh's head kicked back and his open mouth released a primal roar that echoed and bounced in the empty hallway. His boot hit the wall with a heavy smack.

And here it came.

"I've got my uncle strung up in an interrogation shed."

Lee's hand twitched. "What?"

Siddoh's hands were back in his hair. "I think he tampered with the fence himself. Either to make himself look like a hero or to make Thad look like a douche, or both. He knew he could fix it before the guardians got close. I wonder now if he's the reason the guardians suddenly showed up on our shores out of nowhere."

"Jesus."

Siddoh shook his head. "Fuck, Lee." Hands rubbed roughly over tired eyes. "We aren't close, but we were friendly. Hell, closer than I am to my parents."

No, he'd severed ties with most of his family. Lee knew that much.

Siddoh cracked his neck. "I didn't know how his daughter was killed. I thought… They lived downtown back then, and I was away from the estate at the time. I guess I just assumed it was the usual. Wizards. Unfortunate, but…"

But shit happened.

"So this whole crusade against human interaction?"

"He's been behind the entire campaign, at least the latest major wave. What I don't understand is what I expected to accomplish by doing it the way he was. You can't just overthrow a king, and we live surrounded by humans." Siddoh stalked angrily to the storage area doors and shoved hard. The locked double doors resisted with a heavy *bang*.

Lee rolled his shoulders and followed the angry vampire, suddenly wishing this rage was about Alexia. While he and Siddoh had always carried some animosity toward each other, he could let that shit go right now, because for fuck's sake, nobody should have to lock their own flesh and blood in a cell.

Dimly, Lee was aware of an unpleasant rush in his blood. Pain in his neck and jaw. Sadness. Anxiety. Somewhere across the estate Alexia was hurt and upset. That shouldn't be his concern right then, but it was. He cared very much why Alexia felt hurt or upset. He would find her as soon as he could.

"Okay." Lee ignored Siddoh's startled expression when he hooked a friendly arm around his second in command's shoulder. He understood. The two of them had been at odds for so long. "I'm sorry you had to be the one to handle this mess with your uncle. We're approaching dawn. Can your uncle handle staying in the interrogation shed for the day?"

Siddoh nodded. "I think so. He's old, but... I suspect he's sturdier than he lets on. I hope."

"All right." Lee took a deep breath. "Let's set aside our bullshit for now. I can't even remember why we hate each other, can you?" It was all trivial now. Siddoh opened his mouth but Lee cut him off. "Me either," Lee said. "Come on. Let's go hash out what went on in my absence. We'll figure out what to do about your uncle."

~~~

Alexia couldn't have slept if someone had drugged her. Oh, she knew because she'd tried drugging her own damn self. Summer allergies, right? God bless Benadryl. Two of those babies usually knocked her down for a solid ten hours. Only not this time.

Sleeping through the day had never gotten comfortable

for her. Sure, after a late night she could sleep past what she called breakfast time. But all day? Totally different. And now the entire mansion had been emptied of living bodies. Lee had tried to get her to go to the bomb shelter whatchamahoozit with the other folks, and maybe she should have. Sleeping alone in this giant house felt a little like sleeping in a ginormous mausoleum.

Still, the security system had been restored, and sleeping with a bunch of strange vampires sounded equally weird, so Alexia had stayed. For as long as this place remained her home, it was the closest thing Alexia had to familiar. But now she also suffered from a fuzzy head, thanks to the "fog de antihistamine."

So she made coffee. The stress of recent events encouraged her to add some Irish whiskey she found in the kitchen. A little whipped cream. Rainbow sprinkles. Fuck the August heat outside. The way these vampires blasted the AC, she might go ahead and spark up a fire in the common room. Toast a marshmallow.

She sipped a little as she walked down to the common room where they kept the comfy love seat and the awesome TV. Funniest thing, since it was also the room where Isabel received subjects and Thad met with his upper-level soldier guys. Nothing said "multitasking" like a throne and a flat-screen in the same place.

She'd just stationed herself on the love seat when her stupidity thunked her between the eyes. She already sported a major case of the jitters, which made the coffee a bad idea. That she'd already swallowed two allergy pills made the alcohol a bad idea. Dammit, the whipped cream and sprinkles looked tasty, too.

So she swiped the good stuff off the top with her

finger and licked it off. "Oh. Ick." The whipped cream soured almost as soon as she swallowed, apparently past its freshness date. "What a letdown." She was putting her mug down on an end table by the sofa when a flash of light and movement caught her eye up the path outside.

Wait. Outside? Why were the drapes open?

With the house evacuated, the maid staff or whoever usually handled closing the drapes before the morning must have been gone. Alexia recalled hearing that Ivy was still around, but she must have missed covering the windows in this room. Alexia stuck her face against the window, trying to make out what was going on. Whatever it was, it was all the way up at the entry gate to the property. With the trees and the distance, she just couldn't tell.

With the magic restored to the fence, she was probably worrying about nothing. Still... that was exactly where she'd found that cord thingy that Lee had gotten so weird about. And nobody else could check this out. Anton and Tyra could go out in the day, but they were at the hospital guarding Thad and Isabel. She pulled out her phone to call Lee, but stopped. He'd been holed up all day handling some urgent problem with Siddoh.

Alexia pulled the drapes shut. She'd just go check things out. If the fence was really doing its job, whoever or whatever lurked up there couldn't get to her anyway. She slipped down the rear hall and out the door.

She kept to the trees as she threaded her way up the path toward the gate. The oppressive August heat made it hard to breathe after being inside that chilly mansion. She squinted into the sun, trying to see past the trees.

The day had an eye-searing brightness, with a sky so blue and clouds so fluffy that the whole thing looked fake. Dammit, she never remembered to leave the house with sunglasses anymore. Her thumb hovered over Send just in case. She'd call if anything looked funky—if her vision ever returned in this freaking sunlight. And then she'd run like hell.

"Afternoon!" A man leaning over the engine of a battered pickup gave her a wave.

Alexia let out the breath she'd been holding. Oh, jeez. Some guy with a broken-down vehicle. No big. Her chest still held on to a ball of heavy tension, an inkling that something wasn't quite right. Then again, she'd been nervous ever since she and Lee… She shook her head. No. Yeah. Just unspent nerves. That was all.

"Everything okay?" She held up her phone. "Someone I can call for you?"

"Nah. Think I've finally almost got her ready to bend to my will." He grinned. The better part of his face was hidden behind dark sunglasses, but the smile showcased gleaming white teeth and the kind of dimples that probably made panties everywhere hit the ground in record time.

The dimples paired nicely with the muscular arms showing from under his crisp white T-shirt. Still, Alexia's undies didn't even pretend to budge a little bit southward. After getting ravaged by an ancient vampire, could getting laid in the human world possibly hold any thrill? She could hardly consider the possibility. Would it help when Agnessa wiped her memory?

Would she be able to fall in love again someday?

Again? Oh hell… She sure hoped so.

She took a step away, ready to flee back to the house and shower off her latest revelation. She stopped when the man pulled his arms out of the engine compartment. A large bandage encircled one hand. "Hey, are you okay?"

"Oh, sure." That grin again. He reminded Lexi of the kind of guys they put on sexy farmer calendars. "Just a cut. It'll heal."

"Oh. Great. Well." She jerked her thumb. "I'd better—"

"Hey, you mind jumpin' behind the wheel and givin' this thing some gas for me? I'd like to watch what happens while you start it up."

"Oh, uhm…" Okay, this kind of shot her staying inside the gate plan. She didn't want to be rude, assuming the man *was* on the up and up. But Lee was gonna kill her if she went out there.

You don't have to tell him…

No, it didn't feel right to lie the way she had been so she sent a quick text. Better to anger the beast than risk being wrong. "Sure." Rather than open the gate, she scaled the side and jumped down. Call it paranoia, but she wasn't about to break the magic seal with Farmer McDimples standing right there.

"Impressive. Athletic little thing, huh?" He came around the side of the rust and silver truck.

She managed an awkward chuckle. "I never met a dismount I didn't like." Before her parents had gone around the bend, they'd signed her up for gymnastics. Only a year, but it had been fun.

Nerves gripped her when she slid behind the wheel of the vehicle. She made a point of keeping the driver's side door open, but that ball in her chest got heavier. After a few tries, no luck. "Sorry. I guess it's not starting."

"Hang on," the man called. He bent down to fiddle again, and Alexia tapped her hands on the bench seat to calm herself.

Something nagged at her brain. Like that voice that whispered in your head when you'd forgotten something important. Maybe it was all the sunlight. She wasn't so used to it any more. Or being out here with this strange guy. Meanwhile, she'd checked and rechecked her phone. No response from Lee.

"Listen, I'm sorry. I've really got to go. I have… an appointment." Probably to get her ass handed to her by an angry vampire.

No response from Dimples. Where was he? She jumped down from the truck to find him right by the driver's door. "Oh. Hey."

"Hey." He stood uncomfortably close. "I appreciate your help."

"I didn't do much."

"All the same." He licked his lips "I'd love to thank you properly."

The way he stood so close, she was afraid she'd have to introduce his balls to her knee. "I'm… seeing someone." For lack of a better response. "I'm sorry. Are you sure I can't call someone for you?"

"No. Thank you." He backed away, thank God.

Alexia sidled away and speed-walked to the fence. She took a good look before she climbed over. All she could see were trees and the horse barn next to the mansion where they parked cars. Farther down on the property was a stone building used for the same purpose. Beyond the barn she saw a training ring for horses, a single home, and lots of pasture land. Wowzers. That vampire cloaking stuff was some cool shit.

She waved a final good-bye to Farmer Hotness, climbed the fence, and made fast tracks back to the house. *See, Lexi? Everything's fine.*

Except for the massive, angry vampire who waited in the shadows when she got back inside. "I got your text."

"Oh God!" Her pulse sped up to frappé. She waited for him to charge, to growl, but he didn't. Just stared, simmering. "Yeah. I was worried it might be someone messing with the fence again, but it was just a guy with a dead truck battery."

Lee's broad chest rose and fell. He came close, combing every inch of her with his scrutinizing gaze. And was he... sniffing her?

Oh God. Could he smell the truck guy? She hadn't touched him. But she'd sat in the truck.

Lee's stare cut away. "I'm glad you're okay," he said at last. Then he turned on his heel and left her standing there in the hall.

Emptiness filled Alexia in his wake. She'd braced for a lecture, and no lecture came. He didn't care. She'd thought him letting her off the leash was what she wanted.

The pain of his indifference nearly stopped her heart.

Chapter 17

"WHEN DO YOU THINK WE'LL BE ABLE TO RETURN TO the estate?" Theresa made sure to infuse the question with the right amount of hope. In truth, she'd missed Xander in her life more than she'd realized, and returning to the estate would mean his returning to the fight. Leaving her, leaving Eamon Junior.

Here, the night rang with an eerie quiet in the wake of the storm. Nothing but regular city sounds. No fighting or training. For a little while, she could almost forget about their enemies.

"It's best to stay put until I get word that things back home are secure." Xander pulled out his phone as if to indicate he'd received no calls. "I'm sure Lee or Siddoh will call soon."

The nation's capital stood eerily empty that evening. Theresa would bet most of the government buildings, secured with fancy electrical security systems, were locked up tight thanks to the power outages. Fallen branches covered cars and blocked streets. A few lamps glowed here and there, but much of the city remained dark. She hadn't been inside the Beltway in awhile, but even at night after all the commuters were gone she had never seen it so still. So messy.

"You're sure you're okay?"

She smiled and nodded up at Xander, who walked next to her. For some reason he seemed terribly worried about her comfort. She didn't know how to explain that walking next to him made her very warm and light. Having him there comforted her in a strangely familiar way, but at the same time it was all brand-new. He'd stayed and guarded her during the end of her pregnancy and had been there during most of the birth.

Xander, not her mate of a dozen years.

Oh, of course folks had come and gone. Midwives. Other soldiers' mates. Even Commander Goram and the king and queen had checked to see how she and little Eamon were doing. The queen had been especially concerned for their well-being. But nobody had stayed the day on the sofa just in case Theresa needed anything for those beginning weeks of her son's life. Talked. Brought her tea at dusk.

Nobody except Xander.

Now, looking over as he pushed Eamon Junior in a stroller and seemed to sniff the rain in the night air, she reminded herself not to hang her hopes on something he could not be for her. He'd chosen to go back to the fight. She did not want another soldier.

Eamon had been a loving, loyal male. The fact remained, though, that if she had been given a choice, she would not have mated. She'd held out as long as she could. She loved her child, and she desperately, fiercely missed her mate with all of her being. Part of her also held on to anger. How many near misses had he survived, only to go and get himself killed when she needed him most?

Now she was stuck. Alone but not really. Feeling things she shouldn't for a vampire who grieved for a lost mate just as Theresa did. Who she could never truly love. It wasn't appropriate. It wasn't safe. It wasn't—

"It's too bad none of the street vendors are out tonight."

Theresa was startled enough to laugh. "I can hardly blame them."

"Nor I." He turned to smile a playful smile as they passed under one of the few lit street lamps. How on earth did he manage such good humor? Theresa could swear every time she looked in the mirror another fifty years showed around her eyes alone. "But I love soft pretzels. I want one."

She'd forgotten how much a vampire male could eat. Every time she had turned around during the day, Xander had been sweet-talking the hotel room service staff. Just her and the baby? They required so little.

"Should we head back then?" She managed a smile. A glance down told her the little one had conked out in the stroller. How lovely. Ordinarily she carried the baby in the sling to keep her hands free, but Xander had offered to push the stroller, and who was she to complain? How liberating to walk unfettered for a change. "Eamon's asleep anyway, and I believe there's a pear tart on the room service menu that you haven't ordered yet."

Xander's fangs gleamed in the moonlight. "Theresa, just because I've ordered it once doesn't mean I can't eat it again," he assured her.

She smiled and shook her head. Instead of answering, she skipped ahead on the sidewalk. She couldn't reply with words, because the first thing in her head was that when Xander had leaned close, it had appeared very much that he might be leaning in for a kiss. Or maybe she simply *wanted* him to lean in for a kiss. She didn't think she should, but she craved contact with another warm body. Somebody with whom she could connect.

A clatter behind her stole Theresa's breath. Something she couldn't quite place fired a warning in her brain.

When she turned, Xander had shoved the stroller away from himself into the grass off the sidewalk. The dark would have swallowed the form of her sleeping child, were it not for Theresa's vampire ability to see in the night. The wheel caught something that looked like a tree root.

No!

The stroller tipped. Eamon woke and started to cry.

Xander held his gun pointed at a man dressed in what appeared to be monastic robes. The shadowy outline of the figure was made twice as frightening by the eerie illumination of the diffuse light in his hands and the strange chant that fell from his lips. Another came from the side, off in the trees.

"Don't move." Xander spoke slowly, softly. In the dark he caught her gaze for the barest second, and she found herself wishing she could do with Xander what she'd been able to do with her best childhood friend, Andrew, and communicate using only raised eyebrows and blinks.

Surely, Xander had the training to respond, but the desperate pounding of fear in her chest just wasn't accepting logic. And Eamon, he'd started to fuss and cry louder in his stroller, alone in the dark. She didn't know whether or not Xander could shoot both of those men at once.

So Theresa used her power. She hummed Brahms, but not the "Lullaby." The "Requiem."

The attackers dropped to the ground, and their balls of yellow light burst into the air and disappeared. With a choke and sputter, their breathing stopped.

"Theresa." Xander had started toward her, but when the attackers fell, he turned to grab Eamon instead.

She didn't stop humming until the last tiny twitch had left their bodies. When she was sure, she stepped away, shaking. She planted her hands on her knees, desperate to hold on to the contents of her stomach. Only once before had she ever been forced to use her power to kill. She'd sworn she never would again. But nobody had ever threatened her child. And Xander.

"Shit. Holy shit, Theresa."

She managed to rise to her feet so she could take Eamon from Xander's arms with fumbling hands. Thank God he snuggled tight and stopped crying.

Xander knelt down to make slices in the bodies. "Lucky thing they'll bleed out and disintegrate in a short while just like wizards. I hope I can get at least a text through to Lee. The king. They'll want to know."

Oh no.

He stood, putting a hand on her shoulder. "We need to move. You say Eamon Junior gets ill when he has your blood?"

"I haven't… I don't… He spits up some, yes." Everything blurred in front of her. She focused on the places where her baby touched her body. She was pretty sure the rest of her was floating away.

"Fuck. That burst of light could be dangerous. For those with human blood. Possibly also a baby with a weaker immune system. I don't know all the details. If we're lucky, he wasn't exposed. I just couldn't tell. I'm not entirely sure how those guardians spread the plague. The light… the incantation… some combination thereof."

"Oh God." She hugged Eamon tighter.

"I don't know what to think yet. Let's just go."

They went.

———————

The uncontrollable loathing… the very lava that flowed in Lee's veins… *This shit* was the reason he didn't have relationships. When Alexia had emerged from the hall that afternoon smelling of sunshine, leather, and some other male, his body and honor had dictated that he drag her down the hall and fuck her through to the following Thursday. Once he'd checked to be certain she was healthy and safe, his duty demanded otherwise.

Now that night had finally fallen, his first priority was to accompany Siddoh to question Elder Esmerian. Lee might have trusted Siddoh to handle this himself, but he couldn't make the male pass judgment on his own uncle. Lee could pretend for awhile that it gave him something to focus on other than the way Alexia had tied all of his insides in knots.

Wearing only fatigues and T-shirts, they trekked out to the stone interrogation shed on the edge of the property. Apparently feeling the strain of what was to come, Siddoh was already soaking his with sweat.

Lee paused when they reached the door. "Are you sure you don't want me to be the one to question your uncle?"

Siddoh cocked his head to the side. "You're not usually nice. Maybe hooking up with Alexia had finally chilled you out some, huh?"

Lee's fist shot out. It glanced off Siddoh's chin, but the guy moved fast. "Hey. How about you accept I'm trying to be a good guy and leave it at that before I show you exactly how not chill I am."

Siddoh exhaled long and loud. "Yeah. I'm sorry. I'm just… It's my uncle."

"I know. Let's get this done." Lee went to push on the door, but Siddoh's hand landed on his shoulder.

"You'll take good care of her?"

"I'll do my best." Fuck if he knew how, given their extreme biological differences, but one disaster at a time. He jerked his head toward Siddoh. "Let me talk first. I'm back. I'm in charge. You're his family. That's fine. But I'm in charge."

Siddoh drew up tight from head to toe. "Sure. Yeah."

"He admitted to the setup?"

Siddoh looked up to the dark sky, muttering to himself. "More or less. I asked leading questions but he did."

"All right. Let's go." At Siddoh's nod, Lee pushed on the door.

Elder Esmerian stood when they pushed into the room. There was enough leeway in the chains for the old male to sit. No matter what, though, the manacles were heavy and plenty painful.

"Elder. Good evening." Lee stopped just shy of where the chains would end if they were fully extended.

Damned good thing, too. Siddoh's uncle may have done a good job with the old and frail act, but he pulled out all the stops right then. Fangs bared and powers blazing, he lunged forward. And an angry elder was a dangerous elder.

Siddoh drew his knife in response.

"Easy, Elder," Lee said quietly.

"You call yourselves protectors of our race," his uncle spat. "You do not know the meaning of the words."

Lee and Siddoh shared a rare smile, ignoring the nastiness from Siddoh's uncle for a second. Sion Esmerian had been a member of the upper class, an advisor to the king, and a land developer in the early years, capitalizing on the vampire settlement in Northern Virginia when the race relocated there in the early years. He had been "too busy" to fight.

Too busy to protect the race. "Elder, tread carefully."

"I'll show you careful, you—"

"Uncle." Siddoh cleared his throat.

Lee's protective shields buzzed over his skin. He jammed an elbow under the elder's chin. "Okay. Talk to me, old man. What did you hope to accomplish with that stunt? Disabling the fence was a real dick move."

Sounds of choking and sputtering. The elder's Adam's apple bobbed under Lee's arm. "The king left the estate unguarded. An elder fixed the problem. The Council will finally support a vote to go to a majority rule."

"That is not how things operate," Lee growled.

The old male laughed. "It will. You wait. I saved the day in the face of danger."

"Danger you created." Next to Lee, Siddoh stepped up, looking ready to take a piece out of his own flesh and blood.

His uncle laughed and spat blood out of his mouth. Must have gouged himself with his fangs. "You're still young. You have no idea. I was naive like you once. You'll learn."

Very few accused Lee of being too young. Or naive. "Learn what? How to be an angry old asshole? Just because your daughter died—"

"Murdered! She was murdered by a human. You have no idea how dangerous they are."

Lee sneered. "Don't tell me what I know about humans, motherfucker." He'd gone out at dusk and cut the throats of the humans who trapped his mother and sister himself.

"You idiots go out fighting wizards, and meanwhile our kind ignores the insidious devil that we live right beside," the elder barked. "Intermixing of the species is the greatest threat we face."

Siddoh drew a knife. "Greater than the guys who cut us open and eat our fucking hearts, Uncle? Or the guy who came back from the dead to start a fucking plague?"

"The wizards know who we are. They have offered us opportunities to live peacefully. For symbiosis. And we are immune to human disease, such as the plague."

Oh, fuck no. "We cannot rest our hopes on symbiosis with the wizards. They are soulless liars," Lee growled.

Elder Esmerian's face reddened. "Think of the tabloid headlines in the grocery stores. Think of the science fiction movies. The ways humans delight in scaring themselves with monsters. How is that for lying? What would they do if they discovered again that we were real? Think of what that horrible man did to my child. My unborn grandchild. Interaction with humans must be stopped. Your king has ignored it, as did his father, and it is at our peril." Those words were fired with such venom that Lee wanted to check himself for chemical burns.

Siddoh narrowed his eyes at his uncle. "Are you listening to yourself?"

Elder Esmerian's nostrils flared. "I can smell one on you," he hissed at Lee.

Lee stepped back in time for Siddoh's palm to strike his uncle's face. "You risked exposing us all, Uncle. Lotta fucking maybes in your equation. What if you had not put back that barrier in time? What if Lee and his fighters that you look down your nose at hadn't fought off those guardians who came near the property? What if they had made it inside the bounds of the estate and the queen *hadn't* been at the hospital that night?"

"I knew she would be. I made certain."

Lee exchanged a surprised stare with Siddoh. Chills charged up his spine. "How did you make certain?"

The elder huffed a breath through his swollen nose. "The dog. I let it out just before dawn. She's never without the mutt. I knew she'd follow to bring it back."

Fucking hell. "All for revenge."

The elder lifted his chin. "To teach a lesson." He pointed a stern finger as far as his shackles would let him reach. "You have all gone soft. Your acceptance of humans will come back to bite you. Mark my words."

"Lee," Siddoh said quietly, "step back, please."

Lee complied, hitting the cinder blocks on the far wall. He gave passing thought to taking the knife from Siddoh's hand but stood his ground. It wasn't Lee's place to take away someone else's closure.

Siddoh made the kill quick. One firm slice across the throat. Blood spewed, soaking Siddoh's already sweaty clothes.

"I'm sorry," Lee said.

"Don't be." Siddoh shook his arm experimentally. The flesh of his hand had turned black, some residual effect of the elder's powers. "He didn't teach his daughter to be safe about humans, and he's blamed the rest of us for his pain and his failing. Put our whole society in danger. Isabel. He wouldn't have stopped. God damn it, Lee." Siddoh pressed his good hand over his eyes "In a way it was a mercy kill. As far as I know, he hadn't fed in a long time. He couldn't have lasted much longer the way he was burning his powers."

Yeah. They had thought so anyway, before the elder had unleashed his fury. Now Lee wondered.

"Still, you could have let me—"

"No. It had to be me."

It did.

Chapter 18

ALEXIA ZOOMED THROUGH THE DARK IN A FREE FALL. Hands clasped tightly over her face. She'd gotten more used to the sensation, like she was dropping from the Tower of Terror and might never land. She'd been forcing herself to go with the ride rather than fight the fear. She refused to bow down. She refused to accept that it was real.

Something Anton had done had caused this... this endless, haunted roller-coaster ride. He'd tried to heal a new tattoo on her back and, in using his powers on her, had opened up a door in her mind she had long ago sealed shut. A memory she did her best to keep buried. As she lay in the dark and the intense melancholy of Bush's "The Chemicals Between Us" drifted out of her laptop speakers, she didn't try to delude herself that she had ever truly forgotten that horrible night. But hell, day to day she could function, and for that she figured it was okay to feel good about herself.

An image of Lee came to mind. Her awareness shifted, her body heated, and the remembrance changed to a pleasant one: the fangs piercing her skin and his huge arms around her. His body pressing against hers. Thinking of him shouldn't be so comforting.

She wanted him to be there in her bed, his large, solid body keeping her warm in her freezing cold room. *Never gonna happen. You think a little rockin' good sex suddenly changed his mind about what you are to each other?*

She pried her hands from her face and sat up in bed. The light from her laptop monitor glowed softly. She looked around at the place she'd called home these past several months. Despite her insistence that she wouldn't get comfortable here, Alexia could pick out signs that she'd gotten attached. Books stacked on the dresser and even a couple of splurge trinkets like a Swarovski rose from that store in Tysons Corner. Agnessa had talked her into buying the glittery piece of cut crystal, and Lexi had agreed because she liked shiny things. Who didn't?

She'd stuck a couple of pictures around the edges of her dresser mirror. She and Siddoh at a dance club. Isabel, pregnant and trying to knit a blanket for the baby. The dresser was a gorgeous, sturdy piece of furniture. Not quite Alexia's style, but she'd declined all the same when Ivy offered to get her a different one.

She couldn't believe she'd allowed herself to get so attached to Lee. She'd sworn for so long that it was a crush. She'd bought her own lie: he was hot and she'd roll with the attraction until it worked its way out of her system. Like how she'd gotten sick of candy corn by blowing through two whole bags after eighth-grade Halloween.

Well, that theory had worked out so fabulously, hadn't it?

The central air kicked on, and she shivered. *Well, there's one thing I won't miss. The vampires and their chilly tendencies*. Small freaking favors. She kept meaning to ask someone to close the vent over her bed. The ceiling was too high for her to reach, and of course she never remembered when everybody else was awake. She had fleece blankets even in summer. Talk about crazypants.

She could leave here, get her own place, get out of Lee's pissed-off, buzz-cut hair. Keep the air whatever temperature she wanted. Yeah. It was time to take this gig on the road.

After pacing the carpet for a few laps, Alexia pulled her phone from her thigh pocket to text Nessa: Okay. What can you do and how soon can you do it?

She felt like she might hurl as soon as she hit Send. Still. What choice did she have? Things had nearly passed the point of no return.

Agnessa would be going with Lee to the hospital sometime tonight to bless the brand-new royal bundle. If Lexi didn't catch the royal mind-messer-wither before she left the estate, there would be a whole 'nother day to wait. Then Isabel and Thad would be home with the baby, and it would be even harder to say good-bye. Best to leave before she had to look her best friend in the eye again. Not to mention the tiny peepers of that adorable baby girl. She'd never seen a newborn vampire before. Holy wow. Cuteness times infinity.

Alexia flopped on the bed again, wondering what Lee had been like as a baby. He seemed so serious and larger than life that it was hard to picture him coming out of a standard-issue womb all small and wrinkly. Even a supercharged vampire one.

A light knock sounded at her door. "Alexia?"

Agnessa. How did she move so fast on those pricey stilettos she wore? One would think she jogged in them.

Alexia's mouth dropped open when she answered the

door to find Nessa dressed more casually than Alexia had ever seen her. Usually clad in chic pencil skirts, this time the half-succubus female wore a flowing tunic and white pants. White leather ballet flats. As always, of course, her signature diamond choker.

"I have to bless the baby," Agnessa said. "Best to do it in comfortable clothes."

"Uh… sure." Maybe natural fibers channeled to the spirit world better? Maybe this was all fucking crazy? Alexia's pulse kicked up. Fear mixed with sadness as the implications started to sink in. She was about to ask Nessa to take away everything she'd known for nearly the last three years, if she counted the time since she'd first met Isabel. The prospect had been straightforward and logical, right up until the moment when she'd finally gotten ready to push the big red button.

She asked anyway. "So you can still do it, right? My memory?"

Agnessa parted her lips in apparent surprise. "You want me to do it now?"

"Can you?" Please for the love of all that was holy. Otherwise she was going to lose her nerve and be trapped in darkness loving a vampire who didn't love her back and missing her best friend whose life had gone on without her.

Fuck! She clamped her mouth shut so hard she made her teeth do an awful zing of agony, even though she hadn't said the *L* word out loud.

She didn't love Lee. Not that way. Fuck. *You thought it before, remember? When you were helping that guy with his truck…*

Oh, hell, she couldn't love Lee. Could Agnessa take *that* away too? She wasn't going to ask.

Nessa studied her for so long that Alexia got hot and embarrassed. Being scrutinized made her twitchy. She wondered so often what people saw when they looked at her. The man who had tried to take her from her father's house had said she was a "pretty little thing" and she'd make him a lot of money. Alexia wasn't sure she saw pretty when she looked in the mirror, and she definitely wasn't sure being pretty was good.

"You've got everything you need ready to go?"

"Yeah." Alexia nodded slowly. "I parked a car by the rear entrance. I have stuff in the trunk."

"All right. Lie on the bed," Agnessa said finally.

"Uhm, okay." She locked the door behind Agnessa. Awkward and exposed, Alexia did what Nessa asked. Pushed aside the temptation to jump up and yell, "Never mind," before it was too late. She gripped at the soft blanket underneath her. Something invisible and heavy pressed against her chest.

With one hand on either side of Alexia's head, Agnessa paused and leaned over Alexia's bed. "Here's what's going to happen. I'm going to ease you into a trance. Open you up, metaphysically speaking. I'm going to go in and find the things that pertain to your time among us and unthread them. Then, I will need to give you instruction. A new path. Where do you want to go when you're done here?"

"Back to Orlando, I guess."

"You guess? You need to make a decision. Be sure."

Alexia swallowed. "Back to Orlando." She'd been living there when she met Isabel. It was as good a place as any. She'd go there and figure out her shit. "I'll still remember who I am right? How to access my bank account…" What a time for practicality to rear its ugly head.

Agnessa smiled down at her. "I'll do my best." A deep breath, and a porcelain hand with red-polished nails settled over Alexia's eyes.

She'd do her best. Well, on the upside, in a prior moment of paranoia, Alexia had written her ATM PIN and all her other urgent info on the back page of a copy of *The Siren* in her spare backpack. She had cash set aside. She could get a job. She'd be fine. She closed her eyes. *It's okay. How much more can she fuck up my brain than it's already been fucked?* Talk about questions she shouldn't be asking.

The door banged open. The door Alexia was pretty sure she had locked. No, very sure.

"For fuck's sake, I've been looking—*Get your hands off her*."

Agnessa eased slowly off the bed. "There you are. So, you're ready to leave to see the queen?"

Alexia sat up. Had Nessa done anything yet? Didn't seem so. Everything felt the same, mentally speaking.

She looked back and forth between Nessa and Lee, whose chest was puffed with all manner of alpha male posturing. Jeez. How did Agnessa not get… *flapped* by his extreme douchefuckery? Alexia on the other hand couldn't manage to keep her mouth shut around him. "What the crap are you doing barging into my room?"

Lee narrowed his eyes with a growl. "Better question: What was going on in here just now?"

—◆◆◆—

Alexia had dozed off, confused and strangely tired after
Lee had stormed out with his ex in tow. She jumped,
disoriented and sleepy, from her rumpled bed when the
door to her room slammed open wide. *Again.* Thank
God she hadn't paid a security deposit when she arrived
in this place.

"C'mon, girlie." Siddoh stood with one substantial
hand braced on her door to keep it from swinging back
the other way. His face resembled the earlier weather
outside—dark and stormy. "I need to get fucked up, and
I knew just the human to come to for help." Clasped
firmly in his grip was an open bottle of Mondavi
Reserve Cabernet. Her favorite red.

Alexia twisted her head around. "I'm so not sure…"
Lord knew she was the last person to get judgy, but
Siddoh shouldn't be drinking while Lee and the rest
were gone, that was for damn sure.

"Come on, what the hell do you mean? You drink.
You could drink a vampire three times your size under
the table."

An exaggeration, but whatever. She drank plenty.
Often with Siddoh as her partner in crime. Because he
was her oversized, fanged-up Jiminy Cricket. "I drink,
but you don't. You definitely don't drink red wine." Red
wine affected vampires much, much*muchmuch* differently than humans. It was often referred to as the "vampire hug drug." She'd never known Siddoh to touch a
drop of wine.

He gave an exaggerated wink. "Shows what you know."

She rubbed her forehead. Seriously? The world had

practically collapsed around them, and this was how he chose to deal? "Aren't you still…"—she made a sweeping motion with her arm—"y'know… in charge of everything?"

"I've got a guy covering the patrols. Lee will be back soon with Agnessa. And soon after, God willing, Thad and Isabel." He stepped close, hooking the arm that held onto the wine bottle around her neck. "*Entre nous*, sweetheart, I want the fuck out of this leadership shit as soon as possible. What the hell is up with those power-hungry despots, you know? Couldn't goddamn pay me."

The wine bottle smacked Alexia in the cheek. She pushed at it and ducked away. "Yeah, I got that, *sweetheart*. I think I'd want to be sober, though, when the actual guys in charge get back. Or if, heaven forbid, anything else goes wrong?"

She twisted the bottle from his hand, taking a swig for good measure. She could use a buzz right now, and it would keep Siddoh from drinking. Eh. Didn't taste as good as usual, but she drank anyway. She didn't feel so great for some reason. Maybe the buzz would help.

Had everyone lost their minds? Siddoh wasn't like this. He put on a laid-back playboy attitude, but he was always sober and, as far as she could tell, fought harder than anyone. Many nights, Lee wasn't even out there fighting. Not that she blamed him; someone had to stay at the mansion to protect Thad and Isabel. But except for the nights when they were rotating shifts, Siddoh was out there busting his ass. Or he was in the training facility busting his ass. And on his off nights, he put up with her, trying to protect her when she wanted to go out and pretend she had a social life.

Everything Siddoh did was about guarding the safety of others. Getting fucked up on the job made no sense.

"Okay, dude. What's wrong?" She took another drink of the rich, fruity red. Dammit, she usually loved this stuff, but tonight it didn't sit well in her stomach. Maybe it was all the bad juju in the air. Or maybe it was the bla-tantly disrespectful chugging. Somewhere a sommelier was rolling in his grave over the way they were downing a hundred-dollar bottle of wine straight from the container.

She looked carefully at Siddoh's face, trying to make sense of his expression. His eyes, normally a light hazel, were darkened and bloodshot. He held back from saying something, but whatever it was stood there in the room like a big, evil elephant.

"Something tells me you'd get into big trouble with Thad if he came home to find you'd been hitting the sauce in the wake of what sounds like..." She paused and reached around him to shove her door shut. "In the wake of some kind of security breach. Now I know you butt heads with him and Lee plenty, but swilling red wine while you're on duty sounds like pushing things too far."

He ran a hand over his head, and that was when she noticed what else was strange: "Ew, you shaved your head?" He still had hair, but he'd given himself one of those buzz cuts that was even shorter than Lee's. The tousled mess of brown stuff that Siddoh used to have had disappeared. Most of the guys kept it short. Probably a regulation. Her estimation of Siddoh was that he cared more about regulations than he let on, and for some reason, he always pushed the envelope as far as he could without shoving it straight through the shredder. This, however, looked an awful lot like conforming. Or desperation.

"Yeah. Wanted to set a good example."

"For whom? Since when have you given a shit about an example?"

He sagged against the door then, not so much tired as worn out in a sad way. No answer.

Her fingers clenched. "Okay, you know what? I can see that something is going on with you, and I wanna be a friend here because you've been one for me so many times. But I don't know what the right questions are. Can you help me a little? You look like someone backed over your grandmother and your puppy. Or your grand-mother backed over your puppy."

Something. Anything. She didn't even care that her joke was lame or that desperation strained her voice. She hardly even cared at that moment that Lee might never speak to her again. She'd never seen Siddoh looking so desolate. She wanted to help her friend.

Siddoh's fist thumped the door. The painted wood rattled the frame, and Alexia flinched without meaning to. "I killed my uncle."

Somehow, her eyes stayed inside of her head. "Oh my God. Siddoh…"

His head hit back against the door. "I didn't— There was no choice. He let Isabel's dog out at dawn. Intentionally endangered the queen's life. The baby. The punishment is death."

Oh, Siddoh. Her body turned to lead. "But Lee could have—"

"No. I suspect my uncle relied on my relationship with him for leniency, which could not happen. I needed to be the one. Sometimes you need to step up and take charge."

God. Sometimes you did, but holy... Her eyes burned as she pulled him into a hug. "I wish I knew what to say."

He hugged back hard, but pulled away fast. He rubbed his eyes. They were red but dry. If he was anything like her, it might take a decade for what had happened to really come out. If he ever let it out. "There's nothing to say. It's just fucking awful."

The sharp pain of her nails in her palm was nothing compared to what lay inside her, sick and burning. She'd run away from her family because she blamed them for what had happened to her, because she didn't trust them anymore. She couldn't imagine having to kill one of them, though. Siddoh obviously had done what he did with good reason, but that didn't keep it from being awful.

One more reason she didn't belong in this world. It would never be something with which she could truly identify. And Lee was so angry and bitter. She didn't want to let what had happened to her make her bitter. Even more bitter, anyway.

She looked into Siddoh's hopeless eyes. On the other hand, Isabel would be bringing the baby soon... and Alexia couldn't just leave someone who had become like a brother to her when he was hurting. She couldn't go right away anymore, anyway. Not since Lee had hijacked her priestess whateveryacallit.

"Okay," Alexia said. She threw an arm around Siddoh's waist that barely went halfway and steered him to the bed. "Sit down. I may not have any answers, but I know how to distract you for a little while..."

Chapter 19

EAMON'S HEAD WAS BLEEDING, AND THERESA'S NERVES and energy had left her. Using her power to such an extreme had drained her to the point of shaking. She'd pricked her thumb to give the blood to her son so he could heal, but he only cried and refused the offering. The final straw. "Come on, honey. It'll make you feel better." She barely believed her own words.

Eamon turned his head and wailed louder. Panic streaked through Theresa's veins. Heaven forbid he'd been exposed to that spell. That virus. Whatever it was. "Sweetie, Mama needs you to take this blood." She dabbed some on his lips, hoping that would help. Babies only needed a little.

Eamon cried more, but then he seemed to settle. He licked his lips. Little baby eyes fluttered as if they might consider a nap. But the feeding didn't stay down. "Oh, Eamon, no," she whispered. Each time she hoped— prayed—that this would be the time the thing that was meant to nourish him didn't make him ill.

Xander came out of the bathroom, freshly showered and dressed. "What's wrong? Did he get sick?"

"He…" She stood and held Eamon away from her. "I need to find a clean shirt. He spit up again."

"I'll hold him while you change." Xander held out his arms.

"He might do it again. You just got clean."

Xander smiled. "We'll be fine."

Theresa nodded and handed her child to Xander, grateful for a moment of peace. She waited until she'd closed the bedroom door behind her before she allowed herself to cry. She didn't grant herself much time for sorrow, ripping open the packages of T-shirts they'd stopped to grab on their way. She would not wallow. This could be a fluke. It could get better.

But a baby spitting up its own mother's blood certainly was not good.

"Oh God, please…" Theresa fell to her knees in the darkened bedroom and let her head rest on the bed's fluffy white duvet. From beyond the door, the sounds of Xander humming to Eamon reminded her of those men she'd just killed in the park. Her chest heaved. She could try to pretend she'd only used her power to make them sleep, but that would be wrong. She could try to be sorry for what she'd done, but that would also be wrong. Her child had been in danger.

Freezing cold to her core, she swiped the tears from her face and returned to the suite's living room. Surrounded by the white noise of her fear, it took a moment to realize that everything had fallen quiet. She looked around to find Xander on the couch with Eamon cradled in the crook of his arm. "He stopped crying."

"Shh." Xander lifted one long index finger. "I think he's tired."

"How did you—Oh." Her eyes followed Xander's pointer finger. The pinkie finger on that same hand rested in Eamon's tiny mouth. "Well, that's…" Adorable. Heartwarming. *Going to break my heart when this is all over*.

Xander grinned. "I did this once right after he was first born. You were getting checked by the doctor and he got hungry. It helped him go back to sleep. I thought such a thing might work again." He shrugged a shoulder. "Maybe I can be good for something other than firing a gun." Xander's words, said in a light tone, did not match the scowl on his face.

"Are you…" She sat slowly on the other end of the sofa. One hand clasped the other to keep them both still. "… are you angry with me? Am I going to be in trouble? I know I should have let you be the one to handle the situation. I acted without thinking."

"I'm only worried about you." He shifted carefully, gentle with Eamon. "You didn't do anything wrong. I remember my first kill, though. That can be difficult to process."

She scooted forward. "Here, I can take him."

Xander frowned. "Okay, sure. I think he's—ow!" Xander raised an eyebrow. "I was about to say I think he's out, but the little bugger just nipped me."

"Here." Theresa held out her arms. "I should take him. He might get sick again."

"Wait." Xander sat up straighter, watching with interest. "He's sucking on my finger. That's good, right?"

"But…" Her throat clogged. "It makes him sick." She looked around for a hand towel, in case of the worst.

"Are you sure?" Xander smiled down at Eamon in the dark. "He's got a good hold on me. He seems… yeah. Look. The cut on his head is healing, I think."

No. Could he really… Hope fluttered in her chest. "Are you sure?" She dropped to her knees by his side without thinking. "He's really drinking?"

Xander pulled the finger from Eamon's mouth and the squalling started immediately. "I think he wants more." He chuckled.

Theresa couldn't stop the tears. "He's really drinking." She put her hand to her chest. "I'd been…" *Panicked. Terrified. About to vomit myself so many times I'd almost given up on eating.* She shook her head. "It's the worst thing, you know. As a mother. To have the very thing that's supposed to sustain your child, from your own body, and to be told it might be the thing that makes him ill. That you can't take care of him." She kept her gaze firmly fixed on her son in Xander's lap, suckling peacefully on that pinkie, eyelids drifting toward sleep. So unbelievable.

Gratitude mixed with anger and fear. Her own blood made her son ill, but someone else's could heal him? The unfairness burned through her.

"Theresa."

She looked up. Xander's green eyes shone brightly in the dim light. "One way or another, this will all be okay. I'll be here to help any way I can."

Not if you leave us. Not if you get killed. But she only said, "I just can't believe he's taking your blood. You must really be something special."

Xander smiled, managing to pull his hand free of Eamon who had finally dropped off to sleep. He hooked his index finger around hers. "I like to think I am." He seemed to search her face. "And so is his mother."

~~~

Alexia and Siddoh settled on her bed to watch *Dirty Dancing*. No, it wouldn't fix what ate away at Siddoh. Nothing could.

But for the moment? Passion. Angst. Catchy music. Patrick Swayze in his prime. These things would help more than getting hammered. She knew of whence she spoke.

Johnny and Baby practiced their moves together in the summer heat, and she and Siddoh both sighed a little. Best movie ever. Damn, Alexia loved hanging out with this big teddy bear of a vampire. They had fun together. She'd miss doing this sort of thing with Siddoh if she were gone. When.

"Shit, this guy is smooth. I need to learn to cha-cha. Maybe I'd get laid more."

She threw a handful of popcorn at Siddoh's severely shorn head. "You look so serious with that haircut. And how is it you don't get laid with all those tattoos and muscles? You're hot."

He waggled his brows. "You offering?"

She rolled her eyes. "Right. You're also a smart-ass." They flirted all the time. He really did look great, and she'd seen the female staff around the estate swoon behind his back when he wasn't aware. She'd always thought she must be missing something not to have been swept up by his mojo. They'd bumped and swayed together on the dance floor at clubs. Hell, once they even fell asleep together in his bed after he'd had a really intense feeding and she'd been unable to last until the end of watching *Troy*. She could get her cuddle on with the guy, no problem. But there had been no chemistry. More than friends had never been in the cards for her and Siddoh.

He grunted and shook his head without her having to say anything. "Yeah, yeah. I know."

"I'm not the right type for you, anyway. You're look-ing in all the wrong places. Otherwise you'd be mated by now. You're like… old, for crying out loud."

That surprised something like a laugh out of him. "Says the girl who's hot for a seven-hundred-year-old vampire. That guy's practically got one foot on the Council of Elders and the other on a banana peel, for crying out loud. Anyway, what type of female do you think I'm looking for?"

"I don't know, but look at me. Look at Tyra. Bitchy, stubborn, and willful. I think you're attracted to women you know won't work for you. I think deep down what you really want is a nice, traditional girl who will cook you dinner and rub your shoulders every night, but you're afraid that saying so would be bad for your image as the resident ne'er-do-well. What was your mother like?"

He barked a laugh and tossed a handful of popcorn into his mouth. On television Johnny and Baby danced at the Sheldrake. "Trying to put those psych lessons to work, Lexi? Interesting thought, though. Weird. But in-teresting. By the way, my mother and I haven't spoken in a century."

Ouch. She tapped her head. "Ah. See? Mull it over."

He grunted and crossed his ankles on the bed.

Banging on Alexia's door interrupted their conver-sation. It hit the far wall with a hard slam. Again with the slamming.

"Jesus, Lee. Are you trying to break the thing?" Alexia glared, not that the stubborn ass gave a damn.

Like that, Siddoh rose to his feet.

Lee nodded his head. "Siddoh, check in with the

patrols. The grounds and the surrounding area look clear, but I'd like to verify."

"Understood." All business now, Siddoh straightened and nodded to her before leaving the room. No trace of his former sadness or concern remained. There wouldn't be any. Siddoh was all fun and games until a job needed to be done. He pulled the somehow-still-hanging-on-its-hinges door shut behind him without a backward glance.

Lee stood at the foot of her bed with his chest rising and falling, wearing an expression she couldn't read for anything. Was he pissed? That was a safe guess. But Lord knew she was just as likely to tick him off by breathing as if she personally danced right up and kerthwacked him in the junk drawer.

Damn it, though, he was so frigging handsome. Rain still dotted his short hair, and under his jacket, his clothing clung tight to his muscles. Lean. Hard... and she knew now what the whole package looked like.

God, if only that alone could be enough reason to stay.

He stalked up close. "Are you out of your fucking mind?"

She held out the large ceramic bowl she'd shared with Siddoh only minutes earlier. "Popcorn?" On the screen, Johnny and Baby argued in Johnny's room. How fucktacularly appropriate.

He grabbed the bowl and clunked it onto the dresser. "That's hardly a reasonable response."

She huffed and sat back down on the bed. "Well, shit, Lee, I don't know what would be reasonable, since you keep blasting in here right and left with an apparent attempt to remove my door from the frame. I really don't have a clue what you're asking. Am I out of my fucking mind in general? I don't think so, but it depends on one's perspective. I'm the only human living on an estate full of vampires so perhaps I maybe, possibly, just might have a screw or two loose. Can you be more specific?"

He pressed forward. He stopped short of grabbing, but the flex of his fingers and the darkness on his face told her that he wanted to. "You can't do it, Lexi. I'm sorry. You can't have Agnessa wipe your mind. You cannot leave." His voice had dropped to a whisper on that last sentence. She wasn't sure she had ever heard him whisper before a few nights ago. She hadn't known Lee could be soft in any way at all.

She was so busy tripping over the gravelly quiet of his words and his breath skating past her ear, because she'd drawn up to her full height and he'd stooped low, that she nearly let what he'd actually said slip right by her. "Wait. What? What the hell do you mean I can't go?" She pushed at his chest. "What did Agnessa say to you?"

She veered around him, and his arm shot out, closing a hand around her wrist. She tried to swallow, but sharp fragments of a major freak-out made doing so impossible. "You have no right to make me stay. Agnessa said she could—"

"Agnessa cannot be trusted." The hand that held her wrist eased its grip, let go, and found the small of her back. He pulled her close, and very weirdly, the wet warmth of his clothes was a comfort. Familiar, after their little unplanned wilderness bonding experience out in the woods. After the hospital. "She also left out a very important detail. Whether deliberately or because she wasn't paying attention, I can't be certain."

"What are you talking about?"

Lee's other hand slid along her shoulder, that broad thumb stroking her throat. "I drank from you. You drank from me. Enough at this point that you feel me within your veins. You would continue to feel me if you went away."

A shiver started from the crown of her head and chased its way down her spine.

"Now for me, I can eventually drink from someone else maybe. Wash you out of my system," he said.

Now, why did that make her itch to warm up her bitch-slapping hand?

"You, though? Let's say you go back to the human world. Forget about vampires. Never consume blood again. I will always be there. You'll feel me inside you. You won't know what it is, but I'll be there. When I'm angry. Hungry…"

Another shiver. Intense. Whether intentional or not, his hand flattened across her back. His hold on her tightened and she resisted the urge to lean forward. Against the heat of his skin.

"Lexi, I'm serious. You'll go insane."

Chapter 20

LEE'S HAND TIGHTENED INTO A FIST.

"What the frick do you mean I'll go insane?" The look on Alexia's face showed her disbelief. Hell, her expression suggested she thought he might be the one who was nuts. Certainly a possibility.

As he held her there in his grasp, her eyes went back and forth, searching for an answer she couldn't quite seem to find. Her body pulled against his hands, but his fingers held tight. He couldn't let her go, and this was beyond simple duty.

Lee had chewed on this shit the entire drive home from the hospital. He had pounded the steering wheel and clawed the leather seat, even dented the car door with his rage. His confusion. He didn't trust Nessa's motives or the story she'd supplied on the ride to the hospital that what she had done with Alexia had been well-intentioned. For Lee's *good*? The excuse sounded far too convenient.

"Please," he said, "sit down." He trusted his legs and their ability to bear weight about as much as he trusted his ex at that moment.

He could not pull his arms from around her body. He knew the feel and shape of Alexia intimately now. Every slope, every curve. After the encounter he'd had with Nessa at the hospital, he was raw and worn enough that he could admit to needing Alexia's comfort. She had kept up with him through a hell of a lot these past nights, far more than he'd given her credit for. He'd been so busy pushing her away since her arrival at the estate that he'd failed to truly see her.

He could claim it was because she was human. "Lexi…" Certainly Alexia's humanity complicated things beyond measure. But Lee had to stop denying it changed the bone-deep want inside.

Her blonde and brown hair tumbled around her shoulders. Dark eyes narrowed at him, in search of answers. He could always say he loved her attitude. Even when it drove him to distraction, her toughness and her fortitude made him smile deep inside. He swept a palm across her cheek and into her hair, gratified when she pushed the cheek against his hand and closed her eyes.

"Do you feel that, Lexi?"

"What am I feeling?"

That I'm hard for you. Hungry for you. That you are the closest I will ever come to tasting daylight, and I still have the memory of your skin and your blood on my tongue. In my veins. Just as you have the memory of me in yours.

Lee sucked in a breath, waiting.

Her eyes stayed closed while his fingers ran through her hair and down her back. He wrapped his hand around her hair and tipped her head, leaning close until their bodies pressed together every place they possibly could. He nuzzled along her jaw, her throat. "Because of our blood, my body knows yours. Inside and out. Whatever you may think of me, I am not one to play games. Being near you stirs my veins. Makes me want things I shouldn't." He took her chin between his thumb and forefinger. "Please. Open your eyes. Look at me."

She did. Her dark pupils enlarged against the whites of her eyes. He pushed her backward against the pillows of her bed. They carried Siddoh's scent and Lee's anger rose in response. "Now do you feel what I'm feeling?"

She stiffened in his grasp, likely pissed off even as her body's want overrode her anger. Heat pulsed from between her legs. "What I'm feeling is frustrated. You said yourself you and I couldn't—"

"Dammit." He resisted the urge to tighten his grip. To push harder. "Deep in your blood, Lexi. *What do you feel?*"

She played along this time, going still and quiet. Her eyes lost focus and she went limp in his arms.

Lee took another deep inhale, sucking down Siddoh's lingering scent. The other vampire's smell remained on her skin as well. Faint, but there. They hadn't been intimate. If they had, Siddoh's familiar odor would cling more tenaciously to her skin. Still, anger and possessive jealousy swirled deep inside of Lee. This wasn't something he'd had with Nessa. Lee's issues with his ex had been about pride. Saving face.

What Alexia stirred in Lee's veins was... molten. Need.

Her next breath shook. Her gaze refocused on his. "You're angry. But you... you're horny? And you're calling *me* nuts."

He snarled deeply, unfathomably pleased. "So are you," he whispered in her ear. "I can smell Siddoh on your bed. On your skin."

"Sure." She frowned. The light of understanding didn't seem to have dawned yet in her mind. "We were watching a movie. We sat next to each other. It's not like anything happened—"

His nose went to her hair. Threats rumbled from his chest. "I can't stand knowing he was so close to you, Lexi. It makes my blood boil to smell another on your skin." He nuzzled along her low neckline. One whiff of her honeyed blood and his dick got hard. God, she'd changed into a long, sleeveless dress. Fucking gorgeous. So feminine, and so easy to reach down and push up the thin material. To claim her.

Even as her breath deepened and the flush of arousal crept across the tops of her breasts and up her neck, her eyes narrowed. That challenging stare again. Her hands, so small and pale compared to his, pushed against his chest. "Okay, I've got the mcmo," she whispered. "I'm super flattered, but that's not a reason for me to stay here. You said yourself it can't work."

A growl rumbled out of his chest. "You aren't hearing me. That you can read me in your blood is our problem. You can erase me from your thoughts…" He ran a hand over her hair, her throat, the valley between her breasts. His hand stopped over her heart. "You can never erase me from *here*. When I am angry, when I am in pain. Heaven forbid I die before you die, and I very well might. My agonies will be your agonies. My joys will be your joys—"

"You experience joy?" This said with a maddening curl to her lips.

Lee stared hard into her eyes. "For fuck's sake. Without your memories of me and this place, you would have rage and pain and a whole fuck-ton of emotions inside you that you can't begin to make sense of or process. You would lose your fucking mind. Is that what you want?"

Moisture rimmed her eyes. "So I'm screwed then? If I stay here, I'll lose my fucking mind regardless. I am alone in a crowd constantly. I never get to see day-light unless I sneak out without telling anybody, which of course is dangerous. My best friend never has time to speak to me anymore because she's the queen of an entire race of vampires." She blinked rapidly. "Not to be selfish, but I do miss her."

A dull ache spread through Lee's chest. Not his own pain this time. Alexia's.

"You didn't want me before because I was geneti-cally inferior," she continued. "Now you do want me because my blood apparently is helpful to you some-how, but you still don't trust me because I'm buddies with your ex and I'm human."

"That's not true." But it had been. At the beginning, at least, it had been.

She sniffled. "What if things change between us? Now that we've been together, I guarantee no other vampire on this estate will touch me for love or money. So I'm screwed if I stay, and not in the fun way." For a moment, her face twisted into a bit-ter mask. "Besides, you claim it's safer for me here, but I know for a fact that sometimes the safest place winds up being the place you get hurt the most, so I'll never know for sure what or who to trust. That kinda leaves me without options, doesn't it? So I'll take my chances with insanity."

Fuck. Lee had said similar words to the doctor at St. Anne's, and if things had been different, he'd almost be willing to respect her decision and let things go. But things were not different.

Desperation like he'd never known clogged Lee's throat. His fingers tangled in her hair. The white at the top of Alexia's dress clung to her skin because the wet of his clothes had seeped into hers. So damned gorgeous it killed him. His pride had difficulty with the words, but he said them anyway: "Alexia, please. I'm begging you to stay. Not for duty. For me. I want you to stay for me."

With that, Lee crushed his lips against hers.

Alexia's brain went "Kaboom." No other explanation for why one second her hands pushed against Lee's shoulders, why her eyes narrowed at him in disbelief for the ridiculous way he'd barged into her room and started spouting all sorts of nonsense… And then the next thing her hands gripped tightly to his damp shirt with the purpose of pulling him forward. Her thighs widened, one foot sliding up the bed to prop her knee on his lean, muscular hip. Her body, her blood thrumming in time with his.

That same blood rushed in her ear. Urged her to agree, and fuck the cost. Saying no to Lee felt like tearing up a winning lottery ticket. Tearing away a piece of her soul.

Deep in her core she couldn't deny what he'd said. Even as his hard-on nudged between her legs through the barrier of his wet clothes, the hum of his inner desire stirred from someplace inside that she couldn't pinpoint. She swallowed, gasping in shallow breaths as he pushed the hem of her skirt up her legs bit by bit.

She could have stopped him. She should have stopped

him. Lee, for all his posturing, would have walked away if she'd told him she wanted him to leave her alone. If she'd said she didn't want him. Making love to him again would only make it harder to walk away.

"You wear dresses so rarely," he murmured. One hand skimmed her bare shoulder.

"It was easy," she said. Sometimes a sundress was nice because she could just throw it on. No effort. She hadn't thought about the benefit of a rabidly horny vampire gaining easy access after her shower.

Alexia shivered and clamped her mouth tight. No, she couldn't tell him she wanted him to stop, because it would be such a lie. More than a lie. As he gathered her skirt and she mapped out an exposed section of his hard, ridged belly with her hand, she couldn't have stopped touching him for anything in the world. He held her with the intensity of his stare and made her stomach do loop-de-loops. Made her warm inside and out in a way she hadn't been in absolutely forever. Maybe never ever.

He hunched down, his lips pressing to hers again. Oh, good effing Lord, Lee could kiss. That large mouth could be so unbearably firm and gentle all at the same time. Hot. Lush. His tongue slid alongside hers, pushing and challenging. Dueling.

Lee's long fangs nicked Alexia's lip. The tang of her blood barely touched her own tongue before he sucked it off. He growled with pleasure, a deep noise in the back of his throat. Suddenly he lifted her hips, pushing her deep into the mattress, and there was nothing she wanted to do more than wrap around and hang on.

"So fucking delicious." Light and shadow played

over his face. "I don't know how I didn't realize. How I withstood tasting you for so long." His growl echoed through her body and dampened her underwear.

Holy frickin' Toledo. Vampire foreplay.

She reached between them. "Your pants…"

"Let me," he said. His hands went to work, tugging at his shirt, unbuttoning his pants.

She gasped at the delicious slide of his golden, lightly furred skin against her inner thighs. At the stretch and burn as he pushed inside her. *Oh God*. At the fire in his eyes. "Lee…"

He rocked into her, slowly and gently, never breaking eye contact. "God, Lexi… Nobody has ever been in my blood like this."

God, the things he said could turn her brain inside out. Alexia bit her lips together. As he thrust deeper, she dug her heels into his ass and her fingernails into his shoulders. She didn't answer. She couldn't. Right then, with them both half naked and his voice so raw, she would promise him the world. And if she stayed only because he asked her to, would she be giving up every shred of her independence, the thing she perceived as safety, in the process?

Lee shifted, gripping her, pushing them both harder into the bed so he was deep inside. Pressing in all the right places. His free hand caressed her arm, stroking over her shoulder, running a thumb over her throat. Oh… yes.

Alexia's legs tightened around Lee's waist, spurring him deeper. Together, they both groaned. Lee dug his fingers into her hips and thrust faster. Alexia smiled into his eyes, loving the way she turned him on in that moment. Any minute now, her heart was going to bust out of her chest in its effort to get to him.

If only there was a way for them to be together. Really be together.

The sexy dips and curves of his chest pumped in and out right in front of her, rising and falling with each hard breath he took. She longed to sink her teeth into the firm muscle. Remembering how he'd responded before, how he'd enjoyed the pain, she raked her fingers down his back.

"God. Fuck. Yes." Lee adjusted his grip on her. Faster. Sweat collected between the places where their bodies touched, slicking their movement. Fangs long, Lee hissed and threw his head back for a moment. The struggle played over his face as the muscles and veins bulged in his neck.

She remembered the way he'd responded when his fang nicked her lip. "Lee." Her hands came to the sides of his face. She needed to see his eyes. Everything made sense when she could look into them.

His golden skin took on a red cast as his muscles flexed and his body shook. Alexia's pleasure climbed with his. Her legs tightened around him, and as she stared into Lee's eyes, as his pupils dilated, she let her head relax on the pillow. "Take what you need, it's okay."

"What?" He barely panted the word.

"My blood. It's yours. It's okay." More than okay. Right then she wanted to give him everything. Absolutely everything.

His hesitation rippled through both of them. His body tensed and she clamped her thighs around him. They both rode the edge, the pleasure in every nerve coiling tighter. Climbing with every breath, every thrust.

The moment he gave in was the moment she flew into a thousand tiny pieces. Hands under her back, he thrust hard inside her as he pulled close and sank his fangs into her throat, setting off a rolling wave of pleasure. The pinch of his bite created an unexpected shock wave, spurring her to squeeze every muscle, and she was rewarded with the roar of his release as he pulsed inside her. Bruising fingers dug into her flesh but she couldn't bring herself to care. In that moment, knowing she'd wear his marks carried a strange sense of pride.

He'd hardly drunk at all before licking the bite closed.

"You're okay? You had enough?" Blood thundered between her ears even as aftershocks of her orgasm rocked her body.

He leaned down, pressing his forehead to hers. "I'll never have enough of you. Thank you for your gift."

"I'd…" *Anytime*, she had almost said. Was that the truth? Was she going or staying? Her blood was the only gift she had to give. If things were different, maybe she'd try to stay. She'd want to give him the gift of her, for real. But in the end, once this medical problem of his sorted itself out, he would need someone better, stronger than she was. He'd need another vampire.

As they pressed away from each other and the high of what they'd just shared lost its edge, she struggled for breath and faced reality. Really, that was the bottom line: he would always be vampire and she'd always be human.

She couldn't deny that being with him like this made it harder to go. But could they honestly make it work between them if she stayed?

Chapter 21

ABOVE ALEXIA, LEE'S BREATH PUFFED HARSH AND ragged like hers. His fangs had yet to retreat back inside his mouth. Seeing his monster side so prominently only drove home the reasons she was so afraid to believe. If this was just some misguided sense of duty or his need not to fail… If it was about his blood…

Moisture leaked from her eyes. "Listen, this about-face is confusing. You always said you hated humans. I can stay a little longer if you just need more blood…" Her arm jerked. She wanted to wipe away the tears that ran along her jaw, but Lee had her arms trapped. Her emotions were running away without her, and she hated showing him this kind of weakness.

"It's fine, okay? I don't have any plans. I—I wanted to be gone before Isabel and the baby got settled so it wouldn't be so hard." *Before I got so attached to you.*

His face darkened and his head came down, one forehead pressed to another. "You're still not listening, Alexia."

She tried to answer, but the words made her sputter and choke. She balled up her fists and pulled harder against the restraint of his body, not that she expected to get anywhere. She didn't exactly have superior strength against Lee's solid wall of muscle. Suddenly she went full-on panic spazz-out, like a million bugs crawled under her skin and she just had to get away from him. Had to.

"God, will you just—" Her throat tightened. Clogged with screams that couldn't get out. "Please *let go of me!*" She twisted and jerked, yanking her arms and pulling her legs to her chest, ready to use them as leverage.

The effort proved unnecessary. Lee released her immediately, rising onto his knees and backing away practically before she'd even begun to protest.

Still, Alexia's body had pumped up the adrenaline. She jumped against the wall, while her heart kept doing wind sprints and she tried not to shrink down to two feet tall. She took a long, slow, deep breath. "I'm listening, I swear. My ears work perfectly fine. All those years spent in the party scene didn't kill my hearing, I promise you." Alexia giggled nervously but Lee didn't move, didn't quirk a smile, didn't respond at all to her awkward little joke.

She used an embarrassingly shaky arm to wipe tears from her chin. "I hear you saying it's gonna make me crazy if Nessa wipes my memories. You think I don't understand. Thing is, I think what's going on here is you are a truly honorable guy and you'll feel responsible if I leave. But I don't belong here, and you're not responsible.

"I'm used to crazy. I'm used to emotions I can't control or explain. I had a mom put in jail for shoplifting to support my drug-addicted father who wasn't paying attention when some of his dealer friends snatched me out of my bedroom one night. Believe me, that kind of thing doesn't exactly make life conducive to sanity."

He didn't respond, but his lips slackened in apparent surprise. His fingers clenched. "Lexi…"

When he moved to come closer, she pressed back

against the wall, closing her eyes against the searching stare in his bottomless aqua eyes. "No, it's okay. You know, some days are just fine. Some days I'm so intensely angry at the world and I can't figure it out. Then I realize it's right around the day they tried to take me. Some days I'm inexplicably terrified. I can't eat. I can't sleep. I run and dance and drink and all that other stuff to try and get tired. I hate to sleep." Her head throbbed.

"It's just—You think I might go crazy? That it's more dangerous out there than in here? I'm in hell all the time." She tapped her forehead, indicating the nightmares and memories trapped inside. "And the people who promised to love and protect me didn't. So I mean it sincerely when I say I'm grateful for your intention, but you can't give me any guarantees."

Alexia pressed her hands against her eyes as the tears fell, unable to stand the despair and frustration on Lee's face. She couldn't make this okay for him. She didn't even know how to make it okay for herself.

Gently, the back of his hand brushed along her cheek. "Lexi, I'm sorry. I shouldn't have tried to hold you down just now."

"You didn't know."

He tried to meet her eyes. She tried to count spots on the ceiling. Only those eyes were too blue and too hypnotic not to look into. "I remember a time when I tried to carry you over my shoulder and you got so angry you kicked me in the balls," he said with a slight smile.

She crossed her arms over her chest. "Anybody would've been pissed. It was embarrassing and demoralizing. I'm not five." But she smiled some, too, in response to the beauty of his upturned lips. His attempt to understand.

He tipped his chin. "But that's why."

Alexia moved her head from side to side. "Yes."

"Forgive me." Words whispered so softly from this big Sherman tank of a vampire that she hardly heard them.

Alexia's head fell forward against his chest. The apology melted her. For some reason she hadn't expected it... not from him. "It's okay."

"No, it isn't."

She shook her head. "It's as okay as it can be, you know? I figure, all things considered, I function pretty well. Mostly."

He breathed a laugh and kissed her then. Gently, softly, his lips brushed hers, and only for a moment did the tip of his tongue touch his bottom lip before he pulled away again. "I think you're amazing. That's a frightening thing that happened, and look how far you've come. Did they hurt you?"

She shook her head. "I mean it depends on your definition." The pictures entered her head. Being shoved into a windowless van full of tools. The tools and what they might have done to her with them were the scary parts.

"Lexi..." His voice was low and dangerous. "Tell me."

She shrugged again. As if it had all been no big deal. "They shoved me in a van. They hit me. They shot me up with... I don't know, some kind of sedative. I was in there with girls—young girls—who were bloody and restrained, and... God, in the end I got so lucky. Compared to the rest."

She swallowed hard. Her chest and throat ached, and

it was hard trying to remember enough to tell the story without replaying it all in her head. "I had managed to distract one of them, and then I just started kicking and screaming. This one big guy tried to pin me down and pull my clothes off, but I was able to grab hold of some saw-type thing and hit him on the head. It was enough to get away. A couple of the other girls and I managed to hide out until we were sober. I never went back home." The muscles in her neck and shoulders ached from the remembered tension of that night.

He growled quietly, nuzzling into the crook of her neck. His head shook like he wasn't sure what to say, so she squeezed her fingers around his to let him know he didn't have to say anything.

"The hard part was that I couldn't save all the other girls. I wasn't too messed up from the drugs yet, but some of them were stoned or high or just too scared, I guess. Some of them wouldn't run and there was no time to wait."

His arms went around her. "I am so sorry. I wish I could have protected you then, too."

She couldn't help but smile at this, but the ache in her heart was fierce. She'd never told anyone about that night. Not even Isabel. Not really.

Why she had told Lee, she couldn't be sure. What was she honestly hoping that would solve? Maybe it was just time to tell someone she wasn't paying for therapy. "It's all right. I survived. I managed to build a life. It's more than some of them got," she said. And she said no more because remembering the ones who hadn't made it out, wondering what had happened to them, tore her to pieces every time.

"God, Lexi," Lee murmured into her shoulder. "Stay. Please stay. I want you to. I want to make all this shit up to you. Let me make things better. Please."

It looked like Lee. It felt like him. Smelled like him. These just didn't sound like words a gruff, badass anti-human vampire would say. Still, at the mere sound of them, her body had relaxed into his, ready to believe anything. God, she wanted to trust his sincerity. She wanted to give in. "I want to say yes. I'm *dying* to say yes. But you said yourself humans and vampires don't work. How can we?"

He raised his head with a snarl. With one finger he stroked her eyebrow and then ran a hand through the strands of her hair. "I asked before about the color of your hair. You said if I could drink from you without getting ill, you would tell me."

Sadness burned in her chest, but she decided not to call him on his abrupt change of subject. She could only take it to mean he didn't have an answer to her question. "That night they tried to take me, I was told how I was so pretty. How lots of men would pay lots of money to fuck me. I swore," she whispered, "I would never look in the mirror and see what they had seen. Ever."

Before Alexia could blink, the mirror over her dresser had cracked and shattered. Lee's knuckles dripped with blood. Heartbeats passed before either of them spoke. "Then fuck the mirror. You'll be beautiful to me regardless," he said.

―⁂―

Lee pressed his lips again to Alexia's. He'd always hated to kiss. Awkward and tricky with his fangs in the way. With someone else's fangs in the way. Kissing Alexia… perfect fit. He could hardly remember why he had so resisted this before.

He groaned, shifted, and pressed against her mouth. Her body. He wanted to wrap around her. Make promises. Find the men who had tried to carry her off to danger. Who had hurt and scared her. Promise her he would never be the one to cause her pain.

You can't make those promises, can you? He also couldn't let her leave.

Since the day she'd entered his life, Lee had tried to keep Alexia at a distance, convinced it was the best thing for all involved. Now he couldn't let her go. Fuck if he knew how to make it work if she stayed, but the idea of her walking out into the daylight tore him apart.

"Your hand…"

"It'll heal," he said. "You gave me blood. It's a minor wound." He hardly noticed the sting over the pulse of his rage.

He drew her breath into his mouth. Even after their lovemaking, red wine and salty butter lingered. "You've been drinking."

"Some. Siddoh showed up wrecked and chugging wine. I took the bottle so he wouldn't drink it himself."

Once upon a time, he would have gotten angry with her for imbibing. For having vices. He could see that tonight she'd been a friend. And fuck, he'd had vices, too. Before, there had been blood. And now her.

Lee Goram, addicted to a human. Never say never.

The very thought made him want her—need her—all over again. His hand slid between their bodies. Down her stomach. He had to touch her skin again. Making love to her just then hadn't sated his desire, but instead fueled his craving.

He paused, though, as his hand touched her thigh. "Is this okay?"

She nodded with a frown.

Lee understood her confusion. He hadn't asked before, had he? He'd just... taken. He couldn't do that anymore. "I didn't know. About what had happened to you. I'm trying to be..." Gentle. Careful. He didn't finish the sentence aloud, worried she'd be offended by the notion that he wanted to treat her with caution. Still, he needed the assurance of her skin against his again more than he needed to breathe.

So much was clear to him now. He didn't want to act as if she was weak or fragile, but he'd been a complete dick. "Lexi, I'm so sorry. For what you've been through. What I've done."

She sagged against the white-painted wall, her hands pressed flat like she didn't want to touch him. "It's fine. You didn't know."

Then you'll stay. Say it, Lexi. He jammed his tongue to the roof of his mouth to avoid spitting it out like a command. Fuck him, but he was used to giving orders. "I hope so." Females said they were fine when they were the opposite: angry. Angst-ridden. Plotting your demise.

He slid his hand along her shoulder. *Careful.* He'd never been so at odds as with Alexia. Since the morning he'd lost his mother and sister, he'd been decisive. Indecision got you in trouble. Got you killed. Now here he was with a human who turned him every direction but forward.

Finally, he understood her issue. She'd been on the

run for so long. Still running from the men who had tried to take her, even though in all likelihood they were dead by now. Humans who lived those lives didn't survive for long. Maybe she even ran from herself. Lee sure as hell ran from his own demons.

To Lee, making Alexia stay on the estate had been about safety. For her, it had been the same as being locked in the back of that van. She'd been trying to break out around every turn.

He buried his face in that gorgeous hair. "So many reasons the two of us cannot last. Still, it makes no more sense to withhold what I feel for you." Not if it might save her life. Truly, she had no idea. She could stand there with defiance in her dark eyes and toss aside the idea that she'd feel his emotions for the rest of her life as if it was nothing. She didn't grasp the implications. Right now, she had a frame of reference for what she felt when he stirred in her veins. With no recollection that he'd ever been in her life, it honestly would confuse her beyond sanity.

Alexia's breath came in deep gasps. "But how…"

He skimmed his hand along her arm, wrapping around her shoulders. Drawing her close. "I don't know. I'm so out of my element here. Right now I want to make love to you again. I want to hold you. I want to go back in time and kill those fuckers. I want to make it all better for you, and I don't know how." His body throbbed from head to toe. Hot and tight, despite the cooling moisture on her skin. His fangs remained long into his mouth. His primal side, desperate to devour her. Still, this couldn't be about what he wanted.

She shook her head. "What do I do if I stay here?

I've spent these last months getting in everyone's way. Nobody wants me to go anywhere or do anything."

He closed his eyes. It burned that she was right. "I concede that we've been overprotective. I have. Perhaps I can talk to Thad about giving you more daytime freedom."

"Look, I know a little self-defense. I've taken the class to get a gun permit. I'm not totally helpless."

Christ. The idea of Alexia with a gun nearly made his brain leak from his ears. Not that she wasn't competent, but he just couldn't picture… Oh, hell. He nodded, even as dread settled in his chest. "I will talk to Thad." Tension made his muscles burn. "We haven't… there's been no more word of attack from Haig. His guardians have been spotted, but their power pales compared to his. No more cases of plague have shown up in the human hospitals. Nobody has spotted him. He may be dead after all."

Haig returning from the grave may have been another thing about which Lee was wrong. For once, he hoped so. He'd rather look like an asshole than be right. He ignored the cold fear that lodged its jagged blade in his sternum. They'd reinforced the estate again. Things were safer now.

This was all so new. He'd never… Not since Agnessa had he allowed himself to confess feelings for a female, and his emotions had never been of this magnitude. Rarely did he find himself in uncharted waters.

"Can we consider more freedom in general?" She leaned toward him now, looking hopeful.

"All right." God help him. He leaned back so he could see down into her eyes without hunching his shoulders. "What do you mean, exactly?"

Alexia looked up to the ceiling. "I need a way to fit. I've been bumming around and I'm a pain in everyone's ass. It's lonely. If I'm going to stay, I need a job. A purpose. Something."

Lee stood over her and looked down into those bottomless brown eyes. He was going to have to jump and pray to holy fuck that there was a place to land in there somewhere. "I told you. I want to be your purpose. Stay for me."

Chapter 22

ALEXIA LOOKED AROUND HER SPARSE ROOM. THE PINK and white sheets now all rumpled from sex, the few pictures on the mirror, and the turntables set up along the wall were the only decorating she'd bothered doing because she'd always secretly suspected she wasn't going to stay. *This was never supposed to be home.*

She closed her eyes and tried to picture a world where she and Lee made sense. She'd practically died to have him say these things to her. *Died.* For weeks and months, she'd watched and wanted and wondered if he'd ever want her in a million years.

She pried her eyes open. "You have no idea how much this means." Still, there was one problem they couldn't get around. "But what about the biological stuff? I'll die in a few decades. You've still got centuries."

He opened his mouth, but she reached behind his head, pulling him down to land a kiss on that dangerous mouth. Her leg lifted high to wrap around his waist. "You know what? There are so many questions. Let's not dwell on the bad stuff right now." She could tell he was still aroused, and there were better places they could both put their energy. "Listen. Whether I stay another day or another decade, I'm yours, okay? I can promise that much."

Those gorgeous eyes threw heat at her, and even if she shouldn't, she let those big arms of his make her feel safe. She wanted to enjoy him while she could. Didn't want to dream of things she couldn't have. They were both better when they focused on the physical.

That, she could do.

Strong hands slid along her leg and underneath her ass, lifting her like she weighed nothing. Bringing her slowly up the wall until they were level, looking into each other's eyes. She shivered, not from cold and not from fear. Not from some evil-bad encroaching memory. Lee.

Heat. Clarity. Those eyes of his glowed beautiful and bright. Something else lingered in there behind his desire… hurt. Unease. Anxiousness. Something that she wasn't detecting through their blood connection because of her own anxieties, no doubt.

"Lee, what aren't you telling me?"

With a pained snarl, he dropped his head to her shoulder. "It's not—I don't want to burden…" His head rocked side to side on her spaghetti-strapped shoulder.

Alexia wrapped her legs tighter around his waist, ignoring some soreness in her stitched-up knee. Thanks to Lee's blood, it was nearly healed. Speaking of burden, how was he still holding her so easily? Damn, he was strong. "See, here's the thing: You want me to think about staying? You need to share with the class. I need proof that this isn't just fucking around. Throw me a bone."

He groaned and shifted, pushing her against the wall and securing his grip. The move pushed him between her legs, and in spite of whatever had him upset, in spite of the fact that they'd just made love, he was ready to go again.

Men. How did they manage that?

Was he actually trembling? Could've been air-conditioning on his wet clothes. Could've. "The blessing. The prediction for the heiress. 'She will be scarred by someone who has been sworn to protect her.'"

The question in his eyes amazed her. "You can't possibly think that meant you," she said.

His next breath made his entire body shudder. "Guarding the family is one of my primary duties. Of course it could." He winced at something she couldn't see. "My mother and sister died on my watch. I swore I'd keep them safe. I'm supposed to keep you safe. It's no wonder you don't believe."

Oh, Lee. It was like seeing him naked for the first time. Lee, who wasn't afraid of anything. Who could take down half a dozen evil baddies all on his own. He was afraid of not protecting the ones he loved.

She put a hand to either side of his face. The stubble on his cheeks scraped her fingers gently. "You're amazing at what you do. Besides, it could be nothing. You're always saying that for all we know, Nessa's wacko."

He chuckled, kissing her hard. His lids lowered. "You know, I don't want to talk about my ex right now." His voice had dropped, all full of gravel. "I want—Can I—I need you again. Please."

"Hell yeah." God only knew what would happen tomorrow. She had him right now.

One hand stayed on his cheek while the other grappled for his pants. He hissed and shifted to give her better access. It took little time to pop the button fly and peel aside the wet pants, freeing his heavy erection and pushing the pants down. Just enough, anyway, that they had room to maneuver. They kissed again, tongues dueling ever so briefly before he pulled back with a hiss.

"Dammit, Lexi." His pupils were wide and dark. She'd never seen him so wild and so restrained all at once. "I want you so fucking much…" Wow. He was trying to hold back for her. To make her feel safe.

She already did. She'd never allowed anybody to hold her the way he held her now. She'd never relaxed her weight into someone's arms and trusted that she wouldn't fall. Despite what she'd insisted before, she did trust him right then. "It's okay." She looked into those ocean-like eyes. "Go ahead. I'm yours."

He bunched up the fabric of her skirt, and then he was inside of her again. Hot. Hard. Connected. "Oh God, Lee." She breathed his name over and over like it was a prayer for something.

Maybe it was.

Lee ached to drive forward fast and hard, and for the first time, he felt true fear while making love. Deep inside, Lee was a monster. A primitive, primal beast honed into an angry fighting machine over many lonely centuries. To be what Alexia needed, he needed to be something more.

He pushed slowly into Lexi's tight heat, holding her legs with his hands and her stare with his own. He made promises with his body that he had no idea how to deliver. Shifting and reseating himself inside her, he pressed deep to find the right spot that would drive her wild.

She gasped. Her head went back.

"Dammit, Lexi." His fangs, already long and sharp and desperate for a target, scraped inside his cheek. He hunched over and ran his tongue along her jaw, the inviting warmth of her throat... The heat of her skin and her subtle fragrance spurred him to thrust faster as she tightened the grip of her thighs. Each of her petite hands grabbed a handful of his back, nails and all. "More."

"It's okay?" God forbid he ever be the one to scare her. Hurt her. He couldn't. Never again. He'd die first.

Her palm came to his chin. Fingertips and nails gouged into his jaw, forcing his head to her eye level. "Look at me. I know it's you. I'm okay."

Lee responded with a pleased, possessive snarl. Even if she didn't recognize the low cadence of it for what it was, he knew. *I know it's you. I'm okay.* In that moment, with those words, she owned him. *Owned him.*

Fever burned over every inch of his skin. He peeled off his wet shirt and pressed their bodies tight—skin, lips, everything. "Lexi..." He'd run out of words. Seven hundred years on the planet, and he did not have enough words. She had just informed him that he was her safe place. He was unspeakably humbled. Awed.

"Lee..." Her legs squeezed tighter around him. Hell, yes. She was close. Thank fuck. She gripped him hard. His fingers dug into her ass, and she responded by digging hers into his biceps. "Harder," she hissed. Lord, he loved Alexia's spirit. Her aggression. Sometimes even her stubbornness.

Her. Yes, he loved her. So much.

The realization nearly made his chest explode. He gasped for breath and thrust into her with renewed fervor, gripping her tight against him.

Their hearts raced together. Alexia's desperate pants came short and sharp, delicious high-pitched pleas and agreements and praises to God.

"Yes, Alexia. Come. Please." Lee choked out the words, hardly able to breathe.

He adjusted his grip and thrust up, deeper and faster. Riding the edge.

"Your fangs," she gasped. "You need... need..."

"No." Oh, like fucking breathing, he wanted to drink more of her blood. Biology and desire demanded he take from her. The sweet memory of that honey on his tongue called out to him. Knowing that sludgy, angry *glug, glug* in his chest vanished when he drank from Alexia. He pumped deeper. Slower. So close. "I don't need to." She'd already given him so much. He wouldn't take more.

No. He wanted, but he could wait. Right now, he was flying high. On top of the goddamned world because he was balls deep inside of Alexia, and he had just sworn his own private vow to protect her. He would. He fucking well would keep her safe.

He would control his damned vices. He would find a way for them to be together.

This was not duty. This was love. Something he'd sworn he would never do again. Never feel again.

Never say never.

Her fingernails scored his shoulders and her eyes held his. Sweat dripped from her temples, and her hair fell in disarray around her shoulders. Her dress had long ago slipped down her arms. Need shook him hard as he bent to lick across that gorgeous collarbone. If he couldn't have her blood, tasting her skin would have to do for now.

The slick heat of her muscles gripped him tight. She shouted her release so loudly that her cries rained on him from the ceiling.

Then he did the same when her teeth sank into his shoulder. "Oh fuck." It pushed him over the edge. He shoved inside her to the hilt, riding the pulses of his release. "Harder," he grunted.

She complied.

"Yes. God, yes." He hadn't allowed a female to bite him in so long. Even though Alexia's human teeth couldn't pierce his skin the way fangs could, hell on earth, was it ever hot.

She shivered and wrapped her arms around him, her muscles still pulsing and grasping as he spilled into her. Their bodies, rain-damp and slicked with sweat, clung together. He held them both, breathing hard against her forehead.

Neither of them spoke. Lee wasn't even sure what to say. Like nobody else, Alexia left him at a loss. Overwhelmed by emotion in parts of himself he had long thought were darkened and dead.

In Lee's arms Alexia's weight was solid and gratifying. He had thought… He stifled a laugh. He'd held on to this ridiculous notion that she was so small and delicate. She was no such thing. Small, yes. But the way she had met him thrust for thrust and manhandled him… The way she'd kept up with him in the woods. Shit, the way she'd gone after that guardian with nothing more than a tree branch.

So tough, so amazing. Like a tiny tank.

He could see the way she struggled mentally, and now he understood why. She just hadn't been taught how. That part, he could help her with. Or maybe they could help each other. Seven hundred years of mental armor... If anybody could handle his baggage, maybe Alexia could.

Lee took a deep, satisfied breath as he lowered Alexia to the floor. "Lexi, I do have one request. Please don't go sneaking out unannounced again. I know you want freedom, but if you need to leave, please tell me. Tell someone. I'd prefer to have you take Anton or Tyra, but if you must go alone, I'd at least appreciate knowing your location. Just in case."

She disappeared into her bathroom, conveniently avoiding eye contact. When she'd tugged her dress back into place, he took hold of her hand so she had to face him. "You *are* going to stay. Yes?"

She looked like a deer in the headlamp of an oncoming train. "Probably. I think—I know I want to. You've given me an awful lot to think about."

"Probably?" An awful lot to think about. "I see." That was as far as he'd gotten her to budge? "Probably" was not an answer. How could she still be unsure? What else did he need to say?

Her arms went around his waist. Her forehead bumped his chest. "Okay, I want to. I do. I'm scared. We don't have any idea if this can work. And I'm worried that when the lust fades, you'll have regrets. Being with a human is something you were against for so long."

A loud explosion shattered the quiet night. It came from close by. Too close.

"Shit." Well, they wouldn't be discussing it now. He could only hope that later there would be time. His fingers tangled in her hair, and he gave her one hard, short, last kiss. "Stay here. Please, Lexi." *Please stay*.

He reached for his jacket and pulled out a 9 mm. "You said you know how to shoot?"

She nodded.

His chest squeezed hard and painfully. "It's loaded just in case. But stay here. I'll be back."

He hoped.

Chapter 23

HOW LONG HAD IT BEEN SINCE THERESA HAD BEEN HELD? Unquestionably her departed mate had loved her, protected her, cared for her. But he had not been demonstrative in this way, the way Xander had settled her sleeping child in a nest of cushions and pulled her close. The heavy arm that tugged her against his chest made her wonder and want things she never should. The way he breathed now, so quietly and rhythmically against her on the couch, she almost wondered if he'd fallen asleep. With her.

She settled carefully, enjoying the stillness of the dimly lit hotel suite. The closeness. Xander puzzled her. One minute she would think that perhaps he was there to care for her only out of duty, and then his voice would carry hints of endearment that made her wonder if maybe there was something more. He'd sat next to her just now and tended to Eamon so thoughtfully. They were both widowed. Maybe the universe had a message for them. Or maybe she was hoping too hard.

The only other time Theresa had killed with her power, it had been in self-defense. Eamon had been there then and mated her to protect her reputation. She had needed someone, and he had been there. She had come to love and rely on him. Yet raising their son alone had angered and isolated her these past months. Xander, he had been there for her. At the beginning, anyway.

He'd left, though, to go back to fighting. If he left

once, he might again. This harsh realization stung, but perhaps she needed it to. An equally harsh burst of bright light flared from Xander's phone on the table, accompanied by a loud buzz.

His hand shot out. Had he been awake after all? "Cell reception must be back." With one look at the phone, he said, "Shit. Gotta go."

"Everything okay?"

"If they're calling me in, probably not."

"You. Not us?"

He squeezed her hand as he stood. "Hang tight." He made a call and hung up after a series of terse, mono-syllabic replies. "That was Lee. Trouble at the estate. Tyra's coming to transport me."

Whatever was going on, it must be very bad indeed if there wasn't even time for Xander to drive home. Fear clawed at her chest and her throat. Months ago, this was the way she'd lost her Eamon. An urgent call, and then a mortal injury barely a mile from home.

Gone in an instant.

Theresa returned the squeeze on Xander's hand, hers still in his. "You need blood before you go to fight. When did you last feed?" His skin looked pale. He couldn't go out there without proper nourishment.

"Last time I fed from you." This said like a guilty child, caught in a lie.

Her breath stuttered. "That was months ago." She'd given him blood after an injury while he'd guarded her and Eamon Junior. If he hadn't had blood since then, he took a significant risk running into a battle now. "You can't." She held up her wrist, with his hand still clutched in hers. "Hurry. You said Tyra was coming."

He looked like he might argue, but then he didn't. He wasn't stupid. He needed to leave this room charged to full power. She could do this much to help.

His fangs hit her wrist before he even finished sitting. The bite pinched, but not terribly. She could handle this. Even though every time she gave to him, it bound them more tightly together, and it would make saying good-bye that much more difficult.

Especially after what he'd done for Eamon.

Theresa ignored the rush of heat that came from his lips on her skin and the press of his thigh against hers. The deep moan when he swallowed. What did her blood taste like to him? Did he enjoy the flavor? It shouldn't matter. Still, she wondered.

Just as they finished, Tyra appeared in the room. "Sorry to interrupt you guys." The king's sister abruptly offered her back to give them privacy. "Let me know when you're ready."

Xander licked the punctures at Theresa's wrist. "We're done. Let's head out." He gave a curt nod of thanks to Theresa.

"You're sure it was enough?" Truthfully he looked better already, but she didn't want him to leave. That was a foolish excuse and he was leaving whether she wanted him to go or not.

He nodded again, this time with a slight smile. "I am far better prepared." Unexpectedly he turned back, pressing his lips to her forehead. "Thank you."

"Stay safe," Theresa whispered.

With that, he'd returned to Tyra's side. "Let's get this done."

Tyra nodded grimly. "We'll need all the help we can

get. There's a swarm of what look like guardians at the estate. Lee predicts we'll need your power, my friend." She gave a quick nod to Theresa as well, and Theresa bristled, oddly exposed and angry that Xander was being taken into danger. Defending against these attacks was his job. She just didn't want it to be.

Perhaps her next mate needed to be someone safe and far removed from all this action. A doctor or a librarian. Maybe when Eamon Junior was older, she could get out and meet other eligible vampires. Perhaps she needed to move off the estate.

She tried not to watch while Tyra and Xander clasped hands and faded from view. Nonetheless, the hotel suite that had been cozy and warm with Xander there closed in around her. Eamon Junior cried from his nest of cushions and she pulled him close, seeing to his needs and snuggling in with him on the sofa.

"Just you and me alone again," she whispered to her son. "No worries. We'll be fine."

She tucked her baby's still-sleepy body against her chest and kissed his downy head as they settled in to wait, she hoped, for Xander's return.

They *would* be fine. Whether Xander returned or not. Her pure, innocent baby needed a mother who could be strong. Not a mother who relied on a mate. Worse yet, on a fighter who was only around to help once in a while. Wonderful though he was. For her son, for herself, Theresa needed to gather herself together and learn to stand on her own two legs.

But he took Xander's blood without getting sick, when he hasn't been able to take yours. Theresa hugged Eamon tight. She didn't have an answer, but she'd find

one if she had to camp out at St. Anne's and scream at
every doctor in the place. She would find a way to heal
her son.

She'd defined herself as a fighter's mate for too long.

————

Lee had protested against Tyra's mate living among
their kind on the estate grounds since day one. He ques-
tioned Anton's loyalty as a former enemy of their race.
The guy hated to kill, which made him a pansy in Lee's
book. *You say pacifist. I say pussy.*

Still, as he stole up the tree-lined drive that led to
the estate's main gate and found Anton whaling on a
guardian for all he was worth, Lee's valuation of the
male improved further. The grim determination on the
former wizard's face and the bright red glow of his skin
told Lee that Anton flexed his power, and that the guardian he fought was about to eat gravel. Good. That was
good. So the guy could cough up some balls when the
moment demanded.

Siddoh and some of the off-duty patrols crept up and
fanned out along the perimeter. "Where is everyone? I
can feel them, I just can't see them. Well, two can play
at that fucking game," Siddoh whispered sharply as he
turned invisible, and only the crush of grass under his
boots told Lee he headed away.

Most definitely, more would come.

"And what was that explosion?" Lee mumbled under
his breath. If something was out here blowing shit up,
that needed to be his target.

"That was me." Thad stepped forward from the shadows. He threw out a fireball across the wide gravel road

to hit a guardian behind a tree. "Idiot must have been carrying something flammable."

"Jesus, T. What the fuck are you doing here?"

"Defending my home is what the fuck I'm doing here."

"That's my job. Right now your place is with your queen and your child." Regardless, Lee charged his shields, spreading his arms until electric prickles of power danced along his arms. He sidled close to Thad until their bodies touched to ensure that his king would be protected as well.

He caught Thad's tight nod from the corner of his eye. "Being away from them is eating me alive. But you know I can't sit back and let these assholes try to beat down our front door without coming to greet them personally."

"Of course you can. I believe it's what the human leaders do."

"Good for them."

"Dickhead."

Thad cast a narrowed glance Lee's way. "We'll talk later about your insubordination."

No, they wouldn't. For decades before Thad took the throne, Lee had been the one in command and Thad had been the drone. They were friends still, first and foremost. Right now, Lee spoke from love for his friend more than anything. Besides, "if you're still alive in the morning, we can address whatever you want, sir."

Thad chuckled quietly into the night.

Movement across the road. Thad drew his weapon, silencer on. Lee did as well.

"Stay close to me," Lee said quietly. "Stay in contact." So long as Thad touched him, Lee's shields would offer protection. It was the best he could do under the circumstances.

Thad turned, their backs almost touching. Two pops fired. "I know the drill."

"Good. Then while you're at it, keep being a dick." Thad hissed.

Lee slowed his breathing. He took aim and dropped a guardian who'd gone after one of the newbies. He let out a shrill whistle, and the subtle outline of Siddoh's cloaked form moved past him, as did several other cloaked figures.

Thad turned to the side. "Any sign of your old enemy?"

"I'm seeing guardians, but I haven't seen Haig. I'm wondering if this is some smoke-and-mirrors thing that Siddoh's uncle cooked up before his death. Perhaps Haig's ghost is only that."

Out of nowhere, one of the guardians stepped into view, an orb of bright light conjured high in the air.

Lee sounded another whistle. A warning. "If you have a defensive power, step up. Everyone else fall back."

"Shit," Thad muttered. "How would he be able to do something like that?"

Lee shook his head. "The guardians are rumored to all carry Haig's blood. Perhaps they have enough to conjure up more than simple magic spells."

The guardian held a white, glowing sphere the size of a grapefruit, and it grew as they stood. With his shields Lee might be okay, but not all the others. "Thad, go. Get out of here."

"The king does not run, Lee."

"You left a fight once."

"Only to protect Isabel."

Right.

Lee raised his MK23. If he took the guy out, would that thing go flying, or fizzle and die? "Keeps getting bigger," he muttered. "Thad, get behind me. *Please*."

Right then Tyra teleported in behind the whole mess, with Xander at her side.

"All right," Lee whispered. "Firing." One shot and the guardian was down, but the giant ball of light remained aloft. "Everybody out of the way." Then it fragmented. Pieces scattered. Thousands of searing balls of light.

Siddoh uncloaked. "You've gotta be shitting me." He glanced back at the young trainees behind him. "Hit the deck, newbies."

Xander shouted and raised his arms into the air.

All around them, everything went white.

Chapter 24

ALEXIA HELD BACK A SCREAM, SCANNING THE BODIES lying in the marble foyer. *Lee's not here*.

Siddoh lay shirtless and scorched. The lion and cub tattoos on his chest had barely escaped damage. Tears welled in her eyes. So close to his heart.

Next to him on the floor, young vampires she did not recognize. They had to be new, so baby-faced even by the standards of supernaturally slow vampire aging that their skin appeared peach-fuzzy and too smooth to need shaving yet. The biology of it all escaped her. For all she knew, they had decades on her but... no, they couldn't. Their painful moans and groans made her stomach cramp.

She knelt by Siddoh's head. "Where is he?"

"Don't know..." Shallow breathing. "Went back out."

Her heart raced faster. She put a hand to Siddoh's cheek, the one where the flesh still glowed golden and smooth, dusted with stubble. "Are you going to live?" Even as she tried for levity, her chest burned.

He gave a bare nod.

"I'm glad."

"Me, too."

Through a blur of unshed tears, she managed a smile. But his eyes drifted closed and she wasn't sure whether he could actually see her. She rose and headed toward the door, which required passing the horrific, makeshift triage area.

On the far end, Dr. Brayden drizzled blood into the mouth of Jarrek, a young fighter who had guarded Alexia a time or two. The "kid" had oozed intensity and seriousness. Thought very highly of Lee, of his job. Alexia knew the young fighter enough to know that he embraced that whole "honorable soldier" thing all the way down to his bones. The gray cast to his skin and the massive smear of blood under his body turned on her waterworks full force. The grim expression on Brayden's face... "Is he..."

"I think he's going to survive," Brayden murmured. "I know it looks like a lot of blood. It smeared when they put him down. We'll have to wait and see but... he's stable. He's young and strong. I'm cautiously optimistic." He paused with his mouth open, his fangs long when he lifted wrist to mouth so he could lick his own lifesaving wound closed.

Alexia nearly collapsed to the floor. She couldn't help but think that if Jarrek didn't make it and that blood stained the porous marble floor, it would remind them forever that someone had died there. Her heart ached to run outside and scream Lee's name, but she felt like a jerk going to find him when there were all these injured vampires just lying here.

God knew what she could do for them, but she could clean. She'd worked in a restaurant with a marble bar for a short while. God help anybody who didn't clean up a puddle of merlot right away. "I should get something to help you clean up that blood."

Brayden's terse head shake cut her good intentions short. That fast, his white polo shirt was over his head and on the floor to soak up the pool of ick. "There. Good enough for now. Ivy will clean the rest up shortly."

Well, then. Nothing for Alexia to do here.

Anton came in. He looked exhausted, cut, and bruised, but better off than some. The pink cast of his skin gave the image that he'd been at a tanning bed too long. "Hey, Doc, you need me to help you move him?"

The doctor shook his head. "He needs time. Let's get the others."

They lifted one of the young ones and carried him down the hall. Alexia inched toward the door, at odds. Did she stay and watch over the groaning casualties? Try to help? Go back to her cleaning plan?

From his place on the floor, Siddoh groaned and shifted. She hustled back over to him. "Don't. Let me help you."

"Nah." He batted her hand away. "I can move." Bits of burnt skin fell from his body as he sat up.

"Oh, nasty."

"What?" he asked dryly. Amazingly, when his fingers brushed at the burnt places, more fell away to reveal his normal, healthy golden skin below. "I'm not pretty anymore?"

"God, no. You look hideous." Tyra stood over both of them. She reached down and Siddoh took her hand, which was unarguably far better than Alexia helping him up. Tyra could bench-press, like, a fire truck. With all the riders inside.

So Alexia backed away, her breathing still shallow. Where in the crap was Lee?

Voices in the hall. Anton and the doctor. Alexia decided to break for the door at the fastest walk she could manage without running.

And almost got smacked in the chest by the big, brass door handle.

"Fuck, Lexi. Watch where you're going."

Lee. Thank God. "Nice to see you, too." Seriously, there were angry badgers wrestling around her insides, she was so nervous and scared and happy to see him. He was messed up, no lie. Cut and burned, but standing. He still looked strong and able, and she didn't burn with that awful searing pain in her center that told her he was about to keel over.

He'd gotten lucky, so much better than a lot of these guys. His face appeared dark and angry, though, when before he'd been thoughtful and concerned about not wanting to see her go. Had he changed his mind?

Fuck the questions. Fuck them. She launched into his arms so fast he had no choice but to catch her. Legs around his waist and everything. "God, thank God you're okay. I was so scared."

"Of course I'm okay," he whispered. When had Lee ever been so quiet? His fingers threaded through her hair, one rough cheek against hers. With his hot breath against her ear and their hearts beating in time with each other, she could not manage to let go, even though God knew who might be staring.

He was right. All along, she'd wanted to be stubborn and to tell herself she didn't need him the way he said. Not the way he said he needed her. Not after the way he'd treated her in the past. She had her pride. But she couldn't... not after seeing this. He'd walked out that door, clearly not sure if he might come back. And her last words had been, "I'm scared." How fucking stupid.

"I was so terrified." She'd watched the fight from the window. *You aren't always okay*. She didn't say it aloud. She wouldn't, not in front of the vampires Lee commanded.

"I'm here."

"You were right," she said softly. "I'm sorry for being stubborn. I'll stay." God, she loved the responding rumble in his throat.

He drew a deep breath, and his arms squeezed so tightly that she could hardly breathe. "What about your purpose?" He disentangled himself and set her down gently. "Your whole need to find a day job?"

"We'll figure something out," she said.

Tyra ambled over. "Sorry to butt in, but I might have a suggestion."

Lee was as certain as he was of the fangs in his mouth that Tyra's "helpful suggestion" was about to be something horrific that would make Alexia jump for joy and Lee punch the wall. He loved Tyra like a younger sister. Sometimes, though, that younger sister failed to follow orders and came up with ridiculous plans. Dangerous plans. *This is not a drill*.

Tyra had once used Alexia in a harebrained plan that had nearly gotten Alexia shot. Lee still wanted to strangle Tyra for that idea. He glared and took a step back. "What's your helpful suggestion, Ty?"

She gave him a smug look. "Uh-huh. Why you gotta give me that tone, Lee?"

He crossed his arms and stepped closer to Alexia. Fuck it if he appeared possessive. He'd spent too long denying his feelings for Lexi, and now that the proverbial cat was out of the bag, there wasn't any point in denying anything. "Because you've given us all plenty of reason."

She harrumphed.

"I'm working on a plan to reappropriate what used to be the Ash Falls interfaith homeless shelter. The wizards tore it apart this past winter. I don't feel safe opening it back up for human use, but I don't want to leave the folks without a place to sleep. I've got a crew working to renovate some abandoned buildings downtown. Anton's overseeing everything."

She nodded her head toward Alexia and then shot Lee a look of irritation when he bristled, no doubt quite visibly, at Tyra's mention of her mate. "He's spread a little thin. So am I. We could use the extra help."

Alexia turned a questioning look his way.

He frowned. "You know nothing about construction." Then again, he'd thought she knew nothing about guns. "Do you?"

She turned back to Tyra. "That's true. I don't know much. A little plumbing, but I doubt that's helpful."

Much? Plumbing? Dammit, he needed a thousand years with this woman so he could know everything.

She shook her head. "You don't need much. Anton can take you down and explain our plans. Be there to answer questions or let me know if something looks majorly screwed up, like they put a toilet in the middle of the kitchen. Start getting some of the smaller stuff in place. You can help interview potential employees. You have a college degree. You're competent."

Downtown all day. In a shitty part of town.

Unsupervised. *All day*. Something went "ping" in the back of Lee's neck.

"If you don't want me to…" Alexia said slowly. She let the sentence dangle, unfinished, in dead space. Because only one correct answer existed. Lee was being tested, and he could put his foot down and say no if the situation truly demanded, but it would break her heart.

You haven't seen Haig. Only his minions. Which was probably all a scam orchestrated by Siddoh's dead uncle to gain control of the throne.

Tyra shifted uncomfortably. "Listen, why don't you two discuss—"

"No." Lee's nails bit into his palm. "I'm sure it will be safe." He unclenched his fist and tapped Alexia on the arm, forcing a casual gesture. "You'll keep in contact. We'll get you a concealed permit and get you trained with a firearm, like we discussed."

She practically beamed. "Okay."

He turned to Tyra. "My only stipulation is that we wait to make sure this latest barrage of attacks has blown over. It's probably related to Siddoh's uncle, something the old guy arranged prior to his death. A few more days' wait would be wise."

Tyra put her hands to her hips. "Yes. Agreed."

"Okay." Lee turned his back to them then. He walked away for a couple of paces, then back. His stress ratcheted. Lee found himself hating Alexia and then himself by turns for his fear and the concessions she was demanding he make. He turned to her again, noting the fullness of her hair, still tangled and tousled from this last time they'd made love. He thought about the full moon, and what was it she'd said? Birth control. Why had she been sneaking out to get something that prevented pregnancy? Had she planned on getting laid somewhere else?

"How long have you been sneaking out during the day, Lexi?"

She stepped back, giving him a silent look that said, *Excuse me?* "Can't you just appreciate the fact that I've been fine?"

All the times something could have happened to her. He'd never have known. His teeth ached with the force of his anger. "How do we know you weren't the one who led those fuckers right to our doorstep, going in and out so often?"

Tyra gasped. "Lee."

Alexia just stood there. He may as well have slapped her. Slapping her would have been far better.

She turned to where the last few bodies lay. The trainees Lee only knew by number and Jarrek, who appeared to have fallen into a torpor from the gravity of his injuries. Brayden and Ivy together had lifted him carefully to carry him toward the hallway. When she turned back, her face was wet with tears and Lee's hands stayed on his hips because anything he could possibly say would only dig the hole deeper.

He hadn't truly meant for such a shitty, dickheaded thing to come out of his mouth, but he couldn't seem to call the words back. He wasn't even sure what had possessed him to throw out such a ridiculous accusation. Jealousy. Hurt.

So when she turned in the opposite direction from where the wounded were being carried, most likely headed toward her bedroom, he let her leave. Better not make things worse.

"Oh, come on." Tyra's derisive scoff was loud and clear. "You're just going to let her walk away?"

No movement from the east hall once Alexia disappeared. Not that he'd expected any. "She'll cool off." He didn't want to return to the time when things were combative between them. If he followed her now, things would explode.

Tyra's head swiveled. "You need to apologize."

He straightened on an inhale. "It was a fucked-up thing to say, but the fact remains that she broke security protocol. We brought her here to the estate to begin with for her safety. For everyone's. As a human who knew too much—"

"Lee. She didn't ask for this life. She's young." Tyra stepped backward. "And you have to admit, we've all been a little too busy to follow up with her lately. Admit it, until very recently, you were motioning her forward with one hand and pushing her away with the other. How do you expect her to deal with that, plus the fact that she's the only one of her kind living here?"

With a jerk of his head, his mouth snapped shut. Fuck it all, she was right. "You need help moving these guys?"

"Nah." She gestured down the hall. "If I were you, I'd go make sure she didn't sneak out the side door at the end of the hall."

"Fuck." Tyra was fucking with him, but it worked. He made tracks down the hall, stopping in the entryway. "I'll be back shortly. We need to talk strategy."

Tyra nodded. "No shit."

Chapter 25

THERESA'S HEART ALMOST STOPPED WHEN XANDER came into the room and collapsed on the floor. Before she knew what she was doing, she'd discarded the magazine she'd been pretending to read and knelt next to him, touching her hands gently against his skin. "How badly are you hurt?"

"I'll be fine," he mumbled. "Just need to rest."

She tsked quietly. "Xander."

"Theresa." He made a noise that sounded almost like a laugh. "I hate my power. Hate. No fucking use to me ninety-nine percent of the time. Once I use it, I have all the strength of a kitten."

She tried to smile and gave in to the urge to run her hand over his dusty hair. "I would bet you saved a lot of lives tonight."

He shrugged vaguely. "A shower might help. My skin burns like crazy." He rolled and struggled to sit, but Theresa pushed his shoulders. Weak from burning his powers, he went back down easily.

Forgetting the reasons why it might be wise to stay disengaged, Theresa laid her head on his chest. "I'm so grateful you're back. I can't tell you how much I worried, watching you walk out of this room." She ignored the moisture that gathered at the corners of her eyes. The night has been stressful, that was all.

She heard him swallow. His throat must be dry.

"I'm sorry. I didn't want to go. God, you're soft. So... really soft."

She sighed deeply. "Okay. Stay here. I'll start the water."

His eyes opened wider.

Saying nothing further, she headed into the bathroom and turned on the shower, making sure to keep the water nice and cool. The pressure, not too hard. "Come on," she said, when she came back into the room. She gripped his arm and pulled him from the floor.

"Damn." He coughed, struggling to rise from the floor. "You're strong."

"I'm stronger than I look." She'd had to be, after all. Theresa swept her long hair from her shoulders and put one arm around him. When she reached the bathroom, Xander braced his hands against the counter, trying to stay upright, and heat radiated through her body, knowing what she was going to have to do.

They'd certainly gotten close, but injured or not, sharing a little blood paled in comparison to seeing him in all of his natural glory. Steeling herself, she pulled his jacket.

She'd managed to untuck his shirt before he stirred from his daze. "What are you doing?"

Her pulse did a nervous little dance. "Helping you to undress."

"I can..." He turned, reaching for his belt, and landed hard against the counter. "Well, that fucking hurt."

"Let me help you." She assisted him with his shirt, his belt. She hesitated before assisting him with his pants, as much because it seemed like the point of no return as because what she could already see truly deserved to be admired. "My goodness, you're gorgeous." She clapped her hand over her mouth. Saying such a brazen thing aloud wasn't like her.

His hand reached out. It found the back of her neck, and tired though he was, he pulled her forward. "You know where this is going if we continue, don't you?"

"Do you mean right now? Tonight? Or…" It was as if her dress had shrunk a size.

The muscles in his chest followed his breath, rising and falling. His green eyes went dark. "I think I mean all of the above. I've been worried it's too soon for you."

Very hard to breathe. Very. "I think…" She thought of herself. Eamon. What was best, what was logical. The promises she'd made to herself about never again loving a soldier. Her anger when Eamon's father had died.

Then she thought of that moment shortly before Xander had returned. "I thought I lost you, you know?" Tears welled again in her eyes. She couldn't make them stop. "We still share a blood tie. I knew when you fired your power. I knew something had happened to hurt you." Her fingers had tightened around Xander's but she didn't care. She couldn't let go.

Tears slid down her face, and she was only vaguely aware of his thumb wiping them away. "Waiting here alone for you to either return or for someone to give word of what had happened was the hardest thing I've ever had to do. Harder than when I lost Eamon, because then at least I had my community around me. And Eamon was my mate. You and I, we're…"

Xander took her face in his hands. "What are we?"

She sniffed. "That's just the thing. We've been doing this strange dance. I swore I couldn't see another fighter die. Not after losing one mate that way. When I thought I lost you, though…" She leaned forward and kissed him.

Xander's hands bunched in her hair. His tongue carefully probed her mouth, kissing her back. She gripped his hips as his hands came to the tops of her arms, waking up shivers of pleasure as his fingers trailed down her sleeve. He pulled away then, his forehead against hers the way it had been just before he left. His breath came out in heavy, jagged pants.

"I suppose I should have asked if it's too soon for you, too," she said. A shiver of shame crept into her body. Theresa had thought of her own departed mate, her own concerns. She'd thought little of Xander's lost mate, Tam. She should have. "I shouldn't have assumed. I'm sorry." She tried to pull away. "I can listen at the door to be certain you're safe in the shower. I can call someone from Blood Service to see to your needs if you'd rather. But I don't think I can continue—"

He smiled slightly, and then his mouth closed over hers. "Why do you think I haven't fed from anyone else? I fell in love with you and that little boy a long time ago," he whispered. "I stopped guarding you because it got too hard. I've said my good-byes to Tam. I couldn't just move into my fallen friend's life, take his mate and his child. It didn't feel right, and you weren't ready then."

He tucked a strand of hair behind her head. "However. I swore if you ever felt for me what I did for you, I wouldn't let that chance go. You and I both know life can be lost in a blink, Theresa. I see no point in worrying about 'too soon' when there may not be a later."

His words made her want to jump out of her skin and pull him closer. Every muscle twitched with joy, with fear, with utter confusion. "I don't know… My head is such a jumble. I only know that I don't want to lose you again. Having you come back into our lives feels like the greatest gift in the world."

He kissed her again. Nuzzled her throat gently. "Then I would love to be by your side, if you would let me. I want to spend many more nights talking with you. I want to see Eamon grow big and strong." He pulled back, his green eyes serious. "I want to talk to Thad about taking on a role closer to the estate. Something safer. No fighting."

Theresa couldn't hold in her gasp. "But you love fighting."

Xander laced his fingers with hers. "Some things mean more. Now, we've left the shower running and I'm about two minutes from collapsing on the floor. Do you know anybody who can sponge me off and help me with some blood?"

"Yes," she said with a smile, "I do."

Lee's presence loomed behind Alexia, but she refused to turn around. "Lexi, talk to me."

She couldn't stop, couldn't stand still or sit down. Swinging wildly back and forth from her dresser to her bed, she gathered clothing and phone chargers and toiletries—oh, my!—and tossed them into her backpack with all the force her indignation could manage.

"What are you doing?"

"Accusing me of leading those assholes here?

Seriously? Do you want to accuse me of fucking Thad while you're busy being completely ridiculous?" She stuffed yoga pants and tank tops into the backpack. "That was so shitty." Her finger sliced through the tension between them to point at his cocky, handsome face. The wad of cash hidden in her underwear drawer came out, and she stuffed that down inside the bag, too.

She ignored the widening of Lee's eyes. She already had stuff packed and stashed in one of the cars, but it was way the hell across the estate. "So you know, I found the hidden entrance at the back of the property, and that's the one I've been using. Not that anyone around here has noticed." Her favorite navy-blue hoodie went in next. She jerked the pack's zipper. "I told you, I watched out the window. So I know they didn't come to that entrance."

Toothbrush. Toothpaste. Floss. Couldn't forget proper gum care.

Lee grabbed a fistful of thongs and whatnot from the still-open drawer where she'd retrieved her money. He practically threatened her with them. "Aren't you forgetting something? Some of this..." He read one of the tags. "This Victoria's Secret stuff?"

She flopped down on the bed, suddenly tired. "I'm going to head back to Florida, and it's summer so I don't need a coat. I can buy more underwear." That underwear had cost her a good chunk of change, and she just didn't want to give him the satisfaction. God, the idea of leaving shredded her insides. So did the idea of staying with someone who would accuse her of something as hideous as selling the vampires out to their enemies. Even accidentally.

"Lexi, you can't walk out that door tonight. We don't

know if there are still guys out there in the woods around the property."

"If I suddenly happen upon a nest of them, I'll send a smoke signal. But frankly, I think the chances of it are slim. The chances of meeting up with more vampires are slim, for that matter. In almost thirty years on the planet, I had only met Lucas and Isabel before you and Thad showed up to find Isabel for that royal prophecy thing. Your secrets are safe with me, I promise. But this isn't my world.

"You want me to stay here? For you? I was this close, God damn you." She held up her hand, pinching her thumb and forefinger together. "I can't live a life with you constantly second-guessing and mistrusting me." She flung one strap of the backpack over her shoulder and booked it for the door.

He pulled the door shut and stepped in front of it, blocking her exit.

She gave him her best angry glare. "Really? Are we going to stoop to brute strength? Because you know good flipping well that's going the right way to make me want to smack you, and not in any way that's sexy."

His eyes widened and, swear to all the great heavenly bodies, a blush stained his cheeks. She remembered the sex they'd had. The hot, no-holds-barred animal way he'd made love to her that first time in the hospital. The way he'd asked her to bite and scratch him harder. The way he'd wanted more. Her own face heated, too, and she couldn't help the tiny tug at the corners of her mouth. Wow, that had been out-of-control hot.

He reached to tuck a strand of hair behind her ear. "Please."

She shut her eyes for a few hard thumps of her heart. When she opened them again, his eyes were still wide, solemn, and that bold aquamarine color that made her knees quiver. "I've listened. I believed, because I wanted to, that you were honestly sincere that you wanted me to stay and you wanted things to be different. That you wanted to give me more power and freedom, or whatever the hell you said. Maybe I heard what I wanted to…" His hand wrapped around the back of her neck, and she let him pull her in for a moment before she stepped away. "Don't. Don't do that."

"I'm falling in love with you, Alexia."

She couldn't breathe. God, seriously, her throat… She was breathing through one of those thin little coffee stirrers or something. "Lee…" She sat abruptly on the corner of the bed. Her backpack dropped to the floor.

She rubbed her hands over her face. God, she had to look just awful. The tears she'd cried before had dried up, and fresh ones flowed now, because damn—she'd love to pretend it didn't grab her right in the chest to hear that he loved her, but God, it totally did. "Don't pretend you love me if you don't mean—"

His lips covered hers. His hands came gently but firmly to either side of her face.

Tears ran hot and fast down her face. God damn him. She hated to cry. It was worse exposure than standing naked in Times Square in February. Plus it made her throat and chest strain. She just couldn't seem to keep it together around him.

His lips brushed her ear. "If you don't believe me, listen to your blood."

"Lee—"

"Take a deep breath for me."

She hiccupped. "This is stupid."

"No." He pressed close. So hot and solid. "You do this for me. You listen to my blood in your veins, and if you still think I'm a lying asshole, you go ahead and walk out the door. I'll help you pack your things properly." Hot breath brushed her cheek. "Take a deep breath. Close your eyes."

She shivered. And dammit, she did. She closed her eyes. *Inhale, exhale.* "Okay. Fine. And?"

"Again."

She did. No words from either of them this time, and in the quiet that followed came a warm, gentle throb from deep inside her veins. A magnetic pull that drew her toward him so effectively that when her eyes opened, she was clutching at his sides, her nose against his. She hadn't even realized.

"Twenty-five years, Lexi," he ground out. "Twenty-five years since I walked out on Agnessa, and I swore that I would go to ash never letting another female have my heart."

Oh, wow. "And you're saying I..." *Oh God. Don't cry. Don't cry...* But she couldn't stop.

"You have far more than she ever did. You can't go, Lexi. Don't try to say this is only about guilt, because you can be sure that I care for you just as certainly my blood runs in your veins. We are a *part* of each other. And if you think you could leave and I'd never know something had happened to you, you haven't been paying attention." His lips brushed hers. "I would know the moment you were hurt. *And it would fucking gut me.*"

Her tears flowed harder when she put her arms around him.

Chapter 26

SIDDOH GRIPPED ONE DOOR FRAME AND THEN THE NEXT as he pushed his way down the hall. Once everything had looked under control up front, he'd used the kerfuffle with Lee and Alexia as an excuse to slip away.

I'll be grateful when I'm no longer ready to beg for beheading. Always the worst part of a bad fight and the subsequent feeding was that awkward in-between period when you didn't fit back inside your own skin. Times like these, Siddoh half wished he'd just eaten it out there in the dirt. Getting knocked from the top of the food chain to the bottom never sat well. At this very moment, he'd lose a tussle with a garden slug.

The door next to him opened and Ivy rushed out, so busy looking down that she nearly ran the top of her head into his jaw. "Oh." She stopped short, looking appropriately startled. Her hair had been piled in a pretty but haphazard way atop her head, and her face was golden and freshly scrubbed.

Yeah, everyone needed showers after that mess. Not that he'd be getting his for awhile. Siddoh paused, at odds about whether to just keep on keeping on, or to actually make conversation. "I wanted to thank you." His mouth chose Option B without consulting his brain. "For before. Your blood." She, Dr. Abel, and Dr. Brayden had made donations after the fight to get everyone back on their feet. He indicated one burnt hand with the other, as if it was necessary.

"It was… You're welcome."

He hesitated when he shouldn't be, wondering about the things he'd seen before. The tattoo on her back, the red marks. *Get home, Siddoh. None of your business. Long walk to that house of yours.* Still, he found himself feeling as if he should say more. Lacking words. Stalling, probably. Sometimes going home to his empty house was a real bitch, and tonight he'd be doing so minus a layer of skin. "Well. Good night." He ran a hand over his face and pushed away from the door frame.

Her head tipped sideways. "Are you all right? Did you need more blood?"

"No. No," he said too quickly. "Generous of you to offer. I'm sure you donated a lot tonight."

She smiled. Gorgeous smile, that female. Bright. "Therapeutic amounts. Most of them are so young they can hardly drive. They bounce back fast."

Siddoh nodded. His vision blurred some. "Hard to recall being so young."

She sighed quietly. "I know."

He didn't bother pointing out that he had a few centuries on her. He couldn't recall being as young as she was, either. "And yet you're unmated. I find it hard to believe." A rude comment. His filter still hadn't returned. And he wanted to know. She came off as too quiet perhaps, but a competent female. Pretty. Sunshiny disposition, snake tattoos, and potentially self-inflicted wounds aside.

"I—" She looked him up and down. "Goodness, come in here and sit down, will you? You look like you might yet keel over. Dr. Brayden will never want to mate me if I allow one of his patients to die."

What's this now? Siddoh had known Brayden many long decades, and while the doctor kept his personal life very private, he was very certain Ivy wasn't the guy's type. Siddoh pretended selective hearing for the time being.

She led him into her room, a surprisingly austere place done in all whites and creams. Wingback chair by the door. Dresser. Desk. Lamp. The satiny silk blanket on the bed seemed to be her one luxury item.

Funny, with a female like Ivy, he'd expected flowers. Lace. Doilies like the kind her father had in the living room. Something. Before he'd seen the snake tattoo anyway. Now he half expected Alice Cooper posters. Or whoever. Was that guy still "in"? Sometimes the decades blurred together for Siddoh.

"I'm going to sully your nice, white room with my burnt skin. I'm, uh, sort of still molting here."

"I have a vacuum cleaner. Best if we get that stuff off you anyway so you can regenerate." She smiled and blushed brightly as she swept her thumb across his nose and cheekbone, sloughing the dead stuff from his face.

Had any female ever touched him so carefully?

When she leaned in close to inspect her work, tears rimmed her eyes. God help him, he wanted to wipe away the moisture from under her eyes.

He tried to shift in the chair but her body pressed so close. "Is something wrong?"

She knelt in front of him. "My father's dying. He's been cooped up in that house, and he hadn't been able to search for a suitable mate for me..." She fell silent, and for awhile Siddoh thought maybe she'd decided to drop the topic and focus on de-flaking him. He decided that he could absotively bump this into the top five strangest conversations he'd ever had.

"I should probably—"

"He wants to see that I'm not alone," she finished in a hurried breath.

"Of course." Siddoh would bet money that no greeting card existed for this scenario. He should send in a suggestion. *Hey, Hallmark. Howzabout something that says, "Screw your dying father. Why can't a hot, intelligent female like you fend for herself?" Maybe jazz it up with a hairless hunk on the front, or that crabby old woman in her bathrobe. That old lady is a fucking riot. So is this conversation.*

"I'm all he has left. I want to give him peace." Her hands moved again. Gently, methodically. Across his neck, his chest, his arms. Brushing the damage from Siddoh's body and making him brand-new.

Siddoh swallowed when she grabbed a cloth to exfoliate the skin along his waistline and tried to pretend the whole situation wasn't the weirdest thing he'd been party to in the past century. "I guess I've just never been able to get comfortable with the concept of an arranged mating. To me it's like an exchange of property. And then you're committed. For a thousand years, maybe more. Yeeow." She'd pulled at a flake of skin on his arm that still wanted to stay attached.

"Sorry." She stood and dusted his shoulders. "It worked for our kind for a long time, you know. For many it still works. Statistically, arranged matings are more solid. It's only been in the last couple of centuries that we've had formal laws in place for dissolution of the mating pact. *Probably* because of the increase in love matches. Love cools. A business agreement comes with incentives to create a true commitment."

Would she pull out pie charts next? Laser pointers? How could she not believe in love? Even Siddoh believed in love. He wanted to believe it was a thing he would be part of some day. "Have you even gotten Brayden's okay with this?"

She knelt in front of him and gave a sharp stare.

"I'm just playing devil's advocate."

"I can see the things they say about you are fitting."

The words, her glare. Both sliced deep across his exposed chest. He could only imagine. "What things?"

"Look," she said. She knelt down and ran her hands around his side and up his back. "I leave the estate very rarely. My father is traditional. I wish to honor his beliefs. He loves me." She ran her hands over his forearms and rocked back on her heels. "Okay, your upper body is fine."

With the death knell of "the things they say about you" still ringing between his ears, Siddoh held back the knee-jerk zinger of "Why, thank you." Not that they couldn't use some damn levity.

Ivy, however, smiled slightly and said, "You look much better with all the dead skin gone, I mean."

He managed a chuckle. She almost related to his humor. In this stuffy society of theirs, so few females did. Probably why he got along with Alexia so well, with her progressive human ideology and her abuse of the phrase "that's what she said."

He put his hands on the chair. "I can understand," he said, "that you want to uphold your family's traditions."

His voice had gotten embarrassingly heavy and deep. Hard to ignore all that gentle stroking from an attractive female. With hope, *she* didn't notice. He shifted, slightly aroused by her proximity. "But arranged matings are done so little anymore. If this was important to your father, why didn't he set you up before now? I don't think bartering oneself—"

With that, the pleasant massage session was over. She stood so quickly that the stir of air against his new, sensitive skin made him shiver. "There was never time. And then he was put under house arrest." She gave him her profile. Long, straight nose. Longer eyelashes. "You have your values. Allow me to have mine."

He stood as well, a growl rising. "How can you value yourself at all if you're willing to commit your life to a stranger?" Wrong fucking thing to say. None of his damned business.

Her mouth dropped so far open he could have parked a car between those fangs of hers. "I value *family*. And I am about to have none left. You make it sound so awful. Dr. Brayden is a friend and we work together. How is that not a foundation? My father only wants to know I'm taken care of."

"Ivy, you run an entire estate with hundreds of residents on it, practically single-fucking-handedly. You do not need anyone to take care of you."

"I know that. I *know* that. But my father…" Her breath caught.

But her father was dying, and this was what she believed she needed to do. Grief could be a real bastard.

At a loss, Siddoh placed a hand on her shoulder. "Ivy, I'm sorry."

She sniffled. "You know, statistically, arranged marriages are more likely to last."

You said that already. She was trying so hard to prove a point, but was she trying to prove it to him or to herself? "You don't have anything to justify to me. I had no right to pry." He had no right. No reason. All this because she'd given him blood? All his pride about moving with the times. Here he was being closed-minded and backward.

She blinked and nodded, still staring at the floor. Another sniffle. "Are you feeling up to making it back to your house?"

"Yeah." He cleared his throat, backing away carefully to avoid brushing anything with his new, ultrasensitive skin. "Much better now. Thank you."

Brayden had once given Siddoh blood, too. So had a dozen unnamed, unmated donors from Blood Service. Males. Females. Siddoh couldn't believe he'd let Ivy get to him this way.

Her eyes remained downcast. "Then perhaps you should go."

So he did.

───※───

Days had gone by with no attacks. Amazingly, Lee had willingly kissed Alexia good-bye and walked her to the door to greet Anton earlier that morning. They'd talked about moving her stuff down the hall into his room when she got back that night. She'd always sworn she wasn't the type to get giddy and love-struck, but she was practically dizzy with excitement.

She spun around in the center of the dusty, hollowed-out room that was to become the new Ash Falls shelter, already wondering about a good way to thank him when she got home. *Home*. "Whoa." She stopped herself and sobered up, finally taking a good look around the construction area. "That's enough spinning."

The windows had been covered so that the workers could paint with a big sprayer, and the wiring and pipes stuck out all over. She edged close to Anton, who stood with his hands on his hips surveying the mess. "Anton, what the hell am I doing here? I don't mean to sound like a jerk, but not only do I know jack shit about construction, what little Spanish I know tells me these worker guys are all talking about my tits."

Anton, God bless the man, blushed from collar to roots. He was so easy to fluster. "Probably not all of them."

"No." She licked her lips, following the gaze of one painter whose eyes were plastered to the tight-fitting Levi's on his coworker. "Probably not him."

Anton muttered. "Lexi, focus for me, would you please? You wanted a meaningful day job. You want something to do other than Lee—"

"That's what she said."

"Lexi!" Holy cow, his finely bronzed skin really caught fire. "Dammit, that one didn't even make sense."

"Okay," she said. She gave him her best smile. "Sorry, I'm feeling off today. Maybe it's all the nervous flutters. I'll be good. Seriously. Give me the four-one-one."

He blew out a breath. "This is all freaking you out, I bet," he said in a lowered voice. "We haven't gotten to talk much, and I'm sorry. I know you were kinda planning to get the hell out of Ash Falls. Next thing we know, the queen's in labor, the estate's under attack, and you and Lee…" He let out a low whistle.

God. Yeah. Her and Lee. Only in her craziest peyote-induced dreams. "Nuts, huh?"

He tapped a thumb against his bottom lip. "I don't know. Last few months, I've noticed the way he looked at you when he thought nobody knew. Certainly it was no secret how you felt about him. No more nuts than a cast-out, homeless wizard shacking up with the king's sister. If Tyra and I can make sense, then you and Lee can make sense."

She squinted up at him. "Just shacking up. You two gonna do the official thing? Tie the knot, or whatever the vampires do? The official mating ceremony?"

"Eventually. Hope so. She wants to wait until things settle down." He rubbed absently at a bandage covering his forearm. "If they ever settle down." He pointed to a stout, bespectacled man in the corner with a flannel shirt and an armload of two-by-fours. "Okay, so that over there is Ted. He's the guy in charge of the workers."

So they would be moving on. All righty then. "Ted. Gotcha."

"So they knocked down the walls between these two buildings, and there are going to be two floors. Upstairs will be for families. Downstairs, single males and females will be separate like before." He paused with raised eyebrows.

Alexia nodded to indicate she was keeping up.

"Great. So the other thing is we've purchased the building next door as well. It'll be a private school for any, uh… children like me that happen to be spotted coming through here who need a place. You know?"

"Gotcha." She shivered in spite of the mild late-summer afternoon. Something was strange. She had the sweats even though she was chilly, not to mention dizzy and a little nauseous. Maybe all the paint fumes… "Okay."

"So maybe that's something you could help with, too, you know? Some of these wizard kids don't have parents and the ones who do, they need to be educated. That's a whole new problem that the vamp—that our society hasn't handled before. For these kids to survive, they have to be integrated into society or handled somehow. It's something Ty and I are still figuring out. We don't know the best course of action for these kids yet, and if it comes in front of the Elders' Council, they'll all lose their fucking minds. We need to come up with a plan. A program."

She shook her head. "Okay, so for the rest, I just need to what? Supervise?"

"Pretty much. I've been bringing the guys coffee and donuts to be nice. Check in with Ted a lot to make sure they're on schedule. Gonna start getting really cold in a few months. We need this place to be ready as soon as possible. Walls, rooms, electricity, running water. We need a kitchen. I figure you could probably handle ordering furniture and linens and whatnot once they say we're ready to start moving that stuff in."

"I could do that, yeah." Sounded easy, in fact. Except for the fact that she kind of couldn't see clearly. *What's going on?*

"Really, if anything else comes up, all you gotta do is call me or Ty. We can come in to help if necessary, but this way we're available to help out at the mansion with the fallout of that nasty fight, and you've got something to fill your daytime hours other than lying around in your room and listening to sad music or sneaking out the back door."

She blinked to clear her blurry vision and shot Anton a look that she hoped told him to get bent.

He shot one right back.

She couldn't help but laugh at that. "Thanks, Anton."

"No sweat." He threw an arm around her shoulder.

Anton turned away from her. "All right. Let me show you the plans. I know you won't really be able to read them, but it may still help just to have them for reference."

"Com…" She turned to follow. The room swam. "Oh, jeez." She reached to brace her weight on a folding table she was so sure had been right next to her, but her hand met with a whole lot of nothing.

"Lexi?"

The concrete floor smacked her in the face. Hard. "Oh fuck." She reached for Anton's outstretched hand. "That was embarrassing. I don't know if it's the fumes in here or the fact that I haven't eaten much lately. I just got, I dunno, really disoriented." *Like I'd been on the Tilt-A-Whirl a dozen times. Whatever.* The whole running-through-the-woods, stay-or-go roller coaster with Lee had put her stomach through the wringer. Her appetite had been completely MIA for days.

"Here." Anton handed her a chocolate-mint protein bar. "These are great when I forget to eat. They've got protein and the mint helps when you're queasy. Calms my stomach when I forget to eat. Try one."

He knelt beside her, trying to help her up. "Lexi, are you okay? What's going on?"

She shivered again. Everything hurt. "I'm really cold. It's like seventy-five out, right?" It wasn't that late in the year yet. Still August. Her favorite month because of the moderate temperature heading into fall. How could she be so cold?

Shouting nearby. Her hands slid from underneath her. The hard concrete under her head.

"Hey," she mumbled. "Hey…" Nobody seemed to hear her. "Guys, I can't see anything."

Lee. She wanted Lee. He was going to be so upset.

Chapter 27

"HAVE WE HEARD FROM XANDER?"

Lee held his phone as they all gathered in the king's office. Tyra, Siddoh, and Flay formed a semicircle around him.

Flay's head popped up, directing his answer toward Thad's voice, growling and tired from the speakerphone. "Not since he headed back into DC to get Theresa and the baby. I think he needed time to heal."

All at once, agony exploded through Lee's skull. The phone fell from his hand. From far away on the floor, Thad's voice asked if everything was all right.

"Jesus... no."

He looked up to Tyra as he swallowed the bile that rose in his throat. "Tyra, call Anton. Please."

Without a word, she put her phone to her ear. After a pause, she said, "Nothing yet." Her concerned face betrayed the calm in her voice.

"Tyra." Thad's voice was tinny and far away for some reason. "Do you know where they are?"

"He and Alexia went down to the work site."

Lee retrieved the phone from the floor. "You have to go. You're the only one here who can be out in daylight. Something's wrong." Even as he said it, something dark and sharp raced through his veins. He sucked in a breath and rode out the pain. He wouldn't lose his shit now, not with all these waiting eyes on him.

"Tyra," Thad warned from the other end of Lee's phone. "You have no backup."

"Thad." *Breathe in… Breathe out…* "With all due respect, she can go in cloaked. If it's a nest, she returns immediately."

"Following orders and just reporting in is not her strong suit," Thad warned.

"Thad…" Tyra's fingers dug into the back of a chair. Wherever Alexia was, Tyra's mate was also. Not hurt, not yet. Lee presumed Tyra would have sensed Anton's distress, would be acting with more anxiety.

Dammit, the dark pain and not knowing had frozen Lee's bones.

Flay stood. "I'll go." They all looked up. "I have human blood. If we're going from indoors to indoors, a little sun filtered through a window won't hurt me much." Tyra gaped at him. Hell, everyone did. "What? My human blood is a coupla generations removed, but I can take a little sun. Anyway, I was patrolling downtown when the big UV bomb happened. I'm due. Come on."

Lee nodded to them both. He looked to Siddoh, who gave his agreement. Thank fuck. Right now, Lee couldn't count on himself to be objective. He held up the phone. "Thad?"

"Be careful, guys."

The clock on the wall told them that the little hand had only passed noon. Hours. Fucking hours. This time of year, it wouldn't be dark enough for him to leave until maybe eight at night. He squeezed his eyes shut. "Yeah. Be careful, guys. And thank you." His breath left his lungs and would not return.

With that, Tyra grabbed Flay, and both faded from

view. They took a huge risk in simply going to look for information. Tyra would take a power hit, teleporting cloaked with another large body. For the sake of Flay's vampire side, Lee hoped they didn't have to step out into the sunshine. If they got downtown and had to fight… Fuck.

Siddoh, still ragged from the night prior, finally spoke up: "So what's the worst-case-scenario plan here?"

"Worst-case scenario, we don't need a plan because they're dead." Just saying the words made Lee's world spin, but it needed to be out there. God damn, he was freezing. Shivering without control freezing.

"Thank fuck I haven't got you guys on speaker over here," Thad said. "If Isabel heard you, she'd lose her mind."

Lee gripped his own forehead. "I'm being realistic, Thad."

"I know. Let's assume you're going to get her back. How?"

"Worst case, we have the windowless vans. We load up in the back stalker-style like when we took you and Isabel to the hospital. We'll put Brayden and Blood Service on standby." The question was always who to drive in these situations. They'd pasted obscenely illegal tint film over the windows, but it wasn't sufficient to protect a vampire's sensitive skin. Still, if Lee had to, he'd drive the damn thing himself or go up in flames trying. "Depending on what Tyra says when she reports back—"

Siddoh's phone rang. "That was fast." He answered. After a few monosyllabic responses and a terse, "Call us when you know more," the asshole hung up again.

Lee's fingers stiffened. "Status?"

Siddoh took a slow breath. "Tyra says that Anton handled the situation remarkably well under the circumstances."

What fucking circumstances? "That tells me exactly dick. What happened? *Where is she, and when can she get the hell back home?*"

Siddoh grimaced. "I don't have all of that information, which is why I said, 'Call back when you know more.'" He leaned forward. "She got sick, reasons unknown, and passed out at the construction site. Anton tried to heal her, but an ambulance had to be called. She's being taken to a human hospital. Tyra thinks it's County Hospital. That's all I've got."

Lee eased back into his chair. The searing pain returned in force to his chest. A human hospital. No way to get to her. No choice but to wait. They could try to drive down there, but he risked storming into a human hospital covered in brutal sunburn, freaking out the staff and doing more harm than good.

All his power and experience as a fighter, and he could do nothing to save her now. Like the day he'd lost his family.

I knew something like this would happen. In a matter of days, Lee had given in to love, and now some karmic "fuck you" had come along and knocked his newly built house down. He kicked an empty chair, hardly appeased when the carpet cushioned its fall. Now was not the time to come unglued.

"Okay." *Breathe in… Breathe out…* "Let's get back to strategy. She's in good hands. Tyra and Flay are keeping an eye out." His eyes burned. He could not afford to shed tears. Not yet. Thad was right. Alexia would be fine. Lee would accept no other option. "If we get word that she's in trouble, we roll out in the vans. As long as she's stable, safest thing is to wait." Fuck, just saying it burned. "The second night falls, I'm out the door."

Lee went on autopilot, making suggestions and nodding or dismissing others with a wave of his hand. Inside his chest the painful ache, the slow, sludgy *glug, glug* of his heart trudged along. This was the first time he'd experienced such pain since the night Alexia had given him her blood.

He struggled to sit still. If Alexia didn't make it, Lee wouldn't survive. And not only because he needed her blood to heal his heart.

He needed Alexia to heal *his soul*, too.

The night chilled Siddoh's new skin. The promise of fall not too far away and the eerie aftermath of battle hung over what had always seemed a safe enclave. Siddoh's skin still held a strange hypersensitivity, and the only thing that had him willing to wear clothes and weapons was that without it all, his boys might retreat in protest.

His burns had healed nicely. Whatever Ivy might have said about "therapeutic" doses be damned; she'd given him a decent amount of blood. His gratitude toward her did indeed warm him. However, his current mission was a real kick you in the crotch kind of a thing. Particularly if Ivy happened to be visiting her dying father's house.

He nodded to the guard at the door. "How are we doing tonight?"

"Hanging in there," the vampire said. "No visitors this evening."

Siddoh was surprised. He'd have expected Ivy to be over here the second the sun dropped out of the sky, given the reports that the elder circled the drain. Then again, last night had been exhausting for everybody. Ivy might be catching up on rest after giving blood to those who'd been injured.

All in all, the situation was best for Siddoh, who needed to have a talk with Ivy's father. Doing so without his daughter present would be the best, least emotional thing for all involved.

"Good," Siddoh said. "I need a word." Or two. Thousand.

Through the foyer and past Elder Grayson's doily-covered sofa, Siddoh paused at the door to Elder Grayson's bedroom. *So let's recap. Thad gone. Lee gone. Tyra gone. Once again, Siddoh, you've found yourself in charge. Let's not turn this into a habit.*

Anton and Tyra had guarded Alexia all day, and Thad maintained a holding pattern at the hospital. Understandably, the king hesitated to bring the queen and his child home until a clear green light could be given. As soon as the sun had dipped out of sight, Lee had left smoke trails in his hurry to get to County Hospital. God willing, Lexi would be fine. Siddoh did care for that little human, and he wanted her to be all right. And damned if he'd ever seen Lee twisted up over any female before.

Siddoh pushed quietly into the room where Ivy's father lay asleep and open-mouthed against a pile of pillows. A television on the low dresser by the door played the History Channel at low volume. Something about Nazis and medical testing.

Siddoh gagged. He couldn't watch that shit, not even

after centuries of witnessing all manner of violence between vampires and their enemies. He couldn't understand the atrocities humans committed against their own kind. Then again, he could not understand his uncle's actions either.

The chair by the bed creaked when he sat down. "Elder Grayson."

The old vampire's eyes eased open.

"Still in there, sir?"

The elder's head moved slowly, his braid of gray hair coiled next to him on the pillow. "Only resting. How may I help you?"

In spite of everything, Siddoh kind of appreciated that the old vampire seemed to have a spark of life left. "Earlier this week, my uncle disabled the energetic shields that surrounded the perimeter of the estate in an effort to make the king look foolish. He intentionally endangered the queen. I need to know what information you have. How many members of the Council were in on the plan."

These were not questions; they were commands. In deference to the dying elder's condition, Siddoh laid them out as quietly as he could manage while making it very clear that an answer was required. When the old vampire seemed to hesitate, Siddoh said, "At this point, Elder, there is nothing to be gained by taking it to your grave. Dare you continue to shame your daughter with your deceit?"

The elder vampire closed his eyes against the questions.

Siddoh leaned forward. "I think," he said slowly, "that you are decent deep down. You care for your daughter, you care for your race. I suspect that some-body convinced the Council that our king is weak and that the best thing for our race is for the Council to take over."

The elder swallowed. "So many of us have died. Thaddeus Senior was young and progressive in his ways. His son even more so."

Siddoh rubbed at his chin, a thing he did when he was thinking, but immediately regretted the friction on his sensitive skin. "So was this going to be a committee leading the vampires? Or was someone in particular to be at the helm?" He had his suspicions, but he needed to hear an answer.

Elder Grayson blinked and shook his head. "Your uncle approached me. I agreed with his plan."

The old male licked his dry lips, and Siddoh handed over a glass of water from the bedside table. "You sure you don't want to rethink having some blood, old man?" Word from Siddoh's last status update was that Elder Grayson would no longer take blood.

He shook his head. "My time is up. My family resides in the afterlife. My place is with them."

"Everything set to go except for farming out your youngest daughter?" Siddoh's anger rose inexplicably in his throat as he stared at a framed photo over the bed. Elder Grayson sat in the living room of that very same home with his departed mate and three younger females. Ivy, clearly the youngest, smiled broadly and innocently on the far right. Pre-tattoo, probably?

"Our kind thrives on tradition," the elder said. "Ivy will need family of her own when I'm gone." The elder seemed to sink into the bed. "She's innocent. Sheltered."

Siddoh thought of the scars and that snake tattoo, and wondered.

The old male gave a dry cough. "Her power hasn't fully developed yet. When it does, she'll be a danger to herself." He paused for breath. "I lost her sisters at such a young age. Her mother and I grew to love each other. I just hoped…"

A thump in the outer room drew their attention. "Father?"

Siddoh stood but turned back to the elder. "My earlier question, sir. Who would lead the Council if the king is overthrown?" Even if run by committee, there would be a chairperson. Somebody.

"Not sure…" He was looking tired now. "Seemed to be your uncle's plan."

Siddoh's stomach turned as he headed for the outer room to check Ivy. In all of this, Siddoh had the vague suspicion that a puzzle piece was missing. His uncle's daughter being killed by a human had been tragic, but the old male had been on the slow road to death as far as everyone knew. Then again, he hadn't seemed so tragically ill in the interrogation shed, and all roads seemed to lead back there.

In the outer room, everything remained dark and quiet. "Ivy?"

Her long, dark hair framed her face when she lifted her head from her seat at the dining table. Red-rimmed eyes looked at him as she grabbed a napkin to blow her nose. "You were right."

He smiled and crossed his arms. "Now, that hardly ever happens." He sat as gently as he could in the chair across from her. "What was I right about?"

"Dr. Brayden." Sniffle. Blow. Sniffle. "Since my father's ill, I went to him myself about a mating arrangement. He respectfully declined."

Siddoh put his hand over hers. "I didn't mean to be

cruel, Ivy." A quick pat, and he pulled his hand back. He was usually so at ease with females, flirtatious practically out of habit, but something about Ivy made him twitchy. "Brayden's always kept to himself. It doesn't surprise me that an arrangement like that wouldn't be his thing. I think he's one of those mated to his job types."

Apparently Siddoh's words didn't help, because she dropped her head back down to the plastic, oval place mat on the table, crying again. Was it only the hurt of rejection or something heavier?

She'll be a danger to herself.

Siddoh thought about that needle and lighter he'd seen in Ivy's desk drawer. The marks. He wondered if perhaps Ivy wasn't already in danger.

He looked from the lovely, sobbing vampire female in front of him to the bedroom door on his right and back again. Ivy's father lay at death's door. After everything, she wanted to know the man had passed away in peace. Siddoh actually made peace pretty damn well.

He patted Ivy's hand once more and headed back into the bedroom. Ivy's father was awake but glassy-eyed. Clearly short on time.

Siddoh sat beside the bed. "Listen up, Grayson. You're worried for your daughter. You need someone to provide for her and keep her safe. That I can do. Me. You have nothing to worry about. If you'll just explain to me how it is she's a danger to herself."

The elder's mouth opened like he might answer. Or maybe it was surprise. His breath stuttered, and he nodded slowly and closed his eyes. Then, with a short gasp, Elder Grayson was gone.

Siddoh never received an answer to his question.

Chapter 28

LEE TRIED TO REMEMBER THE LAST TIME HE'D BEEN IN a human hospital. The nostril-searing antiseptic smell, the way everyone looked at him like he didn't belong there—a fair assessment but chafing nonetheless. He didn't belong in this massive building full of ill and dying humans for certain. Once he had Alexia, they would go.

Anton met him in the lobby, looking twitchy and out of sorts. "Over here." The former wizard grabbed Lee by the arm and pulled him to the middle of the room, near a cluster of vinyl sofas and tables covered with tattered magazines.

Lee held a snarl. "You're not taking me to Alexia." Not a question, a demand for fucking information.

"Here's the thing: she's actually doing much better."

Lee found his lungs didn't much like the air in this human hospital. Or Anton's response. He grabbed the guy by the arms. "I'm not feeling reassured, wizard."

Anton looked around them both. "I wanted to talk to you before we get up there." His eyes darkened. "She's been dizzy and sick to her stomach. Achy."

Lee shook his head. "Then I need to get up there. She needs my blood."

"Damn it, Lee, I'm sorry as hell about what happened this afternoon."

"You couldn't have known she'd get sick." Lee

almost choked on the words. Strangling Anton right there in the hospital lobby would not be productive, but hell if his fingers didn't itch with the urge. He couldn't strangle Alexia, after all, and it was her he truly needed to have it out with. He'd told her. So many times he'd warned her not to be out alone in the day. Although she hadn't been alone this time. Sending her with protection wasn't enough. How the fuck could he keep her safe? "Take me to her."

Anton nodded and led the way.

"Do they know what caused this?"

The two of them bypassed the information desk and a security guard that Lee could have crushed with his thumb. Up five floors in the elevators, past another desk with nurses, and down a hall lit less harshly than the entrance through which Lee had arrived.

Anton radiated tension with every step, as if he expected that an attack was imminent. "They think she was exposed to some sort of nerve toxin. They asked questions about chemicals she might have come into contact with and took her clothes for testing. I had to go across the road to the gym and get her some sweats as a backup."

"Toxins." Lee's vision swam.

They stopped in the hall, just outside of Alexia's room. The door stood open. Tyra sat in a chair next to Flay, keeping an eye out while a male nurse in green scrubs took Alexia's temperature. Her hair had matted to her face, and her olive skin looked pale. The nurse made a joke that elicited a chuckle from her, which made Lee growl under his breath.

He'd hardly heard Anton's words. "I—Thank you for helping her." *When I couldn't.*

When Lee resumed his charge into Alexia's room, he got slapped in the sternum by Anton's arm. "One other thing," Anton whispered. "I don't think this is isolated to Lexi."

Lee brought his head up. "What?"

"Talked privately with Flay." Anton inclined his head toward the door. "He complained of similar pain. Nausea and extreme dizziness. He nearly ate concrete during his last rotation the same way Alexia did. Refuses to get it checked. You vampires get so stubborn about medical care. He's part human, right?"

Lee held Anton's stare, trying to put the pieces together. *Your acceptance of humans will come back to bite you.* The words of Siddoh's uncle ran ominously in Lee's head. Could it have been more than only hollow threats? Could someone have done something? Given them something?

"They do both have human blood, yes," Lee said. This did not necessarily equal correlation to each other or to the dying warning from Siddoh's uncle. Two estate residents with human blood plagued by the same symptoms could be coincidence.

Lee did not believe in coincidence.

"Yeah." Anton licked his lower lip. "And here's the thing: that gym where I grabbed those clothes for Lexi, it's one of those classy places with a spa and a cafe and a business center and everything. I gave them the impression I was interested in a membership so I could use the business center..." He dug in his back pocket.

The picture Anton produced, printed on cheap paper, looked like nobody Lee recognized. He grabbed it for closer inspection. "Is this a mug shot?"

"Yeah." Anton cleared his throat. "My brother has the power now to transfer wizard powers. I remember when I found out, thinking all he had to do was crack open a prison and he'd have a fresh supply of psychos for his army."

"Fucking insanity," Lee murmured.

"Right." Anton flicked the paper. "Well, this is Baron Ingram, a.k.a. 'the Doctor.' Convicted for an aborted attempt at what was believed to be a re-creation of the sarin gas attacks at Metro Center in DC. Sarin, by the way, is another nerve toxin. Former profession? Oral surgeon and cosmetic dentistry. License revoked on suspicion that he was taking disgusting liberties with the patients while they were sedated for treatment. Vanished from Red Onion State Prison about eight months ago." Anton tapped the picture. "The without a trace kind of vanished. From a maximum-security prison. Around the time my brother took over leading the wizards."

"Holy shit." Lee's fist pounded the wall where he stood. He ignored the angry glare of a passing nurse. Fuck. *Fuck.* "So much for your brother's truce. How has this scum managed to taint Alexia? You think this is your brother's work?"

Anton's agitation had him pacing their small section of hall as if standing still would be his death. Lee had the opposite trouble. His boots remained rooted to the tile, certain that if he moved, he would storm into that room and throw Alexia over his shoulder. A thing he'd sworn never to do again. He needed his arms around her. He needed her to never be out of his sight again. But first, he needed to focus on her safety.

Anton rubbed his neck. "I'm dead certain. Lee. He's

come up with a way to transfer wizard powers to humans. I saw him do it once. With my own eyes. He no longer needs to breed wizards. He finds the right criminal, bestows the power he wants, and *Boom*—" Anton punched his fist into his palm. "He can fucking customize. Breaking one out of prison would be nothing."

"Jesus, your brother's an evil piece of shit. If Lexi and Flay were both exposed to something, it's almost a given that Siddoh's uncle was the insider responsible. Your brother must have hooked the two up somehow. This bastard has to go down." *All of them.*

"Agreed."

So this thing with Haig, the truce. Had it all been misdirection? "I haven't seen your brother since he approached me in the woods and proposed a cease-fire. Where the fuck might he be hiding?"

Anton was thoughtful. "I have some places we can check that we haven't tried yet," he said at last.

"Good. I'm sorry to pull you in on this, but we gotta get this shit done. You, me… Flay, if he's able. We go out after I talk with Lexi and we take this asshole down."

"Roger." Anton's expression was resigned.

"I'm sorry your whole family's evil." *Perhaps the most absurd thing I've ever said aloud.*

"It is what it is," Anton replied.

Lee brushed past a tall, male nurse in blue scrubs who was leaving as Lee and Anton entered. Lee gave the guy a short but pointed stare.

"Lee." Alexia held her hand out. Her expression was equal parts sleepy and stern. "That was unnecessary."

"I thought it would be good for him and me to be on the same page."

"It makes you look insecure."

His hand tightened around hers. He bent down and put his nose against her throat, inhaling to assure himself that even in this odd place, she still smelled the same. "I almost lost you. I can be any fucking way I want to be right now."

Her brown eyes softened. "I'm so sorry."

"So am I. I would like to have been wrong."

She smiled slightly. Suddenly, her face brightened. "Hey, but I'm doing much better. They're hoping whatever is in my system will work its way out on its own. Is it safe to come home?"

He squeezed her hand again and leaned forward to kiss her gently. "It will be. I should give you blood," he whispered, "to help you heal."

She glanced around. "I'm not sure that's safe right now. Whatever I've got going on is weird enough there's been someone in here to poke around practically every five minutes. Anyway I'm feeling much better. Really."

He didn't like her answer, but the windowed walls of her room provided no privacy. He hoped they could afford to wait. "All right. You rest." He kissed her again and motioned to Flay. "Anton, Flay, and I are going out now."

He turned to Alexia. "We're going to take care of this. I'll make it safe."

~~~

Lee pounded the cold, stone walls of an abandoned wizard sanctum. They'd scoured the town over the course of the night, checking every hideout, basement, nook, and cranny that Anton could remember having visited with his brother in their youth. Finally, they had wound up back at the place that had been Anton's home for the majority of his time when he worked for the side of the vampires' enemies.

No sign of Anton's half brother, Petros; no sign of this crazy "Doctor" fucker. No guardians.

Lee lowered his MK23 as he swept the hall. "Lights out, nobody home."

"Actually, we rarely had working electricity," Anton said dryly. "The lights being on or off wouldn't be much of an indicator about occupancy."

"Do we really want to play a game of who had the shittier childhood? Even the winner loses." Lee spat out the words. Strange, he used to pride himself on composure. These days he found it tough to keep a lid on his temper.

Flay appeared from a stairway off what Anton had said was the main gathering area. "I find evidence upstairs of recent habitation. Food containers, spent lighters. Nothing of substance." He held out a small silver canister. "Except maybe this thing, whatever it is. Looks sort of like a nitrous cartridge." He tossed it to Lee, who stuck it in a pocket for later examination.

Lee pointed down the hall from where he and Anton had just come. "The place that Anton says used to be the main living area appears to have been empty for some time."

"As well as the ceremony room," Anton added.

Flay shuddered. "Ceremony, my ass. You cut a vampire open and take out its heart. It's fucking murder."

Back when the sanctum had been a bustling hub of lively wizard activity, a vampire would have been taken to the ceremony room so a wizard could cut out its heart and claim its power. Lee had taken a gander at the place. Tiled walls and floor with a drain in the center for easy cleanup. Disgusting.

He paced, gathering himself. His fingers clenched and released with the urge to dig at the burning in his chest. He needed Alexia. He needed... fuck, exhaustion weighed him down. He let out a breath, acutely aware of the tight bind of muscle on bone throughout his body.

Something far greater plagued Alexia than had shown at the hospital. He didn't claim to know shit about human females, but the roiling sickness, the panic shooting through his veins spiked within him a very real unease that *his* human female was having some kind of serious trouble. "We need to get going," he said.

"There's got to be something we're missing," Anton replied. "For all of his power, my brother likes routine and familiarity. Either he's around here somewhere, or he's gone halfway across the world so there's no way we'll find him. It's not the latter. Given these recent attacks, he'd want to be nearby to control his puppets."

"There you guys are. You know, there are a lot of damn woods around here. You could have left a note or a trail of bread crumbs or something."

Lee turned just as Tyra pushed her way into the room. While her tone may have been light and conversational, her face showed fatigue. She made her way immediately to Anton, bumping her head against his even as she spoke again. "You guys gotta get out of here. Lexi is out of her mind with worry, Lee. Girl wants outta that hospital bed." She stepped back and took a deep breath. Her thumb jerked toward the entryway. "And I don't think you have any idea how close you're riding the dawn. Sky's almost gray out there."

"Fuck." They'd been hunting those evil bastards all night, and this place had no windows. The only way in or out was through a strange portal in the woods. Lee had been too wrapped up in his thoughts. This was why it didn't pay to get distracted. Why he didn't do relationships. Why he hadn't until Alexia.

Lee, as the only pure-blooded vampire in their little group right then, was the one who would take the greatest damage. Funny how all the elders crowed about the importance of purity of the species. That morning, it would be to his detriment.

"One more thing, though," he said. His hands spread wide, indicating the place where they stood. "We need a way to close this off. Make sure the wizards can't use it for their ceremonies anymore."

Tyra's shoulder quirked. "Anton and I can probably make the entrance collapse."

Anton's eyebrows shot up. "We can?"

She nodded firmly. Leave it to Tyra. "Sure. Flay, you get out there and stand guard. Lee, if you can use your shield to make sure Anton and I don't blow each other up, that would be super. You'll have to pull us both out since the portal is really narrow, but it should be a piece of cake."

"Piece of cake," Anton said with raised eyebrows.

Her face was deadpan. "We could go back home and grab some explosives, if you want. But, you know, sun's coming up."

Nausea surged in Lee's gut, and the mere mention of sunlight burned his skin raw. "Okay, let's do this."

He positioned himself in the center of the portal and charged his shields, one arm hooked around Anton's waist, one arm around Tyra's.

They each invoked their powers. Both their bodies glowed red and very hot, uncomfortable enough that if Lee hadn't had the protection of his energy shield, he'd have been as fucked as the now crumbling concrete. Tyra added her ability to make fire, shooting across the arc of the stone doorway, and everything cracked and came apart with a heavy rumble.

A chunk of stone bounced off Lee's head.

"Okay, I think it's about to go," Tyra shouted. "One… two…"

"Shit." A piece of rock clunked Anton as well, and Lee tugged them both through the portal. They all rolled out into the clearing under a dawning morning.

Lucky the leaves were on the trees this time of year, so they'd have some cover. Not so lucky, they also had trouble. Flay had disappeared from sight, and from up ahead came the grunts and pops of battle.

Chapter 29

A FUCKING AMBUSH. GUARDIANS WAITED IN THE woods. Dozens.

Dawn broke through the trees. Lee sliced open the major pulse points on one dead asshole and turned fast to block the hit of a man who appeared human and was coming from behind with a length of rebar, of all fucking things. The pain of metal on flesh already bruised and burnt rang through Lee. He'd run out of ammo. With no other alternative, he'd been forced to drop his shields. With the sun rising and more yet to kill, he needed to conserve power.

He wrapped his raw hands around the metal rod and kicked hard, sending his enemy back into a tree. He followed, running the rebar through the guardian like a spike. The male only laughed, revealing a set of custom fangs. The familiarity hit Lee between the eyes: Anton's photo. "They call you 'the Doctor.'"

"I'd offer to shake your hand…" The man laughed and pulled the rebar from his body. The bloody metal dropped to the dirt at their feet with a wet thump. "There we go. And I'm at a loss. You know me, but I don't know you."

"You're not going to know me, you filthy son of a whore." He scooped the discarded rebar from the forest floor and crunched the man hard enough for him to choke on his balls.

Lee didn't expect a guy who could take a length of metal through his stomach and keep ticking to go down easily, but he got enough of a knee-jerk crotch grab to gain some leverage. He grabbed for the wizard's hair and introduced knee to nose. Blood poured. "Rookie mistake, man. Even with your brand-new super-juiced powers, a vampire will beat a wizard any day in a contest of speed. Shouldn't have left that rebar on the ground."

He spun, still gripping the Doctor's hair, and shoved the man down on his knees. "So what's the deal, Doctor? The fake caps and the nerve toxin? Is your boss having fang envy? What the fuck are you doing helping the guardians? Aren't you one of Petros's goons?"

Petros had been the one to call a truce. Deep down, Lee had known better than to trust that such a thing would hold water.

The fucker laughed. "I answer to no master."

"Yeah, master this." A swath of sunlight cut across Lee's arm. He hissed but held firm as he drew his knife ear to ear, shoving the body facedown in the blood-soaked dirt.

The entire thing had to have been a trap. Lee cursed himself up and down, because it had almost worked. Next to him, Tyra handed over her firearm. "Here. Loaded with one in the chamber. I don't have the silencer, sorry." Good damn thing they were out in the woods.

"Thank you," he said. "We only need to make it to where you parked the car. Hopefully we'll be out of here before any humans show."

He would not call for backup. The only living things in their enclave who could possibly withstand the sun were already out there fighting.

All except Lee himself. The normally toasted tan of his skin brightened more and more as each minute passed.

Up ahead, Flay took a hit and fell. Poor SOB had been pummeled worse than the rest, thanks to acting as Welcome Wagon before the other vampires.

Lee took aim. His vision blurred. With a whispered "fuck" he tried to clear it and find the front sight. He shot twice, glad that Flay was well out of the line of fire.

Another guardian crumpled into the dirt, and Flay was on him, cutting him up before Lee could get there. Down, but not done.

Could Lee say the same about himself?

He clasped Flay's hand and pulled the young vampire up. "Good teamwork, buddy."

"Thank you, sir."

With the sun beating down, they ran the gauntlet. They couldn't kill everyone. The goal was to make it to the car and get out alive. Lee's eyes burned when they reached the edge of the tree line and the full brightness of dawn hit him.

He'd get the others back alive, at any rate. He charged his shields again and turned to Flay. "Get to the car and get back to the estate. Now. Be dead fucking certain you're not followed. Take the rear entrance."

"What are you going to do?" But the young vampire's eyes registered understanding.

"I'm going to hold them." Even as Lee said the words, he drew the gun from Tyra and fired once, twice, taking down two more guardians.

Another volleyed with a cascade of golden radiance and chanting that sounded ominously like the spell used to conjure that damnable plague. Lee grabbed Flay's

arm to make sure the part-human vampire was protected. "Go. Now."

Tyra hesitated but for once followed an order. All but
Lee made their retreat.

Sweat rolled down Lee's back. Deep inside, a ripping
sensation tore through him. Alexia. Hurt. Something.
Worse than before. And he might not make it back to
her. All because of this shit. This fight he'd been part for
so long. He didn't know who else he was.

Lee dodged the punch of another coming at him.
They'd gotten all but a dozen or so, but shit. Daylight.
Exhaustion. Power drain. He couldn't take this many in
his current state, not alone.

Fuck, Alexia, I'm sorry.

Exhausted, he sank to his knees, remembering Lexi
and how fearlessly she'd launched herself at that guardian in the woods not so long ago. He scrambled and tried
to stand. Another guardian tried to kick him in the teeth
and he caught the foot, but barely. He held it, struggling
to push. Still, that muddy rubber print came closer.

Then a crack and a strangled cry. Like that, the boot
was out of Lee's hand, away from his face. Its owner
falling to the ground by Lee's side. What the fuck?
Adrenaline rattled Lee's body. He blinked, desperate
for focus.

The hardened face of the Lee's long-standing
enemy appeared in his blurry field of vision with a
shaking head. "Things have fallen so far from balance,
Commander Goram, one wonders what is true and what
is madness, yes?"

Lee accepted the wizard leader's outstretched hand
with no small dose of hesitation. "I don't wonder a damn

thing. It's all fucking madness." Lee scanned the forest. The sight of Petros's wizard minions fighting against the guardians through the trees convinced him that hallucinations from sun sickness had set in. "What the fuck are you doing here?"

"We had a bargain." He gestured through the trees. "You know as well as I do that the guardians' magic cannot return to power. Nor can the evil my father practiced." He looked down, kicking at the dead Doctor, whose throat Lee had cut. "And it would appear some of my followers have turned on me and sold themselves to the highest bidder, which I cannot abide. I feel it's time to reevaluate my course and that of my kind."

Nausea twisted in Lee's gut. "It does not sit well, owing my enemy a favor." Dizziness swamped his senses as his body heat rose.

Petros met Lee's stare. "I would suggest that perhaps our kind could form a new understanding, but I doubt you'll live long enough to suffer the pain of such a thing."

A deafening crash came through the trees. An engine. The boom of a rifle shot. Lightning sparks. In daylight? One of the guardians turned from its advance through the trees and retreated in the opposite direction.

A large form in a ski mask and head-to-toe body armor emerged from the back of the vehicle. On a late August morning. A statuesque human woman with flowing red hair charged through the woods, wielding an old Polish rifle. "Yeah, you better run, you limp-dicked motherfuckers." She loaded and fired again, letting out a whoop of victory.

"Commander." The masked man revealed himself as Lee took aim against the shade of a tree.

"Number Twelve." The young male Lee had kicked out of training.

The young male wore a concerned smile. "Sir, sorry for not getting here quicker. We thought we picked up on signs of a fight, but Sarah had trouble starting the van. Had a feeling we'd need wheels."

Sarah herself tromped back. "Needs a new alternator. I've got one on order." She pointed. "Let's get him in the van, baby. No offense, sir, but you look like shit."

She popped the doors. Lee turned to Petros, searching for deception.

"Go before you incinerate, Commander. My wizards will take care of this," Petros said. "For now, I'd say we're even, wouldn't you?"

Fair enough.

Lee and Number Twelve—Joshua?—got in the back of the still-running van and took off.

"I need to get to County. The human hospital. My…" Lee hesitated. "My mate." He hadn't said it aloud before. He hadn't officially made that declaration to Alexia. With hope, there would still be a chance.

"I'm on it," the redhead called from the captain's chair up front.

Lee checked out the washed-out newbie fighter through blurry, gritty eyes. He examined the girlfriend, her exposed arm covered with pale, freckled skin as she drove. "I remember you mentioned a girlfriend," he said to Joshua. "You didn't say she was human."

Sarah piped up from the front seat. "Hey, don't knock it 'til you've tried it."

"I—" Lee's heart hammered. He *had* tried, and look where it had gotten him. In the back of a windowless van, almost dead. *And you'd be fucked if they hadn't shown up when they did.*

Twelve had his ski mask off. "It's not that I'm ashamed, sir. I just don't like to invite conflict. You were already pissed at me when we last spoke, sir."

Would it have made him like the young vampire less or more, had he known? Given the way Lee had struggled with his attraction to Alexia, it was hard to say. "You're not burned." Lee noted that Joshua's skin remained unaffected, even after removing his mask.

The young male smiled proudly. "I've been building my tolerance."

Tolerance? "Excuse me?"

Twelve scooted along the floor toward the space between the seats and grabbed his mate's hand. "I want to spend my life with her. Her life. However long we have. I want to be able to be in the daylight with her sometimes. So I work on my tolerance. I started with a few seconds, a minute. Two. Your skin toughens up. You don't burn as easily after awhile. I can go out for a good few minutes now. Longer, if the sun is low or if it's overcast."

Lee propped his head against his fingertips. "I've never heard of any vampire desensitizing to sunlight." Tyra, maybe, but she was a half-breed. She was, in many ways, an exception.

"With all due respect, sir, I doubt many have tried. Nobody gives a shit. Most full-blooded vampires are elitist assholes. We don't mix much with the humans. Plus, you gotta want it bad. Burns like a motherfucker, you know? It's like you're drowning in fire at first. I won't lie. Took weeks before it didn't. I had to feed a lot, so the strain was on both of us. Why would anybody go through that, if not for love?"

The young male asked an excellent question. Lee leaned his head back against the cool metal wall of the van, humbled by this young vampire he'd initially pegged as nothing more than a worthless punk. "Thank you for picking me up," he managed to say through all the rocks and sand in his throat. "I'm grateful. To both of you."

Joshua ducked his head. "I'm glad we were nearby, sir. Sorry I was a piece of shit before."

"We're all stupid sometimes." Himself in particular.

Lee focused on the redhead's pale fingers clasped in the other vampire's gloved hand. They were young, of course, but he sat in amazement at this kid, so openly willing to love a human, even though their time together could be short. Lee and Alexia had both resisted so hard.

He rested his head on his arm to hide the moisture leaking from his eyes. As the van bumped and thumped him toward downtown, Lee wondered whether maybe he and Alexia might actually have a shot at a real future.

Alexia didn't like to think rude things about people, but the lady in the next bed had some truly horrifying shit going on. In the "whatever you've got, don't breathe on me" kind of way. They'd pulled the curtain across the windowed wall for privacy, but Lexi had gotten a gander at the gangrenous fingertips and the body sores while faking sleep. Guilty relief stole through her that her door had been closed when they brought the lady down the hall. Who knew if whatever that lady had was

contagious. The symptoms reminded her too creepily of
that dead kid from the side of Route 9.

Then again, Alexia still didn't feel so hot, either.
Her stomach still churned, but less than before. She'd
wanted to try some crackers or something, only the
hospital staff wouldn't give her anything but clear
liquids and Jell-O. Jerks. The bigger trouble lay with
Lee, wherever he was. Her blood rippled with darkness, pain, and anxiety. Every once in awhile, some
invisible knife would jab somewhere on her body.
She'd bet her favorite coffee mug that somewhere he
was in a fight.

Was he okay? Would he make it to cover before the
sun came up? The questions, the not knowing, turned
her stomach inside out.

The door to her room opened. "Mrs. Blackburn. I'm
Dr. V. How are you feeling?" He paused to pick up
some syringes from a tray just outside the door, slipping
them in his pocket before he entered.

Alexia prayed that whatever those were, they weren't
for her. Needles gave her the freak-outs.

"I'm… fine." She opted not to correct him on his
assumption that she was married. She still didn't have
a solid handle regarding how that stuff worked with
vampires, let alone how it worked with Lee. There was
supposed to be an official ceremony. Still, this physical
connection they shared certainly made it very difficult
to feel any other way than bonded to Lee at the moment. "Great, actually." She sat up straighter to make
her point. "Ready to go."

Dr. Whatever-his-name-was had a handsome face.
Young, tanned skin. Dark hair. Nice smile. Dimples.

"Good, good. Glad you're feeling better. It's important you're feeling well cared for here."

Uh-oh. She didn't trust people who gave her the sunny kiss-ass treatment. Usually that shit came right before something that made her want to set them on fire. "Absolutely. Best hospital ever. Thanks for all the great broth. Still, how soon can I leave? I gotta go."

"I'm afraid we're going to have to keep you a little longer for observation." He reached for something in the pocket of his lab coat, and Alexia stiffened, remembering those syringes. She relaxed when it turned out to be a pen, probably to write "bitch be crazy" in her chart.

"I can have someone observe me at home. I'll call if there's a problem."

"I'm afraid there's already a problem." He stepped closer. Something about this guy seemed wickedly familiar. Emphasis on wicked. "We're seeing the beginning signs of an outbreak."

"Outbreak?" Reflexively, she pulled her thin hospital blanket up higher.

He smiled politely, popping his dimples. "It's the most amazing thing. Cases of bubonic plague started trickling in last week. Today they're coming in right and left. So we have to observe you."

"But I don't have the symptoms." Oh, hell no. She'd googled the hell out of that shit, shortly after Lee told her about his buddy Haig was suspected of coming back from beyond the grave.

"Can't be too careful with these things." He stepped closer. What was up with his eyes? For such a handsome man, his eyes conveyed a wild sort of... mania? "You know, the human race has stopped fearing the plagues. Hospitals no longer keep treatment on hand."

Was that what he had in his pocket? Wait… Her heart almost tripped and fell. Mother-effing hell. She knew why he seemed familiar. Those dimples. Those damned dimples. The band around his arm. The crisp white shirt under his lab coat. Doctors didn't wear white T-shirts to work, did they? Holy shit… That hadn't been just a guy with a busted truck outside the estate's entry gate.

Then she saw the bracelets around his wrists. She'd seen one of those on Isabel the day she'd passed out in the yard.

Alexia's fingers clawed at the tape and tubing on her arms. Legs kicked at the blankets. "I really have to go." Now. *Now.* The periphery of her vision grew dark, the walls closing in on her like the walls of that damned van all those years ago. The heart monitor announced her panic in rapidly escalating beeps. She yanked the clippy thing from her finger that tracked her pulse. She rose to sitting on the bed, curling her knees under her. Pushing down the acid in her throat, she looked for anything she could use to get leverage against him. A table stood between them. A chair. A—

"Doctor." A nurse stuck her head in the room. "Mary left some syringes on a tray. For the patient next door. Have you by any chance seen them?"

Dr. Psycho grinned. He flashed a blinding smile, dimples and all. "I'm sorry. I didn't notice."

The ones he'd put in his pocket. For the patient who probably had the plague.

Alexia's heart hammered as the nurse left. "You're Haig," she said. Alexia curled her toes under her body,

ready to pounce. Grateful they'd let her put on the ridiculously oversized sweats Anton brought for her. At
least she didn't have on a freaking gown. Didn't stop her
stomach from churning.

"You know, humans have forgotten to fear me. To
fear the Great Almighty. My plague once wiped out
millions." God, the man beamed with pride like a new
father. He pulled one of the syringes from his pocket.
"Now, without this? I can bring a swift death to hundreds, thousands, even millions." He leaned close. Not
close enough. "You've all forgotten what to value.
Humanity's numbers have swelled to epidemic levels."

Jeez. "So it's up to you to cull the herd?"

He grinned. "As the Lord has commanded."

"It's been awhile since I went to church, but I hear
they teach things like loving each other and compas-
sion these days. Helping others. Not, you know, passing infectious diseases intentionally. In fact, that sort
of thing is against the law. Anyway, aren't you supposed to be dead?"

A quiet laugh from the psycho. "Yes. Lee. I smelled
him on you. Special, is he not? Strong. He tried to burn
me to the ground." Closer. Hell yes. Closer. She now
noticed a faint webbing of scars across his left cheek and
wondered what he'd done to hide them so well. "I rose.
I'm stronger. I have a duty to fulfill. Quite a shock waking up to find I'd been in stasis for six hundred years,
but my guardians have kept me safe all this time and the
Great One has a plan for me."

He raised his empty hand and began to mutter something that Alexia suspected would only end badly.

Without further thought she jumped, throwing herself

against the doctor. She interrupted his little spell. That was the important part.

As they went down to the floor, she managed to wiggle one syringe from his lab coat, hoping her hunch about it being an antidote for this plague thing was right. She needed it to be right.

His fingernails, surprisingly long, dug into her arm.

Her knees connected with his balls, and he curled reflexively. "Ha. Even evil psychos have squishy balls, asshole." She stuck the syringe into his neck.

Face red, he shouted and pushed it away. The contents spurted all over. Shit, it always looked easy to do that kind of thing in the movies. There was another one, though. She made a fast grab for his pocket but came up with nothing but a pen.

Fuck. The floor.

She scrambled for the other syringe as it rolled under the edge of a cabinet. Every fiber of her screamed to just run for the door while this guy was down on the ground, but she needed to get that damned medicine. If that shot had been for the patient with the plague symptoms in the next room, and she was in the middle of wrestling with the ground-zero outbreak monkey, that shit was probably the antidote. She had every intention of shooting that Haig guy full of his own damned medicine.

He came down on top of her as her hand reached the second vial. A large, hot, unwelcome body. His hands scraped for purchase, tugging at her clothes. For a moment Alexia froze. She fought the urge to recoil, reliving that stifling moment in the van when she was a teenager. The man with the scraggly hair who tried to get her naked. Who tried…

No.

This was not that moment. Alexia was no longer that girl. And she was going to fuck up this guy's game.

She managed to pull a knee underneath her. It gave her leverage. When his hands came around her throat, she had room to make hooks from her fingers to yank them apart. She spun. "Oh my…" God. His neck had gone red, starting from the injection site and spreading across his face.

"I… have… important work to do." His voice had deepened. It sounded labored. And really damn angry. Good.

Pain echoed through Alexia. Lee. Haig lunged forward and she kicked fast, following with the syringe in her hand. Right in the stomach this time.

He doubled over, retching. She didn't have another, but she was pretty sure she'd gotten the job done. She had to go.

She had to get to Lee.

Chapter 30

SNEAKING OUT OF THE HOSPITAL HADN'T QUITE BEEN a one-shot deal. There'd been a commotion in the hall that prevented her from getting far. She'd wound up hiding down the hall in the bathroom, wondering if she'd just killed a guy.

Hoping she had.

Sure, the shakes that wouldn't go away, those were worrisome. For now, she'd chalk it up to the intensity of what she'd come to think of as "extreme sympathy pain." God, wherever Lee was, he needed her. She just *knew*.

She'd tried to call Tyra and Anton. No answer. Siddoh's phone had gone straight to voice mail, which troubled her even more. For all she knew, the estate had crumbled to ash. It killed her not to be there. Were they all safe? Hiding? She was human. It was daytime. She could help, if she could only get the hell out of the hospital unnoticed.

With her stomach still queasy and her skin on fire and the sheer holy-fucking-spitballs panic over the idea of being trapped inside this hospital with that back-from-the-dead psycho while God only knew what was happening to Lee, Alexia crept out of her hiding place in the bathroom stall and stuck her head into the hallway.

"Okay, guys, just let me leave peacefully, huh?" Her visual sweep of the hall turned up nobody familiar.

There had been a lot of bustle outside her room a few moments ago. God, was there any chance she could just get out of here without being seen? She'd totally screwed herself, hadn't she?

"Alexia?"

Alexia jumped back. A woman stopped just in front of her. She didn't recognize the voice at all. Female. Southern-ish. Boots, ball cap, denim shorts and jacket, and flaming red hair. Definitely not a hospital employee, unless they'd done something wildly new with the scrubs at shift change.

"Lexi?" The redhead smiled broadly. "Alexia?"

Alexia crossed her arms over her chest. "Yes?"

"Oh my God. I'm Sarah." She tugged on Alexia's arm, immediately heading toward the exit sign at the end of the hall. "Man, I'm glad I found you. We've got to get you the hell out of here."

"We?"

Redheaded Sarah, who had nearly a foot of height on Alexia, jerked her thumb. "We've got Lee. He's hurt." She looked around. "And security was buzzing about something when I tried to go check in your room."

Alexia went cold. "I think they're looking for me. I fought an attacker in my room. Pretty sure I killed him. He wasn't hum…" She hesitated, looking the redhead up and down. Alexia had never met another human with whom it was safe to be open before. Now that she could, the words seemed strange. "He was—"

"One of those plague guys, right? Yeesh." Sarah pulled a face, grabbing Alexia by the hand. "Come on. Lee's in the parking garage." She handed Alexia her hat and jacket. "Put these on."

Somehow they made it to the parking garage without being stopped. The battered maroon van sat in a rear corner of the garage's ground level, conspicuous in its creepiness. Unlike the sleek vehicles from Thad's fleet, this one had rust holes and Bondo-filled dents. Lee was in there?

She paused, panic rising again. This sort of thing had "trap" written all over it. Sarah's arm jerked when Alexia was no longer following behind. "What's wrong?" She looked to Alexia and the van and back. "My boyfriend and I pulled him out of a fight in the woods. He was outmanned."

"Lee's never outmanned."

"Trust me, everyone is sometimes. There were at least a dozen of them." She shook Alexia's arm impatiently. "My boyfriend got kicked out of their training program, right?"

That rang a bell somewhere in the deep fog of Alexia's brain. Sarah shook her arm again. "Would you just come on? He's in really bad shape."

But not dead? Alexia held back tears. She would have given anything then for hope.

The door to the van opened, and a young male appeared with a battery-powered lantern. He squinted into the dim light of the garage. He definitely had fangs. She recognized him... from the night at the hospital. Lee had taken him to see Thad. Hallefuckinlujah. The redhead spoke the truth.

"Lee? Let me in there." Alexis pulled at the door.

God, he looked awful. Burnt. Bleeding. His head appeared to weigh too much for his neck, the way it rested haphazardly on his arm. Oh God, but his eyes. Bright and blue-green like always. Gorgeous. Staring right at her.

"You're alive," she murmured. Stating the obvious, but oh well. The relief made her all floaty. "Thank heaven."

He hardly moved from his slump against the side wall of the carpeted van. "Funny, I feel like hell."

The van doors closed and the lantern went out, cloaking them in darkness. She was afraid to touch Lee, unused to him looking fragile, but the burns and sores... She didn't want to hurt him. "I'm so sorry. God, I've been worried about you."

His arms came around her. The needle-sharp point of one fang grazed her collarbone. "It's okay. I can handle anything, now. You're here."

———————

Lee had lost consciousness in the van and woke to find Alexia gone.

His vision blurred, but he was immediately, acutely aware that somebody moved nearby. His hand brushed the rough blanket under him. He tensed and struggled to sit, hot all over.

"Hang tight if you would, please. I'm still checking you over."

"Doctor?"

Lee shifted again. Where the hell were they? The place smelled completely foreign.

"Really. Holding still would be excellent right now," Dr. Brayden said dryly.

Lee exhaled in an attempt to relax and let the salty physician do his thing. "So how's it look, Doctor?"

"Like you tried to hold off a band of enemies at daybreak all by your lonesome." The doctor's eyes narrowed sharply. "But I think you'll survive."

Lee craned his neck to see if the door was open into the hall. Where was Alexia?

"If you can hold still, that is," Brayden grumbled. Clearly, the day had been long for everybody.

"I just want to know that Alexia's okay."

Anton stuck his head in the door. "She's okay. She's down the hall in the bathroom. Guess she ate something that didn't agree with her." He looked around nervously and then pulled the door shut behind him. "I don't blame her. It was nice of that human lady to cook for us and everything, but I can't really stomach venison, either. Whatever she put on it tasted funny." Anton gestured up and down at Lee. "You look a hell of a lot better."

Pain stabbed the back of Lee's brain when the doctor pried his lids up to flash a light inside. "Jesus, really? I don't even want to know what I looked like before."

Other eye. Fuck.

"I'll tell you, getting you back here in one piece took a group effort," Anton said. "My healing power, Lexi's blood, and some from that washed-out fighter of yours."

What? "I got blood from that guy?"

"Not ingested. He just slathered some on your burns like ointment or something."

Lee glanced down. Brushed at flecks of dried blood on his arm. "Huh. Newbie paid attention."

Brayden peeled apart the packing for a large bandage. "A human, a vampire, and a wizard…" He slapped the bandage against a still-oozing gash on Lee's arm and paused. "Almost sounds like the beginning of a joke."

Lee frowned. "Everything okay, Doc?" This darker side of Brayden was one not seen too often.

Brayden pressed his lips together. "Anton, check on Alexia, would you?"

Anton stood with the door half closed. A poster for some football player Lee didn't recognize hung on the back, "I can try. Last time I did, she sort of… growled at me."

In spite of his pain Lee suppressed a laugh.

The doctor nodded again, still grim-faced and focused on bandaging Lee's arm. "Check again."

When Anton rounded the corner into the hall, Brayden held up a "just a minute" finger and pushed the door shut. Something unsaid on Brayden's part hung in the air, and Lee waited patiently for an explanation. If one called nearly tearing out his own hair "patient."

"You know…" Brayden drew the words out slowly, his eyes focused on his task of bandaging Lee's wounds. "I loved a human once."

"No." Lee frowned. "I didn't know." Hell, as far as Lee had known, the doctor lived a strictly monk-like existence, leaving his room in the king's mansion only to care for the other vampires at the estate. Sure, the male had been absent from the property over the years on occasion. Not that anybody had given such a thing any thought. He had surgery rights at St. Anne's vampire hospital. Maybe the guy had to go shopping for clothes or personal items once in a while. Or hell, maybe the guy… maybe the guy actually had a personal life of some kind. What a thought.

Brayden didn't stop him this time, busy packing the bag at his feet as he crouched by the side of the bed. "It's not well-documented, given the insular nature of our society and its regard toward blood purity, but I also know firsthand that a human in optimum health can survive a good many centuries on vampire blood." He placed two fingers over Lee's pulse point, pausing to count, probably.

Dr. Brayden. And a human. As Alexia would say, *Holy shitballs*.

The doctor met Lee's gaze briefly and smiled as he stood. "Not as long as a vampire of course, but as it is, you've lived a long life. Chances are excellent that you could have a very good run together. Maybe five, six hundred years. Better than if you were younger, actually. I doubt you'd have to worry about her dying early."

Hope swelled in Lee's chest. The oldest living vampire had made it over a millennium and a half, but twelve hundred or so was more common. If Lee's blood would keep Alexia alive for a handful of centuries, they could live out their lives together. Assuming he didn't die in battle.

His throat tightened. "What of your mate, doctor?"

"Snorkeling accident in Mexico. Not quite twenty years ago." He glanced away then, placing his hand on the bag he'd just packed. "He kept asking for me to take a vacation, and I kept insisting my place was here. Some things no amount of blood can fix."

"I'm sorry." Inexplicably, Lee's throat squeezed shut. Nobody had known that the doctor had been grieving a lost love. Would the outcome have been different for Dr. Brayden and his mate if he'd thought it was okay to tell everyone that he loved a human?

All this time, Lee had been so wrong.

A heavy, grief-filled thump in Lee's chest reminded him of his diagnosis from the hospital. Lee cleared his throat. "Brayden, I saw a doctor over at St. Anne's..."

Brayden nodded. "They faxed your test results. Continue to check in with me. Cut back on feedings unless you're having difficulty healing. Stick to human blood for the time being. You should be fine."

Stick to human blood. The washed-out trainee stepping up and saving his ass. Lee's mind had been well and thoroughly blown. "Thank you, Doctor."

Brayden paused with his hand on the doorknob. "You know… Alexia isn't really my patient. Aside from a few stitches I've only treated her once really, so I don't wish to talk out of turn." His forehead wrinkled pensively. "But I noticed she drinks quite a bit of alcohol. And there's the scent of clove cigarettes on her once in awhile. She really ought to quit those things."

Lee's head tipped to the side. "I'll… talk to her?"

"Degrades the quality of her blood. Not good for her life span, or yours." The corner of his mouth lifted slightly. "Won't be good for the child, either."

Lee stood, grabbing the peeling wall for support. "Doctor?"

Brayden's smile widened. "Three times while you slept she complained of sudden nausea." His head bent as he checked his watch. "If she were a vampire, she'd have been crying out for your blood by now."

"Lee!" Alexia's voice rang out from down the hall.

Lee's adrenaline spike nearly blew off the top of his head. He pushed past Brayden and took off down the hall toward Alexia's voice.

Alexia closed her eyes and prayed for peace in the cool bathroom, hating the chill since the sun had gone down.

In the daylight she'd been able to push open a window and breathe in the fresh country air, the sunshine. Something she didn't get much of these days since living among the creatures of the flipping night.

It didn't sound as romantic when she could hardly hold up her head.

She sat on the edge of the tub, grateful the queasies had passed. With hope or luck or *something,* for fuck's sake, the knot in her gut that called out for Lee's blood would also tell its story on its way out the goddamned door.

Her head dropped to her chest. All the calming yoga breathing in the world wasn't working. Her muttered "Damn you, Lee" was one part pissed-off and one part defeated, just as his boots came into view at her feet.

She hated that her heart sped up. With hope, dammit, her heart fucking leaped at the sight of him.

"I thought…" She brushed another tear from her cheek. *Relax. There's a logical explanation. Deep breaths—don't let your voice shake.* "I thought you couldn't turn me. Vampires can't turn humans. Years ago when Isabel and I first became friends, I asked her, andshesaidandyousaid—" Deep breath. "You *said…*" Dammit, she wanted to wrap around him like a koala.

Lee's hands landed on her shoulders. He'd fallen to his knees on the floor, his warm gaze level with hers. "I can't. We can't. You're no more a vampire than you were this morning. Last night. Last year." He brushed a tear from her cheek and kissed her gently. "How are you feeling? Is your stomach still sick?"

His lips had only barely left hers, but that fat vein in his neck was just visible, and hell that looked juicy. Ew. Ewww. "No, I'm better for now." Fear tightened her chest again. "But I swear, I can't eat anything. Like, I mean, anything. I tried mint tea. I tried crackers." She dropped her voice to a whisper. It was just them in the room, and that other human had said her grandmother was hard of hearing, but saying it aloud felt a little insane.

"I keep craving blood. I can't hold down human food anymore, and I'm craving blood. Doesn't that sound like something out of a bad horror movie?" She sucked in a breath. "And Anton's half brother, Petros, he found a way to turn humans into wizards. And then Agnessa passed me that energy you got so mad about—"

He kissed her again.

She stiffened in his arms but relaxed after a second. She couldn't stay mad. Right now, Lee was her everything. "Lee..."

"I'm sorry to cut you off, but this stress does you no good." He pulled back then, a slight smile on his face. "Wizards acquire magic differently than we do, and I am not convinced that the way Petros is indoctrinating new recruits will work for him, if it ever did. Agnessa... what she passed to you is actually a very gentle healing power. I have come to believe perhaps she intended to be helpful, in her"—he licked his lips—"misguided way."

He smiled. The corners of his eyes crinkled. Mother of freaking pearl, he made her wet when he did that. Had she seen him smile that way before? The way those fangs hinted at appearing and his eyes sparkled from the golden light over the bathroom mirror. Gorgeous. Freaking gorgeous.

Alexia could not return the gesture, her pulse was stuck on overdrive. Maybe it was their blood tie. Maybe it was intuition. Something teased at her, deep inside. Some missing puzzle piece.

"Lexi, I can't turn you into a vampire. None of us can do that to any human."

His hand touched her waist, and though she'd kept her arms clamped to her sides, she grabbed his muscled flank in return. "But?"

"You already know the 'but.'" His breath puffed hot against her ear. "You witnessed it with Isabel. Remember when she first realized she was pregnant? You brought her back to the estate because she needed Thad's blood? Only his blood would do, right?"

She shook her head.

"Lexi."

"No."

"The baby needs it from me."

Lalalala, I can't hear you. "I told you I was on the pill."

He smiled again. So patiently, like she was a silly kid. "You did say something about this… pill."

"I did. I am." Could she sound more like an argumentative teenager right now?

His smile broadened. "I did not accuse you of lies. It is possible that these human methods sometimes fail?"

Alexia buried her face in her hands. "Gah. Yes." The pressure eased in her chest but created a logjam in her throat, and fuck no, she was not going to cry again. "Stupid supernatural vampire sperm."

He laughed. Oh my God. Lee. Laughing.

She couldn't help but chuckle a little along with him, even as tears filled her eyes. "God, how are you not freaking out? This is fucking insane. Lee, I can't have your baby."

Oh shit. He looked like she'd slapped him. "No?"

Her eyes opened wide enough to stretch the skin tight. "Oh, Lee, I don't mean… Look at yourself. Look at me." She gestured back and forth. Alexia was five-three, and if she hit the weights regularly, she topped out at a buck twenty-five. Lee could bench-press an Amtrak train. Huge. A solid foot taller. "You've seen you, right? Having your baby might kill me."

He kissed her again. Hard. Fast. His breath whooshed out like it came from a wind tunnel. "Have I told you how I lost my mother?"

She shivered. "You said humans. I hadn't wanted to pry."

He pulled her closer, so tight his heart thumped hard against her chest. "It was during the great plagues, and some humans had trapped her late in her pregnancy, demanding blood to heal them. She refused because she was with child, so they shoved her out into the rising dawn. The stress had started her labor. Like with Isabel."

Oh, God. The stress of what happened to Isabel must have been horrific for him. He hadn't said a word. Alexia grabbed tighter.

"She tried to get home. I found them both in our entryway, too far gone to save. My father couldn't handle his grief and walked out into the sun."

"Lee…" She put her hand to his stubbled cheek, unsure of what else to say.

He pressed his forehead to hers. "Then all these years later, we nearly lost the queen and her newborn. And these were strong, pure-blooded vampire females, equipped for the task.

"So yes. I am terrified, and I'd rather be dead than

terrified. I am going to be fucking insane, and we're going to all have to deal with me being insufferable because 'afraid' is not a place I will ever handle well." He swallowed hard.

"I am also, however, elated. This is a fresh start. You and I both have our fears. So many of my long-held beliefs have been challenged by loving you. I've been so closed-minded. The very thing for which I've so judged the elders." He kissed her then, on the forehead, the nose. A gentle brush to her lips again. "We will get through it together. We will face our fears. We will adapt."

Warm tingles flooded Alexia's body. "Adapt. Together." The corner of her mouth lifted. He made it sound so simple. And just when she thought it might be, the knot in her gut piped up, tightening and digging in, jabbing her stomach with a thousand invisible forks and knives. Alexia doubled over. "Oh my God."

Solid arms came around her. "Come on. You need something from me, and I'm not going to give it to you here."

She looked around the bathroom.

"Not here," he said again. "Not when there is a perfectly good bedroom right next door. This morning I thought I would die, and here I am, still alive. I'm going to be a father. So if it's acceptable to you, after you drink my blood I'm going to want to make love to you again."

Lee pulled her against the comforting hardness of his chest, and oh… yeah… "God, it hurts. If you can make the pain stop, then that's acceptable."

"Great," he said. He lifted her easily, and she wrapped her legs around his waist. "Let's fucking go."

Chapter 31

LEE AND ALEXIA DID NOT MAKE LOVE AFTER ALEXIA fed. Siddoh had shown up insisting that the king wanted to have a meeting, and even for the mother of his child—holy fucking insanity—Lee would not deny the king. Particularly not at a time like this, not when things had been left so awkwardly before.

Upon return to the estate, Lee left Alexia in her room with strict instructions to wait there until he returned. More of an emphatic request. However emphatic, his gut told him she would not be found in her room by the time this meeting was done. She'd gone all wide-eyed and shell-shocked on the ride back over to the estate, and she was feeling vulnerable. *There will be a pop quiz at the end of this lesson*. Hell, he almost hoped she'd be gone, just so he could say he'd called it correctly. Learning to tease out her habits had become an interesting game.

"I've got something to say," Siddoh whispered to Lee as they made their way into the king's receiving room. "Something you're not going to want to hear."

"Which explains why you're giving me the preamble instead of just spitting it out."

Siddoh huffed a laugh. "I'm beginning to consider maybe your ex isn't such a bad dame."

"You're right," Lee said. "I find your use of the word 'dame' wholly unacceptable. What'd she do to get you on her side?"

"While you were out"—Siddoh cleared his throat—"as it were, I dealt with the death of Ivy's father."

"Shit. I'm sorry."

They sidled in along the edge of the room and took up a standing position at the back. A few other senior fighters were already present. Joshua, the trainee who had saved Lee's ass from the dawn, arrived as well.

"Yeah, well." Siddoh settled back against the wall. "She's having a rough time, but she's tough. Anyway, I found out Agnessa's been advising Ivy's dad. And I talked to Anton while I was over at that human's house picking you up. Apparently Lexi has some low-grade healing energy that helped pull your ass out of a sling earlier. Something she got from Agnessa."

Lee stiffened. "I heard."

Siddoh squared up with Lee, eyeballing him like he was stupid. "Yeah, well. It may suck owing your ex a solid, but it seems like somehow she and her wacky fortune-telling skills knew this day would come."

In this instance, if the dunce cap fit... "I know. I will have to thank her. And apologize."

"I'm thinking." Siddoh turned his back to the wall. "It made Lexi able to amplify Anton's healing power, or vice versa. Point is, it makes that she's human not so much of a deal breaker, if she can help heal you."

Lee nodded. He'd already discarded such concerns. With Alexia pregnant, he would not take the risk of going out to fight. Still, the information could prove useful.

Murmurs and shifts happened around the room. Lee and Siddoh straightened as Thad entered with a purple bundle of fuzzy knitted blanket cradled against his shoulder. Princess Morgan's head poked out of one end, eyes closed and sleeping soundly.

Lee's throat nearly closed. In not very long, he would hold one of those in his arms. Holy hell.

"And another thing," Siddoh whispered. "I believe Agnessa convinced Elder Grayson to request lowering the Council induction age all those months ago."

"What?" Lee's throat opened again, and air rushed in fast enough to make him cough. "Why?"

"I'll explain in a minute. You'll see."

"This better be good. No way am I sitting on that panel of stuffed shirts anytime soon."

"I hear you."

Thad approached Lee, staring hard. One arm hooked around Lee's neck, hugging so fiercely that Lee resisted hugging back for fear of harming the tiny baby held in Thad's other arm. "I sat down and mourned you this morning, my friend," Thad growled quietly in his ear.

Lee's eyes watered. He thumped his friend and king on the back, unable to keep the gravel from his voice when he replied. "I'm glad to be back."

"Okay," Thad said as he pulled away and seated himself. "Two things before we get started." The king wore moccasin slippers with his black fatigues and T-shirt. He held out a length of the fuzzy blanket. "Queen Isabel knitted this herself. It was her first try, and it came out less like a baby blanket and more like a scarf. If you see her, be sure to tell her how good it and she both look."

Nods and murmurs of assent around the room.

"Second." Thad hiked the bundle higher on his shoulder. "I'd like you all to meet Sophie. Named after the queen's late mother."

Louder murmurs. Light applause. The sleepy little bundle snuggled against her father's shoulder and remained blissfully unaware of all of the fanfare. The whole affair was... sweet. Oddly horrifying. That tiny baby had no idea of all the evils that might lie outside the door. With hope, she never would.

"I hear," Thad continued, "that congratulations are in order for Lee, as well."

Dozens of heads and pairs of eyes turned to stare right at him.

This was not the way he had planned to announce his relationship with Alexia. He had not planned to announce it as such, at all. Perhaps Thad, in spite of his youth, was king for a reason.

From across the room, Lee met the young vampire leader's blue-eyed gaze. "Yes. It seems Alexia is expecting."

Then there was more chatter in the room. Siddoh slugged Lee in the arm with a "Way to go, you dog."

Lee slid his gaze to the side. "As if you didn't know. Given your friendship with Alexia, I'm assuming you're the one who leaked the news to Thad."

"Guilty. But still, way to go."

Standing there with all eyes on him, he may as well have been naked. "Thanks. You're not..." Angry? Jealous?

Siddoh shook his head, one hand raised in what appeared to be some sort of oath. "Friend zone. Seriously."

Thad focused on Siddoh. "Okay, Siddoh, Lee. Fill me in on what's happened in my absence."

Siddoh straightened. "Ivy's father has passed away, I'm afraid. As well as my uncle."

Thad bowed his head in quiet acknowledgment. Lee kept silent about Siddoh's omission that he'd been the one to pass sentence against his uncle. It would keep for a private talk with Thad. "We have reason to believe that there is still a threat on the Council, and I believe you should allow the past motion to lower the Council induction age to pass," Siddoh said. "I think the thing to do"—he tipped his head in Lee's direction—"is to have Lee be your eyes and ears on the Council."

Lee pegged Siddoh with a glare. "You said you heard me," Lee growled.

"Didn't say I agreed."

"It makes perfect sense," Thad said amid all the surprised gasps in the room.

Lee looked from Siddoh to Thad's expectant expression. In the moment it took Lee to tamp down his anger, it did make sense. He crossed his arms over his chest, seething.

Lee would not be able to leave the estate to fight now that Alexia was pregnant, for risk of leaving her without the blood their unborn child needed to develop and grow. They still suspected traitors on the Council, and this way Lee could get closer to finding out. Fuck. He turned to Siddoh. "I hate your ass for thinking of this."

Siddoh grinned, but there was a healthy dose of sadness there. "I know," he said, "but it's the best thing."

It *was* the best thing. Fuck.

The bundle in Thad's arms mewled and squirmed, bringing Lee back to the present from his haze of thoughts. Thad calmly shifted in the burgundy velvet and gold chair on which he sat, popping a pinkie in the newborn's mouth to soothe her.

Imagining himself in such a position sent a fresh rush of adrenaline through Lee's body. Would he be able to take to fatherhood so easily? This sort of uncertainty was so new to him. *Because when, in the last six hundred or so years, have you done anything unfamiliar?*

Yet in the last week or so, it would seem literally everything had been brand-new. Love. Alexia. *Horse. Cart. Breathe…*

"There's one last pressing matter," Thad said. He nodded to Number Twelve, Joshua, the newbie who had saved Lee's ass at dawn. "Not only do we owe this young male here a debt for helping Lee out of a jam, but when I brought him back to the estate to thank him properly, we got doubly lucky."

Across the room, the young vampire who had been so stubborn and cocky in training now stood at attention but blushing with all eyes on him. "My father runs a small HVAC repair service for our local community. One of the services we provide is duct cleaning, cuz if you get mold and whatnot in your ventilation system, the whole house can get sick." He shrugged.

"Bigger issue for humans than for vamps, but over time, even a vampire's immune system weakens from breathing toxins daily in their home. This was in with your stuff after the doctor came to check you over." He cleared his throat and reached into a cargo pocket on his pants, pulling out the small canister Flay had found in the old wizard sanctum.

Lee straightened against the wall.

"Noticed a funky smell when I entered the house. The fan on the central air had been cranked unnecessarily high. When I checked, several of these had been rigged in the ventilation system," the kid said.

Shuffling and grumbling and a chorus of "what the fuck" came from all around in response to that piece of intel.

Lee whistled. "Let the kid finish."

Joshua continued. "I think… I mean, I'm no expert. Whatever this stuff was, it was weak enough to get you guys sick over time so you wouldn't notice." He pointed to Lee, then around the room.

Lee looked at Thad, snuggling his newborn. "Thad, the baby." All over again, Lee's body flooded with tension.

Thad nodded calmly. "Joshua here was good enough to go through the mansion thoroughly. We're clear. We've opened every window in the place to get air flowing. Joshua's father is kindly bringing his team tonight to check the rest of the estate."

The fast wash of relief sent cool tingles down Lee's spine. He exhaled carefully, trying not to reveal his jitters. Jesus, all this time he'd tried to keep Alexia here in the mansion so she'd be safe, and she'd been breathing tainted air.

This was enough roller-coaster riding for the rest of his life. "Excellent." He turned to Joshua. "You have my gratitude. For everything."

Lee turned back to Thad. "In light of present circumstances, I'm prepared to offer Joshua another shot at fighting with us, if being on the team is still something he wants."

Joshua stood up straight. "Sir, I'd be honored. Thank you."

Mouths dropped open. Never in history had Lee

given a second chance. In light of this, he added, "You fuck up again, you're out on your ass for good. Don't even consider reapplying."

"Understood."

"Good." Lee nodded. "Talk to your female. You'll need to tell us when you move in whether you'll be with the unmated fighters in the barracks or if you need a residence on the estate for both of you."

It looked like the young male tried to hold back his grin, but couldn't. "Thank you, sir."

Thad dismissed the meeting, and next to Lee, Siddoh shuddered and rubbed his forehead. "Christ, he was like a suicide bomber in slow motion." Referring to his dead uncle, Siddoh's whispered words came out strained and hoarse.

"The question," Lee said, "is how did your uncle team up with the guardians to pull off all this shit?"

Anton slid over. "Wait. Guardians? Was it not my brother who helped that nerve-gas guy escape from prison?"

"Actually I had an interesting run-in with your brother in the woods this morning. He indicated that 'the Doctor' had sold out to the highest bidder. So either the man worked for the guardians or he'd been dealing with Siddoh's uncle directly." The idea made Lee's already wrung-out brain want to sputter and quit. "All sorts of fantastic fucking possibilities."

Siddoh snorted. Not such a bad guy after all, Siddoh. Either of them, actually.

Lee clapped each of them on the shoulder. "All right. Let's all take some downtime to get our heads together. First thing we do tomorrow is have a meeting on this. Figure out what comes next."

Chapter 32

WHEN SIDDOH ROUNDED THE CORNER INTO IVY'S office, the gorgeous sight of her long, dark hair hanging over her shoulder punched him in the gut. She sat next to Alexia, smiling and chatting together while Alexia worked on a knitting project of some sort, and for a second her face was suffused with the warmth that had been absent from it of late.

He smiled at Alexia. "So is this a thing when females get pregnant, the knitting? You look so sweet and demure." He'd seen the girl drunk and dancing on a bar in stiletto boots. Boy, had she done a real switcheroo.

She stuck her tongue out at him. "I've known how for a long time. Honestly it's not my thing. I don't have the patience. Isabel was very upset about her blanket going awry so I told her I'd get the next one started so she had the width right." Sudden realization dawned on her face. "You heard."

He tried to stifle a laugh but couldn't. "You muttered about turning into a vampire and giving birth to a giant when you didn't think I was paying attention. Congratulations, by the way." Bittersweet warm-fuzzies filled his chest. Alexia had never been more than a friend. But wow, a baby.

She smiled back. "Thank you." Her eyes shifted side to side. "Where's Lee?"

"Looking for you, I'd imagine. Might be good to

find him before he gets irritated." He turned then to Ivy, pretending to ignore Alexia's irritated expression. "Ivy, Thad has authorized for you to take a month of leave."

He'd expected relief. He got... terror?

"A month? What will I do for a month?"

Was this a trick question? "Pack up your father's house. Grieve."

"Oh... Yes..." She fiddled with a crystal pen in her hand. Maybe things just hadn't caught up with her yet. "But who will handle manage things here?"

Siddoh dropped into a chair. "What about Lexi?" He pointed at the new mistress of knitting. "You do computer stuff, right?"

Alexia's head whipped up again. "Damn. What?"

"What?" Ivy mimicked.

He gestured between the two of them. "Lexi, you could take over for Ivy for a while, right?"

Alexia gaped at him.

"No, really. Perfect solution. Thad's doing some changing of the guard stuff, and you're great with computers and whatnot. They won't be having visitors or any of that shit for a while because of the baby. Best thing, given your bun in the oven, is to stick close to home."

She tipped her head to the side. "Hmm. Not a bad idea. Thad's okay with it? Lee?"

"We'll talk to Thad. I think Lee would be thrilled not to have you sneaking off in the daylight hours any longer."

Her face flushed red. "Ivy? Is it okay with you?"

Ivy's fingers pressed against the blotter on her desk. She avoided eye contact with anyone. "Of course." She pasted a smile on her face, but her skin was pale.

"Siddoh's right. I need some time off." Her body seemed to relax some. "Besides, you and I need to settle—"

"It's okay." Siddoh's hands came up. His heart performed a weird, wobbly flip-flop. His body heated, and not in the good way, at the idea of her blurting out in front of Alexia that he'd proposed an arranged mating between the two of them. "You and I... We'll figure it all out soon enough."

At that, she seemed relieved.

Alexia shot him a questioning look. He shook his head. *I'll tell you later, Lexi. First I have to go to my room, shower, and try to put away the fact that I had to kill the only family who wasn't ashamed of me.*

He took a step back from the doorway, shifting his gaze away from Ivy, who couldn't quite look at him. "Listen, Lexi, you really ought to go find Lee. It won't be pretty if he has to come find you."

She dropped the yarn and wooden needles in her hands. "He told me to stay in my room. Like I'm a kid. Come on."

A muscle in Siddoh's jaw twitched. He loved Alexia, but boy did she have issues. "He wanted to tell you how the meeting went, I imagine. Why are you being difficult about this?"

"Because..." Alexia looked unsure.

Siddoh rubbed the throbbing muscle. He needed a shave with that shower. "He loves you. Stop testing him. Go."

She stuck her tongue out again, picked up her knitting, and left.

"It's funny," Ivy said quietly. "Everyone said you were sleeping with her."

"Everyone says I'm sleeping with everybody," Siddoh said. The words were out before he could call them back. Perhaps she wouldn't realize the magnitude of what he'd just said. He straightened and took another step away, rapping the door frame with his knuckles. "I'm gonna go. Let me know if I can be of any further service to you. I'm pretty good at moving heavy stuff."

"Siddoh."

When he turned his head, she met his stare this time. Moist brown eyes and a smile so unexpectedly genuine it nearly knocked him over. "Thank you. For everything."

Lee found Alexia in the kitchen with her raw honey and one of her giant coffee mugs. "I thought I'd find you here."

She stopped in the middle of preparing a cup of tea, spoon in one hand and jar of honey in the other. Her shoulders tightened and she did not turn around, leaving Lee for the first time in extremely uncertain territory.

Alexia, pregnant with his child. The set to her back and the chill in his veins said that she might be angry. What had he done? He stood so far beyond comfortable that he needed binoculars to see the line.

"Lexi?" He leaned against the door frame and waited. Thad's cook was in tonight, dishing up what smelled like chicken soup from a giant stockpot. He wouldn't put voice to his deepest concerns in front of the house staff, so he took a deep breath and waited.

She stirred a giant blob of honey into a black mug with a white X on it and turned, her face looking drawn and pale. The sludgy "ick" of illness in his system had returned, this time a faint echo that told him it was Alexia who felt unwell. "What's wrong?"

She held up a finger and he followed as she passed him, making her way down the hall to her room. At one time he would have called himself a moron for following a female anywhere. For keeping quiet because she held up a finger. Now she was sick and he wanted her to be better, and the ghosts of assholes past could go to hell.

She backed against the door to her room and pulled the mug against her chest, appearing to take the peppermint scent deep into her nostrils. "Oh, that's goood." She sighed. "I'm sorry. I wasn't ignoring you." Her eyes drifted shut for a moment. "Isabel asked the cook for chicken soup, and you know what the queen wants, the queen gets, but…" She put her hand on her stomach. "It had garlic." She blew on her tea and took a small sip of her tea. "I couldn't talk to you. I'm so sorry. I was afraid if I opened my mouth…"

He stepped forward, caressing the soft, pale olive of her arm. "You don't need to explain. It's okay."

She opened one eye. "You're lying."

He smiled. "I am. You looked so tense. I felt anger. I didn't know where we stood. I worried." His pulse quickened as he spoke. With Agnessa he'd have never answered that question honestly. He'd have dodged, even with the blood tie, because the honesty would have made him too vulnerable. Naked. Lee didn't do emotions. Not before Alexia.

The brightening of her face said he'd given the right answer. "I talked to Siddoh. Ivy has some time off, so I'm going to take over her duties for awhile." Her arms slid around his waist. "It will keep me close to home."

Home.

"I so like keeping you close," he murmured.

"I thought you would."

"It's okay with you?"

"We'll work it out." She bit her lower lip. "I'm scared, Lee. About plenty of things. About settling down at all." She pressed a finger against his closed lips. "We're going to have to communicate. Trust each other. It's not your strong suit."

He played at biting her finger. "It isn't yours, either."

She glanced away. "Okay, you're right." The way she spit the words out fast, you'd think he'd tortured the confession out of her.

A laugh came out of him then. It dislodged some block long anchored in his chest. He pulled her close and bent down to kiss her gently. "As you say, we will figure it out. I look forward to finally moving you down the hall to my room."

She nodded against him, and when her body went slack, he pulled the tea from her hands so it wouldn't spill. She kissed him back, harder, and deep in his veins a sudden arousal flared.

Oh, well. Okay then.

Still, that faint echo of queasiness remained, and his desire for her warred with his concern for her well-being. He wanted her. So much. And he would not make her ill with the kind of rough-and-tumble lovemaking he so desperately longed for.

"Lee." Her lips moved against his. Whether consciously or not, her legs widened, allowing him to press his thigh between them.

Aha. A brilliant idea popped into his troglodyte brain.

"Lexi." He dropped to his knees, pushing her skirt a little up her thighs. "Is this okay?"

She ran her hands over his hair, massaging the back of his head. He loved that. He loved her. Had he said it out loud? "Love you, Lexi."

Her eyes sparkled with unshed tears. She pulled his lips to hers again. "Love you, too, you big stubborn vampire."

He frowned. "Did I upset you?"

She pursed her lips. "Emotions. Women have them. Humans have them. Pregnant human women have an awful damn lot of them."

He let out a possessive snarl. "*My* pregnant human woman."

She grinned broadly. "All yours."

That was the sexiest thing in the history of ever. His fingers slid beneath her skirt and tugged at one of those tiny pairs of underwear she seemed so fond of wearing. "Lime green," he mused. "I approve." He flipped them onto the floor. "They look better over there."

She laughed. Like music, that laugh.

He nuzzled gently between her breasts. So luscious and perky, she often got away without any bra under her dress, like tonight. He fucking loved those breasts. Would they swell as her pregnancy progressed? Would it be the normal eight and a half months of a vampire pregnancy or longer like a human pregnancy? Would she need regular doses of his blood?

Stop thinking and make love to your mate.

Without any further thought, he pushed the dress over her head and dragged it to the floor. His hands gripped her hips and ass. He buried his lips and tongue to work against the heat of her moist flesh, burying his nose in the soft, dark hair there and—

"Oh God, Lee."

He sucked, licked, and nibbled at her clit until her moans and mewls got louder and her legs shook. Then he sucked some more. He kept his eyes fixed on hers. Her fingers walked along his neck and shoulders, digging in.

"Lee," she whispered again.

He pulled back, smiling. "Is it good?"

She gasped and palmed the back of his head. "So good. Keep going."

So he did.

He worked his tongue feverishly. Thrust his thumb inside of her, rubbing. Fucking. Loving. Over and over, she chanted his name. And as she came apart against his lips, doubling over against his shoulder, he nearly came without ever touching himself once.

No matter how many enemies he had killed with his own bare hands, at that moment he'd never been stronger.

Chapter 33

ALEXIA TRIED TO STRAIGHTEN AGAINST THE DOOR BUT got dizzy. "Whoa. Okay. Little light-headed."

Lee's hands snaked up her back to support her. He stood slowly, pulling her against the hard warmth of his body. "Does that help?"

She nodded against his chest. "Mmm." She shivered with the aftershocks of her intense orgasm. "That was fantastic."

He chuckled, the sound of it rumbling against her cheek, her ear. "Thank you."

"But you know, as much as I like the feel of your clothing against my skin…" She slipped a hand under his shirt. Her fingers slipped over the sweaty definition of his abs, his chest. He gasped when she stroked a thumb over the peak of one nipple. "You are a tad overdressed compared to what I have on. Or don't, rather."

He groaned when she pushed his shirt up farther and helped her pull it off over his head. "I had been thinking that tonight would be all about you," he rasped. "You weren't feeling well."

"Mm-hmm." She nuzzled against his chest, soaking in the smooth skin and coarse hair against her cheek. The flat of her tongue explored slowly, tasting the salt on his pectoral. Sucking those dark, generous nipples into small, hard peaks. She pushed with the pads of her fingers against his sternum until the backs of his legs hit her mattress and he had no choice but to sit. "See, I'm feeling better."

He frowned. "That tea must be something."

She wiggled her eyebrows. "Oh, yes." It hadn't really been the tea.

He narrowed his eyes. "You're lying."

She pulled a fake pout. "This isn't fair. There will be no mystique in our relationship if we can always call each other on our lies."

He crossed his arms over his chest.

She crawled into his lap. He was hard. Obviously, gloriously hard. "It was the garlic that made me so queasy. Getting away from the kitchen helped." She went to work on the buttons of his fly. "And I had some raw honey in the kitchen. Works wonders."

He dropped his hands to the bed. "So you don't like garlic?"

"Not anymore."

"Hmm." He nuzzled at her throat. "I don't like garlic, either," he murmured.

"You don't?"

"Not anymore."

Oh. That was so the sweetest thing ever.

He nuzzled at her throat again. A tip of fang scraped her skin.

"Do you need blood?"

"Not me," he said softly. "You."

It could keep, though. No pain dug at her insides, not like before. She pushed a hand against his chest. "Lie down. I wanna ride you." She gave him her best wicked grin.

She popped the last button and tugged his pants

down. His erect cock came free, and she managed to get his fatigues about halfway down his muscular thighs before she realized a problem: she'd forgotten to remove his boots first. Oh, well.

He gave her a knowing grin. "Now what?"

They both laughed. Planting a firm hand in the center of his chest, she pushed him back onto the bed, helping him pull the rest of his clothes off before she straddled his thighs. "There we go." She giggled.

Perfect sex was for perfect people. Neither of them was perfect, so they could have imperfect messy sex and it would be amazing because it was the two of them.

Lee groaned like he might die when he filled her, and she could admit satisfaction at the sound. At him wanting her so much. She bent down to nuzzle her nose against his, even as her hips rose and fell.

"How's that?"

His head dropped back on the bed. "You're going to kill me." His hands gripped her ass. "First night we met, I knew you'd look gorgeous on top of me. I was right."

"Just don't say things about killing..." But she squeezed tight around him and rode faster, leaning down and brushing her breasts against his chest. His moans and groans of satisfaction and want put her on top of the world.

His hands touched her everywhere. He squeezed her ass and stroked her back, massaged with firm fingers and then sent featherlight strokes down her arms. Light flicks of his tongue over her nipples drove her to the edge of orgasm but wouldn't... quite... push her over. "Gah." Made her insane.

His breath grew heavy and ragged. Chest and abs

heaved. Damn, those abs. His bottomless aqua eyes stared her down intensely. He had to be close. *Had* to be. His fangs had grown outrageously long.

Without warning he struck. Not her. Himself. "Quickly, Lexi." He held his bleeding wrist up to her mouth.

Unbelievably, her second orgasm hit as soon as his blood washed over her tongue. She broke apart on a scream that was muffled by his arm and her need to swallow. Lee, on the other hand, did not hold back. God help them if anybody in the neighboring ZIP codes had a problem with the noise.

He bucked underneath her, roaring with such might she worried perhaps she'd hurt him. Had she taken too much blood? His heart. Oh God. Was it his heart? "Lee, are you okay?"

He pulled his arm away, licking the wound shut in a hasty, sloppy manner. "Fine." He panted. "Lexi. Holy"—his head rocked side to side—"shit, that was amazing."

"Seriously?" Sweat trickled down the side of his face. "You're sure you're all right?"

He puffed a breath. "Okay? I'm fucking great."

She shivered again. "You had me worried. I think everyone heard you."

He touched the side of her face, and she couldn't stop herself from leaning into the touch. "I can live with everyone knowing I got laid." He blinked. Smiled. "I'm sure everyone will be hoping it'll improve my asshole disposition." His thumb swiped a bead of sweat from her temples. "My God, I've never had sex so amazing."

She leaned down, cheek on chest. His heart made a steady boom, boom, boom in her ear. Comforting, knowing what she knew now. "Seriously? Seven hundred years and you've never had hot sex before?"

As soon as she said the words her body went cold. What a stupid question. Certainly, he had. And if he lied she'd know. Stupid.

"Plenty," he said matter-of-factly. "But never like this. Never with someone I loved the way I love you. Never with the future mother of my child."

"Oh my God, you're unbelievable." Sudden tears burned behind her eyes. It was the perfect answer. *He* was perfect.

If only he would stop making her cry.

Lee swept a tear from Alexia's cheek. "Are you kidding? I thought in my lifetime there were no surprises left. I never imagined anything so amazing."

Her fingers crept up to the two black hearts inked into his rib cage. "Is it okay for me to ask why you only have two? You said your father died that day as well."

Yes, he had. Lee exhaled long and slow, leaning to place a kiss on her forehead. "I have spent centuries carrying unspent rage toward my father for walking out into the sun that morning." He squeezed Alexia briefly. "I was devastated by the loss of my mother and sister, too." He sniffed, blinking away the burn of his own sorrow. "Hell. I was the one who found their fucking bodies. You wouldn't believe how many times I've bargained with history. If only I'd found them a few minutes sooner…"

He shook his head and swiped at his eyes. "I thought he was a coward, and it hurt like hell that my only remaining family chose to leave me alone rather than stay so we could survive together." Alexia rested her head on his chest and his heart thumped harder.

"So," she said, "you've come to expect the ones you love will leave. And I've come to learn that I have to leave before I get hurt." She kissed him gently. "We're a pair, huh?"

Lee thumbed a lingering drop of blood from the corner of her mouth. "We are," he murmured. His hand stroked her belly. "But I've promised to trust. You've promised to stay. Together, we're creating something new." Great hope and excitement swelled in his chest. "Right now, knowing I have that much, I feel fucking on top of the world."

Her answering grin shone brighter than the dawn had been on that single morning he'd been forced to greet its brilliance. Her laugh, even more beautiful. "It's still so hard to believe. I remember the night we met. You were so angry."

His hand touched the satin of her cheek. "I worked very hard to lock away anything that might allow me to feel. Meeting you pissed me off because I wanted you from that first moment. I knew you'd be trouble when I couldn't get you out of my head. Then the more I knew you, the more I wanted to show all of myself."

"Oh my God." She rolled onto her back. "Lee." Tears rolled down the side of her face.

He gripped her hand. "It's all okay now. You're mine."

"I am. I'm yours. I just can't seem to stop crying." She sniffled. "I'm sorry."

He rolled to his side, twisting their legs together. His arms wrapped around hers. "Don't ever apologize. I'm just so grateful that we have each other." He kissed her temple. "We face the future together. Your blood has healed my heart, and your love has healed my soul. I know the doctor tells me that we have the promise of many years, maybe even centuries. For that we are truly blessed. Yes?"

She nodded, returning his kiss. "Yes."

"We're going to have a family."

Alexia released a small gasp. "We are, aren't we? Holy fricking cow, we are…" She turned, kissing him again. "Oh my God, I love you."

"I love you, too."

Epilogue

"Here." Alexia unfolded the small blanket and held it out to Isabel. Made with a fuzzy, synthetic yarn, it had wound up being a colorful array of stripes in blues, pinks, and purples. "I meant to just get it started for you, but then I got into the zone."

Isabel laughed. "And while you were in the zone, you got in the car and went to the craft store for more yarn?"

"Tons." Alexia tugged at a strand of hair that had the gall to slip from behind her ear. "It's amazing what you do when you're in the zone."

Next to Isabel on the bed, baby Sophie slipped a tiny fist free from her swaddling, squirming until half her upper body was out. Isabel frowned. "She'll be awake soon. She's like Houdini. No matter how well I wrap her, once the arms are out, that's all she wrote."

Alexia laughed. "She's beautiful, Izzy."

Isabel grinned. "Thank you." She slipped a pinky finger inside her sleeping daughter's tightly curled hand. "She's clearly very talented. We're so proud."

Alexia leaned her hip on the edge of the four-poster bed. "Will you have to have another?"

Isabel's look of alarm was priceless. "Why?"

Well, color her stupid. She'd just assumed... "Thad needs an heir, right? Someone to be king someday when he kicks the bucket?"

"Oh." Isabel seemed to relax. She shifted on the

bed, and Sophia wiggled, too. "I don't know. Maybe this little one takes the throne someday and her mate is the supporting cast. Maybe we try for a boy. If we do, we don't have to do it soon. It's common for vampire siblings to be decades or even centuries apart, thanks to our biology. Thad doesn't like the idea of having a male only to be king. There are a lot of questions to be answered. Either way, it's a very long way off. With hope, Thad is a good many centuries from stepping down."

Alexia nodded. "A lot of questions to be answered. Yeah. Well, maybe Lee can help, now that he's going to be on the Council."

A knock came from the doorway. "Did someone say my name?"

Ho, baby. His hair had grown. Not long, but enough that he could comb it back, and the charcoal suit hugged his sturdy frame nicely. Veeery nicely. "Look at you." Her breath caught.

"Looking very handsome, Lee." Isabel smiled approvingly. It was a nice thing because once upon a time Isabel had suggested to Alexia that perhaps she'd be better off giving Lee a pass.

Alexia had tried. Really, she had.

"Thank you." He smiled self-consciously. "May I come in?"

Looking at his face now, Alexia couldn't figure out why she had tried so hard.

She turned to face him. "Is it uncomfortable?"

"It's"—he held his arms out—"different."

"You do look very nice. Gorgeous." She brushed a hand down the lapel. "I know it will be a big change."

Thad came in. "Temporary, we hope." He clapped a

hand on Lee's back. "I appreciate you having my back on the Council. You have no idea."

Lee grunted. "Anything. Still, you think anybody will talk around me, knowing my loyalty to you?"

Thad lifted a shoulder. "My hope is that you can convince them otherwise. Or somebody's tongue slips. And if you get nothing, you get nothing. There's no reason this has to be a career move." He nodded to Alexia. "That's between you and your woman, once the baby comes. I'm modifying the language of the Council law. Induction will no longer be mandatory. We don't want cranky assholes like you on the Council against their will."

Lee barked a laugh. The two clasped hands, pulling each other in for a brotherly hug. "I guess we'll see how the Council reacts."

Thad shrugged his shoulders. "Who knows? Maybe the trouble died with Siddoh's uncle. Haig's body was reportedly found at the hospital after Lexi fought with him, and nothing's been heard from the wizard leader in a month. Perhaps we're truly entering a time of peace."

"I hate to hope," Lee said, "but…" He grinned at Alexia. "Never say never."

Alexia absorbed the picture in front of her. Two vampires. Friends, fighters. Planning to investigate a potential enemy inside the Elders' Council. How did this become her life?

Isabel threaded her fingers through Alexia's. "I'm glad you stayed," her friend whispered.

Alexia nodded. "So am I." Truly.

Across the room, Lee and Thad clasped hands. Lee reached out to her. "You're coming with me to the ceremony?"

"Of course." She didn't give a shit if the whole thing was faked for Lee to be Thad's spy. She wouldn't miss his induction ceremony for anything. She would stand next to him as his mate, and all those stuffy old goats could take their human interaction bill and put it in a place where the moon glow couldn't ever shine.

They left Thad to say his good-byes to Isabel. Lee pulled Alexia close and kissed her firmly when the door to the royal suite closed behind them. "Okay," he breathed. "Ready?"

She smiled up at him. "With you, I'm ready for anything."

Acknowledgments

Many, many thanks to my brilliant editors, Deb Werksman and Cat Clyne. Also to Susie Benton, Skye Agnew, Beth Pehlke, and everyone else at Sourcebooks who have been so fantastic in helping to see these books to fruition.

Mary Calmes and Damon Suede, your friendship and counsel has been a lifeline, and this book wouldn't be what it is without you. I truly don't know where I'd be without you both, and I'm so grateful. Kimberly Kinkaid, mad love for the eleventh-hour helicopter reading! Amy Lane: "douchefucker." Erica Goode: big vat of coffee = <3.

Thank you to Chad Byers and Patrick McKinley Johns for lending me your patience and expertise. Also, of course, for your military service. Knowing you both is such an honor. :)

Writing can be solitary, and I'm grateful beyond measure to the community of authors near and far I've been blessed to meet who have offered help, advice, and support. I hope I've been able to do the same in return.

A bazillion squishy hugs to the readers, reviewers, and bloggers who continue to be so supportive. Extra-special thanks to Viviana Izzo and "The Staab Mob" for all the awesomeness! Thank you to Sharon Stogner and Jillian Stein for going the extra mile (and the martinis).

To my friends and family, the wonderful folks who

care for my kids, and *most of all to my Tom*, thank you from the bottom of my heart for your love, support, and patience. I couldn't do it without you.

About the Author

Elisabeth Staab still lives with her nose in a book and at least one foot in an imaginary world. She digs cats, coffee, sexy stories, and friendly things that go bump in the night. Find out more at ElisabethStaab.com.